TAM...
VIP P...

BY

KATHERINE GARBERA

AND

PROMOTED TO
WIFE?

BY

PAULA ROE

MILLS & BOON

"I really do want to know the man behind the flash."

"Good. I hope you find him to your liking," Nate said.

"You're impressing me so far."

He took another sip of his drink. The February breeze blew around them, stirring a tendril at the side of Jen's face. Each time the wind blew, the strand of hair brushed over her high cheekbones and caught on her lips.

He reached up and brushed it back, tucking it behind her ear.

"Thanks," she said, but her voice was softer, huskier than it had been moments earlier.

He couldn't stop touching her skin. He stroked his finger over her lower lip until she pulled back. Her lips were parted and her breath brushed across his finger.

"I can't think when you do that," she said.

"Then don't think," he replied.

Dear Reader,

I'm addicted to the reality TV show *Dancing with the Stars*. I don't know what it is I love about it, but I can't resist watching it every week while it is on and using everyone's phone to text in votes! That show is where the seeds of this story started.

I was thinking about the couples on the show and what if a romance developed between them. From there the story morphed and changed into what it is today. Nate Stern is a former baseball player who has returned to his home in Miami to help his brothers make their club in Little Havana, Luna Azul, the hottest, most desired ticket in town.

Nate has done his part. He loves the playboy lifestyle he has and the fact that he always has the most beautiful women on his arm. Life is good and a lot of fun for Nate, who hasn't been serious about anything since he stopped playing ball. But then he meets Jen Miller, the dance instructor at Luna Azul, and everything changes.

He thinks she's a lot of fun and that they will have a good time together, but things turn a bit more serious than either of them expected.

I hope you enjoy meeting Nate and the other Stern brothers.

Happy reading!

Katherine

TAMING THE
VIP PLAYBOY

BY
KATHERINE GARBERA

Published in Great Britain 2011
by Mills & Boon, an imprint of Harlequin (UK) Limited,
Eton House, 18-24 Paradise Road, Richmond, Surrey TW9 1SR

© Katherine Garbera 2011

ISBN: 978 0 263 88327 5

51-1211

Harlequin (UK) policy is to use papers that are natural, renewable and recyclable products and made from wood grown in sustainable forests. The logging and manufacturing processes conform to the legal environmental regulations of the country of origin.

Printed and bound in Spain
by Blackprint CPI, Barcelona

Katherine Garbera is the *USA TODAY* bestselling author of more than forty books. She's always believed in happy endings and lives in Southern California with her husband, children and their pampered pet, Godiva. Visit Katherine on the web at www.katherinegarbera. com, or catch up with her on Facebook and Twitter.

This book is dedicated to my wonderful daughter who has started her life as an adult. I'm so very proud of everything she's accomplished and look forward to watching her continue to grow and make a good life for herself.

Acknowledgements

Special thanks to my editor, Charles Griemsman, for his insight in making this book really shine!

One

The rhythm of Little Havana pulsed through Jen Miller as she parked her car on one of the side streets of Calle Ocho and made her way to Luna Azul. *Blue Moon*…they were rare in real life, almost as rare as second chances, and she was glad for the one that the Stern brothers had offered her by hiring her to be the salsa teacher at their Miami-based nightclub.

The club itself was a rarity. The Stern brothers had created a scandal when they'd purchased the old cigar factory in the heart of Little Havana and turned it into one of Miami's hottest clubs ten years ago. Something that still outraged certain members of the Cuban-American community today.

She pulled the strap of her large Coach bag higher on her shoulder as she walked through the grand entrance of Luna Azul. She stopped as she always did to catch her breath. Nothing said glamour the way the club's

Chihuly chandelier and ceiling installation did. It was a depiction of the night sky filled with a large blue moon. It was also the basis for the club's logo and the colors of the uniform of the entire staff.

Walking through the door each night made her feel as if she was a part of something lasting, and she was very happy to be working here.

The fact that she got to dance again made her even happier. Three years earlier, when she'd made a bad decision based on her heart instead of her head, she'd been banned from competitive dancing.

But now she was back at the barre so to speak and teaching her favorite of all the dances she knew. *The salsa.*

The dance was created by Spanish-speaking people from the Caribbean and even though she was about as white-bread-American as one could be, the dance felt as if it had been created for her.

As she headed into the club, she saw that the main stage was being set up for tonight's performance of XSU—the British rock band that had taken the American pop charts by storm the year before. Her sister and her best friend had both begged Jen to get them tickets for tonight's event and she'd managed to.

She was hoping for a glimpse of the rockers as well but she'd be working during their first set.

The club was divided into several different areas. The main floor in front of the stage was a huge dance area surrounded by high-stooled tables and cozy booths set in darkened alcoves. On the second floor, where she spent most of her time, was a rehearsal room with a small bar and then a mezzanine that overlooked the main club. But the real gem of the second floor was the balcony that opened off to the left and the stage set in the back.

It was there that every night Luna Azul re-created the
famous last Friday celebrations held on Calle Ocho. Up
there every night was like a feast day for Latin music
and dancing. The hottest Latin groups performed there.
Regulars and celebrities mingled to the sexy salsa beats
of the Latin music.

And she was at the heart of it, Jen thought. She taught
the customers how to do the salsa, giving them a little
knowledge to help them enjoy the music that much
more.

As Jen walked into the rehearsal room, her assistant
greeted her with, "You're late."

"I am not, Alison. I'm right on time."

Alison lifted one eyebrow at her. She was funny most
of the time but she had a thing for punctuality that Jen
simply didn't.

"You're lucky no one has stopped by to check on the
classroom."

"Alison, chill. The classroom is ready and we are
ready. I brought a new CD with me."

"Which one?"

"Just a compilation of some of my old favorites. I
want to have something different for tonight's class."

"What's special about tonight's class?" Alison
asked.

"We have T. J. Martinez signed up."

"The third-base player for the Yankees?"

"Yes. And since he's good friends with Nate Stern, I
thought we needed to make a good impression." Keeping
the club owners and their friends happy was the name
of the game.

"Maybe you should have arrived earlier."

"Alison, I don't mind a little ribbing, but you have to
drop that. We have thirty minutes before class starts."

"I know. Sorry, I'm bitchy today."

"Why?"

"Marc is leaving for Afghanistan for another deployment."

"When?" Jen asked. Marc was Alison's brother and they were very close. Alison often said that he was all she had.

"Three weeks. I…"

Jen went over and hugged her friend. "He'll be fine. He always is. And I'll help you through it."

Alison hugged her back and then stepped away. "You're right. Now tell me more about the songs we are using tonight."

Jen knew that Alison needed to lose herself in the music so she could forget about her life for a while. Jen wasn't sure she could be as brave as Alison. Having a brother who was a warrior and would always be called to a battle somewhere in the world was hard. She saw it on her friend's face every time Marc got deployed.

The music soon echoed through the empty dance hall as Alison and Jen began their routine. Alison was an okay dancer, though she would never have made it in the competitive world of dance as Jen had. But for Luna Azul she was more than competent.

"I like this," Alison said.

"Great. I want you to add a little more hip twist at the end of the sixth beat like this," Jen said, showing her.

"Very nice, Ms. Miller."

Jen stumbled and glanced toward the door to see Nate Stern standing there.

He was tall—at least six feet in height—and had thick blond hair that he wore cut close to his head. He had the kind of deep and natural tan that everyone wanted and wore his clothes with a stylish panache that she honestly admitted she envied. He had a stubborn-looking jaw with a small scar on his chin from a baseball accident when he was ten.

Why did she know these things? She shook her head. One of the reasons she'd applied for this job was that she'd always been attracted to him. She'd seen his picture in the paper when he'd been a rookie for the Yankees and she'd been smitten.

"Thank you, Mr. Stern. Is there something I can do for you this evening?" she asked.

"I'd like a private word," he said.

"Alison, will you leave us?"

"That's not necessary," he said. "Please join me on the balcony."

She took a deep breath. She hated following orders or letting anyone else be in charge. "Keep practicing."

Alison nodded as Jen led the way out of the rehearsal room and out to the balcony. She tried to be nonchalant but she couldn't help her nerves. This job was literally her last chance in the dancing world. If this didn't work out she was going to have to stop dancing and take Marcia, her sister, up on that secretarial job at her law office. And that was the last thing she wanted to do.

"Is something wrong?"

"No, quite the contrary. I've heard nothing but good things about you and I wanted to come and see for myself."

"So you'll be attending my class tonight?" she asked.

"Yes, I will be."

She almost scowled at him but years of performing for judges enabled her to keep her smile on her face. "That will be wonderful. I believe one of your former teammates is signed up for our class as well."

"Yes, Martinez. I thought I'd tag along and see how you handle having a celebrity in your class."

She almost rolled her eyes. Honestly, did he think she was going to treat T. J. Martinez any differently than she did her other students? "Do you think I can't handle it?"

"I have no idea," he said. "That's why I'll be dropping by."

She was furious but kept calm. "I'm a pro, Mr. Stern. That's why your brother hired me. You don't need to attend a salsa class to ensure I do my job."

He tipped his head to the side. "Did I offend you?"

"Yes, you did."

He gave her a quick grin, which changed that arrogant-looking face of his into a very charming one. "I'm sorry. That wasn't my intent. Celebrities are the key to our continued edge over the other clubs in Miami, and I don't want to chance anything disrupting that."

She nodded. "I understand your concern. I can promise you tonight's class isn't going to damage Luna Azul's reputation one bit. And I will enjoy having you in my class."

"You will?"

"Yes," she said, turning on her heel and walking back toward the rehearsal room. "Because afterward you will owe me an apology for doubting my skills."

His laughter followed her into the hallway and she smiled a bit to herself as she entered the classroom. She had to be in top form tonight and she had absolutely no doubt that Nate would be as challenging in the classroom as he'd been beforehand.

Nate watched her leave, wishing he'd come up here a long time ago. She was funny, spunky and very cute.

Her legs were long—so damned long—and her body was lithe. She was quite a dancer and that was apparent in the graceful way she moved.

He stayed where he was on the patio and stared out at the sky as it darkened into twilight. It was February, and there was a light chill to the night air. The scent of the Cuban food that the patio kitchen was preparing carried on the breeze.

He'd done what he needed to do to keep up the club's image. After all, he was the face of Luna Azul. Funny that a non-Latino would be the face of the hottest club in Little Havana, but the Stern brothers had turned to what they knew best when they'd started their business nearly ten years ago.

Nate was the youngest of the three Stern brothers, Justin the middle one and Cam the oldest. It had been Cam's idea to take the failing cigar factory and turn it into a club. Justin was a finance whiz kid and he'd looked at the numbers and decided if they invested their trust funds into the club, it could make them money.

At the time, Nate had been more interested in his budding baseball career and had merely signed a paper agreeing to the terms. But when a shoulder injury forced him out of the game two years later, he'd been very glad for Cam and Justin's decision to buy this place and open a club. And Nate had quickly found that he had something to contribute to the business.

His A-list contacts from the celebrity world.

As much as he loved to play baseball, he was also a Stern through and through and he loved to socialize. Something that the society pages had noticed when he'd first gone to New York to start his career. And Nate had been careful to make sure he stayed in the news.

He used his celebrity to bring attention to the club and

to stay current. Even though he hadn't played in over six years he was still one of the top-ten most recognizable baseball players.

"What are you doing up here?" Justin asked as he came out of the kitchen area. He was two inches taller than Nate and had dark brown hair. They both had their mother's eyes and their father's strong jaw, a feature all the Stern men had.

"Talking to the salsa teacher. T.J. is going to be in her class tonight and I wanted to make sure she could handle it."

"Jen must have loved that."

"Do you know her?" he asked, feeling a twinge of jealousy at his brother's familiarity with Jen.

"Not well. But I interviewed her for the job and she's very confident of herself. She doesn't like to be questioned."

"Who does?" Nate asked.

"Not me. I have a meeting downtown with the community leaders tomorrow. They want to have their say about our tenth anniversary party."

"How many times are we going to have to prove ourselves before they accept that we are a part of this community now and not going anywhere?" Nate asked.

"They'll never be satisfied," Cam said as he joined his brothers on the patio. "What are you two doing up here? I need you downstairs to talk to the band when they arrive."

"I'm on it," Nate said. "I've got the society reporter from the *Herald* coming. And I'm positive we are going to see Jennifer Lopez tonight. She's in town and her people said she'd drop by. I've got calls in to the internet celeb-site stringers so we should get some good coverage."

"Great. I like the sound of that," Cam said.

"I know you do, that's why I spend all night partying."

"Ha. You do it because you like it," Justin said.

"Indeed, I do. I guess the Stern genes run true in my case. I'm not meant to settle down."

"Like Papa?" Justin asked.

"Yes. I think that's why he and Mom were so miserable," Nate said.

"That and the fact that she was so…cold," Cam added.

Nate turned away from his brothers. Their mother had never wanted children and had done her best to spend as little time with them as she could. It had affected them all in different ways. For Nate, it was that he didn't trust women to really know their own emotions. He always knew that women were going to leave and they always did.

"I guess we all know what to do tonight," Cam said. "How are your talks with the community leaders going?"

"Slow. I invited a few of them to join us for tonight's show so they can see how much a part of Calle Ocho we are."

"Good. Keep me posted," Cam said.

"I will."

Nate and his brothers went back downstairs. Standing in the nearly empty club, Nate glanced around at the decor. It was hard to tell from looking at the place that this had once been a cigar factory.

As a boy, he'd never thought about the future. Once he became a professional baseball player, he'd always just assumed that he'd continue playing until he was in his thirties and then transition to a sportscaster career. But when he'd been injured so young…his dreams had changed and morphed into this.

He wasn't bitter about it. To be honest, he figured he'd ended up exactly where he needed to be and he was very happy about that.

"Nate?"

He turned to see T. J. Martinez standing in the foyer under the Chihuly glass ceiling. "T.J., my man. How was your flight down here?"

"Good. Very good. I'm ready for some action tonight. Ready to mix it up with you."

"Me, too," he said, shaking hands and giving the other man a one-armed hug. "I heard you signed up for dance lessons."

"Mariah insisted that I take them. She said the teacher is the best and that I'd be an idiot to miss out on the classes. Of course, Paul said the teacher was hot."

"You can see for yourself tonight. The first class starts in about thirty minutes. Do you want to have a beer?"

"Yes. I'll catch you up on the team news. There's a rumor that O'Neill is going to be traded."

Nate led his friend to the bar and they chatted about baseball and the players they both knew. It was still early and the club wasn't open to guests yet. But Nate wanted some private time with T.J.

Nate tried to concentrate on the conversation, but his mind kept drifting back to Jen. He didn't attribute much to it, though. Sure she was sexy and spunky—two things he'd always been attracted to. And talking about baseball and his glory days always made him want to go on the prowl.

"Let's go. Don't want you to be late to your class."

"Are you coming with me?"

"Yeah, why not? I haven't been to a salsa class yet and as you mentioned, the teacher is…well-qualified."

T.J. tipped his head back and laughed. Then they finished their beers and headed upstairs. There was no reason for Nate to be in this class except that he wanted to see Jen again. And that was all it took, he thought. That was a perk to being his own boss—he could do whatever the hell he wanted.

He walked in the door of the rehearsal room and Jen glanced up from a turn she was doing. Her hips were swaying and the pulsing sensual beat of the salsa music echoed in the background. He felt the rhythm of it down deep in his soul, and his shoulder started to throb the way it did when something big was about to happen. That old injury was like a dowsing rod for spotting trouble.

Two

The music swelled around her and for once a man distracted her. Well, that wasn't true—she'd been distracted by men before but not like this. Nate Stern was making her conscious of each sway of her hips. She felt the material of her long skirt against her legs and when the side slit parted to reveal her thigh, she felt his gaze on her.

His gaze.

Not another single person in the room was registering for her. *Just him.*

Why?

Why Nate Stern? This had disaster written all over it. She couldn't be attracted to her boss. The last time she had been attracted to someone with authority over her it had ended badly.

Her sister Marcia would roll her eyes and say that

Jen never learned. She had to learn, she thought. She couldn't start over again.

To add to her troubles, Nate's friend T.J. might be a rocking third-base player but he couldn't find the rhythm of the songs she'd played to save his life. It shouldn't be that hard. The strong Latin beat was easy to hear.

Alison was working with some students at the back of the classroom as Lou Bega's "Mambo No. 5" came on. She used her remote to pause the music. This was the song that the class danced to every evening to open the club. Then Alison and Jen would go into the back and come out twenty minutes later to do a flamenco routine.

"Okay. Is everyone ready to show us what you've learned?" Jen asked. "When you signed up for this lesson you probably didn't realize it but you are going to be the stars of the opening number tonight."

There were a few good-hearted groans from the men in the room and a smattering of applause.

"The important thing to remember about the music is that it is sensual. It reflects the rhythm of the night. You should feel it pulsing through you. And don't worry about looking silly, you all look wonderful when you are dancing together."

"I don't think I can feel anything except when someone is going to try to steal third," T.J. said.

"I have to agree, Mr. Martinez."

"Call me T.J.," he said with a charming grin that revealed his perfect white teeth.

"I will. Since you are our celebrity tonight we would like to invite you to lead the conga line into the room and then, of course, have the first dance."

It was their standard procedure to ensure that the classes got the utmost attention. According to Nate

Stern, it was a nice way to drive business to the lessons. Everyone wanted to be in a class with a celebrity.

"I don't think I'm the right guy for that."

Jen smiled at him. "I will make sure you are."

She hit the button to turn the music back on and walked over to T.J. Nate was watching every move she made and she felt as if she had a spotlight on her body.

She gave him a pointed stare and he just grinned back at her. That was when she decided to show the annoyingly handsome man that she was made of tougher stuff than he thought she was.

She'd been dancing since she was thirteen. Let's face it, she thought, there wasn't a time in her life when men hadn't been staring at her body. And tonight…well, tonight she wanted Nate to see her and to want her. She knew she was an okay-looking woman most of the time, but when she danced…she was beautiful.

"I'm not an athlete, T.J., so you will have to tell me, does baseball have its own cadence?"

He nodded. "It might, ma'am, but all I hear is the sound of the bat hitting the ball."

She nodded, trying to think of another way to reach him. How was she going to make this work for him?

"Do you mind if I touch you?"

"Not at all," he said with a grin.

She smiled back at him. Walking around behind him, she put her hands on his hips. "Just stay loose and let my hands move you."

He nodded and she counted the beat of the music under her breath. And then she started to move his hips. He tried to move his feet but stumbled. "Just stay still and learn the beats."

"I don't think that method is working, Ms. Miller," Nate said. "Let me show him how it's done."

She looked at her boss and then put her hands up and stepped back.

But instead of going to T.J., Nate came to her. He put his hands on her hips. "Move so I can feel the rhythm."

His low tone was meant only for her ears and she responded to it. She counted the beat so he'd hear it as loudly as she did inside of her head and then she started to move.

Nate, unlike T.J., moved with an innate grace and natural ability that made dancing with him…well, not work. He put his hands in the proper position for the dance. One hand on her hips and the other holding her hand, his eyes met hers and the other people in the room faded away. In that one moment, Nate wasn't her boss or some local celebrity.

He was her partner, her man, and she let the dance take over. Their gazes met and held as they danced. Nate understood sensuality, and in his arms she realized that she was more than the dance instructor.

The salsa was about heat and sex. It was a seduction, a promise of the evening to come. She felt the barriers she'd been trying to put into place to keep him back start to shake and then fall.

This man wasn't going to let her keep him away if he wanted to be closer. And as the music faded and they stopped moving, she knew he did want to be near to her, or at least she knew that she wanted to be near to him. She wanted to feel his hands on her hips again. To feel his big hand holding hers and watch his dark obsidian eyes as they moved together to the music.

* * *

Nate didn't know why he felt so possessive toward Jen. She was nothing more than a pretty face and an employee but when she'd touched T.J., he'd seen red. And he didn't like that.

Once he held her in his arms, he knew what the problem was. He wanted her. And wanting her was complicating his rather simple plans for an enjoyable evening. But dancing together had also shown him that she was interested in him, too. She watched him, her gaze heated under his as they moved and when the music stopped, he started to pull her to a corner of the room.

But the applause stopped him and Jen bit her lower lip as she stepped back.

"That is what we need to see from everyone," she said. "I'm going to observe you all dancing and then we will be ready for our big debut."

"I don't think I'm going to look like that," T.J. said.

"Don't worry about it," Nate said. "I'll take your place. Unless you have an objection, Ms. Miller."

Jen flushed and shook her head. "You are a very good partner, Mr. Stern."

"Call me Nate," he said.

She nodded. She turned her attention back to the class.

"Why didn't you tell me you had something going with her?" T.J. asked.

"I don't. That was just a dance."

"That was sex on a cracker, man. That was so much more than a dance," T.J. said. "I guess there is no chance for me."

Nate shrugged. It was a connection, and one that he didn't feel all the time, but he knew it wasn't rare. It was just lust. Tonight he was on the prowl. Ms. Miller was attractive and there was something about her that made him curious. Maybe it was her mouth with the full lower lip that he knew would feel right under his. Or her nipped-in waist and long lean dancer's body that he sensed would feel right in his arms.

Hell, he already knew that it felt right here. That she felt right when she moved with him. He wanted to explore it further but he was aware that he was her boss and long-term relationships weren't his thing.

Which could make working together in the future a little uncomfortable.

"What are you thinking, man?"

"That women are complicated."

T.J. laughed. "Understatement of the year. I don't think I'm ever going to figure them out."

"The dances?" Jen said coming over to the two of them. "You should probably stop chatting if you want to master them."

"Sorry," T.J. said. "I think I'm a lost cause."

"I'm not ready to give up on you yet. Maybe Nate can help you with the footwork. He seems to know his way around the dance floor."

"I think I'd rather practice with a beautiful woman than with this retired pitcher."

"Ditto," Nate said.

"Well, I have other students who need my attention as well. And I'm not getting through to you," she said. "Nate, why do you think that is?"

He realized she was being sincere. She wanted to help T.J. and that was the first time he realized that the dance lessons were important to her. He'd been too busy looking at her body and watching her sensual moves to pay attention earlier.

"I'm not sure. T.J. is used to using his body as a blunt instrument and dancing is more subtle, isn't it?"

"Yes, I think you're right. How about a line dance?"

T.J. groaned. "No. My sisters have tried rather unsuccessfully to get me to Electric Slide with them."

She laughed. "Does liquor help? Some people can't let go of their preconception that others are watching them dance until they have a few drinks."

"Not even a keg of beer could relax me," T.J. said. "But I appreciate your trying."

"It's my job."

"And you are very good at it," T.J. said. "I'd put a good word in with your boss but I think he already knows how good you are."

Jen glanced over at him. "Does he?"

Nate nodded. "You are very good."

He realized she was flirting with him just a little and he silenced the voice in the back of his head that had said she was off-limits. Her interest was all the permission he needed to pursue her.

She went back to the front of the classroom and told everyone to take a five-minute break. Then they'd practice the dance they were going to do to open the show one more time.

Nate followed Jen out of the room. She stopped in the hallway when she realized he was behind her.

"I'm sorry that T.J. isn't getting the dance."

"That's fine. You've gone above and beyond trying to teach him."

She nodded. "I'm not sure that you and I should dance together."

"Why not?" he asked, stepping closer to her.

She wrapped one arm around her waist and tipped

her head to the side. The high ponytail that held up her pretty brown hair brushed against her shoulder. He reached out to touch the end of it. Her hair was soft.

"That's why," she said. "I'm starting to forget you are my boss, Nate. And I like this job."

"Dancing with me isn't going to compromise your job," he said. "Luna Azul doesn't have a fraternization policy."

She wrinkled her brow. "I know that. But if something…"

"What?"

"It would be awkward and I really like this job," she said, then turned and walked away. And he let her leave realizing that she was concerned and that he had no idea who she was beyond a pretty girl that he was attracted to.

Jen wanted to just dance into the night with Nate. To pretend that her actions would have no consequences and that she could give in to the powerful attraction and that everything would be fine.

But she wasn't the young girl she'd once been. And she'd paid the price for making a bad decision based on her desires before. She wasn't about to make the same mistake twice.

It didn't matter how nice he'd felt when he'd held her in his arms. Or how right they'd fit together as they danced. It didn't matter.

But it did. She was always looking for a man who made her feel the way that Nate had when they'd danced together. It wasn't just the dancing but how he'd kept her gaze and how they'd just instinctively found the rhythm of each other. That kind of dancing was rare and she wanted to do more than just salsa with him.

She wanted to pull him close while the soul-sex sounds of Santana played in the background.

Stop it.

She needed this job. This was the new Jen Miller. No longer a creature who was ruled by what felt good or right, she now followed the rules. Put family first and was a good girl.

She had to remember that. Marcia had given her a place to stay when she'd needed it and she had promised her sister that she'd changed. That she'd embrace…well, being someone new.

Marcia had always thought that Jen was spoiled and to be honest, she was. She'd had talent from the age of eight. She'd been a dance prodigy and everyone had expected great things from her. And for Jen, those things had come easily.

Crashing at age twenty-six hadn't been in her plans and leaving the competitive dance world behind hadn't been, either. If she wanted to dance—and let's face it, she didn't know how to do anything else—then she needed to keep this job.

And that meant staying away from Nate Stern.

"You okay?" Alison asked, joining her in the hallway.

"Yes. I'm just trying to catch my breath before we go on."

"You and Nate…"

"I know. We have dance chemistry."

"In spades. I think you should capitalize on it," Alison said.

Sure, it was easy for her to say. She didn't have to go out there and dance a sensual dance with a man who was all wrong for her.

"How?"

"Have him come back every night."

"I doubt he has time for that. He's a busy man," Jen said. "Are you ready?"

"I am. Are you going to hang around and wait for XSU to perform?"

"Probably. You?"

"Yes. My boyfriend is meeting me here."

"How's it going with him—Richard, right?"

She nodded. "Pretty good. It's not a forever thing, but we have fun together."

Jen wanted that. Some guys she could have fun with and not lose her heart to. But she'd never been able to do it. Maybe it was simply the way she was wired but she didn't do casual. That's why Nate worried her.

If she could be like Alison and just have fun with him…why couldn't she?

She was starting over—why not start over with her attitude toward men? Why not have some fun?

"How do you keep from caring too much?" Jen asked.

Alison shrugged. "He's not the one so it's just fun. I don't think about anything except having a good time with him. If he's too busy to make it to something I'm doing, I call someone else."

Jen didn't know if she could do that. She wanted to.

"Why?"

"I…I wish I could be like that."

"You don't even date," Alison said. "We've known each other for eighteen months now and you haven't met a guy for coffee."

"I know. I'm just not into the casual scene but maybe I should be. I mean, I don't want to spend the rest of my life alone."

Alison smiled. "Want to come and hang with Richard and me tonight?"

Jen shook her head, then realized that she needed to do something different. "Okay. I'll do it."

"Good. Richard always has his posse with him and there are at least two guys I know who will be interested in you."

She swallowed. "What if I can't do it?"

"Then it's no biggie. They aren't exactly looking for a commitment."

She reentered the rehearsal room. Nate was standing off to one side, talking on his cell phone and she stared at him. And it hit her.

She didn't want to just learn how to lighten up and have fun with any friend of Richard's. She wanted to do it with Nate. He was the only reason why she was even considering changing her ways.

She wanted to spend more time with him but it didn't take a rocket scientist to know that Nate wasn't a long-term dating kind of guy. He always had a new woman on his arm and he was always in the papers. He was an arm-candy kind of guy and she'd never been an arm-candy kind of girl.

Wanting to be with him was understandable. He was hot and flirty. He made dancing feel the way she wanted it to. And he had the kind of dark eyes that she could lose herself in. But that didn't mean that she should pursue this any further than on the dance floor.

Hell, for all she knew he didn't want her for anything other than publicity for the club. Shaking her head, she put on "Mambo No. 5" and got the class ready to conga out into the crowd as she heard Manuel, the deejay for the open-air room, start warming them up.

"Everyone get ready."

"I know I am," Nate said. She felt his hands on her hips and she stumbled over her first step. She stumbled! That never happened.

But Nate caught her, and his hands on her hips as she led the way into the main room were all she thought of. She knew whether it was wise or not she wasn't going to deny herself the chance to get to know Nate better.

Because he was exactly her kind of man.

Three

Nate glanced around the crowded balcony club area and spotted just enough A-listers to make the party interesting. Leaning forward, he whispered in Jen's ear.

"That's Hutch Damien over there. Let's get him in this conga line."

"I don't know him."

"I do. Head over that way," Nate said.

He directed Jen as the line snaked through the tables. She had no microphone on, the deejay did all the talking in this club getting patrons on their feet. She left the conga line and approached the velvet ropes.

"Wanna dance?" she asked in that flirty way of hers.

"I never turn a pretty lady down," Hutch said with a grin. He hopped up and Nate moved back in the conga line to make room for him. The music swelled and Jen snaked through the room gathering up many of the people who all wanted to say they danced with Hutch Damien.

Hutch was a bona fide Hollywood superstar who'd started his career as a teenage rapper, but not with that hard-edged gangster rap—more of a sophisticated and fun sound that had him climbing the pop charts. He had movie-star good looks that he capitalized on to make films that people loved. And he was a genial guy.

Nate and he went way back to before his playing days when they'd both been rich boys at prep school. Since that image didn't jibe with Hutch's public persona of a rapper who made good, they seldom mentioned that fact to anyone.

Jen led them into the middle of the dance floor and then moved off to the side as the music ended and the deejay played "Hips Don't Lie" by Shakira.

Nate left T.J. and Hutch on the dance floor as a group of women came up to dance with them and probably grab a picture or two on their cell phones.

Jen was nowhere to be seen forty-five minutes later. He sent a message to Cam checking in to see if there was anything he needed from him. Then he tweeted about the club, talking up Hutch and T.J. on the dance floor.

He pocketed his phone and sought out his friends in the VIP section. He quickly found Hutch and T.J. and sat down with them. But Nate couldn't stay up here all night; he needed to make sure that there were celebrities throughout the club.

Nighttime was his busiest time but he loved it.

"Where you going?" Hutch asked him when he got up.

"We have a band performing downstairs."

"Not until ten," Hutch said, glancing pointedly at his watch.

Nate grinned sheepishly at his friend.

"There's a girl…" T.J. said.

"There's always a girl for our Nate."

"Yes, there is always a girl. I think you'll like her."

"So she's for me?"

"No," Nate said. "She's mine."

"Fair enough, who is she?" Hutch asked.

T.J. took a sip of his rum and Coke and leaned over the edge of the table, his eyes skimming the dance floor. Jen was in the middle doing a flamenco dance. "There she is. The dark-haired one dressed in red."

"Nice," Hutch said. "She works here?"

"Yes," Nate said, leaning back against the padding of the banquette. "Dance teacher."

"What's her name?" Hutch asked.

"Jen," Nate said.

The fact that he was going to bring her up here said more than he wanted it to. His friends understood that he rarely invited someone who wasn't a part of their group to join them. They were the same way. But Jen was different.

"I like her," T.J. said. "She's funny and knows how to move her body. And this one got jealous when she touched me."

"I am not jealous of you," Nate said.

That was one thing he'd never been. Even when he had been injured and had to quit playing ball he'd never envied those who still played. He didn't waste time dreaming about what might have been. He lived his life to the fullest and if that sometimes meant he had to course correct then he did it.

"I know, man, just joshing with you. Go get your girl before she disappears," T.J. said.

Nate glanced back at the dance floor. Sure enough, Jen and her assistant Alison were taking bows and leaving the club. For the night, he knew.

Nate stood up and walked through throngs of people in the club. He stopped to sign autographs for Yankees fans and posed for pictures with scantily clad women. He kept his smile in place even though he was impatient and wanted to get to Jen.

Cam texted him that there was some kind of problem with the guest list and Nate knew he needed to get down and take care of it, but he was afraid to miss Jen.

Afraid?

He shook his head and began making his way to the front desk instead of waiting for her. He walked down the grand staircase and looked at all the people crowding the dance floor and tried to take some satisfaction from it. This was his life. Luna Azul—the blue moon. Which had been the name of their father's boat when they'd been growing up.

They spent long lazy summer days on that yacht, just his dad and his brothers. Away from their shrew mother's demanding voice. Away from the shore where everyone wanted a piece of Jackson Stern, the PGA golf phenom. Away from the real world on the ocean where they could just be themselves.

And Nate had thought naming the club after that childhood oasis had been a stroke of genius, but then Cam was good about doing those kinds of things. Finding a connection between the past and the present.

He got to the VIP desk just as he caught a whiff of a familiar flowery scent. He glanced over his shoulder and saw Jen standing there.

"Sorry about this. I was told my sister and her friend would be able to get in tonight if I left their names here."

"Of course they can," he said, realizing that this was fate. Jen and he were destined to spend this night together.

Jen had been trying to avoid Nate. Having his hands on her hips during the conga had made her too aware of him. And she knew that she was on the verge of doing something stupid once again so, of course, there'd be a problem with Marcia and her friend getting into the club tonight. And it seemed fitting that Nate would be the one man they'd call to fix it.

"I'm so sorry," she said again.

"It's not a problem," Nate said. He turned to Marcia and smiled at her. "I'm Nate Stern."

"Marcia Miller, and this is my friend Courtney."

"Pleasure, ladies. Give me a few minutes and I will get this straightened out," he said.

He walked back over to the VIP desk and Jen wanted to disappear now while she still could. This was embarrassing. She didn't want to bother him.

"Is this okay?" Marcia asked.

"Yes, it's fine. Nate will take care of it."

"I don't want you to get in trouble," Courtney said.

"I won't," Jen said. She hoped she was right. The club policy was that two comp tickets a month were issued to the employees and she hadn't ever used hers. So she knew that she was technically in the right.

"It's fine," she said again.

Marcia reached over and rubbed her arm. "Nate Stern? Is he your boss?"

"Sort of. You know who Nate is, Marcia, don't pretend you don't."

"I do. It's odd that he seems to be handling operational things. I thought he was a playboy."

Jen shrugged. "That's his image and it works for the club but he's doesn't strike me as someone who's just loafing around waiting for a free ride."

"That's reassuring," Marcia said.

"I know it is."

"How do you know him?" Courtney asked.

"He was in my dance class tonight…one of his friends had signed up and I guess he tagged along to make sure it went smoothly."

"Has he done that before?" Marcia asked.

"No and I've had bigger celebs than T. J. Martinez in the class."

"You had T.J.—"

"Yes, stop drooling, Courtney."

"Ha. I'm not drooling, but he's hot. You have the best job."

"You're just saying that because all you do is Excel spreadsheets all day."

"Very true," Courtney said. "He's coming back."

Jen glanced over her shoulder to see Nate walking toward them. He held up two tickets, which he handed to Courtney and Marcia. "Have fun, ladies."

"We will. Thank you, Mr. Stern," Marcia said.

"Call me Nate. And you should thank your sister. There was just a mix-up with the list you were on," he said.

"Thanks, Jen," Marcia said. "Are you coming with us?"

She nodded.

"Can I have a word before you go in?" Nate asked.

"I will meet you both inside in a few minutes," she said to Marcia and Courtney.

As they left, she turned to Nate. "What's up?"

"Do you have plans for this evening?"

She wrinkled her brow. "I'm meeting my sister and her friend."

"I guess that sounded stupid," he said.

"Just a little bit. Why did you ask?"

"I want you to join me."

"Why?" she asked.

"I think you would be fun to hang with."

She tipped her head to the side to study him. She wanted to say yes and thought about what Alison had said earlier about just having fun. She couldn't ask for someone who knew how to party better than Nate.

"Okay."

"Wow, did you really have to think on it?"

"Yes," she said. "I'm not...I don't make snap decisions."

"I'll remember that. Do you need to check in with your sister?"

"Yes. Why don't you come and hang with us for a little while?"

"That wasn't what I had in mind."

"What did you have in mind?" she asked. She had no idea why she'd agreed to this and she might be in over her head. She should have eased herself back into the dating scene with one of Courtney's financial analyst friends or someone that worked at her sister's law office instead of jumping straight from stay at home every night to Nate Stern.

"You and me burning up the dance floor."

She looked up at him. "I'm not your kind of girl, you know that, right?"

"No, I don't. I think you and I are going to get along very well."

"That's what I'm afraid of," she said under her breath. But in for a penny in for a pound, she thought. She wanted this night and this man so she was going to go for it.

"Come on, Nate. See if you can keep up."

He laughed a full robust laugh. It made her smile just to hear it. He was that kind of guy. The kind that knew how to enjoy life, and she realized she needed someone like that. She needed to learn how to go with the flow.

He took her hand in his big one and led the way into the club, over to where Marcia and Courtney waited. She tried to tell herself that she was in control of this but she had the feeling that Nate was and she wasn't sure what the outcome would be.

Marcia and Courtney left at midnight but Nate wasn't ready to let Jen go yet.

"Stay," he said when they were in the lobby under the beautiful Chihuly glass sculpture depicting the night sky.

"I'm not sure that is wise," she said. "I have to work tomorrow."

"Not until the evening. Stay and play with me, Jen," he said.

"I...okay, why not? What will we do now?"

"There's an after-party for the band. It's up in your court—the rooftop club."

"Okay. But I can't stay past two," she said.

"I won't hold it against you if you change your mind."

"Are you really that confident of yourself?" she asked.

"Of course. I know that you are enjoying yourself and your sister told me that you don't have enough fun."

"She said that?"

"Yes."

"What else did she say?"

"That you were her little sister and she'd hurt me if I hurt you."

Jen flushed. "She's just overprotective. Our mom worked a lot when we were growing up and Marcia was the one who always had to watch me."

"Some habits never die," Nate said. "It's the same with Cam and me."

"I can see that about him. He's like everyone's older brother here."

"He takes care of family. If you cross him…well, I wouldn't."

"Me, either," Jen said.

"Do you know him well?" Nate asked. It seemed odd to him that he'd just met Jen today and that his brother might have known her longer.

"Not really. But he asked me to serve on the tenth anniversary celebration committee."

"Yes, I am to be on that committee, too, so we will be seeing a lot more of each other."

She glanced down and he wondered at her expression. But then T.J. came over and slung an arm around his shoulder. "Buddy, how's it going?"

"Good," he said, realizing T.J. was drunk. He was reluctant to stop talking to Jen, now that he was finally learning a little about her, but T.J. needed him.

"Let's find a table to sit down and chat."

"Nah, I'm making the rounds. Did I tell you that I'm a single guy again?"

Nate shook his head. "I heard it through the grapevine."

"Everyone has," T.J. said.

"I think I see a table in the back that will be nice. Why don't you two go grab it and I'll get us some drinks," Jen said.

"Not a problem, Jen. As soon as we sit down, Steve will send my usual drink order over," Nate said.

"I don't think he'll know what I want, so I will tell him and then join you both," she said.

"Thanks," Nate said, leading T.J. through the crowds to the table that Jen had spotted. T.J. was rambling a little about being single again.

"I hate it, man. I'm not like you. I don't like the party life. I want to go home with the same woman every night. Have a nice little house in the suburbs, ya know?"

Nate patted him on the shoulder. "I do know. It will work out when you find the right girl."

"The right girl? I doubt there is one out there. We don't meet nice girls, ya know?"

Nate started to agree but then glanced up to see Jen walking toward them. He thought that they did meet nice girls in their lives but they never knew how to treat them. And he was torn for the first time in recent memory. He wanted to be more of a gentleman for Jen than he normally was but he had the feeling that it was too late for that. He scarcely remembered how to be a gentleman.

"I don't think guys like you and me know what to do with a nice girl."

"Could be," T.J. said as he looked at Jen. "Did you tell the bartender to bring me another rum and Coke?"

"No, sorry. I told him Coke straight up."

"I need the rum, Jen. I think I could samba better with rum."

"I don't know about that. And I was teaching you the salsa."

"Damn. I guess I'm not impressing you," T.J. said.

"You already have when I watch you play," she said.

"I am a hot third-base player."

"You are a stud on the baseball diamond," Nate agreed.

"I am. I think I'm going to head over to the bar and see if I can get them to add a little rum to this Coke," he said. "Not that I don't appreciate the thought, Jen."

"No problem," she said.

T.J. got up and left the table. Nate watched his friend go and hoped that he'd find some kind of peace in the alcohol.

"Thanks for giving us a minute," Nate said.

"It's okay. I have friends, too. I know how it is when you need some privacy with them," she said.

"Sit down," he said, gesturing to the seat next to him.

"I was thinking I should head out," she said.

"Why? What changed your mind?"

She sat down in the chair next to him perching on the edge of the seat. "This isn't my scene."

"Why not? It's not different than being downstairs with your sister," Nate said.

"Maybe not to you, but this isn't my crowd of people. There are celebs everywhere and people are taking photos with them and I think there are only two groups here."

"What are they?"

"Those who belong and those who are hanging on. And I don't want to be that," Jen said.

She reached over and took his hand in hers and he noticed how delicate her fingers looked with those long pink nails of hers. "I like you, Nate, but this is your world, and being here for just a short time has shown me that I don't belong in it."

"You could if I invited you in."

"I could," she said. "But for how long?"

Four

Nate shrugged. "Life can be pretty crazy."

"I know it can," she said.

"Sit down, Jen. Tell me what brought you here."

She swallowed hard enough for him to see and shook her head. "That's not a good topic of conversation."

"Why not?"

"Because there's a samba playing and I'd rather dance."

And just like that she changed the conversation. He was no longer thinking about who she was and where she'd come from but rather how nice it felt when they'd danced together earlier.

He stood and led her to the dance floor. As soon as they were there he turned and she started dancing. The samba was a very quick-moving dance but he followed her moves perfectly.

When he'd been old enough to notice girls, he'd

realized that they liked to dance and if he knew
how—no matter how much ribbing he had to take from
his friends—he'd be very popular with the ladies. That
had worked to his advantage and he'd liked it.

Jen was a great dancer, her lithe body moving in time
with the music, but she also kept eye contact with him
and soon the dance felt as if it was just between the two
of them.

He found the rhythm and their hips swayed in the
same motion. He drew her closer to him as they moved
and felt the brush of her body against his. He kept his
hand steady in the small of her back even when she
would have stepped back.

She looked up at him, confusion and desire evident in
her gaze, and he knew that something had just changed
between them.

The lust that had been there from the first moment
they met was now blossoming into something stronger,
something more solid. And as the song built up to the
ending, he drew her into his arms and kissed her.

She didn't think of the past or the future. She just
lived in the now.

Somehow the night slipped away from her and though
she'd meant to leave after one dance, one dance turned
into just one more and she spent the night on the floor
with Nate. For the first time since she'd been forced to
leave the competitive dance world she felt alive.

It bothered her that a man was the reason why. And
she knew that this night was a one-off. There was no
way she'd ever be with Nate for more than this night.
His crowd of friends consisted of people that she read
about in glamour magazines and on the internet gossip

websites. And though they were unfailingly polite to her, she knew tomorrow they wouldn't recognize her.

"I need a drink," Nate said, drawing her off the dance floor. "You might be used to dancing that much but I am not."

"I didn't notice you falling behind," she said.

"I've got the stamina," he said with a wink. "Plus, I couldn't let a girl out-dance me."

"A girl? Women don't like being called girls," she said to him.

"Ah, I meant it in a nice way. My dad was real old-fashioned when it came to ladies and we were never allowed to call girls women. He thought it was too harsh."

Jen shook her head and had to laugh at that. "I guess it's okay then."

He hugged her close with one arm. They were both sweaty from dancing so much and she liked Nate's musky smell. She leaned in closer for just a second before she realized what she was doing.

"Don't," he said, stopping her by holding her tighter. "I like having you close."

"I like it, too," she said, softly. She looked up into those dark obsidian eyes of his.

"Good. Now how about another mojito?"

"I think water would be better," she said. She was already buzzing a little from the drinks and the dancing. And from Nate, she thought. He went to her head faster than any other man she'd ever been with. Maybe that was because in the past, a man would have had to compete with her dancing career, but now she was simply a woman. And this man…well, he was addictive.

"Water first," he said. "Then mojitos…I don't like to drink alone."

"I'm sure that's not an issue. You always have someone on your arm."

"Not always," he said.

And as he walked away, she realized there was more to the playboy that she'd first suspected.

When he returned to her side, he led her out of the crowded part of the club and behind the stage where there was a roped-off area. There were not a lot of people back here—in fact, it took her a few moments to notice it was just the two of them.

He handed her the water and she drank it down, grateful for it after all the dancing they'd done.

"I love this view," he said, pulling her closer to the railing that ran around the edge of the roof.

She glanced out over Little Havana and toward the Miami skyline. She could make out the bright lights on the Four Seasons Hotel, which was the largest building in Florida. It was a breathtaking view.

"I can see why," she said. "Tell me about this club and how you ended up here."

He arched one eyebrow at her. "I would have thought that was all common knowledge."

She shook her head. "Not really. I mean I know the headlines and the speculation, but I want to know the real story. Why did Nate Stern leave baseball to help run a club in South Florida with his brothers instead of pursuing a career in front of the camera?"

She finished her glass of water and set it down on the wrought-iron table. Nate took her arm and led her farther away from the club sounds as the deejay played Santana. There was a padded bench set amongst some tall trees. The night breeze surrounded them and she felt more comfortable in her own skin than she had in years.

"If I tell you my secrets will you tell me yours?" he asked.

She nodded. "I'm not nearly as interesting as you, but if you want to know about me, I will tell you if you get me a mojito."

"Good."

After a brief trip to the bar, he came back and he handed her the mojito, then gestured for her to sit down. He sat next to her, stretching his long arm behind her on the bench and drawing her closer to him.

Nate didn't like to talk too much about the old days. He did it with guys like T.J. because they expected him to and frankly that was the only thing he and T.J. had in common. The old days.

But reminiscing about what was instead of focusing on what is had never seemed wise to him.

"I think you asked about why I'm here," he said.

"I did. I've always thought…well, since I started working at the club you seem the least likely to actually be happy here in Miami. Why didn't you stay in New York or head to L.A.?"

He shrugged. He'd thought about it. But to be honest, he had been injured and unsure and he'd needed the support of his brothers around him. And frankly, they weren't going to give up their homes to move across the country.

"It just felt right," he said.

She laughed as she turned to look up at him. "I can't believe you made a decision based on your gut. I mean one that would change your life."

"Why not? When I played baseball I made gut decisions all the time." It was one of the things he thought had made him stand out.

"I never thought about it like that."

"Most people don't. So that's it. My brothers were here. I'd invested in the club so I technically had a job, at least on paper, and my sports career was over so I came home."

"You sum it up like you are stating facts," she said, her voice soft and pensive. "Was it really that easy or did you struggle to give up your dream?"

"My dream?"

"Baseball," she said.

He had had a rough patch but had worked through it. "The sad thing about me, Jen, is that I realized I didn't want to be just a baseball player."

"What did you want to be?" she asked, moving closer to him.

He knew he could talk about himself all night with her as an audience. Most people didn't listen well and were just waiting for a chance to talk about themselves but Jen was engaged in what he was saying. He wasn't sure why. Did she really want to know the man he was?

"Famous," he said. "I know, shallow, right?"

"I wanted that, too," she admitted.

He thought she was being kind and trying to make him feel better about his rather shallow goals. Cam always said that Nate was too pretty and that had made him believe he could skate through life. But Nate ignored what his brother said. He'd worked hard to be good at baseball and he'd done it because he thought it would pay off.

In a way, it had.

"Really?" he asked.

"You think I'm joking around?"

"Of course not. But I don't know anything about you.

I know you weren't a baseball player. Our paths would have crossed before tonight."

"Indeed, they would have," she said.

"So?"

She took a deep breath and then a sip of her drink. The mojito was smooth and minty and he saw her savor it as it went down. Since she hadn't lingered over her drink like that before, he suspected she didn't want to talk about herself now.

"Tell me, honey. Your secret is safe with me."

"Honey? You don't know me well enough to call me that."

"Jen, I will before the night is over."

"Isn't that a little presumptuous of you?" she asked.

"No. You are just as interested in me as I am in you."

She nodded. "I am. I hate to say it but I really do want to know the man behind the flash."

"Good. I hope you find him to your liking," he said.

"You're impressing me so far," she said.

He took another sip of his drink. The February breeze blew around them stirring a tendril at the side of her face. Each time the wind blew, the strand of hair brushed over her high cheekbones and caught on her lips.

He reached up and brushed it back, tucking it behind her ear. "There you go."

"Thanks," she said, but her voice was softer, huskier than it had been moments earlier.

"What did you want to be famous for doing?" he asked.

He couldn't stop touching her skin. It was soft, maybe the softest he'd felt in a long time. The women he usually kept company with were concerned about their looks and how they appeared to others—seldom did they let him touch them except in bed when they were making love. But Jen let him touch her face.

He stroked his finger over her lower lip until she pulled back. Her lips were parted and her breath brushed across his finger.

"I can't think when you do that," she said.

"Then don't think," he replied. He tightened his arm along her shoulders and drew her closer to him. Her mojito glass brushed against his chest wet and cold.

She licked her lips and her eyes started to close as he lowered his head. He wanted this night to go on forever but he knew he couldn't sit here on the rooftop another minute without kissing her.

She tempted him on so many levels and he wasn't sure how to deal with a woman who had that effect on him. He wanted to pretend that it was simply the unknown and the curiosity of being with someone who seemed so natural here with him. He didn't have the feeling she was with him because she wanted to meet his famous friends or have her picture in the papers.

And that was a heady aphrodisiac.

Jen was surprised by her reaction to Nate—a non-dancer. She shook her head reminding herself dancing wasn't her life anymore. It still was a shock to think of her world the way it was now.

"I'm sensing you aren't thinking about kissing me anymore."

She pulled back, nibbling on her lower lip. The smell of hibiscus filled the air from the potted plants that were stationed near the edge of the railing.

"No—I mean yes. I was thinking about you. How different you are than the other men I've dated."

"I don't want to hear about the other men in your life," he said, his voice sounding tight.

"Why not? I'm just your one-night girl, right?" she asked. It was imperative to her that she keep her focus here. No matter that Nate was a life-changing man for her. The first guy she'd wanted to kiss since Carlos.

He tipped his head to the side, staring over at her. "Normally, I'd say yes, but I'm jealous, honey. I don't want to hear you talk about other men when you're with me. I want to be the only man on your mind."

She understood that. She was finding herself struck with an uncharacteristic shyness as they sat here alone. It was because he was so different for her...no, he wasn't, she thought. She was the one who was different. She wanted to own this change and not let it own her.

"You are staring very fiercely at me."

"I'm sorry. I just had an epiphany."

He leaned in. "That you should be kissing me?"

"Actually, yes," she said. She should be kissing him. Like Alison had said, life was short and having fun wasn't overrated.

She leaned over and let the shyness that really wasn't a part of her drop away. She was a woman who had always been comfortable in her own skin. She hated that Carlos had stolen that from her.

And Nate was just the man to give it back. Nate Stern was the man she'd regain her womanhood with because she was tired of just existing. It was time to start living again. She glanced up at the full moon and made a promise to herself that starting this moment she would live with no regrets.

She leaned in close and Nate's pupils dilated. "That's more like it."

Yes, it was. She brushed his lips with hers. His were firm and full and when he parted them the warmth of his breath brushed over her. He smelled like the minty mojito and she closed her eyes to just enjoy this moment.

To take from this night the gift it had given her in Nate.

He drew her closer to him. She felt the warmth of his body and slowed this moment down in her mind. The way she did when she was dancing. She wanted to capture every bit of this evening so that when she was old and gray and she told her grandkids about kissing the famous Yankees baseball player she'd be able to do it right.

Then his lips brushed over hers again and she stopped thinking about the future or capturing anything. She thought instead of the way his flesh felt against hers. She thought of the way his lips parted against hers and his tongue pushed past the barriers of her lips and teeth tasting her deep.

The way he took control of the entire embrace, the same way he'd taken control of her night. *Control.* It had always been something she prided herself on but now it hardly seemed worthwhile.

His arms were big and strong as he wrapped them around her and she felt the muscles of his upper arms, the strength in him. Though he was no longer a professional athlete, Nate Stern was still a very strong man.

She put her hands on his shoulders and pushed back to look at his face. The genial smile he'd worn all night was gone and in its place was a fierce expression.

"Too much?"

"Maybe," she said. "Maybe. I came to work tonight expecting everything to be the same, Nate, and now it's not."

"Good. Life should never be predictable."

She shook her head. "Yes, it should. How else do you find your balance if life is always throwing you off?"

He stood up and drew her up beside him. "You find it in the people."

"Family?" she asked as he led the way to the railing.

"Or the city," he said. "Miami never changes. Not really. Not at its heart. Sure there is a different political climate sometimes but for the most part, the beach and subtropical climate encourage a more laid-back approach to living."

His arm around her waist was strong and guiding as he brought them to a stop at the far end of the railing. The sounds of Luna Azul's rooftop club were even more muted here and she looked out over Calle Ocho and Little Havana.

"Did you grow up here in Little Havana?"

"No. I grew up on Fisher Island."

"Oh," she said. She'd known that from the reading she'd done on him and his brothers before she'd taken this job. But the way he spoke about Miami, well, it had sounded as if he knew the city. The city she'd grown up in. Being middle class—okay, lower-middle class— she'd grown up in a far different neighborhood than the affluent community of Fisher Island.

"You?"

"Here in the city."

He tipped her head up. "Then you know what I mean."

She closed her eyes and thought of the city and the rhythms of the Calle Ocho. She thought of the struggling lower-middle class who still knew how to have fun and remembered birthdays spent on the beach.

"Yes, I do."

"Show me what you see," Nate said. He moved around so that he stood behind her. His chest and front pressed along her back, his hands settling on her waist and his chin resting on her shoulder. "Show me your city."

She started to point out the places she knew and what she heard when she was there. "Each part has a different rhythm, a different feel to it."

"Like dancing?"

"Just like dancing. Some of it is hip and current, other parts sensual and emotional, some parts are the blues… the vibes all resonate around me."

"Show me," he said again, turning her in his arms and kissing her the way he had when they were sitting down. But this time he pulled from her so much more than a response to a kiss. He pulled out the song that she heard in her head. The song that was the very heart of who she was.

And she shared it with him with the sensual undulation of her hips. And the way she rested the curves of her breasts against the firmness of his chest.

Five

The sun was just coming up over the horizon when they arrived at his penthouse apartment in a skyscraper downtown. Nate had seldom enjoyed an evening as much as he had this one and he knew it was due to the fact that he was with Jen.

She stood in his foyer looking sleepy but happy and in this moment, Nate felt as if the night was a success. Somewhere between all the kisses and caresses he'd realized that despite the fact that she was a dancer and spent her life with people staring at her body, Jen was shy about letting anyone touch her too much.

He pulled her into his arms. He didn't care about the city or what she thought of it, he wanted her. Had wanted her from the moment she'd sassed him in the club earlier. And the entire night had just reinforced that longing.

"I like this place," she said as she walked across the Italian marble floor.

She stood in front of the floor-to-ceiling glass windows in his living room. "This view…"

"Incredible, isn't it?" he asked, coming to stand behind her. He put his arms around her and drew her back against him.

"I had fun tonight," she said. "I didn't expect to."

"Why not?"

"This wasn't my best day," she said.

"I thought you enjoyed yourself," he said, leading the way to his modern kitchen. He directed her toward one of the high-backed stools at the counter.

"Tonight has been fun. But it started out worse…I'm tired, so I'm not making sense. I meant to say you made a bad day better."

"I'm glad. What was bad about it?"

"Just some news I was hoping would be different."

"What news?" he asked as he started gathering the ingredients for omelets from the refrigerator.

"Remember earlier tonight when you asked me about my secrets?" she asked. She didn't look up at him but instead traced a pattern on the Mexican tile countertop. Her finger just ran across the pattern over and over again. He was struck by how long her fingers were. He wondered what they'd feel like on his skin.

"I do, indeed. Does the bad news have to do with your secrets?" he asked. He really hadn't thought she was hiding much. She was a dancer and a choreographer. What kind of secrets could she have?

"Yes, it does. I don't know what you know about my past," she said, glancing over at him.

"Not too much. If I had to guess I'd say you were a dancer."

"You'd be right on the money. Dancing has been my life for as long as I can remember. And I made a mistake a few years ago and haven't been able to compete since then," she said.

"What kind of mistake?"

"One that involved a man," she said. Her eyes were wide and weary as she watched him and he kept his face neutral.

"It's funny, Jen, but a woman ultimately led to my change of profession."

"Really?"

"Yes. When I was injured I had been engaged and while I was recovering, she decided to move on to a different player."

"I'm sorry."

"I'm not. Obviously, we weren't going to be happy together. I learned a very important lesson from her, one I haven't forgotten," he said.

"What was that?" she asked.

"That I'm not cut out for marriage," he said.

"To her," Jen said. "Why did you tell me?"

"So you wouldn't feel like you were the only one to make a mistake because of love. What happened with your 'mistake'?"

"I was forbidden from competing in the Latin dance competitions. I filed an appeal," she said. "After a lengthy review, the verdict stands and I'm still not welcome to compete." Her shoulders fell. "I'm never going to compete again."

"That's okay. You are going to do other things," he said. "At the club every night you share your love for Latin music and dances with someone new. That has to count for something."

She shook her head. "It's not the same."

"No, it's not. But that is life, isn't it?"

"Yes, it is. I am still struggling to figure out where I'm going to fit in without competition."

"How long has it been since you competed?" he asked. He thought she'd been working at Luna Azul for at least a year.

"Three years. I filed a protest as soon as it happened. And I don't want to sound like I'm full of myself but things usually work out for me. I just expected this to do the same."

"My dad used to say that everything happens for a reason," Nate said, hearing his father's voice in his head. "We might not understand the reason but it's there."

She tipped her head to the side and studied him. "Do you believe that?"

"Yes, I do. I'm going to tell you something I don't let most people know," he said, leaning across the counter so that their faces were close.

"What is that?"

"I couldn't have been as content playing baseball as I am with the life I'm living now."

"Really?" she asked, sounding a bit skeptical.

"Truly. I get to see my brothers every day. I'm paid to entertain my friends and make sure that people have a good time. Is there a better job in the world?"

She nodded. "I see what you mean. I do love dancing and I'm able to do that every night."

She got a far-off look in her eyes and he knew there was more to the story than she was letting on. "I guess I had gone as far as I could in that career. It was time for something new."

"And you get to spend the morning with me," he said.

"Wow, Nate, don't sell yourself short," she said with a laugh.

"I never do," he said, kissing her.

* * *

Nate's advice made sense and she liked the way he gave it out effortlessly and didn't try to pretend that he had all the answers. He was more than she'd expected him to be, but then he'd been surprising her all night. She should be used to it.

"I'm not really hungry," she said at last. She hadn't come back to his place to eat and they both knew it.

"I'm not, either."

He came around the counter and drew her to her feet. "Want to see the rest of this place?"

"Yes, I do."

He led the way down the hall to his bedroom. On the walls were exquisite pictures in bright colors that reminded her of Mexico City. His home was very modern and now. But it wasn't a cold, modern decor, it was very warm and inviting and Jen was amazed that she felt so at home here.

She drew him to a stop under a portrait of him wearing a Yankees cap. "When did you take this?"

"Season opener. My dad wanted it…he was so proud of me for going pro. He came to every game if it didn't interfere with his playing schedule. This hung in his bedroom at our home on Fisher Island."

"When did he die?" she asked.

"Two weeks after I got injured. He didn't know I'd never play again," Nate said. "I'm glad."

"I think he'd still be proud of you," she said. She knew that her parents would have been proud of her no matter what she did. Marcia always said that parents just wanted their kids to be happy. Usually she was referring to her own seven-year-old son Riley.

"I'm not sure. Why am I telling you all this stuff?" he asked.

"People tell me things," she said. "I think I look like the girl next door and people just feel comfortable with me. You probably do, too."

"Girl next door? What do you mean by that?"

"Just someone comfortable. You know, the kind of girl you can tell your secrets to."

"You called yourself a girl."

She mock-punched his shoulder. "I do it all the time, but that doesn't mean I like hearing a man call me a girl."

He smiled. "Just when I think I have you figured out you do something else to surprise me."

"I hope I'm not so easy to figure out," she said. No matter that she told him about her dancing suspension. She usually played her cards closer to her chest. But to be honest, she had no idea how to deal with this life now that she had no direction. And opening up to Nate felt right somehow.

"You're not. You are very complex," he said, pulling her into his arms. "And very beautiful."

He leaned in close and whispered in her ear, telling her how sexy he found her body and how much he wanted to touch her all night. His breath was warm and she liked hearing what he said.

He made her feel like she wasn't incomplete. And that was it, she thought. Since she'd had her appeal denied, she realized that she'd felt broken, but here in Nate's arms none of that mattered.

She twined her arms around his neck and lifted herself up to kiss him. His mouth moved hungrily over hers and she lost herself. His hands skimmed down her back and settled on her hips. He pulled her closer to him.

The feel of his strong, muscled arms around her

made her feel very delicate and feminine. She had never been with a man who felt like Nate did. He was strong, muscled, his body still in shape from years of being an athlete. There was no way for her to pretend he was anyone other than Nate Stern.

Her blood flowed heavier in her veins as he moved his hands over her. She knew that Nate was in control of this embrace. She was letting him set the tempo and as much as she wanted him, she wasn't ready to take the lead in anything between them. He lifted her off her feet.

"Wrap your arms and legs around me," he said.

She held tight to him as he walked them into the bedroom. He sat down on the edge of the king-size bed. His hands roamed up and down her back as she looked down at him.

He tipped his head up and kissed her. There was passion in the kiss but also a note of tenderness and it was the tenderness that won her over. She held his face in both of her hands and plunged her tongue deep into his mouth. He reciprocated, tangling one of his hands deep in her thick hair.

He held her tight as passion overwhelmed her.

He leaned back and she straddled him on the bed. He palmed her breasts, cupping and fondling them gently. She undid the buttons of his shirt and he slowly drew her blouse up her torso. She liked the sensation of the cloth against her skin. She stopped what she was doing and tipped her head back, enjoying the moment.

His hands were warm against her flesh and he draped the fabric over the top of her breasts so that it hung there. His big hands encircled her waist and drew her down toward him.

She felt the warmth of his breath against her nipple

the minutiae of Zac Prescott's life, after working twelve-hour days and scrimping each dollar, she finally had enough to start her own business. Her week off was supposed to pave the way for her resignation, to ease Zac into it. Instead she'd ended up as his personal on-call service.

Pound, pound, pound.

"Dammit, George." She grabbed the door handle and yanked it open. "Can you stop with the— Oh."

"What the hell is this?" Zac Prescott stood on her stoop, all angry male, a piece of paper crumpled in his clenched fist.

She took a cautious step back. Zac wasn't a yeller. The one and only time she'd seen him lose it was during a call from his father, close to a year ago.

"It's my resignation," she replied calmly.

Zac's olive-green eyes narrowed. "Why?"

What was the collective noun for a group of butterflies? A swarm? Whatever it was, they were doing a number on her insides. Zac Prescott was dressed in sharply creased dark gray pants, a pristine white long-sleeved shirt and a silk tie with blue-green swirls that she'd given him last Christmas. He cut an impressive figure, but it was the face that got her: a beautiful, rugged package that was the result of a dark, brooding father and a blond-haired, green-eyed Swedish mother. The elegant, almost artistic compilation of all-male angles and tanned clean-shaven skin tightened her insides and sent hot sexual awareness pounding through her veins.

She blinked, forcing the delicious ache aside. "Because I quit."

"You can't quit." He surged forward, and Emily had no choice but to give way. His broad body invaded her space, his larger-than-life presence sucking away the very air in her small one-bedroom apartment. It was overwhelming—he was overwhelming.

She took a measured breath, and his distinctive, fresh-yet-sinful scent teased her nostrils, filling her senses, making her head spin with delicious memories. She bit off the hitch in her throat and gently closed the door.

He'd paused in the middle of her lounge room, a clear contrast she'd never known had died and left his Gold Coast apartment to her. So she'd moved clear across the country to Queensland and started over with barely healed wounds and a brand-new hard-ass attitude. She'd scraped back her hair, donned her glasses and shoved herself into monochrome business suits and sensible shoes in order to play the part of a serious professional. And it had paid off when she'd landed the job as Zac Prescott's personal assistant two years ago.

"Maybe it isn't as bad as you think," AJ was saying now.

"No, it's worse." Emily sighed. "I've had it with men."

AJ spluttered on whatever she'd been drinking. "So after a bunch of idiot boyfriends, a false misconduct threat and a loser ex-husband, you're gay now?"

"No." Emily stifled a laugh. "I meant I've had it with getting emotionally sucked into their games, their baggage, their whole mess-with-your-head thing."

"Ah! You're finally coming over to the Dark Side?"

Emily did laugh then. "At least the Dark Side has sex without commitment."

"But that's *me*. You're Angel to my Spike. You're the hyper-organized good girl with the strong moral compass, the one looking for Mr. Right."

"Yeah, and look where that's gotten me." Emily tilted her ear to the narrow hallway. "Someone's at the door."

"Damn. I told that stripper-gram *after* seven."

"Ha, ha. Look, I'll see you tonight. Eight-thirty at Jupiters, right?"

"Yep. And I expect to hear more details then. Happy twenty-sixth birthday, Em."

Some birthday. Emily clicked off the phone, then scowled as the thumping on her screen door became ever more impatient. "All right, I'm coming!"

Probably her grumpy old postie complaining about her missing letterbox again.

She grabbed an elastic from the bookcase as she passed, pulled her hair back, then secured it low on her neck. It wasn't just men who were the problem—she was. After two years of organizing

"Have you not been listening? He's my boss. I finally had a strong, respectful work relationship going and then I go and do something stupid. Talk about déjà vu."

"What do you mean 'had'?" Emily heard a loud bang down the line: AJ had slammed a door closed. "Details."

Emily groaned, tugging off the towel turban that held her freshly washed hair. "I've been on leave for the past week. On Thursday night he called me from the office, blind drunk. I drove him home, got him in the front door, we stumbled...and it sort of happened."

"Ah, the old 'stumble and kiss' routine."

Emily scowled at her distorted reflection in the dark TV screen. Zac being drunk didn't excuse her behavior: that she'd been secretly lusting after a completely-off-limits guy this past year only compounded her stupidity.

"It's not funny. I panicked, shut myself in at home and spent the weekend thinking."

"That's dangerous. And...?"

"And then I quit. This morning. By e-mail."

"Oh, Em! The drunken kiss aside, why?"

"You know why." She ran a hand through her still-damp hair, twisting the ends around her fingers. "I can't go through another misconduct accusation again."

"But Zac isn't like that—that other jerk lied!"

Emily sighed, self-anger congealing into a lumpy mess that sat heavily in her belly. She'd thought talent and dedication got you ahead in the corporate world, not how blond your hair was or how short your skirts were. She'd always dressed professionally, always worked hard for her temping jobs, believing that one day an employer would recognize and reward her business skills.

And four years ago they had, but not in the way she'd assumed. The permanent position at one of Perth's top accountancy firms had come with strings, as she'd found out at the office Christmas party six months later. The first time she'd put on a miniskirt and a nice top, a managing director had groped her on the balcony.

Emily shuddered. She'd been twenty-two, humiliated and alone in the world. No family, no home, nothing—until some uncle

One

"You did *what?*"

Emily Reynolds yanked the phone from her ear and winced before readjusting it back under her chin. "I kissed my boss."

"Wait. Back up," her older sister AJ demanded on the other end. "You kissed Zac Prescott."

"Yep."

"The guy God built just to make a woman whimper with joy."

"The same."

"And you, my little sister who hates surprises and runs the man's company with clockwork efficiency?"

"No need to rub it in—*I know* I'm the dumbest female on the planet." Holed up in her apartment on her comfy two-seater, dressed in her bathrobe and with ankles crossed on the coffee table, it was easy to believe that last week had been just a figment of Emily's overactive imagination. But the telltale warmth on her skin gave her true thoughts away every time.

"Emmy, you are the *luckiest* female on the planet! Was it good?"

Despite wanting to be a vet, choreographer, card shark, hairdresser and an interior designer (although not simultaneously!), British-born, Aussie-bred **Paula Roe** ended up as a personal assistant, office manager, software trainer and aerobics instructor for thirteen interesting years.

Paula lives in western New South Wales, Australia, with her family, two opinionated cats and a garden full of dependent native birds. She still retains a deep love of filing systems, stationery and travelling, even though the latter doesn't happen nearly as often as she'd like. She loves to hear from her readers—you can visit her at her website at www.paularoe.com.

All the characters in this book have no existence outside the imagination of the author, and have no relation whatsoever to anyone bearing the same name or names. They are not even distantly inspired by any individual known or unknown to the author, and all the incidents are pure invention.

Published in Great Britain 2011
by Mills & Boon, an imprint of Harlequin (UK) Limited,
Eton House, 18-24 Paradise Road, Richmond, Surrey TW9 1SR

© Paula Roe 2011

ISBN: 978 0 263 88327 5

51-1211

Harlequin (UK) policy is to use papers that are natural, renewable and recyclable products and made from wood grown in sustainable forests. The logging and manufacturing processes conform to the legal environmental regulations of the country of origin.

Printed and bound in Spain
by Blackprint CPI, Barcelona

a moment before his lips closed around it. She held his head again as he suckled her through the lace of her bra. Everything in her tightened as he caressed her.

She tried to reach behind her to unfasten the bra but he held her wrists. "Not yet. I want to do it this way."

"You do?"

He nodded.

She reached between their bodies and found the hard ridge of his erection. She stroked her hand up and down over him through the fabric of his pants.

"Do you like that?" she asked as he arched his back and moved his hips against her stroking hand.

"Very much. Want to get naked?" he asked, with a grin.

"More than you can imagine, but I thought you wanted to wait."

"Touché," he said, snaking his hands around her back and undoing the clasp of her bra. He pushed the fabric up out of his way and then lifted her off his lap. "I can't see you in this light."

He rolled over and turned the bedside light on. "Take your blouse off."

She removed it and her bra as he took off his shirt. The muscles she'd noted when he'd carried her were visible now. His pecs well-developed, his arms all sinew and strength.

He had a light dusting of hair on his chest and it tapered down to a thin line, which disappeared under his belt into his pants.

She stood up next to him. She caressed him from his neck down his chest. Swirled her fingers over his pecs and thumbed his flat nipples before letting her touch go lower.

He stood there and let her explore him. She liked the

way the hair on his chest abraded her palm. She liked the warmth of his body and the strength in him.

She leaned down and let her lips follow the path that her hands had. She nibbled on his neck and felt his hands on her back, sliding up and down. Rubbing over her spine and then moving slowly back up.

She felt him lower the zipper at the side of her skirt and the fabric pooled around her feet. She stood there in her flesh-colored bikini panties. He took her hands in his and held her arms away from her body.

"Someday, I'm going to ask you to dance for me when we are alone," he said.

"I might," she said. "But only if you do something for me."

He nodded and brought his hands to his belt. Slowly he undid it and drew it through the loops on his pants. He tossed it on the floor and then pushed his pants down. "Come here."

"No, you come here," she said.

He arched one eyebrow at her and came over to her. She pushed him down on the bed and gave him a minute to get situated before she came down on top of him. She put her hands on his shoulders as she straddled his hips. She rubbed her feminine center over his erection and felt his flesh flex under her.

"Like that?" she asked.

"Hell, yes."

He gripped her hips and rubbed her over his penis. She tipped her head back as she enjoyed the sensation, which spread out all over her body. Gooseflesh spread down her arms and her nipples tightened.

Nate leaned up and ran his tongue over her nipple and her flesh tightened even more. She shifted her shoulders

so that her nipple brushed over his lips before he closed them around it and suckled her deeply.

"I want you," Nate said.

"I know," she whispered. She leaned down over him, rubbing her self against him.

"Why aren't we completely naked?" he asked.

"I…I don't know. I thought you'd like to do the honors."

"Indeed, I would," he said.

He pulled her flush against his body and rolled them to their sides. Then his hands swept down over the curve of her hips. He tugged on the waistband of her panties lowering them slowly. She lifted up to help him and he pulled them down her legs and tossed them on the floor.

"Lay on your back," he said. "I want to remember how you look on my bed."

She liked that idea, so she rolled over. "How do I look?"

"Like a siren beautiful enough to tempt a man from the sea. To tempt me into dangerous waters."

She lifted her knee up and parted her legs. "Surely I'm not dangerous, Nate."

He shook his head. "You are the kind of danger I love—highly addictive."

He stripped his own underwear off and stood next to the bed completely naked. His erection was long and wide and she bit her lip at the thought of having him inside her.

She reached out and touched the tip of his shaft and it became even more engorged with blood. She ran her finger around the edge of it and then wrapped her hand around him.

His hips canted toward her. He had one knee on the bed and his hands on her thighs before he pulled back.

"Damn. Are you on the pill?"

"Yes," she said. "I'm a dancer...I can't afford to get pregnant unless I am ready to retire."

"Good. Then we don't have to worry about a condom," he said.

"Actually..." she said. "I want you to wear one. You are a bit of a player."

She hated to say that especially since they were so intimate right now but she wasn't going to be stupid about her own health.

"I guess you have a point. Give me a second," he said. He left the bed and was back in less than a minute.

"Come to me."

He nodded and came down on top of her. But he supported his weight with his elbows and his knees at first, hovering over her. He kissed a path from her neck down to her sternum and then nibbled at her belly button.

Everything inside of her clenched as moisture pooled between her thighs. She wanted him inside of her. She didn't want to wait another minute but she also enjoyed what he was doing too much to ask him to stop.

He slid lower between her open thighs and she watched him as he looked down at her body. He parted her nether lips and leaned in to stroke his tongue over the bud at her center.

The touch of his tongue was electric and she jerked on the bed. No man had done this before. She wasn't sure she liked it at first but Nate took his time lapping at her most sensitive flesh until she put her hands in his hair and held him to her. She was so close to an orgasm and she didn't want him to move...not yet.

He slipped one finger into her and she moaned. Her legs moved on the bed, and around his head. It was too much as he added a second finger and continued to stroke inside of her.

"I'm going to come," she said.

He lifted his head and looked up the expanse of her body at her. "Do it."

He lowered his head once again and she felt the careful scrape of his teeth against her intimate flesh. Her muscles tightened and her climax roared through her. She clutched his head to her body as her hips jerked off the bed.

She kept spasming and he kept his hand between her legs as he slid up her body. He positioned himself between her thighs and waited poised at the portal of her body for a minute. The feel of the tip of his manhood there made her crave more of him.

She put her heels on the bed and lifted her hips trying to take him deeper but he shook his head. "I want this to go slowly."

"I want you inside me, Nate. Now."

Taking his time, he slid inside her body inch by inch and once he was fully seated he waited until she moved her hips and then he started thrusting slowly inside. He felt so damned good inside of her.

He thrust more quickly and his hands tightened on her hips. He brought his mouth to her neck and kissed her there whispering dark words of passion in her ear until she felt like she was going to come again. She reached down and clutched his buttocks, drawing him closer to her with each thrust. He moaned her name as she came again.

This time was so much more intense. She couldn't stop her body from thrusting up against him. His hips

began to pump frantically into her and then he called her name as he came.

He held her in his arms, rolling to his side when he was able to. The sweat dried on their bodies and Jen looked up at him in the light cast by the bedside lamp. That was the most intense experience in her life. And Nate Stern was not only essentially a stranger but he was also effectively her boss.

What had she done?

Six

The morning sunlight was muted through the roman shades on the windows. Nate normally didn't like for a woman to stay too late in the morning but he was in no hurry for Jen to leave. She lay cuddled next to his side with her head resting on his shoulder and her arm wrapped around his waist.

The soft exhalation of her breathing stirred his chest hairs and he felt something close to contentment with her in his arms. She looked peaceful and ethereal in her sleep.

The sheets pooled low on her waist revealing the curves of her breasts and the slope of her hip. He reached out to trace the line of her body. She was a dancer, long and lithe yet still had a feminine curve to her.

What was he going to do with her?

He should be hustling her out of his bed and instead he wanted to draw her closer and lay here until she woke.

Then he wanted to make love to her and spend the day with her.

He stared down at her trying to figure out what it was about Jen that was different. Part of it was the obvious fact that she wasn't in his crowd and seemed to have no desire to use his connections to get anywhere.

She was the first woman he met that needed nothing from him. To be fair, she worked for him at the club, but that had nothing to do with him personally.

"Why are you staring at me?" she asked, shifting on to her back.

"You are incredibly pretty," he said.

She seemed to get more beautiful as he spent more time with her. He loved the fuller curve at the bottom of her lip and how she pursed her lips when she thought he was joking with her.

"I'm a real Mona Lisa," she said.

"You are a very interesting woman, Jen," he said, leaning down to kiss her. "I could look at you all day."

"I'm not sure—"

"Don't think about it," he said, putting his finger over her lips. "Let's spend the day together and enjoy the time we have."

"What will we do?" she asked. "I have to be at work at five."

"Me, too," he said. He rolled over on his back and reached for his iPhone, which was on the nightstand. He pulled her into the curve of his body. She cuddled close to him the way she had when they'd been sleeping and he liked that.

He opened the weather application on his iPhone and saw that it was going to be a perfect day for sailing. "Want to go out on my yacht?"

She laughed. "Do you say that to all the women you date?"

"Yes. I don't have etchings to show them so instead I invite them to go boating."

"I'd love to go out on your yacht. But I don't have a change of clothes to wear," she said.

"There's a boutique in the lobby of this building," he said. "What size do you wear?"

"Um…six," she said.

"I'll order some clothing for you."

"No, that's okay. I think I'll go home and shower and change. I can meet you at the marina later," she said.

He shook his head. "That won't do. I want to spend the entire day with you."

"And you're used to getting what you want?" she asked.

"I am," he said. He didn't always get what he wanted but she didn't need to know that right now.

"Why should I stay?" she asked.

"I asked you to. I want to get to know you better," he said.

"I guess I can't argue with that," she said.

"I'm very glad to hear that. My housekeeper should be here now. What would you like for breakfast?"

"I'm a light breakfast eater," she said.

"How about a croissant and fruit?" he suggested.

"That's fine."

"Good. You go shower and I'll take care of every detail for our day. You can use my robe until your clothes arrive."

"Thank you," she said. He kissed her before she got up and watched her walk across his bedroom.

As soon as she was gone, he focused on organizing the day for the two of them. He kept himself busy so he

wouldn't think about making love to her again. He felt a bond growing between them. And that was dangerous for him. He should have hustled her out the door when he had the chance but he wasn't really good with should-haves.

He dressed in a pair of casual pants and a T-shirt and walked out into the main living area of his apartment. The sun shone over Biscayne Bay and glistened on the lap pool on the terrace.

"Good morning, sir," Mrs. Cushing said as he entered the room.

"Morning, Mrs. Cushing. I have a guest for breakfast and we'd like something light—fruit, croissants, coffee and juice. I think we'll be ready to dine in about thirty minutes on the patio."

"Certainly, sir."

"I'm expecting some packages from the boutique downstairs. Will you check and make sure they are here before breakfast?"

"I will. Anything else, sir?"

"I won't need you for the rest of the day once you serve breakfast. I hope you will enjoy a free Saturday."

"I enjoy all the free days you give me," she said.

"I'm glad. Thank you."

"You're welcome, sir," she said.

Nate went back into the bedroom and heard the shower running. He was tempted to join her in there but wanted her to have some time to herself. And if he joined her, it would be more than sleeping together. More than a one-night stand. Besides he wasn't building a relationship with Jen no matter how much it might seem like he wanted to do just that.

While Nate showered, Jen sat on the rooftop patio of his home next to the lap pool looking out at the glittering

Biscayne Bay. The view afforded by this condo was breathtaking but to be honest, it wasn't the stunning vistas that were on her mind. It was Nate Stern.

She knew that yesterday had been tough—the International Ballroom Dancing Federation had denied her appeal. She'd never dance again. But to come home and spend the night with him…why had she done that?

She didn't regret it. She tried not to have regret in her life because as Marcia said, regret was useless unless a lesson was learned from it.

Her BlackBerry pinged and she glanced down at the screen to see it was a text message from Marcia.

Are you okay?

She took a deep breath and thought about what she was going to say to her sister before she texted her back.

Fine. I'm at Nate's. Sorry I didn't call sooner.

There was no reply for what seemed like forever and then her phone rang.

"Hello, Marcia."

"Jen, what are you thinking?"

Jen had asked herself the same thing more than once and she still had no idea. "I don't know. I do know that my old life is completely gone and it's time to try something new."

Marcia sighed. "Sweetie, just be careful. Deciding to have a different attitude isn't as painless as you might think."

"Was it like that for you?"

"When Riley was born?"

"Yes," Jen said.

"Sort of. I knew before he was born that I was going

to be raising him alone and that wasn't what you and I were taught was a good family for a child."

"I know. But Riley has turned out great," Jen reminded her sister.

"He has, but it was hard. And I had no choice with him. From the moment I learned I was pregnant I wanted him. This change for you is your doing."

Jen didn't point out that so was her sister's pregnancy. Marcia was eighteen months older than her and thought she was always right.

"I am taking control of my life," Jen said. "Yesterday when I got that letter continuing my suspension and realized that the old life I had was completely closed to me, I thought it's time to figure out who I am."

"And being with Nate is going to help?" Marcia asked.

"I have no idea, but I was impulsive for the first time in my life. You know I've never done anything that wasn't to forward my dance career from the time I started dancing. Literally, Marcia, I can't remember a time when dance wasn't the focus of my life."

"I know. I remember how dancing took up every second of our lives."

"I'm sorry," Jen said. "I know that wasn't fair to you."

"You're talented, kiddo. I forgave you a long time ago for being so good at it."

Jen laughed. "Thank you."

"For forgiving you?"

"No, for being my big sister and loving me."

"Not a problem. Where is Nate?" Marcia asked.

"Showering. I'm on his patio overlooking Biscayne Bay. The view is incredible."

Jen stood up and walked around the pool and sat on

one of the padded benches next to the water. "It's like I'm not even in the city."

"Enjoy being in that different world," Marcia said. "But remember that being impulsive always has consequences. And eventually you are going to have to come back to earth."

"I will. I'm working at five today but will be home by ten tonight."

"I'll see you then. Are you off tomorrow?"

"Yes. Why?"

"Riley wants to go to the park with his favorite auntie."

"Tell him it's a date," Jen said and hung up.

"Who do you have a date with?" Nate asked, stepping out on to the patio.

She hung up the phone and then turned to look over her shoulder at Nate. "Riley…my nephew. We usually spend Sunday together at the park. I take him for the morning and let my sister sleep in. It's the one day a week she can."

"I want to hear more about your family," he said.

The housekeeper brought out their breakfast and then left. Nate gestured for Jen to come sit down at the glass-topped table.

When she was seated next to him, he poured them both some coffee. "What does your sister do?"

"She's a lawyer," Jen said.

"So she's smart like you," Nate said. "What kind of law does she practice?"

"Family law. She does divorces and custody hearings," Jen said. "I don't know how she does it, but she really likes it. Her job is really demanding and with Riley she has no free time."

"Where is Riley's dad?" Nate asked.

"He's not in the picture. Having kids and a family wasn't what he wanted. But Marcia did, so they went their separate ways."

Nate put his fork down. "I don't understand men like that. I know guys who make that same decision. But a child is a part of you…I couldn't abandon a part of me," he said.

Jen was surprised to hear him say that. Surprised that family meant as much to him as it obviously did. "Family is important to you."

"Hell, yes. You know how you talked about not being a dancer anymore and not being sure who you were without that?" he asked.

She nodded.

"I was the same way with baseball and I saw a lot of 'friends' drop me when it was clear I wasn't going to be able to play anymore. But my brothers—they just said come home and we will do something together. Something that will be an even bigger adventure than baseball was."

"Did you regret it?" she asked.

"Not once. I wouldn't be here with you now if not for that long-ago injury."

She wanted to pretend that his words didn't make her heart melt but they did. She knew then what Marcia had warned her about. The consequences of spending the night with Nate—and now this day with him—were that she'd forget he was an impulse. She'd forget they were just supposed to be having fun and maybe start caring for him more than she should.

The sea breeze blew across the deck of the boat, stirring Jen's hair around her face. She wore a pair of dark cherry-red round-frame sunglasses, which went

perfectly with the sundress he'd bought for her. It was a deep navy blue with a V-neck and a tie at the back. He'd gotten her a light sweater to wear over it since it was cool on the water.

She sat at the stern of the boat and he watched her from the flybridge. Ordinarily, he'd have a crew onboard but today he wanted to be alone with Jen. To have her completely to himself. He knew that this would be the only day they'd spend together like this for a while. He had a busy social calendar and it was important to the club that he always have his picture in the society pages.

And unfortunately, Jen didn't have the kind of headline-grabbing presence he needed. But he couldn't regret spending the day with her. She was what he needed and he was enjoying every minute of it.

When they were out to sea and out of the shipping lanes, he dropped anchor and joined her at the back of the boat.

"This is so nice. I haven't been out on a yacht before."

"Do you like the ocean?" he asked.

"I do. But there never seems like enough time to just take a day and go out on the water like this. Thank you, Nate."

He sat down next to her. "You are very welcome."

"Why did you bring me out here?" she asked.

"I wanted you all to myself. Away from the distractions of the club and of our real lives."

She nodded. And he wondered what she was thinking. He couldn't see her eyes behind the lenses of her dark glasses. And when she got quiet, he felt as if she retreated to someplace he couldn't follow.

"I saw a picture of you on this yacht…sitting right here. I think it was in *Yachting Magazine*."

He nodded. "With the Countess De Moreny. She was thinking of buying one of these Sunseeker boats and I let her try mine out."

"You looked quite friendly with her, intimate," Jen said.

"I was. I like Daphne," Nate said. "Is that a problem?"

Jen shrugged. "You seemed almost too perfect last night and today and I have to remember that you are a player. That I'm not some woman you are just going to fall for. Please don't let me forget that."

He knew that he was dealing with someone who wasn't used to the world he traveled in. And he'd already decided that was part of the reason she was so appealing to him. But he didn't want to have to remind her not to care about him.

He wanted her to care.

He wanted her to think about him all the time and when they were apart he wanted her to try to get back to him. And he knew that wasn't fair.

"I'm not playing with you, Jen," he said at last.

"I never thought you were. For me this was a crazy dare. Something that I probably wouldn't have done at any other time, but for you, this is your life. A different woman every night and a lot of fun. I have to remember that we're essentially two very different people," she said, pushing her sunglasses up on her head.

He saw fear and caution in her gaze and he knew that she was being as honest with him as she could be. She wanted to be sure she didn't get hurt, and he didn't want her to be hurt.

"I would never do anything to hurt you," he said.

"Not intentionally," she said. She slid out of the

padded bench until she stood on the deck. "Give me the tour of this floating luxury craft. I want to be able to tell my nephew all about it."

He let her change the subject because there was nothing more he could say to change her mind. He knew he'd simply have to do whatever it took to make sure she knew how important she was to him. He wasn't about to let her waltz out of his life easily.

"Does Riley like the water?"

"He loves it. He's an avid deep-sea fisher…well, as avid as a seven-year-old can be. But he always talks about being out on the ocean. Marcia and I take him out on a fishing trip at least once a month," she said.

"What has he caught?"

"He got an eighty-pound, yellow-fin tuna the last time we went out. It took both Riley and the captain to bring that thing in. Want to see a picture?"

"Yes, I'd like that."

She pulled out her cell phone and hit a few buttons. A minute later she turned the screen of the phone toward Nate and showed him a little boy standing next to a fish that was almost taller than him. The boy had thick dark hair and, he noticed, Jen's eyes.

"He looks so proud," Nate said.

"He was. Marcia had the fish preserved and mounted and it's hanging over his bed now," she said. "I don't think I have a picture of that in here."

Nate put his arm around her and took the phone from her. "How about a picture of you and me on the yacht so you can show him when you get home."

"That would be nice," she said.

Nate wrapped his arm around her waist, and Jen put her head on his shoulder as he extended his arm out far enough to get both of them in the picture.

"Smile now," he said, taking the picture. He looked at the screen and saw that the photo had turned out very nice.

He glanced down at her to make sure she was still smiling and she was looking up at him. "Things like this make me wish you were a different man."

He had no reply to that. He knew what she wanted to hear from him—words of commitment or at least a promise to move in that direction. But they were words he couldn't say. He'd made a promise to himself a long time ago that he'd never marry. That he'd never settle down because his father had said that Stern men weren't the kind that took too well to marriage.

And Nate had believed that after his broken engagement. So he'd steered clear of women like Jen. Women who could make him feel more than just fleeting pleasure and a sense of fun.

But somehow she'd snuck in, he thought. Last night she'd been a pretty girl that he wanted. Today she was starting to grow on him. Starting to make him want to make promises he knew he'd never be able to keep.

"Um…why don't you take some photos of the living quarters for Riley. I'm going to check the radar and get us ready to head back to shore."

She didn't say anything but turned and walked away. And he knew that was for the best. That the only way they were going to both be okay was if both of them walked away from each other now. He knew that a part of him would regret it but better to end things now before they had really even started than later when they'd both be hurt worse.

Seven

Nate drove her back to the club to get her car but she was reluctant to let the day end. He stood there in his chinos, deck shoes and T-shirt wearing a pair of Armani sunglasses and looking like temptation itself. Was it any wonder she didn't want him to leave?

"Want to have lunch with me? I don't have your stunning view at my place, but we do have a nice Florida room and I make the best grilled-cheese sandwiches in the world," she said. Standing next to her car with him made her feel more vulnerable than she would have guessed. But in the bright light of day, back in her real world, she knew how fleeting her time with Nate really was.

"World's best, eh? I can't pass that up."

"I'm glad. Do you want to follow me?"

"I have to stop at the office and check in with my

brothers. Give me your address and I'll meet you there in an hour."

She gave him the address, which he entered into his iPhone, and then he gave her his cell phone number and took hers. "So we can get in touch with each other if we need to."

He kissed her and then helped her into her car. She watched in the rearview mirror as she drove away. He stood there until she turned the corner.

She tried not to second-guess inviting him over. Marcia should be at the office and Riley usually had soccer in the afternoons.

But when she walked in the door, the first thing she heard was the sound of kids' voices and she knew that Riley was home.

"Aunt Jen. We won our game!" he said, running into the foyer to see her. "Lori brought us back here to have cupcakes and Coke."

"Great idea. Best way to celebrate," Jen said, even though that much sugar would make her nephew bounce off the walls.

Jen followed Riley down the hall into the kitchen where his nanny Lori and her son Edward were both sitting at the table. "I didn't know you were going to be home."

"It's okay. Do you need to head out? I can watch Riley until Marcia gets home."

"Actually, yes, I do."

"Then you can go if you need to," Jen said.

"Not yet, though," Riley said. "Edward and I are going to trade Silly Bandz."

"Go do that, but make it quick," Lori said.

"I thought you'd be home when I stopped by," Lori said once the boys were out of the room.

"I had a date," Jen said.

"A date? Good for you, girl. You spend too much time working and staying home."

Jen didn't know about that but she nodded. Edward and Riley ran back into the room before she had a chance to comment. The boys were busy chatting about the Bandz they'd exchanged.

"Come on, Edward, let's go."

Riley was disappointed to see his friend leave but got over it quickly. He was talking a mile a minute about the game and his game-winning goal. She listened to him and reminded herself that having her nephew in her life was one of the best things she experienced.

"What did you do today?" he asked.

She waggled her eyebrows at him. "I went out on a yacht."

"You did?"

"Yes. Want to see some pictures?"

"You bet," he said.

Jen showed him the photos she took and when she got to the one of her and Nate, Riley asked who he was.

"That's Nate. He's my friend that owns the yacht."

"Do you think I can go out on his boat?"

"I don't know, Riley, I will ask him."

"Thanks, Aunt Jen. Do you want to play Mario Kart?"

"Not right now," she said. "Why don't you have a game while I make some lunch? Nate is going to come over and join us."

Riley went into the living room and she soon heard the sounds of his Wii game powering up. She turned on the radio and looked around the kitchen. It was a nice area with a butcher-block island, stainless steel appliances and granite countertops. She'd moved in

here when she'd first come back to Miami after being kicked off the competitive dancing tour.

Marcia had invited her to make this her home and together they had shaped this house up nicely. There was a photo of the three of them in Little Italy eating at Ferrara's bakery when they had visited New York last summer so Riley could see where his grandmother had grown up. The refrigerator was decorated with Riley's latest art projects and in the corner was a glass door that led out into the Florida room.

Beyond that was the backyard with a soccer net and a water feature that Jen had done herself after taking a Saturday morning class at the local hardware store.

She liked this place, but she'd never really intended it to be her home. She'd always assumed she'd be going back on tour and this place would be a base of operations.

But now, this might be it. And if it wasn't, she'd have to find her own place. Maybe something close by so she could still see Riley and her sister and help them out when they needed it.

She sat down at the breakfast bar realizing she had no idea what she wanted. This was a major crisis. The future was wide open and as of this moment, she had no idea what to fill it with.

She reached for the phone to call Nate and cancel, realizing that she didn't want him to come to this home. She didn't want to show him her life and see in his eyes that this wasn't what he wanted. Did she really need further proof that they weren't after the same things?

No, she knew she didn't need more evidence of that, but what she did need was to figure out what she wanted. And in the meantime, Nate was fun and a distraction.

As long as she remembered that she'd be okay and they could enjoy each other.

The radio started playing Gloria Estefan and the Miami Sound Machine's "Rhythm Is Gonna Get You" and she stood up to dance to it.

"Auntie! It's our song," Riley said, running into the kitchen. She laughed as he danced around her just as she'd taught him. They raised their hands over their heads and clapped to the beat as they both swiveled their hips to the music. They were laughing and clapping and dancing when the doorbell rang and she realized that dancing was still her life, just in a different way now.

Riley greeted Nate when the door opened. The sound of music floated down the hall and Jen stood behind her nephew laughing and swaying to the music. Nate paused there for a minute, seeing something that contradicted his personal experience of how women and sons got along. He knew that Jen wasn't the boy's mother but they were enjoying each other. He could see that from the expression on both of their faces.

"Hello, Mr. Nate," Riley said, holding out his hand for Nate to shake it.

Jen came up behind her nephew and put her arm around him as Nate shook his hand.

"Nice to meet you, Riley."

"Auntie and I were just dancing to 'our' song."

"What's your song?" Nate asked.

"'Rhythm Is Gonna Get You,'" Jen said. "Do you know it?"

"I do. It's a fun song," Nate said.

"Yes, it is. We danced all over the kitchen," Riley said. "Do you want to play the Wii while Auntie Jen finishes making lunch?" He glanced up at Jen.

"I know I enticed you over with grilled cheese. Is that still okay?"

Nate nodded. "Do you need my help?" he asked.

She shook her head. "I'll be about fifteen minutes."

She walked into the kitchen, which was off the main hall, as Riley led Nate into the living room. They had a plasma screen TV and a very comfy Italian leather sofa. Riley sat on the floor on a big pillow and offered Nate one that was tucked in the corner.

"I haven't played video games in a long time." This wasn't what Nate had expected. It was a little too domesticated for his tastes, and his instincts were screaming for him to run. Leave this house and go back to his real life.

"It's okay. I will go easy on you," Riley said.

Nate took the controller and played with the boy but his attention wasn't on the racetrack or the game. He glanced around the room.

This place was homier than his house. There were touches that showed a child lived there but you really got a sense of the women who called it home. On one wall were photos of Jen and her sister Marcia as girls and through their entire lives. He saw Jen in a skimpy Latin dancing costume holding a trophy. He saw Marcia standing on the steps of the courthouse holding her briefcase and grinning at the camera. And there was a photo of Jen holding her nephew in the hospital standing next to her sister's bed.

The two women were all each other had and their bond was just as deep and strong as the one he had with his brothers.

He knew women were caring so that didn't surprise him, it was just this was the first time he'd been involved

with a woman who was like that. Even his own mother hadn't been a nurturer.

He sank deeper into the comfy couch and realized he could let himself get comfortable here. Not just in the house but in this life. But it wasn't his. He knew better than to try to pretend to be someone he wasn't.

"You lost," Riley said.

"I guess I did. Jen said you have a yellow-fin tuna in your room."

"Yes, I do," he said, hopping up. "We have to clean up before I show you. If I leave the controllers out I won't be able to play again for a week."

Nate nodded and helped Riley put the pillows back in a basket next to the entertainment center and the controllers away in the cabinet. Then Riley led the way to the stairs and up to his room.

The tuna was the dominant feature in the room. The bed was covered in a light blue comforter and there was a desk in one corner. Three toy boxes were lined up under the large plate-glass window. The walls were painted a sunny yellow color.

"I couldn't believe it when I caught that fish. I wasn't strong enough to land it by myself," Riley said. "Do you like fishing?"

"I do. I don't go often," Nate said. The last time he'd been was more than three months ago when Cam had insisted they all take a trip to St. Lucia.

"Why not?"

"Busy working."

Riley shook his head. "I don't understand why grown-ups work all the time. You finally don't have to go to school and instead of enjoying it…well, Mommy likes her job so that's why she does it. Is that how it is for you?"

"I guess it is. Do you think you'd enjoy working?"

"I know I'm going to," Riley said. "I'm going to be a fishing boat captain and spend all my time fishing."

"Sounds like a good plan," Nate said. When he'd been Riley's age he'd declared he was going to play baseball for a living so he knew that kids could make their dreams happen.

"Did you always want to be in business?" Riley asked.

"Nah, I used to play baseball."

"Really? I didn't know that. How come you don't play anymore?"

Nate wondered at kids and how they had no filter or fear. Riley wanted to know something so the kid just asked. "Let's head back downstairs and I'll tell you."

"Okay. Do you still play sometimes?"

"I don't play anymore, Riley. I got injured and had to change jobs."

Riley stopped on the stairs and looked back at him. "I'm sorry. I know I'd hate it if I couldn't fish."

Nate reached out and ruffled the kid's hair. "I can play now for fun, I just don't have the time because I'm always working."

"My best friend Edward's dad is like that. That's why he started coaching our soccer team. So he could play and relax…at least that's what Lori says."

"Who's Lori?"

"Edward's mom and my babysitter. Mommy and Auntie Jen can't be here all the time."

"Work?" Nate asked, getting the picture that the adults in Riley's life spent too much time working as far as the kid was concerned. He didn't want to care. This kid didn't matter to him if he was going to part ways with Jen. And he was going to leave her alone after

this. Their lives were different and he wasn't willing to give up his lifestyle for her.

"Yes. But I know that they have to so I can have nice things and we can live in this house...don't say I was complaining about it, okay?"

Nate nodded just as Jen entered the foyer to call them to lunch. Riley was an interesting little kid and Nate liked what he learned about Jen from watching her with her nephew.

Nate had insisted they go to the local sports store and get a baseball bat, ball and gloves and go to the park and throw the ball with Riley. Riley was ecstatic and kept saying that Nate was obviously a man who knew life was about more than work.

Jen felt bad for her nephew because she and Marcia were gone more than they were home. But today made up for that.

Nate was patient as he talked Riley through how to throw a ball. "You are doing good."

"Your turn, Auntie Jen."

"I'm not as good at this as you are," Jen said. And then proved it by tossing the ball and completely missing Nate who stood with his glove ready to catch it.

Riley shook his head. "That was pitiful. Show her like you did me."

Nate walked over to her. "Get ready, Riley."

Nate walked over to her and stood behind her so close that she felt his body through the fabric of her clothing. He leaned in low.

"Bend your knees a little," he said.

She did what he instructed.

"Now, hold the ball like this," he said, showing her the proper way to hold the baseball.

He spoke directly into her ear sending chills down her spine and making this into so much more than just a kid's game in the park. He made her want to turn in his arms and kiss him. But Riley was waiting and hoping for some spectacular results.

"Next, bring your arm up like this. No, relax. Let me move your arm for you."

She did and the ball fell out of her hand on the ground. "Sorry."

"Its okay," he said, bending down to pick up the fallen ball and letting his hand stray to her hip where he caressed her as he stood back up. "Okay, ready?"

"I hope so. I'm a dancer not a baseball player," she said.

"I think today you will be both," Riley said.

"I will be," she said.

"Remember how I showed you to move your arm. Get ready, Riley."

"I'm ready, Nate. Come on, Auntie Jen, throw it to me."

Jen wound up and threw the ball. This time it went all the way to Riley who caught it and then whooped with joy. Nate put his arm around her waist and pulled her back against him for a quick kiss. "Great throw. You have the makings of a real player."

"I doubt that," she said.

Riley tossed the ball back and he and Nate played while she watched. Jen didn't want to risk messing up her record after that perfect throw. She had so much fun that she forgot that she was going to be cautious around Nate.

Her cell phone rang and she glanced at the ID to see that it was Marcia.

"Hey, there," Jen said by way of greeting.

"Hello. Where are you guys? Your car is here but you aren't."

"We are at the park playing catch."

"Catch? You stink at that."

"Ha, that's what you know. I'm much better today."

"Is Nate with you?"

"Yes, he came for lunch and then took Riley here to play."

"Really? That doesn't seem like the man I met last night," Marcia said.

"There's more to him than meets the eye," Jen said, watching Riley and Nate toss the ball back and forth. "We'll be home in a little while."

"Okay. Thanks for watching Riley this afternoon," Marcia said.

"I enjoy it. I love him."

"I know, but thanks all the same."

"It's no biggie," Jen said, hanging up the phone.

Nate led the way back over to her. "Was that your sister?"

"Yes. Mommy's home, Riley, you ready to go and see her?"

"Yes! I can't wait to show her how I can throw."

"I'm sure she will be very impressed," Jen said.

"Will you stay and throw with me, Mr. Nate? I don't think Auntie Jen will be a good partner for that," Riley said looking up at Nate.

"I'd love to, bud. I can't stay long, though. I've got a busy night ahead of me."

Riley tipped his head to the side. "Do you work at night?"

"That's when the club is open."

"You work with Auntie Jen?" he asked. "Are you a dancer?"

Nate laughed. "No. I own the club with my brothers."

Riley nodded. "Sounds like a good job."

Nate patted the little boy on the shoulder. "It's pretty good but there isn't enough time for baseball or fishing."

"But you are the boss," Riley said. "You should change the rules."

Jen laughed at the way Riley said it. That made perfect sense to him, but she'd love to see Nate tell Justin and Cam that they needed more time for fun. She was pretty sure those two would think he'd gone off the deep end since Nate's life was already one big party.

"I should do that," Nate agreed. When they got back to the house Nate walked them to the door.

Jen watched her nephew go inside, then turned to Nate. She couldn't read his expression but he'd kept his keys in his hand and had almost turned to walk back to his car. It was as if he couldn't wait to get away from here.

"Nate?"

"Hmm?"

"Thanks for everything you did with Riley today."

"No problem. I think he's the first kid I've been around since I was a child."

"My life is so different than yours," she said. But hadn't she truly known that from the beginning? They came from different worlds and that was part of why she liked him so much.

"Yes, it is. Well, I've got to go," he said.

"Bye."

She watched him walk away, realizing how good Nate was at making himself fit into whatever the situation was. Because it was only as he drove away that she

realized he'd been the perfect uncle figure to Riley the way he'd been the perfect date to her last night.

She thought he was multifaceted but now she was afraid he was simply a chameleon used to changing his colors wherever he was. No matter how kind he was to Riley, Nate hadn't really wanted to spend time with her nephew and that, more than anything else, should serve as a reminder that he wasn't the settling-down kind.

<u>Eight</u>

"Hello, boys, thanks for taking time out of your busy schedules to meet with me," Cam said as he joined Justin and Nate in the VIP lounge at the back of the club on the first floor.

The place was empty except for staff as they had an hour before it opened.

"Not a problem. What's up?"

"We need to start working on the tenth anniversary celebration in May. Justin, I'd like you to reach out to the local community and try to get them involved in this. They are bringing in some big-shot lawyer from Manhattan to oppose overexpansion so if you can make sure they aren't up to anything that's going to cause us trouble, I'd appreciate it."

"I'm on it, big bro. There is a community open house tonight and I'm going to attend to see what's on everyone's mind."

"Good. Nate, I need you to pull out all the stops and get us some big-name A-listers for this thing. Not just people who will stop by, but celebs to headline the street party."

"I will hit the phone and see who I can get. What do you want them to do? Hutch will come and do a rap show I'm sure, but what else do you want?"

"I'm going to have Jen Miller choreograph a dance show that will run on Saturday night. I want to showcase everything the club has to offer."

"Okay, that's not a problem," Nate said. "I'll let you know in a few days who can make it. Are we still talking about Memorial Day weekend?"

"Yes," Cam said. "I am meeting with an event planner next week to approve invitations and coordinate our print media for the event. It's important that the Latin community feels a part of this. When you are at that event tonight, Justin, will you see if you can get some volunteers to help with this?"

"I will do that. I talked to our merchandise department and they are going to go ahead with the commemorative cigars. I got the final legal wrangling taken care of so we can use the old labels from this place along with our logo."

"That's going to be great," Cam said. "Boys, I can't believe we've been doing this ten years."

The rest of the meeting went by rather quickly and Nate found himself reluctant to leave. He wanted to talk to his brothers about their mom. For the first time in a long while he wanted to discuss her and figure out if his impressions and beliefs were the same as his brothers'.

Justin got up to go but Nate stopped him. "I...I went out on a date with Jen last night."

"Our employee?" Cam asked, his eyebrows furrowing in a way that Nate knew from his youth meant trouble.

"Yes. I didn't do anything inappropriate like threaten her job security, so chill out."

Cam stood up and leaned over the table. "Did you sleep with her?"

Nate didn't answer. Jen was private. What had happened with her wasn't for public consumption. "That's neither here nor there. I was letting you know because I might go out with her again."

He wanted to say she was different and see if his brothers had any clue as to why she would be the woman to make him react like this. But he would never ask them about that. He would never really be able to talk about her because that wasn't the kind of thing a man did.

"Good for you," Justin said. "I don't really know her, but if you are thinking of dating her, I say go for it."

Nate glanced at his middle brother. Justin looked the most like their mom out of the three of them. "Legally that's okay?"

"As long as you don't put her job on the line I think you're fine. I can draw up an agreement for you both to sign…"

Nate shook his head. "That doesn't sound good to me. Jen's different. She lives with her sister and her nephew."

Cam came around the table and sat down in the chair that Justin had vacated. "Family is important to her. She's not like the kind of girls you usually hang out with."

"I know that," Nate said. Cam was falling into big-brother mode. It didn't matter that he and Justin were

adults now; Cam still felt that he had to watch over them and give them advice. "I can handle this."

Justin nodded. "He's a big boy."

Cam shook his head. "I don't care too much about that. I'm more concerned with the fact that I don't want to lose a valuable employee. She took my dream for the rooftop club and made it viable."

"You did that," Nate reminded his brother. "She's just talented enough to know how to get people up on their feet."

"Which is what makes this club so successful. Just play it cool, Nate. Don't let this get to be more than she can handle. I don't want to have to replace her."

Cam walked away before Nate could say anything else and he just watched him leave. Justin stood there for a second but Nate got up and left as well. He walked out of the club and started down Calle Ocho. He stood on the corner and looked back at Luna Azul.

He wasn't going to do anything to ruin the success he'd found here. He was too old to find another new career, especially since he really liked this one.

And he refused to be the man who stole this from Jen. She had a life here with Riley and her sister and he didn't want her to have to move on. He saw how much not being a competitive dancer had affected her and he knew she was putting her life back together piece by piece. The very last thing she needed right now was a man who was just looking for fun.

No matter that he wanted to be more than just a casual guy in her life, he knew he couldn't be. Because even though what he felt for her was intense, he knew it would burn out eventually and they'd both have to move on.

* * *

Jen woke Monday morning to the sounds of Riley and Marcia getting ready to leave. One of the nice things about her job was that she didn't have to rush out of bed every morning. She got up and put on her robe before going downstairs.

She hadn't heard from Nate yesterday but she knew that she wouldn't. They were both feeling their way through this thing—she was reluctant to call it a relationship because she wasn't sure she was ready for it yet.

"Morning, Auntie Jen," Riley said, giving her a hug.

"Morning, Riley."

"Mommy, I'm ready."

"Great. I need to talk to Auntie Jen. You head out to the car."

Riley nodded and went out the front door. Marcia stood in the doorway so she could remotely unlock the car and keep an eye on Riley.

"I left the newspaper out for you."

Jen glanced at her sister. "I don't read it."

"You'll want to this morning. There's a picture of Nate in it with some woman—a Spanish royal or something."

Jen nodded. She'd just said they weren't dating so why would this news hurt. "It's fine. We're just friends."

Marcia reached out and hugged her. "I can come back after I drop Riley off if you want to talk. I'm not due in court today."

"No, don't do that. I have a meeting at eleven at the club to talk about the tenth anniversary celebration. Besides, it was just one date."

Jen didn't want to talk about this. She wanted to hide

away until she figured out why she felt so hurt. She knew he wasn't the kind of man who was going to give up his jet-set lifestyle for her after one date.

"I'll be fine. Have a good day."

Marcia pursed her lips. "I know you'll be fine. But that doesn't mean this won't hurt. You didn't need this now."

"Marcia, stop. I'm trying to get it under control in my head. Don't make me hash it out or I'll start crying."

Her sister hugged her again and then turned to leave. "Call me if you need me."

"I will."

Jen closed the door on her sister and nephew and leaned back against it. She didn't want to go and look at a picture of Nate with another woman. Especially since she'd dreamed about his arms around her all night. She'd dreamed of them being on that yacht of his together and making love on the sundeck.

She put her hands in her hair and stood there for a minute trying to get her head around the idea. It didn't matter that she'd already thought he might not be serious about her. She didn't want to see the proof that the very next night he'd gone out with someone else.

But she wasn't a coward and she never ran away from anything. She walked into the kitchen and saw the coffee mug her sister had left for her next to the paper. There was a Post-it note on it in Marcia's handwriting warning her that there was a picture of Nate inside.

She poured herself a cup of coffee and then took the mug and the paper outside with her. She sat down on the bench next to the water feature and let the scents of the garden surround her. The sweet smell of jasmine mingled with the scent of hibiscus in the air. The sound

of the water flowing in the fountain soothed her troubled nerves.

She took a sip of her coffee and then set it on the ground at her feet before she opened the paper. The *Miami Herald* didn't have anything as lurid and gossipy as the New York papers but they did have a society page owing to how many celebrities made South Florida their home.

The picture was...she looked away and then made herself look back at it. Nate had his arm around the other woman and she was laughing and looking up at him. The same way that Jen had looked up at him. She'd been pressed to his side and she knew the weight of his arm on her shoulder...knew how it felt to be that close to him. And this hurt.

She tossed the paper aside and picked up her coffee mug. She walked around the garden wondering what to do. Alison had said that men who were fun liked to have fun. And that the only way to be successful in that kind of dating situation was to realize it was all about fun.

But to be honest, Jen had no idea how to do that. She wasn't a fun girl. She wanted it to mean something that she'd had sex with him. And that they'd talked about their pasts. She needed it to mean more than just a bit of fun.

And that wasn't Nate's fault. It was her burden. She was the one who'd been impulsive and jumped before seeing where she'd fall.

This was what her sister had tried to warn her about. But there was no way that she could have heeded that advice. There was something seductive about Nate. It wasn't just the sex, though, that had been earth-shattering. It was more the man behind the image.

If he'd just been the charming playboy then she'd

have expected this, but he'd seemed to be more than that. Now she was going to have to deal with the fact that he'd moved on. That was what he did.

She took another sip of her coffee. She couldn't hide away here or even quit and try to find another job. There weren't that many high-level clubs that needed Latin dancers. She just wasn't going to find another job like this and she didn't want to leave her home again.

She'd had a lot of time to think yesterday while she'd been watching Riley and it had occurred to her that not getting back on the dance circuit had been a good thing. It was time for her to start settling down and thinking about family.

Forget that at the time she'd spun silly fantasies in her head of Nate giving up his playboy lifestyle and settling down with her. The truth that she'd discovered yesterday still remained. She was ready to start looking for a home. To start making a life for herself.

And she didn't want to have to start again somewhere where she had no roots, no family and no friends. She refused to let Nate Stern drive her away from the job and the community that she'd started making her own. She'd just stay away from him and he'd never know how much that one night of fun had cost her.

Nate had reached for his phone to call Jen but stopped himself. If he'd come to any conclusions after meeting with his brothers, it was that he needed to break things off with her. And he had in the only way he knew. He'd moved on.

Countess Anika de Cuaron y Bautista de la Cruz was the sister of one of Nate's oldest friends, the Spanish Count Guillermo. Gui and some friends owned a string of European nightclubs called Seconds. So taking his

sister out for the night was the least that Nate could do. They were like family.

And last night that had been the best that Nate could do. Somehow none of the other women he'd been dating casually had seemed right. There was only one woman he wanted to spend the night with and it was Jen.

But he wasn't the right kind of man for her. She deserved someone who could give her more than he could.

So here he was at a meeting where he didn't want to be trying to figure out why she wasn't looking at him. They were seated in the executive boardroom at the club's downtown Miami offices. Justin sat at one end of the table with his assistant, head chef Antonio Caruso sat next to him and head of security Billy Pallson was next to him.

Jen had taken a seat two down from Billy on the opposite side of the table from Nate. Nate had enough "relationship" skills to know that she was pissed off at him. Though that was what he'd anticipated when he'd gone out with Anika and made sure that their photo had hit all the papers—local, national and international—he still didn't like it.

"Let's get this meeting started," Cam said as he entered the room. His executive assistant, Tess, followed him along with another woman who Nate didn't know.

"This is Emma Nelson, the event planner I've hired to help us organize the party," Cam said. He then introduced everyone at the table before giving Emma the floor.

She handed out action item lists for each venue and it wasn't long before Nate realized that he wasn't paying attention to anything except Jen. He watched as she took

notes, watched as she took a sip of her water and then looked away when she glared over at him.

He didn't understand it but it seemed that he wasn't ready to be done with Jen. Hell, he'd known that last night when he'd gone out with Anika but that didn't mean he could change it.

But Jen deserved a chance to have her dreams and he wasn't the kind of guy who could give them to her. He'd seen that at her home when she'd danced with her nephew, and in the park when she'd played baseball with him. He'd noticed the way her gaze lingered on him as he'd played with Riley. He'd have had to be a fool not to have been aware of the sexual tension there just beneath the surface when he'd taught her to throw.

Hell, right now he wanted her. If he had his way he'd tell everyone to leave and make love to her on this boardroom table. Jen wasn't the kind of woman who elicited a soft reaction from him. She called to him. Called to the passion inside of him and he wanted to answer that call but he knew that it would mean taking a chance on caring for her.

Caring for her? Since when had he become someone who talked to himself in euphemisms? His entire life he'd never let anything stand in the way of what he wanted.

Glancing across the table at Jen, seeing the way the sun brought out some blonde highlights in her dark hair, reminded him of how she'd looked out on his yacht.

He wanted to see her there again. He didn't want to back off because Cam had made him think that Jen wanted more from life than he could give. He wasn't the kind of man who gave up what he wanted and he wasn't going to give up Jen.

No way.

"Nate?"

"Yes?"

"Emma asked who we have booked on the main stage," Cam said.

"Hutch Damien. He will be doing his rap show and I think he'll want to coordinate with Jen and her dancers to use them on the stage as well. Jen and I can meet later to discuss that."

Hutch would be a big draw. He had been compared to Will Smith, and for the anniversary bash, Nate had asked him to include some Latin beats in the background.

"Good," Cam said. "Who else?"

"Ty Bolson and his wife, Janna McGree, will come and do a concert as well. They have a huge country music fan base. I'm not sure how you want to coordinate that. I've also asked my former teammates from the Yankees to come and hold a pitch competition."

"Sounds great," Emma said. "I think since the focus is on Luna Azul we should have the concerts in the club. But maybe have them do one or two songs outside. I can set up a stage on the street if you think we can get the community to agree to letting us have the block party."

"Justin was working on that," Cam said.

"I attended a meeting last night of comunity leaders and I have another meeting set up today to try to talk to them. Right now they are reluctant to agree to anything. They have filed an injunction to keep the marketplace we've acquired from being rebuilt. I'll be meeting with their lawyer to discuss the details."

"Thank you, Justin," Cam said. "Billy, as far as security goes, what do you recommend? We want this to be a free event but not a free-for-all."

"I have my guys set up a perimeter so that we cover

the entire area outside the club. Inside, I'll have our usual coverage and a few extra teams."

Cam nodded. "Emma, will you need to meet with Billy to discuss this?"

"I will need to meet with everyone one-on-one to discuss the details. We have a lot to do," Emma said.

The meeting started to wind down and Nate saw Jen gathering all of her notes. He had a feeling she was going to make a fast break for it.

"Jen, do you have time to stay and meet with me about the show?" Nate asked. "My office is just down the hall."

She looked up at him and then she nodded.

"Sounds good," Cam said. "I want everyone back here this time next week. We will be meeting weekly until the party. Thank you."

Everyone left and Jen stood there in the boardroom waiting for him. "I don't know where your office is."

"I know. I will show you the way."

He led her to his office at the end of the hall. His secretary offered them drinks but Jen declined, and then they entered his office and he closed the door behind them.

"You are very good at that."

"What do you mean?" he asked.

"That you know how to show a girl a good time, and that's all."

Nine

Jen should have known that she'd run into Nate. Should have figured that just because she'd decided to avoid him that it wouldn't happen. Should have known that she'd still want him as soon as she saw him.

It didn't help matters that he looked so good today. His shirt was left open at the collar revealing his tanned neck. His pants were fashionable and fit him perfectly. The fact that he kept looking at her wasn't helping either. Because in his eyes she saw things she thought she wanted to see. She thought she saw regret and a desire to give things a try.

But she knew she was fooling herself. That was just her imagination going crazy. Hadn't she already learned her lesson when her relationship with Carlos had taken dance away from her?

Was she going to be one of those women who never made smart choices when it came to men?

"Thank you for agreeing to meet with me now," he said.

"Did I have a choice?" she asked.

He raised an eyebrow at her. "Yes, you did."

"I know. I'm just out of sorts today. Tell me what kind of dancing you think we'll need for Hutch's set. I've only heard a couple of his songs on the radio so I'm not as familiar with him as I should be. Do you think we can get him to come down and rehearse with us?"

"I don't want to talk business first. I want to sort out this business between us."

"What business? We went out on a date and 'hooked up.' That was it."

Nate shook his head. "We didn't hook up. Things between us aren't that casual and you're not that kind of girl."

"It doesn't matter, you are that kind of man."

"I guess you saw the photo of me and Anika?"

"Yes, I did. I knew you weren't the relationship kind, Nate. So that photo didn't tell me anything I didn't already know."

Nate walked over to the window and looked out at the city. He wasn't sure what he was really looking for, just knew that he didn't want to face Jen anymore. She had made a statement of fact and her words shouldn't bother him but they did.

"I don't want you to think that you mean nothing to me."

"I don't. I think we both weren't ourselves and that's why we were able to connect. But I…I don't want to let you drive me away from this place. It's my home and since I'm starting over, this is the best job for me to do that."

Nate turned to face her. "I get that. I realized while

we were in the meeting today that I want more from you than I thought I did. Actually, that's not true. I knew it from the beginning but I was afraid you'd turn out not to be the woman I thought you were."

She nibbled on her lower lip, something he knew she did when she was nervous. "Who do you think I am?"

"Someone who cares deeply about the people she surrounds herself with. I know that my connections and my friends aren't the reason why you were with me the other night. And that is something I'm not used to."

"I get that, Nate. I'm not sure what you want from me," she said.

"I want a chance to date you. To get to know you and see if there's anything between us besides sex."

She nodded. "That's honest."

"Yes, it is. I'm not going to lie to you, Jen. Not about anything. There are going to be times when I have to go out with different women and I'm going to have to get my photo in the papers but that's publicity and that's for the club. That's not about you and me. Can you handle that?"

She tipped her head to the side studying him and he hoped she'd find what she was looking for when she looked at him.

"I might be able to. I can handle you working with women but I don't want to be made a fool of. If we're going out I need you to be monogamous with me. I'm not willing to settle for being part of your harem."

That startled a laugh out of him. "I don't have a harem. Never have wanted one, either. I just want to have fun. And I think you and I can enjoy the hell out of life together."

"I can handle that," she said. "I'm not in a place to

get serious either, but I like you and to be honest, I'm not ready to move on."

He came around his desk. "Good. Let's seal the deal with a kiss."

"The deal? This isn't a business arrangement."

"I know. Hence the kiss," he said.

She smiled at him and it was the first time today that he'd seen her seem happy. He was glad he'd talked to her. Glad he'd decided to go after Jen. She was the kind of woman that he'd regret not knowing if he let her slip away now.

She walked over to him and kissed him softly on the lips. He put his arms around her and drew her close. Holding her made him realize that he'd feared he'd never get to hold her again.

He tightened his arms around her and then realized what he was doing. He didn't want her to know how much she meant to him. Even now when they'd only really had one date—but what a date. He'd wanted their time together to never end.

He had to find a way to bind her to him. To keep her close to him without giving up any more of his emotions. Because caring for Jen would be his downfall if he didn't handle it the right way.

Jen had thought she'd never feel his arms around her again and she was so glad that she was back here now. She rested her head on his chest right over his heart and heard the strong beating of it under her ear.

He skimmed his hands up and down her back before settling them on her hips. She felt his erection stir, nudging her at her center. She looked up at him as he lowered his head to kiss her.

His lips rubbed over hers and then his tongue traced

the seam of her lips. She parted them and invited his tongue to come deeper into her mouth, which it did.

His tongue tasted her in long languid strokes and she forgot everything. She was back in his arms, the one place she'd dreamed of being since he'd last left her on her doorstep.

He leaned back against his desk and pulled her against him. His hands continued to skim her body and she found she couldn't get enough of touching him. She wanted more. She wanted his clothing out of her way so she could feel his flesh against hers.

She reached between their bodies, stroking him through his pants. She ran her finger down the zipper and then reached between his legs to cup him.

He widened his stance so she could keep her hand where it was. She played with him with one hand and then brought the other down to slowly lower his zipper. She felt the fabric of her skirt being drawn slowly up her legs and then Nate's hands were on her buttocks. She felt him stroking her through the thin material of her panties.

Once she had his zipper lowered she reached into his pants to stroke his rock-hard length. He grew even harder under her touch. He turned and lifted her up onto his desk. His pencil jar spilled and the noise was startling, when she pulled back from kissing him, she looked up into his eyes.

His pupils were dilated with desire. His skin was flushed and his body was aggressive in trying to assuage his needs. His hips thrust between her thighs, his hands working to draw the fabric of her blouse up her body.

She felt his hands against her stomach and then higher as he palmed her breasts.

She reached lower and finished undoing his pants,

freeing him from his underwear. He was thick and hot under her hand and as she stroked him, he whispered in her ear.

Telling her how much he wanted her. How much he couldn't wait to be buried deep in her soft warm body. And then she felt him between her legs. One arm wrapped around her waist, he lifted her up as he pulled her panties away from her body. He got them as far as her thighs before he had to step back.

In an impatient move, he shoved them down her legs and then put his hands on her thighs and spread her legs wide. "Are you ready for me?"

"Once you get a condom."

She nodded and reached for him, drawing him closer to her. He stepped back between her legs. Bracing his hands on the desk beside her hips, he probed at her opening with the tip of his manhood. She was wet and ready. Desperate to be one with him again.

And this time he plunged deep into her. Took her like he meant to make her his completely. He thrust deeply into her again and again until everything in her body seemed to focus on that point of contact. She felt herself getting closer and closer to the edge until she went over. She opened her mouth to say his name but he kissed her and captured the sound.

He thrust into her two more times before he came, his hips jerking forward as he filled her with his essence. She was breathing like she'd run a race—she felt as if she just had. She wrapped her arms around his chest and rested her head on his shoulder.

She took comfort from having him here with her. She knew that she hadn't been ready to move on and no matter what she'd said to him, Nate was important to her.

"That was one hell of a kiss," he said.

She smiled up at him. "You go to my head."

"Good," he said, he pulled slowly out of her body and reached around her for a box of tissues. He handed her a couple and then cleaned himself off. "I have a washroom through that door if you want to clean up."

She hopped off his desk and bent to pick up her panties. "With any other man I might be embarrassed now."

"But not with me?"

She shook her head. "Everything always feels natural with you."

He nodded. "I'm glad to hear that."

She went into the washroom and used the hand towel to clean up. Her hair was tousled and her lips were swollen. Even though she righted her clothing, it wouldn't take a detective to figure out what they'd been up to in his office.

But she didn't care. He said that they were going to try to date each other and she wasn't going to be embarrassed by anything that happened between them.

Nate was the kind of man who lived life with passion. For a long time she'd channeled all of her energy into dancing. It was about time she got out of the rehearsal hall and into the real world. Nate was the perfect man to share this with.

She tried to caution herself as she looked in the mirror not to get in over her head but she knew it was too late. It had been too late since the first time she'd danced with him.

Nate was different and she cared about him. That was why that photo had hurt so much this morning. Why sitting across the boardroom table had been such

agony and why she'd agree to just about anything if it meant she'd see him again.

She opened the door to rejoin him and he told her he'd be a minute in the washroom. She walked over to the plate-glass windows and glanced out at his view. The city sprawled as far as the eye could see.

"You okay?" he asked when he rejoined her a few minutes later.

"I am. I feel a lot better about everything."

"I'm glad. Now what do you say we talk business."

"Sounds good."

She had no idea what the future held for them but she was sure that she wasn't going to be just existing and that made her feel really good about her life post-dancing.

The next few weeks flew by as he balanced his new life. He had no regrets about dating Jen. It was turning out to be one of the best decisions of his life. He was finding that he didn't need to actually date famous women to get their photos in the paper. In fact, the more he included different groups of his famous friends in the club's events, the more he found that some of them had settled down. And that most of them didn't miss their old single days.

It was an eye opener for him. He was happy just being with Jen but thoughts of the future made him a little edgy.

For one, he wasn't too sure about the details of her past and why she left the competitive dancing world behind.

So when Carlos Antonio showed up at Luna Azul and demanded to see Jen one Friday afternoon, Nate felt like he was closer to finding the truth she'd been keeping to herself.

"She's in a class right now," Nate said as they stood in the VIP ticket area under the Chihuly glass ceiling.

"I will wait," Carlos said. Carlos wasn't very tall and he was slim. He was well-dressed and appeared to be in his early forties.

"Let's go up to the rooftop club. Jen will be leading the class out there to help open the dance floor."

"Who are you?"

"Nate Stern, I co-own the club with my brothers. And you are Carlos Antonio, correct?"

"Yes, I am the world-famous dancer."

Nate rolled his eyes. This guy was a pompous ass from what he could tell. He'd been hassling the girls at the ticket booth for almost forty-five minutes before they'd paged him to come and take care of this guy.

"That's where you know our Jen from, then," Nate said.

"Indeed, it is. Have you heard of me?"

Nate shook his head. "I don't follow ballroom dancing. I'm more into sports."

He saw the other man flinch. Keeping in mind that this man was probably a friend of Jen's, Nate thought he should stop needling him. "Sorry about that. I know little of the world of dance."

"Most people don't," Carlos said. "I will go with you to wait for Jen."

Nate led the way to the rooftop club and found a seat for them both. "What can I get you to drink?"

"Jack Daniels on ice."

Nate signaled the waitress and placed the order. "Do you live here?"

"No. I'm here for a competition and thought I'd stop by and see Jen."

Nate wasn't getting much from this guy. He was glad

when the music turned to the familiar "Mambo No. 5" and he saw Jen and her students come out on the dance floor.

She glanced over at him but when she saw who was sitting next to him she lost her ready smile. And her rhythm as the song began. But then she found it again and led the class.

Nate glanced over at Carlos who was sitting back in his chair looking self-satisfied. Nate had the feeling that Carlos had wanted to rattle Jen and that he was pleased that he had.

Nate's first instinct was to reach over and punch the guy. But he restrained himself.

"Why are you here?" Nate asked.

"I told you to see Jen. We have unfinished business," Carlos said.

"I don't think you do. I know for a fact that Jen has left that world behind."

"Do you? Or did it perhaps leave her behind?" Carlos asked.

"Either way she's out of it now," Nate said. He wondered if Carlos was an old partner of hers come to gloat over the fact that he could still dance while she was out of that world. Nate knew men like that. Had encountered more than one player who had treated him that way after he'd been forced to retire.

"I think you should leave," Nate said.

"I'm staying until I talk to her," Carlos said. "You can leave me here if you want to."

Nate did just that. He walked over to the stage and waited for Jen to finish leading the class. He knew she had to go backstage and change into her flamenco costume for the show with Alison in a short while, but this wasn't something that could wait.

When the lesson was over, she rushed into the dressing room before he could catch her. But as soon as she came out, he cornered her.

"Who is Carlos and what does he mean to you?" Nate asked as soon as they were alone.

"He was…I can't go into this now. There's not enough time to explain. Suffice it to say that he's the reason I'm not dancing anymore."

"I will have security throw him out," Nate said.

He turned to go get Billy, but Jen stopped him with her hand on his arm. "Wait. I want to hear what he has to say. Maybe he knows a way to convince the appeal board to consider my request one more time."

Nate didn't like it. He didn't like the fact that Carlos might be able to help her or that she might want to return to the world of competitive dance. "I thought you were happy with the life you are building here."

"I am. I just want to hear what he has to say."

"Okay. Let me know if you need me. I'm going down to the main club."

"Nate, it's nothing to worry about. I'm not going to change my mind. I just need to know why he's here."

He nodded. "I can respect that. Send me a text when he's gone and I'll come and join you."

"I will," she said. Then she leaned up and kissed him, and he let that quick embrace soothe the savage part of him.

The part that wanted to go back to that table and lift the world-famous dancer up by his lapels and tell him that Jen was his now. And this was his world and he wasn't welcome in it.

Ten

Once their dance routine was over, Jen changed out of her flamenco costume and bade goodbye to Alison. She was anxious to see why Carlos was here. She hoped he'd finally stopped saying she'd slept with him to ensure a better score if he were to judge one of her competitions. She wanted him to admit that their affair had started out of their friendship. She wasn't sure she'd return to the world of dance competitions but she would like to have her name cleared.

And he was the only man who could do it. Carlos had gotten word that their affair was common knowledge and gone to the other judges behind her back. Telling them that his guilt wouldn't let him continue to sleep with her. Though he hadn't judged her in an actual competition, the appearance of impropriety was there. The damage was already done.

Being demoted from the world stage to a regional

judge had punished him for their fraternization, but he had been able to stay in the competitive dance world, something that she hadn't. Why was he back now?

She knew that Nate wasn't too happy that she wanted to talk to Carlos and she wondered what he'd think if he knew that she and Carlos had been lovers. That was something she didn't want to find out. Things were going well between her and Nate and she didn't want to rock the boat.

She forced herself to take her time instead of racing back out to the table where Carlos waited for her. She pulled her hair up into a loose chignon and fixed her makeup. She wore a pair of skinny jeans, strappy sandals and a blousy top that tied on the side of her waist. Nate had promised to take her on a midnight cruise of Biscayne Bay and she was looking forward to that. If Carlos had good news, she'd be able to tell Nate more about her past.

She entered the club and saw Carlos sitting by himself watching the room. She wondered sometimes what she'd seen in him as a man. She had long suspected that her infatuation with him stemmed solely from the dance. They'd taught kids together as part of an outreach program when they'd been on tour and Carlos had been a different man on the dance floor. He'd been a special guest judge because of his reputation in the dance world.

He stood up when he saw her approaching and she smiled at him. "Good evening, Carlos. It is such a surprise to see you here."

"Good evening, Jen."

He sat back down and she did the same.

"Why are you here?" she asked.

"The competition is in town."

"But you aren't judging in it," she said.

"Very true. I heard that you'd appealed to the board again to reinstate you."

"Yes, I have. I want to have my name cleared."

"I need you to let this drop," Carlos said.

"Why? You didn't lose anything. I did. I want my name back."

"You're not going to get it," Carlos said. "You should stop trying to make that happen."

"You are probably right. So why are you really here?"

"I need your help," he said.

"What?"

"You heard me."

"Why would I help you?" she asked.

"You owe me."

She didn't even want to imagine how it was he thought she owed him. "What exactly do you need?"

"A recommendation as a dance instructor at the Calle Ocho School."

"Why me?"

"Your bosses own the marketplace where the dance studio is. So use your connections and I will get out of your hair."

"Will you tell the board what really happened between us?"

"Let that go," he said. "You can't go back. Holding on to the past is keeping you from moving on."

That wasn't true. She'd moved on. But she still wanted to clear her name. "I'll see what I can do, but I don't know if I will be able to help you out."

"I can make things rough for you, Jen. Tell Nate why you had to leave dancing before."

She shook her head. "He doesn't care about what happened in the world of dance."

"Just do this for me, Jen. And I'll be out of your hair."

She doubted it. Seeing Carlos again reminded her that she'd been stupid once when it came to men, and she didn't want to make the same mistake twice.

"I'll see."

"Make sure you do it. You know that Luna Azul is having trouble with the local business leaders and I'm not afraid to use my friends in this neighborhood to make their business dealings even more complex."

She did know that. But she thought it was ridiculous that Carlos was threatening her. She could quit if it really would hurt Luna Azul.

"I'll do what I can."

"You'll do what I ask or I will make life really uncomfortable for you. If I don't get this job…"

"What? I can't guarantee you a position, Carlos."

"You better hope you can. If not, it's going to take a lot of money to keep me quiet."

He got up and left the table. She sat there watching him, wondering how she'd ever let herself get involved with someone like that. He had no morals at all and was a complete jerk.

But that didn't mean she was going to be able to ignore him. She knew she had to let not only Nate but also Cam, who was her immediate boss, know what Carlos had threatened.

Her phone vibrated in her pocket and she glanced down at the ID screen to see a text from Nate. He wanted to know if she was okay.

She swallowed hard and knew that the mistakes of her past were going to be a very real threat in a few

minutes. She didn't relish the idea of telling Nate about Carlos but she really had no choice.

She sent him a text saying that Carlos had left and she'd come and find him in the club.

"No need," he said, coming up behind her. "I'm here. Are you really okay? You look pale."

"I…can we go someplace and talk?"

"Sure. Why?"

"Because a club isn't the place to discuss this."

"What happened? Annie told me that it looked like you were fighting with Carlos."

One of the club waitresses spied for Nate?

"How did Annie get in touch with you?" Jen asked.

"I asked her to keep an eye on you and let me know if you got in trouble."

"Nice. Don't you trust me?" she asked, feeling bruised by her encounter with Carlos. She needed Nate to just accept her the way she was and back her up.

"You, I trust. That Carlos guy, not so much. What did he want?"

"I can't talk about it here," she said.

"Then let's go," he said.

She'd expected him to lead her to the backstage area where they'd talked the first night but instead he hustled her downstairs and out to his car. "Let's drive to the beach and you can tell me what's going on."

"Sounds good," she said. She needed time to figure out what she was going to say and how she was going to tell him that her past was threatening his future.

"Do you want to tell me while we are driving?" he asked.

"No. I need to think about this."

"Is it bad?"

"I don't know yet, but then Carlos has always been bad news."

"Carlos is a little jerk, Jen. And I don't mind showing that little dancer boy that you are with a real man now."

She shook her head. This was going to be a lot more complicated than she'd hoped.

As Nate walked down the beach with Jen, he reached out and took her hand in his. He hoped she knew that he was on her side. He wanted her to understand that he wasn't going to stand by and let anyone threaten her. Nate hadn't liked Carlos from the moment he'd met him and that was saying something.

"What did Carlos want?"

"A job and money, I think. Though he didn't tell me an amount," she said, tucking a strand of hair behind her ear.

That was the last thing he'd expected. He thought he might have to worry about Carlos talking her back into the world of competitive dance. He saw how good she was at dancing and he wasn't clear why she'd left.

"Okay, let's break this down. What job?"

"One at a dance school in the marketplace that you guys bought."

"We're not going to influence anyone to hire him."

"If you don't, he's going to use my past to bribe me into paying him."

"Why would he want money?" he asked, not following.

She nibbled her lower lip and then looked away from him. "There is no easy way to say this, Nate. I made a very stupid decision several years ago and had an affair with him when he was a judge for the World Competitive

Dance Federation. That's why I got kicked off the tour and banned from competition."

"What?"

She wrapped her arms around her waist and spoke so softly he had to lean forward to hear her.

"I know it was a stupid thing to do but I never asked him to cheat or do anything like that. We seemed to have a lot in common and I thought we were friends."

Nate drew her closer to him. He didn't like what he was hearing. "You had an affair with Carlos?"

"Yes. Tonight I had hoped he was here to help me clear my name. Remember, I told you the night we met that the board had denied my last appeal. But Carlos didn't come to help me."

Nate put his arm around her shoulders and pulled her close. "Instead, he wants money from you or what?"

"He said that the local leaders are already angry with the club and that if we don't help him, his word will be all it takes to ruin your business dealings."

Nate was angry. Carlos was an idiot if he thought he could intimidate one of the Luna Azul employees. It didn't matter that he himself was involved with Jen; the Stern brothers would stand by any of their employees, as long as they hadn't broken the law.

"Okay, here is what we are going to do. Justin is not only a financial wizard but he is also a lawyer—our corporate lawyer—and he's very good at what he does. I'm going to call him and we are going to figure out how to stop Carlos."

Jen pulled back. "I don't want everyone to know that I had an affair with him."

"I don't see why anyone has to know that besides Justin. He's smart about these kinds of things," Nate said, remembering that Justin had helped Cam with a

false paternity suit years ago. "Let me talk to him and we'll figure this out. You aren't helping Carlos or paying him a single dime and we are going to get your good name back."

"I don't want to hurt the club," she said.

"You won't," he assured her. "When are you supposed to help him?"

"I don't know. I'm supposed to meet him at the Hallandale dance competition and let him know my decision."

That didn't leave a lot of time. "We need to meet with Justin as soon as possible and get his thoughts on this. Frankly, the only solution I can think of is beating the crap out of Carlos. It would make me feel better but I doubt it would help the situation."

She smiled at him. "You'd beat him up for me?"

"Sure would. I don't like guys who threaten women."

She leaned up and kissed him. "Thank you. That's one of the sweetest things anyone has ever offered to do for me."

"Not a problem, honey," Nate said. He wasn't kidding about hurting Carlos. Normally, Nate wasn't a violent man but to think of someone who'd been intimate with Jen and betrayed her then come back into her life to twist the knife…well, it made him livid. "I'm going to give Justin a call."

She nodded. "If you think that's the best idea, then okay."

"I think it's the only solution. Blackmailers are only successful when someone is willing to pay them. We need to stop this now before it gets out of control."

"I agree. I want him out of my life forever. I am so tired of him screwing me."

"We're going to take care of it," Nate said.

He called Justin's cell and his brother answered on the first ring. "We need to talk."

"Now?" Justin asked.

"Yes. Jen just received a blackmail threat and I want it eliminated."

"What are the circumstances?" Justin asked.

"Can you come to my yacht and we can talk there?" Nate asked. He thought they needed to get the details hammered out tonight.

"I can. Give me about forty-five minutes to get there."

"That's fine. I've got Jen with me. Thanks, Justin," Nate said.

"Do you want me to call Cam or are you going to?" Justin asked.

"I'll call him," Nate said. "See you later."

He hung up and turned to Jen. "Justin is going to meet us in forty-five minutes at the yacht."

"Who else do you have to call?"

"Cam," Nate said.

"They are going to think the worst of me," Jen said. "I know that what I did—"

"No one is going to judge you. He's blackmailing you and threatening the club. It has nothing to do with what you did when you were dancing," Nate said.

"I'm so sorry I ever got involved with Carlos," Jen said. "He has cost me so much. I really don't want to have to leave Luna Azul, but if you think it's best I will do it."

"You aren't leaving the club," Nate said. "I'm going to make this right."

"It's not your fault."

"No, nor is it yours. You made a bad choice but it led you to my door. I'm not going to let it be something you regret."

Jen tried to relax while they waited for Cam to appear. Nate had given her a glass of pinot grigio and she sat on the yacht deck under the stars, listening to the faint sound of Nate and Justin talking. Soon they rejoined her, taking a seat next to her on the bench.

"Tell me everything from the beginning," Justin said.

"Well, when I came out to the rooftop club Carlos was sitting with Nate," Jen said, thinking that was the best place to start.

"No. Tell me what happened with Carlos and why he thinks he can use that to blackmail you."

"Should we wait for Cam? I don't want to have to tell this too many times," she said.

"No, Cam will just want to know what our course of action is," Justin said.

Nate slid closer to her and took her hand in his. Feeling his support made her heart swell and she knew she was falling for him.

"Carlos and I had an affair while I was dancing on the tour and he was a judge. I was careful to never talk to him about the competition," she said. "And he never actually scored an event I competed in."

"How did the affair start then?" Justin asked.

"Does that matter?" Nate asked.

"Why don't you go and call Cam? See what's keeping him," Justin said.

"No. I'll keep my mouth shut. Just don't badger her," Nate said.

"I'm not," Justin said. "So?"

"We met at a kids' dance class. The tour sponsors dance workshops at each city we go to in order to introduce competitive ballroom to kids. He and I were partnered in a five-city gig. After the first day, he invited me to dinner and we just had a lot in common."

"How long did the affair last?"

"Just those three weeks," she said. "As soon as I went into the ballroom after sleeping with him, it felt wrong. I told him it didn't feel right and the next week he revealed to the judging board that we'd slept together and that I had seduced him to help improve my scores."

"What did the board do?"

"Suspended both of us. Carlos was demoted to a regional judge. I thought we could work together for an appeal and approached him to ask him to recant what he said and just talk to the board on my behalf…I thought that was why he'd come to the club tonight."

"But that wasn't the case," Nate said. "He wants help from her."

"Let her tell me," Justin said. "What does he want from you?"

"He didn't say. Actually I'm supposed to meet him in two days' time to tell him my decision. He really wants a job with the dance school in the marketplace you guys own. He's hoping I can influence the decision. He implied that if I don't help him, he'd come after us for money."

"What did he threaten?" Justin asked.

"To hurt the club's standing in the neighborhood. If I don't help or pay him he's going to stir up a lot of bad publicity."

"Okay," Justin said. "Let me think about this. Did anyone else know about your affair?"

"My partner Ivan."

"Did he see the two of you together?" Justin asked.

"He had dinner with us when Carlos asked me out."

"Why didn't you ask him to vouch for you?" Justin asked.

"I did. He wrote a letter but they said since he was my partner, they couldn't count on him telling the truth," Jen said. "Ivan was pretty upset because my being suspended effectively shut him out as well. That was another reason the board didn't accept his version of the story. They said he'd say anything to stay in the competition."

Justin nodded. "Courts of law are different. I'll need a sworn statement from Ivan. Would he give us one?"

"I'm sure he would," Jen said.

"I also want to talk to anyone who was at the workshops you conducted."

"I can get you the names, but we only have two days," she said.

"We'll get this together in no time. I'd like to talk to the cops about setting up a sting and having Carlos arrested for trying to blackmail you."

Jen sat back against the seat and glanced over at Nate. "What do you think about that?"

"I think it's brilliant. It will shut Carlos up and get your good name back."

"That's my thought," Justin said. "Once Cam gets here I want to see if he agrees to us using the club for the setup. We can control it a lot more if he does it in the club."

"Control what?" Jen asked.

"Who is there to witness him threatening you," Justin said.

"Who is threatening Jen?" Cam asked as he walked down toward them.

"Carlos Antonio. And he's threatened the club as well," Justin said. "I'll catch you up on what I've learned."

"Walk with me," Cam said. "It's been a long night and I need a drink… Nate, you don't mind if I help myself, do you?"

"Not at all," Nate said.

His brothers disappeared into the galley and she turned to face Nate. "Thank you for doing this for me."

"You're welcome. I didn't like that guy from the moment I met him," Nate said.

"Why not?"

"He just seems too slick."

"He is that," Jen said. "Not at all like you. I think I thought he was this older chivalrous guy and all the time he was playing me."

"I'm not playing you," Nate said.

"I figured that out in your office," she said. "I'm not playing you, either."

Eleven

Jen wasn't really sure what to say once she was alone with Nate. His brothers had left after working out a rough plan that involved her calling Carlos to the club in the morning. Now it was a little after two a.m. and Nate showed no signs of being tired.

He was wound up and raring to go. Looking for a fight but not with her, for her. The times in her life when she'd needed someone on her side had been rare and she'd always had Marcia, but this was the first time she'd relied on someone who wasn't related to her by blood.

She wanted to pretend that was no big deal and that having Nate on her side didn't mean the world to her. But it did. It meant more than she wanted it to.

"Do you want to spend the night here on the boat or should I take you home?"

"I'd like to stay with you tonight," she said.

"I'd like that, too. Did you call your sister and let her know what was going on?" Nate asked as he handed her another glass of wine.

"No. I don't want to upset her in the middle of the night. I did text her to let her know where I am, though."

"My brothers would be pissed if I didn't tell them what was going on," Nate said.

"She will be, too, but she can't do anything right now and I know she needs a good night's sleep. She's going up against Riley's father in court tomorrow."

"He's a lawyer?"

"Yes. And each time she faces him, it's important to her that she does her best and wins as much as she can."

Nate shook his head. "I get that. Must make it hard on her to see him all the time."

Jen nodded. "The worst part is he still wants to be with her. He just doesn't want to be a dad. Can you imagine that?"

"No, I can't," Nate said.

"Have you heard back from Hutch about the anniversary party?"

"Yes, he's coming in this weekend and you'll have a chance to meet him and work with him."

"I have a few ideas that I think he'll like. I've been listening to his music on my iPod."

"I know. We don't have to talk about the club," Nate said.

"Sorry. I just want to make sure you know that all the help you and your brothers are giving me, it's not wasted."

Nate pulled her close to him and kissed the top of her head. "I already knew that."

"This has been the strangest day. I never thought that Carlos would act like that."

Nate took another sip of his wine and moved around on the bench until he was stretched out lengthwise, and then pulled her close to the side of his body. "Comfy?"

"Yes."

"Good. It's hard to say how someone will react. I had the same thing happen with Daisy."

She tipped her head up to look at him. The night sky was beautiful, clear and filled with stars. The half moon was moving toward the west but the night was still nice. After the turmoil brought on by Carlos, this was exactly what she needed.

"Daisy was my fiancée."

"I didn't know you were married…"

"Never made it to the altar. She was looking for a Yankees player who didn't get injured so when I did, she moved on to the guy who took my place."

Jen shook her head. "That's the most… I'm angry, Nate. She wasn't worthy of you."

He laughed and hugged her close. "No, she wasn't. But I couldn't see it until it was too late. We all fall into relationships like that."

She thought about that. Even Marcia—her smart sister—had fallen for a guy who wasn't everything she'd thought he was. "Why do we do that?"

"I have a theory."

"I bet you do," she said. "What is it?"

"That we find these people when we most need them in our lives. I know for me I needed Daisy when I first started playing because she gave me a reason to get away from the field. She taught me how to relax and enjoy life."

She thought about her time with Carlos. "Carlos gave me a glimpse of what life might be after I stopped dancing."

"But you didn't end up teaching kids," Nate said.

"No, I didn't. I ended up teaching the rich and famous…not so different from kids."

"Ha. I think I'll mention that to Hutch when I pick him up at the airport next week."

"No, don't. I doubt he'll want to work with me if he thinks I called him a child."

Nate laughed. "He will think it's funny. He's a good guy who doesn't take himself too seriously."

"How did you meet him?"

"I met him when we were kids but that's not important," Nate said.

"Yes, it is. I don't want to think about Carlos and what he did. It makes me feel really small and sad. Do you mind talking to me?" she asked. She'd already revealed her vulnerability to Nate tonight—there was no hiding it from him now. She needed to just lie here in his arms and forget that life wasn't perfect.

"I can do that," he said.

He held her closer to him and stroked her hair as he talked about meeting Hutch Damien at boarding school and the trouble they both got in. She enjoyed that. It made Nate all the more real to her and that was exactly what she needed him to be.

Nate carried Jen to his bed and tucked her in before going back up on deck to stare out at the sea. He needed some time alone to figure this out. He didn't like the fact that he'd wanted to physically hurt Carlos. He hadn't been kidding about that.

"Nate?"

He turned to see her standing in the doorway. She leaned there watching him, her hair flowing free around her shoulders.

"Yes?"

"Why didn't you come to bed?" she asked, walking over to join him.

"I couldn't sleep," he said. "And I didn't want to disturb you."

"That is precisely why I couldn't sleep. I like having your arms around me, Nate. I've grown accustomed to you."

He wanted to warn her not to rely on him. That the more deeply they came to care about each other, the more panicked he felt at living up to her needs. But he didn't.

He didn't because she chose that moment to wrap her arms around him. "Dance with me in the moonlight?"

"There isn't any music," he said.

"I will sing for you."

"Can you sing?"

"Sort of."

He chuckled. "I have a stereo system on the yacht. What do you want to hear?"

"What's your favorite song?"

"Slow or fast?"

"I guess I'd say that depends on your mood," she said.

"I love Dean Martin. I know he's not hip, but he is cool—the ultimate cool, you know what I mean?"

"Yes, I do."

"And he sings the perfect songs for holding a woman in your arms."

"I'd have to agree. Dean is a great one for romantic standards. What about a fast song?"

"'Shine a Little Love'…ELO."

"Jeff Lynne is the best. Let's dance to ELO."

"Tonight?"

"Yes. We need something that will make us forget about everything. That's the power of dance."

Nate fiddled with the iPod and the docking station and found "Shine a Little Love." Soon the music was blasting from the speakers and Jen stood on the deck in the moonlight beckoning to him. Her hips were swaying and she drew him closer to her.

She brushed by him and touched him with each move she made, and he felt powerful and together with her. He forgot about his anger toward Carlos—and toward Jen a little for getting herself in this situation.

The night breeze blew across the deck. Jen put her hands up in the air as she twirled and clapped and sang along with the music.

"You're not a bad singer," he said.

"Let me hear your singing voice, Mr. Stern," she said.

He danced closer to her, pulling her into his arms and singing into her ear. She tipped her head up and looked him in the eyes.

He had no idea what he was going to do with her but tonight with the half moon hanging in the sky and calm waters all around them, it didn't really matter.

All that mattered was the way Jen felt in his arms. When the song ended, she took his hand. "Slow dance with me."

He felt her hands make their way under his shirt. She tucked her fingers into the back of his pants and held her to him as they swayed to the sound of the breeze blowing over the bow of the ship and the water that lapped gently against the boat.

And in that moment he knew that no matter what his logical mind might be thinking, he didn't want to be anywhere else. Even with her problems and the complications that Jen brought into his life, she enriched it and gave him something he'd never thought he'd find.

"Thank you," he said.

"What for?"

"For this. For tonight. For dancing with me even though you have every right to distrust all men thanks to Carlos."

She went up on her tiptoes and kissed him. Brushed her lips over his and then held the back of his neck and buried her face against his shoulder. "You are easy to trust."

"Am I?"

"Yes, very easy."

Nate wanted to live up to her expectations of him but he was very afraid that he wouldn't be the man she needed him to be.

But tonight there was no need to worry about disappointing her. He lifted her in his arms and carried her back down to the master suite and laid her in the center of the bed.

"Tired of dancing?" she asked.

"No. I just wanted to make love to you."

"I'm glad."

He took his time taking his clothes off and then removed hers. He kissed every inch of her body and then caressed her until she was moaning his name and begging him to enter her. He was on fire wanting her so badly but he needed to savor it tonight. Needed to take her slowly so that he could wring every ounce of pleasure from both of their bodies.

And he did. When he finally thrust into her, she came in a rush and he followed her with his own climax. He thought he'd never recover from the intensity of it. He curled himself around her when they both came down and tucked her close as they both fell asleep.

Jen was nervous the next day as she waited inside the main room of Luna Azul for Carlos to arrive. This plan had been gone over many times and she knew all she had to do was pretty much let Carlos do the talking. Nate, Justin and Cam were all waiting a few feet away along with a couple of Miami's finest detectives. Thanks to the ceiling's design, if you stood on the far end of it the voices on the other side were clear. It had been designed in the same style as the whispering gallery in St. Paul's Cathedral.

The door opened letting in the bright Florida afternoon sun and Carlos. He walked over to her looking very confident. Now that Nate had mentioned it, he did look a little too slick for his own good.

"I see you changed your mind," Carlos said by way of greeting.

"I haven't," she said. "I just wasn't sure I heard you right the other night. The music was so loud."

"Give me a break. You know what I said. If you don't agree to my terms I will make sure your new bosses know all about your past as well as making you and this club the reason why I cannot teach in Little Havana."

"What are your terms?"

"Since you don't seem willing or able to help me get a job teaching at the dance academy, I think a hundred thousand dollars will do it."

"For what? I don't have that kind of money."

"No, but your bosses do. And rumor has it you are

dating one of them…Nate. I should have guessed that when I met him the other night."

"That's crazy, Carlos. I'm not going to be able to convince Nate to give me that kind of money."

"For your sake, I hope you can," he said. "You cost me my job, Jen, and my reputation."

"That's not true. You cost yourself your reputation. You asked me out and yet they blamed everything on me."

"I did, but the panel found I was at fault as well. I was demoted to the regional circuit, if you recall…I'm not meant to live in Indiana, Jen."

"I'm sorry," she said. And she was sorry. Carlos had tried to make her the scapegoat but she at least had something else to turn to.

"Maybe I can help you get the teaching job here?"

"It's too late. I don't want to teach. And I won't have to. I will expect the money tomorrow."

"I will try…"

"Better use all your wiles, Jen. Don't mess this up or you're going to be out on your ass again."

She shook her head as Carlos turned and walked away. As soon as he was gone she walked over to Nate and the other men.

"You did great," Justin said.

"Do you have enough to arrest him?" she asked.

"Not yet. We will need to catch him taking the money," Detective Elder said.

"I don't think I can get that kind of cash."

"We have it," Cam said. "The cops will arrest him as soon as he takes it from you."

"Great," she said. This didn't sound like her idea of a good plan, but she knew they had to follow the

proper channels, or Carlos wouldn't be arrested. And she wanted him in jail.

"So we have until tomorrow?"

"Yes. I will get the money," Cam said.

Cam and Justin stayed with the detectives and Nate led her back to the rehearsal room.

"How are you?" he asked when they were alone.

"Okay," she said because she didn't want to let on how much it bothered her that she was still paying for the mistake of letting Carlos into her life.

"Don't worry about this too much. We will get him. I can promise you that. Standing outside listening to him threaten you—it was all I could do to keep from going after the guy."

She smiled up at him.

"Why are you smiling?" he asked.

"You make me feel very cared for," she admitted.

He nodded. "Don't forget it."

"I won't," she said. "I'm just sorry I brought him here to you guys."

"I'm not. I didn't want you to have to deal with him on your own."

"Me, either," she admitted. "So what are you doing today?"

"Celebrity golf tournament," he said. "Do you have time for dinner tonight?"

"I can't. Alison and I are meeting with the show dancers from the main room to go over some new routines."

"I guess I'll have to try to make it up to the show tonight."

"I'll look forward to it," she said.

Nate left her alone in the rehearsal room. She pondered how close they'd grown over the last few days.

Last night she'd almost told him she loved him. She knew that she cared that deeply for him.

But she had no idea if he was ready to hear that or if he'd ever be. For all she knew, if she ever confessed her love he'd run for the hills.

"You're early today," Alison said as she came into the rehearsal room.

"I couldn't let you keep beating me here."

Alison laughed and they continued joking around with each other as they warmed up. "You're in a good mood today."

"Life is good," Jen said and realized that she meant that. Her life was very good right now. Probably in the place that she'd long wanted to be in. And she was very happy to be finally finding it.

"Life is good with me, too. I talked to my brother today."

"When does he ship out?"

"Another week. We are having a party at the beach house this weekend. Want to come?"

"I might. Can I bring a date?"

"Yes. Who would it be?"

"Just a guy I've been seeing." She didn't want to say that she was dating Nate Stern. They had been keeping a low profile so far. But what kind of relationship could they have if they were both keeping each other secret from their friends?

"Well, let me know if you are going to come."

"I will. Have you done a lot of country-type dancing?" Jen asked.

"Just some line dancing but this tape Ty Bolson and Janna McGree sent calls for more than line dancing."

"Yes, it does. I think we should incorporate some of your line dancing into it. That way our patrons will

be able to dance to the music. Not everyone can do a country waltz."

"That's true," Alison agreed.

They spent the rest of the afternoon working on a few routines and then recorded themselves on video for Ty and Janna. "I think this will work better for the event."

All the while, Jen tried to keep her focus on work. Not on the man she was fast falling in love with.

Love.

No. She couldn't love a man like Nate. He wasn't the kind of guy she wanted to fall in love with but it was too late. She already had.

Twelve

Nate stayed out of the club the next day when it was time for Jen to make the money exchange with Carlos. He knew that if he were there he'd once again be battling with himself to go and take Carlos out.

The forty-five minutes he spent outside waiting were the longest of his life. They rivaled even that time when he waited for the doctor to tell him he could no longer play baseball. He knew then that Jen meant more to him than he wanted to admit.

He should drive away. Get the hell out of here and do something that was fun. He needed to go back to his playboy life but he couldn't. Not while Jen was in there dealing with a scumbag.

He waited in his car until the cops escorted Carlos out of the building. It was over. He didn't need to worry anymore about Jen.

He hurried inside and found her. She was visibly

shaken and he wanted to pull her into his arms but he
knew that doing so in the club in front of his employees
and her coworkers wasn't a good idea. So instead he took
her to his home.

"Do you want to hear about it?" she asked, as they
entered his apartment.

"No. I don't. I'm glad he's been arrested and I hope
you never have to deal with him again."

"Me, too. Thank you."

"Justin did all the work on this one," he said. "Go sit
down while I pour us both a drink."

"Make mine club soda. I have to pick Riley up from
school this afternoon."

Nate made both of their drinks nonalcoholic and
came to sit next to her on the leather couch. "Why are
you picking him up?"

"Marcia has a late appointment with one of her clients
and the normal sitter isn't available."

Damn. He'd been hoping to have her to himself this
afternoon but he forgot that with Jen came her family.
She had commitments and a life that had nothing to do
with him.

"Do you want to come with me? Riley wants to show
you his baseball skills. He's been showing off what you
taught him at school."

"Has he?"

"Yes, he talks about you a lot. Marcia said we'd been
neglecting him by not having a man in our lives."

Nate thought they probably had been, but two women
wouldn't think of having a guy around for a little boy.
"I…can't," he said.

He wasn't a family guy and it was time for Jen to
realize that. Today had shown him how vulnerable he
was where she was concerned and he needed to make

sure she never knew the power she had over him. That kind of feminine power had ruined his father.

"Oh, okay. Are you available on Saturday?"

"For?"

"A beach party that Alison's throwing for her brother. She's got a house on Marathon Key. He's being deployed again to the Middle East and she wants to give him a good send-off."

"Alison from the club?" Nate asked. He thought that she was a dancer but he wasn't sure.

"Yes, she's my assistant."

"I think I'd like to attend. Let me know what time it is."

"I gave Alison the night off so she'll be there all day. It's a drop-in party."

"We could take the yacht down to her place," Nate suggested.

"That sounds like fun…do you think Riley and Marcia can join us?" Jen asked.

"I don't think I can handle your entire family," he said. To be honest, he knew he couldn't. They made him feel uncomfortable in his own skin and made him wish…well he was a different man. The kind of man who could make Jen's dreams of family come true.

She shook her head. "Well, okay then. I didn't realize my family was hard to handle." There was an awkward silence.

Jen left a few minutes later to go and pick her nephew up from school. As Nate watched her leave he was struck by the scariest thought he'd ever had. He imagined this was what life would be like if they had a child of their own.

He'd never considered having kids, though he knew that he might someday. But Jen was the first woman

he'd met that he could conceive of as a mother to his children.

He quickly turned his attention away from that thought.

That Saturday, back on his yacht after a pleasant but long day, Jen relaxed in the living area in front of the plasma screen TV. Nate was watching the highlights of the Miami Heat game while she rested her head in his lap.

"Thanks for a great time," she said. Realizing that most time spent with Nate was great. In fact, since the mess with Carlos, they'd grown so close that it was hard for her not to tell him she loved him.

Only her fears that he might not love her, too, and that he was still afraid of commitment kept her quiet. But she didn't like to live her life hiding something as big as her love for him. She had started this new life when she'd met Nate and that life was meant to be better than the one she'd left behind.

How could it be if she was afraid to tell him that she loved him?

"It was a fun day. I didn't realize your sister was going to be there."

"She's friends with Alison as well. Thanks for giving them a ride back on your yacht despite the fact that you're uncomfortable with my family. I know Riley enjoyed it."

"It was nothing."

"It meant the world to Riley and to Marcia."

"I'm still not your sister's favorite person."

Jen was aware of that. No matter how many times she'd explained to Marcia that Nate had his picture in the papers with other women for the club and not because he

was dating them, her sister just didn't like it. She thought a man should honor his commitment to one woman.

"She just doesn't want to see me get hurt," Jen said.

Nate clicked off the television. After Carlos, he could understand how her sister would be worried about him hurting Jen. And given the fact that he was trying to figure out how to protect himself from caring too much about Jen, he thought maybe Marcia should be worried.

"How could I hurt you?"

Jen sat up, tucking her leg under her body to face him. "By…"

"What?"

She had no idea how to say the words out loud. *By not loving me,* she thought in her head and just kept staring at him like she'd been struck mute.

"You can tell me. Is it the fact that I had my picture in the paper with those two models this morning? You know that was club business and had nothing to do with romance."

"We spend so much time together, I'm not afraid that you are seeing someone else behind my back. Besides, I know you well enough now that you'd tell me if things were over between us."

"Yes, I would. I still don't know what's going on between us, Jen. I keep expecting that we'll grow tired of each other or start to drift apart but the opposite is happening."

Each word he spoke made her feel stronger about the love in her heart and she knew that she was going to tell him how she felt. Tell him that she loved him. And she had the feeling that he'd confess to loving her, too.

"That is exactly how I feel, Nate. I wake each morning looking forward to the part of my day when I know I

will see you. And sometimes when you surprise me by dropping by early…well, I get so excited just to see you."

Nate reached out and pulled her close in his arms, hugging her tightly to him. He whispered something into her hair that she couldn't understand.

"What?"

"Some days I just have to see you," he said. "When I know our schedules are busy and we might not have time for each other, I make time."

She smiled up at him, knowing she was doing a horrible job of hiding what she felt at that moment. "I know that's hard for you with your schedule."

"Not hard at all. Now tell me what you were going to say," he encouraged.

"I have been thinking about us all day, Nate," she said. "When we were on the yacht, it made me realize that we could have a family…that we were already becoming a family together and I want that to continue."

"I'm not ready for a family yet," he said.

"I know that," she assured him. Because she did know that he wasn't ready for anything beyond a commitment to her. She wasn't sure she was. She only knew that having Nate in her life and by her side was the most important thing for her right now.

"I meant that I'm looking to my future and seeing a family. That isn't something I'd anticipated. I mean, when I couldn't return to dancing I thought that…I thought that I didn't have a future. But being with you has given me back dreams."

Nate kissed her softly on the top of the head. "I'm very glad to hear that."

"Nate, I'm not sure you are ready to hear this but…" *I love you,* she thought. I love you. Why was it so hard

to say those three little words out loud? There was never going to be a better time to say them than right now.

"Yes?"

"I...I love you," she said. She spoke the words softly, and he leaned in as if he had trouble hearing her.

But then his eyes widened and he looked down at her. "What did you say?"

"I love you. You're the man I've been waiting for all my life and never knew that I needed. But being with you has completed me in a way that I never expected. I didn't realize I was incomplete without you. Not until this very moment.

"And I know that you might not be ready to hear those words, but I can't keep quiet anymore. The words have been growing inside me for a long time. My love has been growing for you," she said.

He kept his arm around her, letting her speak, but he had nothing to say. She sat there next to him so afraid she'd just made the biggest mistake of her relationship with him but then he moved and drew her closer to him.

"Jen, you mean more to me than I can say," he whispered against her hair.

He brought his mouth down on hers and she felt in his kiss all that he didn't say. He held her so close and kissed her so carefully that she knew they were going to be okay.

Nate didn't want to think about love or the fact that she scared the crap out of him with that confession. Each day he was with her...he wasn't going to think about that right now. Instead, he was going to do what he did best—make love to her. He wanted to have her

lithe body under his again so he'd feel in control and not so unsure of things between them.

He reached for the hem of her T-shirt and pulled it up over her arms. She shifted on the couch to straddle his hips and he leaned back against the pillows looking up at her slim body, the mounds of her breasts encased in the pale yellow bra.

"You have such a pretty body, honey. I can't get enough of touching you," Nate said.

She smiled down at him. "I'm glad you like it. I like your body, too. Will you lean up and take your shirt off for me?"

He did as she asked. And her hands immediately went to his chest, stroking and petting him. "I love the way you feel."

"Do you?" he asked, unhooking the back of her bra and drawing the straps down her arms.

"Yes, I do," she said, shifting forward so that the tips of her breasts brushed over the light covering of hair on his chest.

He shuddered, enjoying the feel of her nipples against him. She shivered delicately and rubbed herself over him as she took his mouth with hers. He let her set the pace for their lovemaking tonight.

He just wanted her. When she took the lead in their passion it was a full-out turn-on. He felt so hard and ready, it took all of his self-control to wait for her.

He put his hands on her waist and shifted on the couch so that he could take her right nipple in his mouth. He teased her with his tongue at first, circling her areola and then gently closed his lips over her and sucked gently.

She dug her hands into his hair and pulled him closer to her. Her legs shifted next to his hips and she rubbed herself against his erection.

"You feel so good, Nate."

He kept teasing her nipple with his mouth and brought his fingers to her other one, plucking at it gently until she was squirming and calling his name.

"I love the sound of my name on your lips."

"Nate."

"Yes, Jen. Tell me what you want," he said. He wanted this to be for her. To show her how much the gift of her love meant to him.

"I want you, Nate. I want to feel the hair on your chest against my breasts. I want you inside me and I want to be together with you—completely yours."

He wanted that, too. He almost came from her words and the remembered feeling of being inside of her. He put his hands around her waist and lifted her up so he could reach between them and free himself from his underwear.

Her hands immediately went to her own pants and she had them off in a minute. Then he was holding her naked in his arms. Here was where he wanted and needed her. Here was where he knew they were doing what they needed to do.

She came down on top of him and let the humid warmth of her center rub up and down his aching hardness. He ran his hands up and down her back and then put them on her hips and drew her up and over him.

She moaned his name again and this time he came up to kiss her neck. He dropped nibbling kisses along the length of it until she shifted, trying to bring the tip of his erection to the portal of her body.

But he made her wait for it. Even though he was close to coming, he wanted this orgasm to be stronger than any of the other ones he'd given her. He wanted her to

always remember this night and the passion between them when she thought of loving him.

She reached between their bodies and stroked her hand up and down his length. A drop of precum beaded at his tip and she caught it with her finger and rubbed it around the head of his sensitive shaft. He felt another drop on the tip.

"I need to be inside you now," he said.

"I thought you wanted to wait," she said, a teasing note in her voice.

"Not anymore. You are too much temptation for me tonight."

"Good. I want to be the woman who pushes you over the edge," she said. "You are too controlled in life."

"But not with you," he said. "Never with you."

He didn't like that she made him react the way she did but that was the truth of it. Jen was the one woman he couldn't control his reactions around. Maybe that was why he loved her.

Dammit. Did he really love her? He was trying so hard to keep her at arm's length. Sure he said it was to keep her from getting hurt, but he knew he was also trying to protect himself.

He hadn't the first idea of how to love a woman other than like this. Reaching between her legs he tested her passion and found her wet and wanting. He pulled her down on his rock-hard length. She tipped her head back and moaned loud and long.

He felt his spine tingle with the need for release but he held it off, wanting her to come first. He found her most sensitive spot and stroked it until he felt her inner muscles tightening around his shaft.

"Nate…"

He kept touching her and thrusting in and out of her

body. She grabbed his shoulders and dug her nails into him as another orgasm rocked through her. This time he wanted to come with her and he pulled her down closer to him.

He felt her hot breath against his neck and her velvet perfection around him as he jetted his orgasm deep inside of her. He came long and hard, calling her name and holding her tightly to him.

He held her like that until they both started to drift to sleep and still that wasn't enough. He woke her in the night and made love to her again. And in the morning when he dropped her off at her house and drove away, he knew he was going to have to figure out either how to live with his fear of commitment or live without her.

Thirteen

Jen didn't realize that Nate hadn't told her he loved her until two days later when she noticed that he was avoiding her. She hadn't seen him since that night on the yacht and to be honest, she was worried about that. He'd made passionate love to her and she'd thought…well, he had a hard time with commitment, so maybe that had been his way of showing her how he felt. Instead, she thought it had been his way of keeping her busy until he could get her off his yacht and out of his life.

She had a troupe of local dancers that were working today on the country routine they'd be doing on stage with Ty and Janna. The group was good and she saw some real talent in the bunch. And two of the dancers had that hungry look in their eyes that she remembered from when she was younger. Of course, she'd never wanted to do this kind of dancing but now she wondered

why she hadn't. The choreography was fun and she really enjoyed it.

"Let's take it from the top."

She cued up the music and then called out the rhythm to the dancers. She sat in the front of the room watching everyone carefully and looking for mistakes but her mind wasn't on the dancers, it was on Nate. Carlos had been a fling so when things had ended between the two of them, it had been expected. But with Nate…she'd invested more of herself.

That hadn't been her plan but it had happened just the same, and she had no idea how she was going to move on from this. She knew she couldn't just let him drift out of her life. If he wanted things to be over, then she was going to confront him and find out for sure. She needed Nate. She loved Nate and she wasn't going to give up without a fight.

She hit the stop button on the music. "Back row, I need to see more passion from you. Let's start again with the back row in the front. No matter where you are on stage I want you to be one hundred percent engaged. If you can't be, then I will find another dancer to take your place."

The dancers went through the routine again and Jen started to see them come alive in the dance. The same way she knew she'd come alive with Nate. When the session ended and she dismissed everyone, she glanced up to see Cam standing in the doorway.

"Do you have a minute?"

"Yes. What's up?"

She wondered if he was here to fire her. If Nate had sent his big brother to get rid of her she was going to hunt him down and give him a piece of her mind.

"I'm in an awkward position."

She felt tears sting the back of her eyes. "Just say it. I think I know what's coming."

Cam walked farther into the room. "I doubt it. Do you know Russell Holloway?"

"The New Zealand billionaire? No, I really don't run in those circles."

"He wants your number," Cam said.

"I'm not interested in any man but Nate. You can tell him thanks, but no thanks."

"Not for dating you," Cam said. "He wants to hire you. Are you okay?"

She felt stupid when he said that. What had she been thinking? This situation with Nate was making her paranoid. "I'm tired."

"You have been working nonstop on the tenth anniversary celebration and I'm really happy with that, but don't kill yourself for the club."

"I'm not going to. Why do you think Russell Holloway wants to hire me?" she asked.

"He told me he was going to try to steal you away. He heard from some of your more famous students that you are one hell of a dancer and I think he wants to add a stage show to his clubs."

"The Kiwi Klubs are world-famous. I mean, everyone has heard of them."

"I know. It would be a position with a lot of exposure for you."

"Are you unhappy with me?" she asked.

"Not at all," he said. "But it's a good opportunity and I didn't feel right not letting you know."

"I couldn't leave Luna Azul," she said. "Not after all you guys did for me."

Cam handed her a business card. "You make the decision that's right for you. That's what we did when we

went to bat for you. After you talk to him let me know what he offered, we might be able to match his offer."

Cam left a few minutes later and she sat down on a stool in the back of the rehearsal room. She wasn't looking to travel the world and be a choreographer for the Kiwi Klubs. But it couldn't hurt to talk to him. Especially if things weren't going well between her and Nate.

She needed to have options and to keep them open. Working at Luna Azul was one of the best things that had ever happened to her—hell, it was the best thing. *Period.* But she knew that if Nate and she didn't make it she wasn't going to be as happy here.

She looked at the business card and wondered what Russell Holloway would say if she called him. She was confused. Life was easier when all she had to do was think about dancing and about the moves that the choreographer had taught her.

She realized how unpredictable life was. She'd had an inkling of it when she'd been forced out of her safe world of competitive dance and when she'd seen her sister give birth to her son all alone.

But this was different. This was her having to make a decision and deal with the consequences. In a way, the impulsive leaping was easier. There was no time to debate the outcome.

But that was what she did all afternoon. Debated with herself. She stared at that card. Even dialed the number more than once and hung up before the call connected. She had no idea what to say to Russell Holloway. Mainly because the one person she could turn to for advice wasn't around for her to get it from. She wanted to know what Nate thought. He was more than a lover to her, he

was also a trusted friend and she knew she didn't want to lose him in both areas of her life.

Nate was having a pretty crappy day by the time he got to the club and Cam's office. "What's up?"

"Just some news about Jen. But what's going on with you?"

Nate furrowed his brow. "Speeding ticket, Lori O'Neil is demanding I go out with her tonight or she's going to stop mentioning the club in her celebrity blog and I have to fly to New York to film guest spots on two different shows."

"Sucks to be you and have to go out with a beautiful woman and be on TV."

Nate glared at his brother. "*Don't*. Don't try to shame me into remembering that I have a great life and that I don't have anything to complain about."

Cam shrugged those big shoulders of his. "I guess I don't have to then. Seems you know that you have nothing to bitch about."

"Yeah, I know it but it doesn't change the fact that I'm having a really pissy day."

Cam laughed. "I'll give you that."

Nate threw himself down in one of the large leather guest chairs in Cam's office. On the paneled wall was a portrait of Cam standing in the foyer of their boyhood home dressed in a tuxedo. "Don't you wonder why Dad had those paintings of us done?"

Cam shook his head. "He wanted to create a legacy for us to pass on to our children."

"Are you thinking of having a family?" Nate asked his brother. That very thought—a family of his own—had been on his mind too often lately. "I always believed us Stern men made better bachelors than husbands."

Cam shrugged. "I feel the same. I mean business is a lot easier to figure out than a woman."

Nate laughed. "Tell me about it. Who are you dating?"

"None of your business."

"A secret love?"

"Not really. Not love. Just sex."

Was that what Nate had with Jen? Was it just really good sex? "Have you ever been in love, Cam?"

"One time," his brother admitted. "But it was a long time ago and I was young."

"What did it feel like?"

Cam quirked one eyebrow at him.

"I know that's a silly question but I'm not sure if I know how to love. I mean you and Justin are my brothers and we're blood so I know I can count on you. But a woman…how do I know if I love her or not?"

Cam came around his desk and leaned back on it. "I have no idea, Nate. I wish I had an easy answer for you. But women are complicated and I have no idea how to unravel the mystery of them."

"You're not really helping me," Nate said.

"I know. I'm sorry about that."

Nate thought about the fact that Cam, who was very smart and very sure of himself, wasn't sure of love. Did that mean he had been right in thinking that the Stern men weren't meant for love?

"On a related note to this woman talk—Russell Holloway called me this morning and asked if he could have Jen's number."

Nate went very still. "Why?"

"He's heard some good things about her and he wants to offer her a job."

"I hope you told him to step off."

Cam shook his head. "That's not my call. I gave Jen his message and his business card. It's up to her if she wants to take the job."

Nate didn't agree with his brother but he kept that to himself. He needed to talk to Jen anyway—it was something he'd been avoiding since she'd confessed her love.

He hoped he hadn't driven her straight into Russell's hands by ignoring her the past few days.

"What's the matter?"

"I don't want her to work with Russell," Nate said.

"Then tell her how you feel. I don't know a lot about love but I do know that women are big on talking."

Nate knew that, too. "Do you think talking would have fixed the problems between Dad and Mom?"

Cam walked back around his desk and sat in his leather executive chair. "I don't know that anything would have helped them. They weren't suited to each other."

Nate had thought so, too. Their dad had been so warm and caring and always put Nate and his brothers first, even over his pro-golf career. Made them feel so important to his life. Just the way Nate had observed Jen doing with her nephew. He wondered if he could feel the same about her.

"I don't know what to say," Nate said at last. "To Jen I mean."

"What do you want her to do?" Cam asked.

Nate wanted her to stay, but saying that would let her know that he was as vulnerable to her as she was to him. It would even the scales in the balance of power between them.

He'd heard once that the power in a relationship belonged to the one who cared less. And he was

beginning to believe that was true because Jen had all the power. And that was what scared him. He just figured out that it wasn't love. It was the fact that he was going to have no power over anything with her if he admitted how much she meant to him.

And to a man like him, a man used to controlling the world around him, that was almost like saying he'd lose the ability to breathe. It was unthinkable.

"I don't know," he admitted to Cam. "I want her to stay but I'm not sure how to say that to her."

Cam nodded. "Let me know what you decide. I want her to stay for your sake, Nate. If you want Jen don't let her go."

"Aren't you concerned about the club, too? She's a very good dancer."

"There are other good dancers in South Florida, bro, but only one Jen where you're concerned."

Nate knew that Cam had a point and was very glad that his brother had told him about the offer. Even though it was the work day he had a reason to see Jen. Not knowing what Jen was going to do was making him a bit crazy so instead of avoiding her, he sent her a text and asked her to meet him at the park where they took Riley to play baseball. Time to find out what she was thinking and where she wanted her life to be.

Jen was eating an early dinner with Riley and Marcia when she got Nate's text message. Riley had finished his dinner and asked to be excused to the living room.

"Who was that?" Marcia asked once Riley was out of earshot.

"Nate." Jen hoped that he wanted to talk because he'd had time to think about her confession of love and

maybe he was ready to move on to the next level of commitment with her.

"What does he want?" Marcia asked.

"To talk, I imagine. Why are you still treating him with distrust?" she asked her sister.

"Why aren't you? He hasn't been around for a few days. Is there something wrong between you guys?"

"I don't know. Can I ask you something…not about Nate?"

"Sure, go ahead," Marcia said.

"I got a rather strange message today."

"What? What was it?" Marcia asked.

"Cam said that Russell Holloway is interested in talking to me about working in his Kiwi Klubs."

"Do you know what you would be doing?" Marcia asked.

"Same as what I do now except you know he has an entire chain of clubs all over the world. My guess is that he'd want me to develop shows for each of the clubs that is unique to their location and then train a dance instructor at each place."

Jen played with the food on her plate. She'd been around and around this in her head and she still couldn't decide if she should call him or not.

"Does he want you to live in New Zealand?"

"I'm not sure where he's going to want me to live. But I like living here with you and Riley."

Marcia sighed and then put on her big-sister face. That serious expression she got when she was about to give advice and make it stick. "You'll never know what it is you are passing up if you don't at least talk to the man."

"Okay. I can talk to him, but what about our family?"

"Jen, we're always going to be family no matter where you live. In fact, you'll probably have a home of your own before too much longer if you stay here. Don't let me and Riley make this decision for you."

Jen shook her head. "This is too hard. It's not like a dancing competition, you know. I loved that and I had to travel but this is my livelihood."

"It's life," Marcia said. "Life is complicated."

"Thanks for nothing," Jen said with a small smile.

Marcia reached across the table and took the fork from her hand. "I wish I could tell you what to do and know that that would be the right decision, but I can't. I won't. You have to do this on your own."

"I know that. I'm just not sure what I want."

"Well, until you talk to him you don't even know what he wants."

"That's true," she admitted. "I guess I'll give him a call. I can't really leave now because of the tenth anniversary celebration at Luna Azul. I'm really busy there."

"Stop making excuses. If you don't want to call him then don't," Marcia said. "But make sure you are making this decision for yourself and not based on me and Riley or even Nate. If Nate loves you he'll follow you wherever you go."

Marcia made it sound so easy. "How do I know if he loves me?"

"Did you tell him you love him?" Marcia asked.

"Yes."

She raised both eyebrows at her. "And…"

"He didn't say anything. I mean he said thanks and that he cared for me and thought I was beautiful…"

"Oh, sweetie, I don't know what to say. What does your heart tell you?" Marcia asked.

Jen leaned back in her chair and thought about her sister's question. Her heart was just focused on Nate. She dreamed about him all night every night. Woke up the past two nights feeling afraid and alone. She wanted his arms around her and she slept better when he was with her.

"That I love him," Jen said. "It all comes back to that. It doesn't matter if he wants me or not, I still love him."

Marcia shook her head. "I know that place and it sucks being there. But you have to make decisions that make sense to you."

Jen had the feeling that Marcia was talking about her own relationship with Riley's dad and not about Jen and Nate anymore. But Jen knew that there were similarities. "Why is love so hard for us?"

"Why should it be easy?" Marcia asked.

"Have I ever mentioned how much I hate it when you answer a question with a question?" Jen asked. "You always do that when you don't have the answer. Why can't you just say I don't know?"

Marcia bit her lip and looked down. "I'm your big sister, Jen, I'm supposed to have the answers. I mean, it's just you and me and Riley and I'm the one who has to know what's going on."

Jen reached for her sister and leaned across the table to hug her. "I'm grown-up now. We can take care of each other, okay?"

Marcia nodded. "What are you going to do?"

"I don't know yet. I'm going to go meet Nate and see where that leads and then I'll decide if I should call Russell. I don't even really know anything about his clubs except their name. And that cute little koala bear logo they have."

"I don't know much about them, either. I will see what info I can find on the internet once I put Riley to bed."

"Thanks, Marcia. I mean for always being here for me and giving me a place to live when I made a mess of my life."

Marcia got up from the table and ruffled Jen's hair as she walked into the kitchen to put the dishes away. "That's what family is for."

Fourteen

Nate sat on a bench under one of the palm trees and watched Jen walking toward him. Her hair was loose and blew in the spring breeze. Her legs were bare beneath a miniskirt and her shoulders bare under the sleeveless top she wore.

She took his breath away. Just looking at her made him realize how much he'd missed her the past two days. And now he had to deal with playing it cool and seeing if she was going to leave him and go work for one of his friends. It didn't matter that he knew she wouldn't be leaving him because she wanted to. He knew he set it up when he'd ignored her confession of love and not told her how he felt. He still wasn't sure he'd be able to do it.

"Hello, Nate," she said, sitting down next to him.

"Hello, Jen."

"Why did you ask me to meet you here?" she asked, pushing her sunglasses up on her head.

She looked tired. Like she hadn't slept in a few days. He wondered if being apart had caused an ache inside her like the one inside him.

He knew he should start off with their relationship stuff but to be honest, the thing that was really on his mind was if she was going to leave him. Leave South Florida for New Zealand and Russell Holloway.

"Have you talked to Holloway?"

She shook her head and pulled her sunglasses off her head and back over her eyes. "No. Is that why you wanted to talk to me?"

"Yes."

"Oh, well, I haven't decided if I'm going to call him yet. I'm really busy with rehearsals for the anniversary celebration. I want to think about this before I make a decision. The last time I did something impulsive…well, let's just say it hasn't worked out as I'd hoped."

"Do you mean me?"

"Yes, I mean you. We haven't seen each other in two days because you have been avoiding me and instead of talking to me about that, you want to know what my job plans are."

Nate knew she had a point and felt that this wasn't going at all the way he'd planned. "It's a valid question, Jen. You are at the stage of your life where you are redefining yourself. I want to know if you are going to walk out the door."

She wrapped an arm around her waist. "Would that matter to you?"

"Of course it would. I care about you, Jen. More than I can say, but it's there," he said.

"I need more than that, Nate. I told you I love you and

that's still true today but I don't want to be like the other women you've dated and see you in the papers all the time and think what might have been. It would be easier for me to pretend that this meant nothing. That I could get over a broken heart by calling Russell Holloway and making plans to leave you and Luna Azul.

"But I know it's not that easy. I didn't fall in love with you on a whim. I fell in love with the man I got to know over the past few weeks. The man who talks to me in the middle of the night and isn't afraid to let me see the person behind the flashbulbs."

Nate had nothing to say to her. Everything she said made her more vulnerable and put more power in his court but he felt like the weak one. The scared one. And one thing he did remember his mother saying was that no woman wanted a weak man. That weakness was the most unattractive thing about any human, most especially a man.

"I want to say the right thing here, honey, but I really don't know what that is," he said, opting for honesty and hoping she'd understand all that he didn't say.

"That is lame. I told you I love you."

"I know that. I'm not trying to be lame."

"No," she said, standing up. "Why can't you say you love me? You can say you want me, but there's no mention of love. Why is it? Do you really not care for me?"

Nate knew this was getting out of control and he had no idea how to fix it. "You are getting upset and that's not the way to have this conversation."

"I'm not upset—I'm disappointed that I've finally found a man I can love and he can't say that he cares for me."

"You know I care for you, Jen."

She shook her head. "That's not enough."

She turned to walk away and he was scared that she might really walk out on him. That this would be the last moment they had together.

"Jen, wait. I can do better," he said.

She glanced back at him over her shoulder. "I know you can. I think that if it is so hard for you to admit how you feel for me then maybe you don't really love me.

"And that's okay. I can see why I'd fall in love with you. But I'm not from your world and you are used to a level of sophistication that I don't have, and maybe my normal life is just not exciting enough for you."

Nate stood up and walked over to her. The Florida sun beamed down on both of them. It was such a nice day he didn't want to let her go. Didn't want to end this relationship with her on a day like today.

"Don't say that. I like the life you and I have. These weeks we've been together have been the most exciting of my life. I've been the closest I've been to peace since I quit playing ball."

"I'm glad," she said, quietly. "I want that for you."

"Give me a chance to prove myself," he said.

She took his hand in hers and then rose up on tiptoes to kiss him. "If you don't love me then there is nothing else to say. I can't do things in half measure and staying with you, loving you while you don't love me, would kill me, Nate. I don't want to live like that."

Jen did what she did best when her life fell apart and that was pouring herself into her work. Almost three days passed before she called Russell Holloway's office and got his secretary. She put Jen through right away.

"This is Holloway."

"Um…hello, this is Jen Miller. Cam Stern gave me your number."

"Jen, it's about time you called me. I have heard a lot of good things about you and I'd love to meet with you in person to discuss an offer."

"A job offer?" she asked.

"Yes. I don't know if you are familiar with my clubs…"

"Mr. Holloway—"

"Call me Russ. Everyone does."

"Okay, Russ. I've heard of your clubs. What kind of job did you have in mind for me? Would you want me to travel to all the locations and train the dancers?"

"Yes, and choreograph new shows. I hope you don't mind but I asked Cam to send me footage of your flamenco show from the club. You are really very talented."

She was flattered. After all the ups and downs and heartache she'd experienced in the past few weeks, it was nice to have a man just say nice things to her. "Thank you."

"You don't have to thank me for telling the truth. Now what do you say?"

"Do I have to give you my answer right now?"

"I can wait a few days," he said. "I'm going to send you a ticket to London."

"Why London?"

"I'm going to be visiting the Kiwi Kensington Klub and you can join me there. Give me your answer then, okay?"

"When is it? I have a lot of rehearsals for the Luna Azul tenth anniversary coming up in May so I can't afford too many days away."

"I like that work ethic," he said with a laugh. "I won't keep you more than a few days."

"Okay. I'll come see you but there is no guarantee I'll take the job."

"I understand," he said.

She phoned Cam and asked for a few days off and then flew to London. She had a glimpse of the life she could have. The Kiwi Klub was bigger than Luna Azul. And it would be very busy and she'd have a chance to reach more people with her dance than she ever had before, but London was cold and rainy and she missed Miami.

She missed Marcia and Riley and she knew in her heart of hearts that this wasn't what she wanted. She'd be taking the job to run away from Nate.

The next morning when she saw Russ she told him her decision.

"I'm sorry, but I guess I'm more of a homebody than I thought I was. I miss my family."

"It's okay. I used to be like that, so I understand. If you ever change your mind, call me. I will always have room for you on my staff."

That was a sweet offer but she knew she wouldn't take him up on it. She was tired of running.

So she flew back to Miami and went back to work. She spent every waking moment at Luna Azul. Trying to prove herself. It had somehow become important to her to make sure she spent as much time there preparing for the tenth anniversary celebration as possible, even though she knew Nate was busy and never showed his face around the club anymore.

One night, when she was alone working on a routine, she heard a voice behind her. "It's time for you to go home."

She glanced at the door of the rehearsal hall and was surprised to see Cam there. He had been riding everyone hard at Luna Azul presumably to ensure that the extra publicity they were getting due to their anniversary celebration wasn't wasted.

"Not yet. I want to practice some of the things from the notes that Hutch sent me tonight. My dancers need to have it nailed before he heads back home."

"They are good and so are you," Cam said. "You need rest. You do know that's important."

"Yes, I know it," she said. But she wasn't going home to rest. She hadn't had a good night's sleep in close to two weeks. Not since she'd broken up with Nate in a sunny park on what should have been the best day of her life. Instead, she'd been sleeping fitfully and never really finding a moment's peace.

"Why are you still here at almost midnight?" he asked. "Why didn't you take the job that Russell offered?"

"I'm here tonight because I'm a perfectionist," she said. "As for your other question, why do you care?"

Cam walked farther into the room and stopped in the middle of it. "I care because my employees are like family to me. I want to make sure that you're okay."

"I'm fine," she said.

"Even though you and Nate are no longer dating?" Cam asked.

"I don't want to talk about this with you," she said. She started gathering up her things. "I'm going to go home now."

"Not yet. Since you're still here and I know my brother isn't sleeping…what happened between the two of you?"

Jen didn't think she could do this. Marcia had tried

to get her to talk but she hadn't been able to. She didn't want to tell anyone that Nate didn't love her. Though his constant partying since they'd broken up was evidence enough.

"I can't talk about this. Seriously, what are you doing here? It doesn't matter how exhausted I am. I can always dance. I'm going to make sure your show rocks."

"I have no doubt about that," Cam said, moving around the room with a casual grace. "What happened to break you two up?"

"Please don't make me rehash this. Why don't you ask Nate?" she asked.

"I can't. Lately he's a total jerk to anyone who tries to ask him anything personal."

Jen soaked up this information. Saddened to hear Nate was having as rough a time as she was. "He seems to be recovering nicely."

"What?"

"He is out partying every night. The women are more beautiful than ever and I saw an interview with him from New York…he didn't seem that broken up about not having me in his life."

"He's good at hiding what he feels. You should know that by now."

Jen crossed her arms over her chest. "I do know that, but I can't make him feel something he doesn't, you know?"

Cam nodded. "He asked me to check in on you. Unlike Nate, you aren't in the papers every day and he has no idea if you are okay."

"I'm okay," she said.

"Truly?"

"No, Cam, I'm not okay. I have a broken heart and I have to be in the same physical location as the man I

love and not see him every day. It's torture, but there's nothing I can do about that."

He nodded slowly. "I see your point. So you've been working a lot."

"What else can I do?"

He gave her a self-mocking grin. "You are asking the wrong guy. All I do is work because it keeps me from being alone with myself."

"I'm sorry. At least I can blame this bout of workaholism on Nate."

"True enough. I have my own demons and they don't come from a place of love."

"I'm sorry," she said, realizing the slick golden boy had his own issues and problems.

"Don't be. I have no regrets."

"Me, either, Cam. Tell Nate I don't have any regrets."

Jen gathered her bag and slung it over her shoulder. "Did you want me to take that job that Russell offered?"

"Only if it was something you wanted. I'm not sure what you want from your career here. Working for Russell will give you exposure to a different world of people."

She started walking toward the exit and Cam followed her.

"I do know that. I could maybe even try my hand at dancing in another part of the world," she said to him. "Thank you again for helping out with that Carlos mess."

"I'm just glad that he is being prosecuted and will have to spend some time behind bars. That should make him think twice before he tries to come after anyone again."

"I agree. Thank you."

"You're welcome. I know that you could try competitive dancing if you moved to New Zealand. Why aren't you?"

"Cam, why are you asking me this? Frankly, it doesn't seem like the sort of thing that would be on your mind."

Cam put his hand out and touched her shoulder. "It's not for me. It's for Nate. He can't figure out why you are staying and he's tearing himself up for maybe making you give up the chance of a lifetime."

She blinked at Cam. Nate would try to make this all about him, and in a way it was. "I decided to stop running away. Money and prestige aren't important to me. Roots and family are and I'm not about to give either of them up."

She brushed past Cam and walked down the hallway and then out of the club. She stopped under the streetlights and looked back toward the rooftop. She thought she felt Nate watching her but she knew that couldn't be right. He had already moved on.

Nate watched Jen exit the club and walk slowly up the street to her car. He'd done this every night since they'd been apart. He couldn't stand the thought of anything happening to her. On the nights that he couldn't be here he asked one of his brothers to watch out for her.

Even though they'd broken up, he couldn't let her go. He couldn't get her out of his mind. She haunted him constantly and it was all he could do not to run back to her door and beg her to forgive him. To tell her he'd give her everything he had even though he couldn't love her.

He heard footsteps behind him and turned to see Cam walking toward him. "What did she say?"

Cam just shook his head and leaned against the railing at the edge of the rooftop area. "I think you need to talk to her yourself."

Nate pushed his hands through his thick hair. "Do you think I don't want to? I want to go to her but I'm afraid I'll say anything to get her back. And I don't want to steal her future the way that jerk Carlos did."

"You aren't going to do that. That young woman knows exactly what she wants. She's staying here, I suspect, to be near you."

"What?"

"Yes. She knows that she'd have a different life if she took the job that Russell offered, but that's not important to her. In fact, she told me that the only thing important to her is family and building a life here in Miami."

Nate turned away from his brother. He was tempted to go after Jen right now. But he knew that he couldn't. He knew that if he went now he would have no idea what to say.

"I want her back, Cam."

"Then get her back, Nate. There is no reason for the two of you to be so miserable apart."

"She's miserable?"

"I doubt she's slept in the entire time since you broke up. She's thinner than she was before and she spends every waking hour here at the club rehearsing for the anniversary celebration even though now we aren't sure we are going to be able to have it since the community board is throwing every legal obstacle in front of us that they can."

She was pouring herself into dancing again but this

time the ones to benefit would be the Stern brothers and Luna Azul. "I didn't want that for her."

"What did you want?"

Nate tipped his head back and looked up at the starry sky. "I want her. I need her in my life, Cam."

"What's stopping you from having her?"

His own stubbornness, he thought, and the fact that he was afraid to admit the most important thing of his life.

He loved her.

That was it. He'd known it for a while but had been afraid to define what it was he felt for her. He wanted to pretend that he could control his emotions. Could control how he felt about her but now that they were apart, he'd come to realize he wanted her even more than he'd thought he could.

It wasn't just the physical side of things, though he did long to hold her naked in his arms again. He wanted to make love to her over and over again to reinforce the bonds of love between them. But he also just wanted to sit quietly with her in the morning as they started the day.

"I need your help," he said to Cam.

"Um, what the hell do you think I'm doing by talking to Jen at midnight?"

"Shut up, Cam. This is serious. I need to get Jen back and the only way I'm going to do that is to prove to her that I love her."

Cam nodded. "Tell me what you need."

"I think I need to do this right. I'm going to ask her to marry me. I want to make up for the way I acted when she told me she loved me."

"Again, Nate, what can I do?"

Nate didn't know. He was still trying to figure

everything out. And he was operating from a place of fear. What if it was too late, and she'd already decided he wasn't worth her time? What if she'd fallen out of love with him?

He needed to stack the deck in his favor. "I need her sister and her nephew on my side."

"I don't think I can help you there."

"I know you can't. Will you ask our party planner, Emma, to help you plan the perfect dinner up here under the stars?" Nate asked. The event planner would know what a woman wanted. "Tell her I want the perfect romantic fantasy that every woman has for the night she gets engaged."

Cam didn't seem too happy about the request, but he nodded. "I'll do it."

"Great. Now I have to do everything else."

"When is the dream night going to take place?" Cam asked.

"Tomorrow night. I think…will you call Jen tomorrow and tell her to take the day off. I'm going to arrange for a day at the spa for her…to make up for all the long hours she put in here at the club."

"Okay. Anything else?"

"No, that's it. The rest is up to me."

After Cam left, Nate stayed there on the rooftop garden area making notes and a long list of all the things he had to do. When he had the list finalized he got in his car to head home but found himself in Jen's neighborhood sitting in front her house.

He knew it was crazy but he needed to be closer to her. Now that he'd admitted to himself he loved her, he wanted to go to her and tell her. He needed to try to fix everything that he'd nearly let slip away.

He hoped he could fix it. Prayed that he hadn't

ruined everything by letting her walk out of his life. Because he'd just realized that his mom had been wrong about men and weakness. Sometimes, Nate realized, something like love could make a man weak in one sense but having the right woman love him back could make him stronger in his entire life.

Fifteen

Jen tried to relax at The Boutique Spa at the Ritz-Carlton in Coconut Grove. She'd been surprised when a courier from Cam's office had arrived at her home at ten this morning and told her she was taking the day off. He wanted her pampered and rested before she arrived at the club at five o'clock tonight.

She'd almost turned down the offer of the day off but the courier had told her she had no option. He was to take her to the spa and stay with her to drive her home when she was done relaxing.

She had been massaged and pampered like a princess and she loved every second of it. She had a manicure and a pedicure and a facial and that made her a little sad because she was going to be glowing and beautiful when she left the spa but the only man who she wanted to see—Nate—would never know.

She had to stop thinking of him all the time. But that

was hard. She still had the picture he'd taken of the two of them on his yacht stored on her phone and she found herself looking at it more and more often as the days went by. It was exactly two weeks today since they'd broken up.

She wished she could report that she no longer loved him, but that wasn't about to happen. Her heart was stubbornly sticking to Nate as the man for her. And she didn't know how she was going to keep going until she fell out of love with him—if she ever did.

Her phone rang as she was finishing up at the spa. "Hello, Marcia."

"Jen. I have the afternoon off and thought we could meet up and go shopping," her sister said.

"Meet up where? I have one of the Luna Azul employees who is driving me around today."

"I'll come pick you up and we can go to Nordstrom's and do a little dress shopping. I need something nice to wear to a dinner with the partners next week. I think they are going to offer me junior partner."

"Really?" Jen asked. "I'm so excited for you, sweetie. All of your hard work is finally paying off."

"Yes, it is. And yours will, too. I want to have a girls' afternoon."

"Okay," Jen said. "I'm so relaxed from my massage and treatments. That sounds like the perfect way to continue my day off."

"Good. I'll be there in fifteen minutes."

"Okay. Do we need to get Riley after school?"

"No, Lori is picking him up. The boys have a project they are working on."

Twenty minutes later, Jen was seated in Marcia's Audi convertible driving toward Nordstrom's. They spent the rest of the afternoon trying on dresses and both walked

away with two new purchases. She had fun with her sister just laughing and for a few moments she forgot her heart was broken.

That was an eye-opening thing because for the first time, she realized she could still have a good life without Nate. It wouldn't be as happy as it could be if he'd loved her back, but she wouldn't be a miserable woman with her broken heart.

Her cell phone pinged just as they got home and she glanced down at the screen to see it was a text message from Nate.

She hesitated for a moment then opened the message. *I need to see you tonight. Please meet me at the rooftop club at five-thirty.*

"Nate wants me to meet him tonight. Why do you think he wants that?"

Marcia shrugged. "I'm not sure."

"Last night, Cam tried to convince me that I should have taken the job with Russell. Do you think that Nate is going to try now?"

"I don't think so."

"What if he does? What if Nate doesn't want me around anymore and he tried to get Cam to let me go…"

"*Stop.* That's just crazy talk. Get dressed, then see what Nate wants. I think you should wear that red dress you got today and make him realize all he's missing."

Jen glanced over at her sister. "You think so?"

"Yes. Let him see everything he gave up when he walked out on you."

Technically, she'd been the one to walk away. But she didn't argue with her sister. Instead, she sent Nate a text telling him she'd meet him later that night for dinner.

She didn't let herself hope that he might have changed

his mind. Maybe her talk with Cam had convinced Nate's brother that she was sticking around for a while and Nate wanted to make sure they had no hard feelings between them.

She had no idea what he wanted. She only knew that the thought of seeing him tonight excited her. She had missed him. And even if this was the last time they were alone together, she wanted to make the most of it.

She took her time getting dressed. Made sure her makeup was flawlessly applied and then she did her hair. She let the long thick length stay down and when she put on her slim-fitting red dress and the killer stiletto heels she bought to go with it, she knew she looked good.

In fact, she thought she looked as beautiful as Nate had always told her she was.

She walked out of her bedroom and Marcia whistled. "You are going to knock that man on his ass."

"He's used to sexy women," Jen said. She'd never been in this situation before. "I'm almost afraid to go tonight."

"Don't worry. Everything will work out okay."

"Are you sure?" Jen asked.

Marcia laughed and shook her head. "No, I'm not, but I want it to work out for you, Jen. One of us deserves to be happy with the man we love."

She took those words with her as she drove into Little Havana and to Luna Azul.

Nate was beyond nervous as he waited for Jen to arrive. The rooftop garden had been turned into a mini-paradise. There were flowers everywhere and Emma had pulled out the stops by bringing in fountains and trees adorned with twinkle lights and brightly colored Japanese lanterns.

The path from the rooftop entrance to the place where they would dine had been carpeted and rose petals sprinkled to lead the way to him and the table. Nate wore his tux and had a bottle of champagne chilling.

In his pocket was an antique engagement ring he'd found after spending several hours going from jewelry store to jewelry store searching for the one ring that seemed made for Jen.

Now he had everything in place. He'd made this area as perfect as he could and the only variable left was the human factor. The one thing he couldn't control.

In his mind he'd rehearsed what he'd say to her. But he always hesitated when he got to confessing his love. He had no idea how those words were going to sound when he said them and he was a little afraid she'd throw them back in his face.

But he wasn't going to let those fears stop him. Tonight he was going to ask her to marry him. He was going to tell her he loved her and they were going to have a chance at having a life together.

He'd invited his brothers and her sister and nephew to join them later in the evening for dessert and he really hoped they'd all be celebrating.

His phone pinged and he glanced down at the screen. The text message was from Cam.

She's here.

Wish me luck, Nate texted back.

He cued the music on his iPod and had Dean Martin ready to go as soon as she arrived. There was little to do but wait.

As soon as he saw her, he forgot to breathe. She was beautiful. No, she was the most beautiful woman in the world. He couldn't do anything but stare at her. And

when she stopped walking and just looked at him, he was afraid she was going to turn and leave him.

"You are gorgeous," he said. "Come over here."

"Thank you," she said, but stayed where she was. "You are very handsome in your tux."

He bowed his head to acknowledge her compliment. "Please come to me, Jen."

She shook her head. "I think I'm dreaming, Nate. I'm afraid to take another step and wake up and find…that this isn't real."

"What would convince you that this is real?"

"You."

He understood what she meant. He went to her and took her hand in his, brought it to his lips and brushed her knuckles with his lips. "Does this feel real?"

"Yes. Why are you doing this?"

He put his fingers over her lips. "I have everything planned. Come over here and sit down and I will tell you."

"You have a plan?"

"Yes, and it's very important to me that this night go right."

"It is?"

"Yes. I want to make up for the pain I've caused you."

He led her to the table and seated her and then turned back to face her. But she was so beautiful he couldn't really think of the words he'd rehearsed. He wanted to be calm and cool but the thought that she wasn't really his was paramount in his mind. He needed to tell her everything.

"I love you."

"Are you sure?" she asked.

"Yes," he said. "Damn. This isn't what I'd planned.

But I want you to know that I have loved you for a long time and I was just too afraid to tell you."

She licked her lips and he groaned wanting to taste her mouth under his.

"Do you still love me?" he asked.

"Yes, I do. I have come to the conclusion that I will always love you."

"Good. I want…" He stopped talking and got down on one knee in front of her. "I want you to marry me. Will you do that, Jen? Will you take a chance on me and go on the best adventure of our lives by spending the rest of yours with me?"

She just stared at him and he realized he'd forgotten to get the ring out. He reached in his pocket but she stopped him by putting her hands on his shoulders. "Are you sure about this? If you ask me to marry you, I'm not going to let you change your mind later."

"I've never been surer of anything in my life. Losing you hurt me in ways I didn't know I could be hurt. The past two weeks have been like trying to live when I can't catch my breath. I need you, Jen. I love you."

"Oh, Nate. I love you, too. I…but will you stay out of the papers with other women?"

"Yes!" he said.

"Then, yes, I will marry you."

He took the box from his pocket and removed the ring from it. He slowly slid it on her ring finger and then drew her to her feet and into his arms. He kissed her slowly and held her close to him.

"Thank you for loving me. You've made my life so much richer by being in it."

She laughed up at him. "You've done the same for me."

They dined together under the stars and talked about

their future. He didn't let go of her hand the entire time and realized he didn't want to let go of her ever again. And when their families joined them for dessert, Nate realized how full his life was. They discussed Luna Azul's tenth anniversary, and their wedding plans.

The future that had seemed uncertain when he'd had to leave baseball now looked so bright. He was positive with Jen's love in his life that he had it all.

* * * * *

"Pack for the weekend."

Finally dismissed, she nodded before turning on her heel and walking out the door. A weekend with Zac Prescott. She swallowed the swell of unbidden excitement with a forceful gulp.

She didn't want to want Zac… Damn, she refused to want a man who blithely made decisions about her life without even asking her. A man who didn't want her the way *she* wanted him to want her.

And yet, he'd kissed her. Flirted, even. Didn't that tell her something?

She tossed the notebook on her desk. Zac had crossed the line, invading her private life—a shameful, personal part of it—without invitation. Embarrassment and anger churned around in her stomach, replacing the fleeting desire. Relying only on herself had become a way of life. She didn't need saving.

Not even if her personal white knight was Zac Prescott.

Dear Reader,

Many lifetimes ago, I worked in a corporate office: thirteen years as a PA, then eventually, office manager. And unfortunately, men like my hero, Zac Prescott, were nonexistent. Which is maybe a good thing—can you imagine trying to get any work done with a gorgeous alpha male in the next room? Of course, that's my heroine's downfall. Emily is so focused on her career that she's forgotten how to enjoy life. And with Zac, there's definitely enjoyment to be had!

Yes, the black sheep of the Prescott family finally has his story! And this book also marks my first set in the beautiful Gold Coast in Queensland—one of my favourite places in the world. For Aussies, a surfers holiday is a rite of passage—lazing on the pristine beaches, shopping, surfing, clubbing and generally soaking up the glorious laid-back atmosphere. I love it! (Can you tell?) And as you delve into Zac and Emily's romance, I hope their little corner of my world comes alive for you, too.

With love,

Paula

PROMOTED TO WIFE?

BY
PAULA ROE

to her humble collection of neatly arranged possessions. She crossed her arms as Zac's gaze raked over her, taking in her makeup-free, damp-haired presence.

You're practically naked. Heat pooled as she drew the ties of her threadbare robe more securely around her waist. That intense focus was narrowed right in on her. He had a way of staring as if he was picking through all her secrets yet revealing none of his. A complete contrast to Thursday night, when he'd been unguarded, almost vulnerable. It had dragged her in quicker than Southport's killer rip tide.

"You can't quit," he stated again, that dark frown still creasing his perfect face.

She blinked. "Why not?"

"Well, for one, your temp—Amber?—sucks."

"It's Ebony. She came from Marketing as a favor to me."

"She's stuffed up the filing system."

"I see." With a keen eye, she watched him massage his neck. Two years of close personal contact had taught her a headache was brewing in that brilliant head of his. For one second she felt sorry for him.

"And she puts sugar in my coffee."

Oh, boy. I've spoiled him. "And let me guess…she doesn't remind you to eat?"

Zac scowled, still rubbing his neck. "And her God-awful perfume gives me a headache. It isn't funny. Everything's gone to hell this past week. I need you back."

Oh, Lordy. Her bones melted like ice cream in summer, her body held up only by sheer will. She wanted to groan aloud but instead took an unsteady gulp. "You need me?" she repeated faintly.

His nod was brief and spare. "For some insane reason, Victor Prescott is about to name me as his successor."

"Your father? What…to VP Tech?"

"Yep."

Whoa. Stunned, Emily felt her jaw sag. Zac never talked about his past, including his family: it was as if he'd emerged onto the Gold Coast's construction scene fully assembled and commanding a million-plus annual turnover. Sure, she knew his father was the iron-fisted CEO of a billion-dollar software company, but that was about it. Zac didn't pay her to gossip with his employees.

"That's why you were…" She paused delicately but he brushed away her hesitation with an imperious wave of his hand.

"Drunk in my office, yes. Not a good impression for the cleaning staff."

Her boss never drank at work. And that was why he'd called her, his loyal assistant, to get him home. *Great.*

"Zac," she sighed. "I spent two years being the best damn assistant you ever had. I organized your work and personal life without comment, without complaint. I soothed clients, I arranged last-minute meetings, business trips and dates. I worked overtime and weekends more times than I can count—"

"I didn't realize you hated your job so much," he interjected stiffly.

"I don't! *I didn't.* It's…it's just time for a change."

"And helping me sort out this mess with VP Tech isn't enough of a change?"

"No…yes. I just—I'm leaving, okay?"

Silence fell for a moment, thick and palpable, until Zac said slowly, "So tell me who's lured away my assistant—the best damn one I've ever had—" his mouth tweaked "—when I need her the most?"

There was that word again. *Need.*

Crazy fantasies suddenly flooded her brain, ones that involved more than a stolen kiss. Like being touched all over by those incredibly masculine, long-fingered hands…

She blinked and smoothed back a nonexistent lock of hair, waiting for him to mention That Night. But as time ticked by, all he did was glare at her. That's when it finally hit.

He didn't remember.

Emily felt the flush start low, then gradually spread up her neck. It finally settled on her cheeks, twin burning indications of her foolishness. While her mind had played out that kiss over and over all weekend like a CD on repeat, apparently Zac hadn't lost a second's thought about it.

Well, what do you expect when this VP Tech thing's just dropped in his lap?

"Are you going to say something?" he said now, crossing his arms.

She sighed. "I can train someone else."

"I don't want anyone else." He shifted his weight, one hand going to the base of his neck again. Emily watched in fascination as he absently massaged, his triceps in mouthwatering relief against the straining shirt. "Of course I'll give you a pay rise."

"But I don't understand why you'd get... I mean—" She stopped.

"Why do I suddenly get handed a software company? Or what happened to my stepbrother, who's been the undisputed heir apparent?" His gaze turned wily as it swept her flushed face. "Have I piqued your curiosity?"

"No," she lied.

He gave her one of those casual grins, one that never failed to flip her stomach. "You sure? It's a mess. We'll have to arrange meetings, reschedule my appointments. You know you're itching to sort it out."

"I'm the last person motivated by morbid curiosity and office gossip."

"No," he said, his eyes running over her again in unhurried deliberation. "That's true. So think of it as a promotion—I'm prepared to double whatever offer you've got lined up."

"Money isn't the point." She turned on her heel and walked over to her couch, desperately needing space to clear her head. "Zac, you're a workaholic," she said, picking up her discarded towel, then flicking a glance over her shoulder. His expression had turned cautious. "And that's not a bad thing, it's just... you expect me to be one, too. I want to be in control of my destiny—be my own boss and make my own decisions." She lifted her chin defiantly. "I'm going to university to get my small-business degree. I'm starting my own company."

"Doing what?"

"Personal organization. You know, time management, life coaching, getting clients on track with—" At his ambiguous silence, she scowled. "You know, just forget it. I've already signed and paid for the first semester. In lieu of two weeks I won't take my last paycheck."

In all her years working with Zac Prescott, she'd been the consummate professional, beyond gossip, beyond reproach. She'd never returned his light banter or gotten beyond the standard noncommittal answer to his "how was your weekend?" inquiries. Like the rest of his thirty-strong office staff, she suspected he saw her as a solitary career woman of average height and weight, someone who'd blend into a crowd, someone definitely not eligible for the "I've dated Zac Prescott" club. Which made Thursday's kiss all the more humiliating, because apparently it was forgettable. Just like her.

Even though she'd made her bed, lying in it was distinctly uncomfortable.

He frowned as she stood there, the towel damp and heavy in her hand. She'd never deliberately defied him…until now. It was fascinating the way his jaw clenched beneath that warm, smoothly shaven skin. *And you know exactly how warm it is. And how smooth. And how it smells—like stealing forbidden kisses in an orange grove, exciting, fresh, exhilarating…*

Mortified, she quickly busied herself with collecting last night's take-out containers from the coffee table as her treacherous heart began to speed up.

He followed her into the kitchen.

"Listen. If you're hell-bent on going, I can't stop you. But it's only October. You've got nearly five months before the term starts, so why not work for me until then? Help me sort out this stupid stunt of my father's."

"I don't—" She abruptly turned from the sink, but he was there, a huge wall of wonderful-smelling, rock-hard muscle. She just managed to stop herself from smashing headfirst into that broad chest. Before her body could start its annoying little joyful hum, she took another step back. The movement was not lost on him, judging by the way his brow creased.

"Are you annoyed because I dragged you from your vacation on Thursday night?"

In incredulous silence she stared at him, eyes wide, until irritation began to bubble up inside. "You think my change of career direction—one I'd been planning for many months now—was precipitated by your demand that I drive you home? Without thanks, I might add?"

"Guess not," he muttered. Then, stiffly, "Thank you. For driving me home."

"You're welcome."

His gaze fixed on hers, holding it for seconds longer than necessary before he glanced away and shoved his hands in his trouser pockets. If she'd expected something, anything to indicate their prior carnal knowledge, then she was disappointed. Firm lines bracketed his mouth, and she watched irritation surge across his expression before he tamped a lid on it.

I was right—he doesn't remember.

"I don't normally drink in the office," he said suddenly.

"I know."

"Yeah." He returned to his scrutiny, making her insides squirm. "You do."

The warm morning sunlight coming through her tiny kitchen window seemed to thicken then, wrapping around her body and creating an uncomfortable ache low in her belly. As she glanced at his mouth, the night came flooding back in all its illicit glory. She'd spied the half bottle of tequila on his desk, seen the belligerent gleam in his eyes, even in the darkened light of his office.

"I need to get dressed," she blurted out now. Automatically his eyes flicked over her state of non-dress, which only made her breath catch. "And you need to go."

"Are you going to think about my offer?"

"Will you go if I promise to think about it?"

"Only if you'll actually think about it," he said. "We both win here. I get you for another five months and you get a massive incentive. Win-win."

"I promise I'll think about it."

As she followed him down her hall, watched as he opened the door, then crossed the threshold, she knew she wouldn't—couldn't—go back to work for Zac. Not after that kiss. She didn't need more chaos, not when she'd spent her whole childhood fighting for order.

He paused on the peeling deck before turning back to her with a thoughtful expression. "How did my car get from the office to my house?"

Her mouth involuntarily twitched. "That's one mighty nice vehicle."

"I let you drive my Porsche?"

"Sure." She couldn't completely hide the smug smile. "You were quite drunk."

He rubbed his chin with a dark scowl. "And you got me into the house without help."

"Yep." Her arm had been around his waist, his delicious warmth distracting her as she'd steered him through his front door. And then…

Anyone could've made the mistake. He'd stumbled, she'd only just managed to retain her balance, they'd turned at the same time. And their lips had met. And met. And kept on meeting, until Emily had managed to wrench free and escape.

A stupid lapse in judgment that had paradoxically brought clarity to her life plans.

With a sigh, she tightened the belt on her robe. "Goodbye, Zac. I'll let you know what I decide."

Like never kiss your boss, then believe everything will be normal. Been there, done that, been trying to burn it from my mind ever since.

Zac barely heard the soft click of the door behind him, too caught up in his frustration to notice. Past the wooden railing, down the rolling grassy slope of the apartment block perched high on Currumbin's Duringan Street, the long waveless estuary locals called The Alley glittered in the early morning sun, a tempting sight for those inclined to call in sick and spend the day lazing on its sandy banks.

Not Emily. She was an employer's dream: always prompt, superefficient and highly intelligent. She knew what he needed before he needed it. She knew how he had his coffee, she reminded him to eat, she always came in under deadline.

And she was an amazing kisser.

The stairs creaked beneath his feet, an aural protest to echo his own irritation. He wasn't confident Emily would return, which meant he had to think up a Plan B.

Emily blinked a lot when she was uncomfortable. It was like a nervous tic, those thick, impossibly long lashes fluttering away over navy-blue eyes obscured by glasses. He'd noticed it the first time he'd casually asked about her weekend. Intrigued and amused, he'd been compelled to test his theory. The confirmation had come when they'd finally negotiated a major contract and he'd struck up some friendly banter to relieve the tension.

She'd also blinked like that after he'd kissed her.

He paused on the path, the cheerful mid-spring warmth doing nothing to ease the headache sluggishly throbbing away. Damn, how many prompts did he need to give a woman? But she'd steadfastly refused to acknowledge that kiss.

A kiss that had rocked his world in more ways than one.

It had, just for one moment, taken his mind off this entire VP Tech fiasco and all the lingering anger it dredged up. Just one moment, and yet long enough for a powerful need to arrest his brain, rush into his groin and conjure up all sorts of delicious, slick images of Emily in his bed.

She wasn't only the best damn assistant he'd ever had: she'd somehow managed to pique his interest to the point that focusing on work had become a major effort these last few months.

And for the first time in months, he wanted. Wanted with an unrelenting intensity.

He scanned the watery view, automatically picking out a handful of his company's early designs on the opposite bank, lingering on the smooth clean lines of those multimillion dollar homes with a deep flush of pride. Once-average homes that he'd single-handedly redesigned, rebuilt and flipped for a profit. And even now, with full-time staff and a corporate development

department, he still designed. Yes, he could now afford to pick
and choose his clientele, but those original projects were still a
humble reminder of how far he'd come.

His days were perfectly streamlined. He enjoyed his work, the
women he dated and his life in general. He had peace—unlike the
years that had come before, years of constant emotional upheaval,
of stress and migraines, sleepless nights and endless, conflict-
filled days.

He'd worked like a demon for his new life. If his father had
taught him one thing, it was that nothing worth having ever came
easy.

Especially when it came to pursuing a woman.

He'd persuade Emily to return and then take the time to find
out if his fuzzy memories were correct, that she'd been an eager
and willing participant in that kiss.

He glanced back up to her apartment door, to the closed blinds
across her living room window.

Waddyaknow. The same day his life had taken a crazy turn,
he'd finally gotten an answer to months of idle speculation about
what lay under Emily's severe business suits. She'd fronted up
at his office without her trademark glasses, dressed in a baggy
T-shirt and ratty Ugg boots, a worn denim skirt cupping a
perfectly delicious curvy butt.

His assistant hid a smoking body. Why?

If he closed his eyes, he could still feel the imprint from those
luscious breasts as she'd walked him into his house. *Oh, yeah.*
She'd been into that kiss even if it hadn't lasted for more than
three nanoseconds.

Deep in the fantasy, the stranger was almost upon him before
he clicked.

The man was built like a brick outhouse: a bouncer's massive
body crammed into a sleek suit, all restrained menace beneath
the sheen of barely there respectability. It wasn't just the man's
overwhelming physical presence that set off warning bells as he
passed Zac on the narrow garden path, giving him a bare nod.
It was the focused, almost mean aura in that smooth coffee-

colored face, the way those shrewd eyes skimmed over Zac before returning to his purpose.

Zac had seen that look before. Hell, he'd faced it down too many times in his line of work. Unfortunately, the construction industry brought with it a certain type of thug who thought they could bribe and terrorize their competitors.

Zac slowly turned, watching the man take the stairs, then continue on.

Emily's apartment was the only one at the end of level two.

Swiftly, Zac backtracked, the wooden balcony above providing cover just as he heard Emily's door open.

He glanced up through the wooden slats. She'd left the security screen locked. Smart girl.

"You Mrs. Catalano?" the big dude said.

"It's actually Miss Reynolds."

Zac frowned. Since when the hell had she been *married?* But then, there were a thousand things he didn't know about her, though not from his lack of gentle probing.

"But Jimmy Catalano's wife, right? Daughter of Charlene and Pete, younger sister to Angelina?"

There was a pause where Zac thought he'd heard Emily drag in a shocked breath. "What's this about?"

"Jimmy owes my boss money."

"Who's your boss?"

"Let's just call him…Joe."

When Emily finally replied, it was with the same tenor and firmness she used when dealing with his most demanding clients. "I'm sorry, but Jimmy died seven months ago."

Zac swallowed his surprise. His assistant was hiding more than killer curves behind that superefficient persona.

"I heard," Big Dude was saying. "And I'm sorry for your loss." His tone implied anything but. "Joe is a compassionate businessman. He gave you longer than most to come to terms with your grief. Now he wants his money."

"What money?"

Zac angled for a better view and caught the movement of Emily's door closing. The Big Dude's slap on the screen rang out, startling her and jerking Zac to attention. A surge of fury propelled him forward, but at the last minute, caution prevailed. In tense silence, he waited.

"You were Jimmy's guarantor, which means his debt is now yours," the man continued roughly, losing patience.

"I didn't sign anything."

There was a rustle of papers. "That's your signature, right?"

"It looks like mine. But I didn't—"

Big Dude sighed, as if her denial disappointed him. "You got fourteen days to pay."

Emily paused, then said firmly, "Then I'll see you in court."

The man's sudden laughter, deep and menacing, sent a chill rippling through Zac's skin. "A wife of a guy like Jimmy knows the drill—no cops, no solicitors. My boss doesn't waste money dealing with the courts. Geddit?" He let that ambiguous threat settle before there was a rustle of cheap material. "Here's my card." A snick of paper and a groan of mesh: he'd shoved his card in her screen door. "Let me know when you have the money." He paused, his voice suddenly softer, more ominous. "Your sister is a nice-lookin' girl. She's what…thirty or so? And just got a brand-new car, too—"

"You stay away from my family."

The panic threaded beneath Emily's granite words stabbed straight into Zac's heart. His hands tightened into fists.

"Hey, I was just making an observation." The man's hands went up in mock defense. "You know, *you* could always pay off the debt in other ways…"

The vicious slam of Emily's front door, followed by the click of the lock, was the final straw. As the man's chuckle floated down the stairs, white-hot fury seethed up, choking off Zac's breath, taking with it common sense and self-preservation.

He straightened, pulling his shoulders back, then gently rolling his neck to work out the kinks. Then he stepped into the path and barred the way.

The man strolled down the stairs, a smug smile still on his

face. When he spotted Zac, his expression flashed into menacing caution.

"Hey, mate," Zac said casually, forcing his fists to slowly unclench. "You got a minute?"

Two

Residual annoyance punctuated Emily's stride as she stalked into the foyer of the office building on Thursday morning. On Monday night, after a few drinks and a deep discussion that became way too serious for a birthday celebration, AJ had confirmed Emily's doomed realization.

She had to go back to work. The cops could do nothing about a vague verbal threat without proof, and a complaint would no doubt piss off this "Joe," which was something she so didn't want to do. His intimidating thug had done more than rattle her: he had forced memories of her former life to the surface where they'd sat, alternately irritating then panicking her until the early hours of the morning.

You could always pay off the debt in other ways.

The thug's rough suggestion still made her skin crawl. Jimmy had voiced that disgusting thought once, and only once, which had been her impetus to walk out. She'd rather pay up and defer her course than settle her ex-husband's debts on her back.

If you weren't dead, Jimmy, I could just kill you.

The security guard held up a hand, scrutinized the ID card around her neck, then waved her on through.

Her face burned as she reached the elevators. How many times had she walked through that reception area and been stopped by the same guard as if he'd never seen her before in his life? For the other pretty things in the building he smiled, nodded and barely glanced at their identification. For her, she was no one worth remembering.

The elevators pinged open and she got inside, cramming in with the other workers.

Every instinct rebelled against handing over her hard-earned cash, but being married to a professional deadbeat had revealed a dark underside to Jimmy's seemingly carefree life. Through all the lying and the cheating, she'd never forgotten one important fact—debt collectors were deadly serious about their money.

Money was replaceable. Her and AJ's well-being were not.

So last night, through alternating tears of frustration and anger, she'd worked out her course refund, then rung The Thug—aka Louie Mayer—to negotiate an extension on the due date. After he'd laughed himself into a coughing fit, he'd finally got out, "Sure. I'm a sucker for a chick with a great pair of tits. I'll talk to Joe. Call me on Monday, blondie."

Humiliation burned as she finally got off on the twentieth floor. Her credit rating was shot thanks to Jimmy, which left selling her apartment—out of the question—or stealing or gambling. *Irony, thy name is Jimmy Catalano.*

Muttering under her breath, she swooshed open the pristine glass doors that proclaimed Valhalla Property Development in elegant gold script.

She went through the motions of stashing her bag, then turning on the computer before tackling the mess the temp had left on her desk.

"Ah, great. You're here."

She whipped around, her eyes landing on Zac framed in his doorway. Seeing him there, dressed in his signature business shirt, pants and precisely knotted tie, something strange happened.

Her mind emptied. As her heart upped tempo, breath catching, her skin began to tingle. The sensation was not unlike an intimate breath swooping over her flesh, goose-bumping her entire body into a sensitive bundle of nerves.

She offered a thousand colorful reprimands to her self-control, even as she felt her nipples stiffen beneath her blue silk shirt.

"Everything okay?"

If you could call wanting to see your boss naked *okay.* "Just peachy." She forced out a tight smile.

"Then let's get started," he said, clearly oblivious to her state. "Come on in."

Emily swallowed and picked up her notepad.

After she sat and Zac relaxed into his plush leather chair with graceful ease, his green gaze swept over her from head to toe. Nothing new—Zac always studied people with a silent intensity that flustered or flattered, depending on the recipient. It hadn't bothered her before. But now...

She felt the sudden overwhelming urge to squirm, to fiddle with her hair, straighten her collar and do a thousand other self-conscious girly things she'd thought she was immune to.

She followed his eyes as they lingered seconds longer on her hair, her mouth. Blood zinged through her veins, sending twin shots of panic and excitement to every dormant inch of her body.

She was reacting like any red-blooded female under the gaze of a charismatic, attractive man. And that scared the hell out of her.

"You wear contact lenses."

The question threw her and she answered unthinkingly. "Yes."

"But not to work."

She flicked the edges of her notepad under her thumb, over and over. "No."

"Why not?"

"I like glasses." She paused, then deflected calmly. "So what do you need me to do regarding VP Tech?"

He leaned back in his chair, his expression almost teasing. "You know, you look much better without them."

"Thank you. I assume you'll want to issue a press release about your new acquisition—"

"Did you get your blue eyes from your father?"

"My mother." She pushed her glasses back up the bridge of her nose, floundering at his intense interest. Zac had a virtual buffet of women to choose from thanks to his gorgeous looks, masculine command and charm. Charm that she'd come to realize was completely unaffected, as effortless as creating his award-winning designs. He was a man who appreciated and loved women, a natural flirt. So why the hell was he flirting with her and why…?

Oh, no. She quickly turned the page of her notebook, desperate to focus somewhere else. The kiss. What else could it be?

Hot mortification flooded her cheeks and she crossed her legs, demurely straightening the long black skirt over her knee. But when she shot him a glance from under the lowered lashes, his eyes remained locked on her warm face. His mouth curved into a small, teasing grin, and for one second she felt a desperate desire to kiss that mouth.

She cleared her throat. "Back to VP Tech…"

Zac leaned forward, his elbows on the desk, hands clasped. "I'm not taking my father's company."

"Sorry?" She blinked. "I thought you said—"

"I have Valhalla. This is obviously a stunt, not a genuine offer. We haven't really spoken in years, and I know nothing about the software industry."

"Oh. So why…?"

"I don't know. But Victor got my attention by threatening a press release unless I discussed it face-to-face." The muscle in his jaw clenched, a rare burst of anger quickly reined in. "We'll leave for Sydney early tomorrow, meet with my father and brother, then concentrate on the Point One project. We'll fly home Sunday morning."

Emily nodded as she noted down the times, but inside a hard lump of apprehension began to form. Zac and close quarters did not mix, not when she had a dozen other worries on her plate. She needed her inner strength, and fighting with this overwhelming urge to get intimate with her boss took too much of it.

She rose to her feet, determined to focus on her job. "I'll make the arrangements."

"Thanks."

When Zac's attention returned to the papers on his desk, an odd feeling of disappointment swept her. What did she expect, the man to throw himself at her feet with slavish thanks? *A simple "it's good to have you back" wouldn't go amiss…*

"Oh, before you go…"

She turned, flushed with faint hope.

"Those debts your ex-husband owed? You don't need to worry about it. I paid them off."

She stilled.

Zac's brows shot up in quizzical expectance, but she could barely choke out the words.

"You did *what?*"

"I paid off the debts. So you can—"

"You didn't. Please tell me this is a joke."

He frowned, clearly not anticipating this reaction. "I don't joke when it comes to money. I paid it in full Monday night."

Her insides crashed to the bottom of her sensibly shoed feet. "What the hell were you thinking? I've already—" She turned away, tunneling a hand through her hair, destroying the neat coiffure in the process. "I got scammed. Again."

"What are you talking about?"

She whirled back, hot anger pulsing low in her throat, choking her breath. Jimmy's betrayal, the thug's visit and now Zac's revelation welled up, pounding against her walls of restraint. She could practically feel her self-control slipping from the tight knots she'd bound them in.

"I've already deferred my course," she said tightly. "I'm picking up the refund check this afternoon… I even got an extension on the due date…" *And Mayer had known and was going to take my money anyway.* Her head felt like it was going to explode. Not since she'd been ten years old had she felt so insignificant, so powerless. First her deadbeat parents, then Jimmy, now Zac—

Zac studied his conservatively dressed assistant with mounting confusion. He could see the tension winding her up, from the pulled-back shoulders, down the painfully rigid spine, to the white-knuckled grip on her notepad.

She finally spoke in a cool, clipped voice he knew all too well. "You didn't need to do that."

"It was nothing—"

"Don't." Her eyes slashed at him behind those protective rims. "Don't you *dare* tell me it was nothing. I know how much Jimmy owed." She took a breath then said, "So. That means you have me, guaranteed, until I can pay you back."

Zac frowned. "That's not why I did it."

Her look was riddled with skepticism. "I see. So why did you do it?"

"Because you were in trouble. Because I could."

"And it works out great for you, right?"

Zac stared at her. "You're out of line, Emily."

"And so are you," she shot back before clamping her mouth shut, but not before he caught a glimpse of her barely hidden disgust.

Disgust. At *him*. Irritated now, he scowled.

Pride. That was the last thing on his mind when he'd stopped Louie Mayer on Monday morning. Admittedly, he had intended to deck the guy—hell, he *still* wanted to. But instead he'd slapped down a bundle of notes for Gold Coast's number-one bookie in some noisy nightclub later that night. And throughout the entire adventure, Emily's pride hadn't entered into the equation. He'd never even entertained the thought that she could take his gesture the wrong way.

But she had, judging by that subzero glare boring into him.

So much for his impulsive good deed. He couldn't ask her out now, not when she was all fired up like this. The implications, her misinterpretation…man, it was an invitation to disaster.

Dammit all.

He gathered up his frustration, forcing it into the backseat. "Look, this is simple. It's not about enslavement or blackmail or anything else. You didn't have the money. I did. You were threatened— Don't deny it," he added as her mouth opened. "Or would you rather owe some criminal than me?"

Her mouth snapped closed and he could see her throat working, swallowing hard. Her composure cracked a little. "No…"

"So there you have it. At least I won't threaten your family when you don't pay up."

Her chin shot up, a defiant gesture that would have made him smile if he weren't so annoyed with himself. "Oh, I intend to pay."

"I know you will." He nodded firmly. "You're Emily Reynolds."

"What's that supposed to mean?"

This time he did smile. *Well, well.* He'd finally managed to dig under her professional armor. There could be hope for him yet. "Over the last two years, you've shown yourself to be highly efficient, reliable and completely professional."

At her embarrassed confusion, he paused. He'd been generous with her workplace performance reviews, hadn't he? Given praise where it was due? Yet her obvious discomfort at his summary niggled at him. "Which is why," he continued carefully, "You're going to be my event manager for the Point One complex."

"The new executive apartments in Sydney?"

"Yes. No relocation necessary—you can do it all from the office via videoconferencing. And it's more pay, a bigger challenge," he reminded her.

"But—"

"You're not up to it?"

"No. Yes!" She took a quick breath. "But we normally use Premier Events."

"I'm looking to start a new in-house department, and you know our staff and our contractors. You should talk with Jenna in Accounts about a budget and get together a list of suitable people you want on your team. When we're down in Sydney—"

The phone on Zac's desk rang. He glanced at the display, frowned, then picked it up.

Emily knew the caller had to be family the instant he spoke. No one else could tense up his shoulders, flatten his mouth and bring such a wary expression to his eyes. But as she made to leave, he halted her with a sharp gesture.

She stood there, an unwilling eavesdropper, until he finally clicked off the call, his green eyes bearing residual irritation as they refocused on her.

"As I was saying, we'll inspect the Point One site and meet the people I've been dealing with. Pack for the weekend."

Finally dismissed, she nodded before turning on her heel and walking out the door. A weekend with Zac Prescott. She swallowed the swell of unbidden excitement with a forceful gulp.

How could she focus on the incredible opportunity he'd just given her when her heart hammered crazily in her chest? Sure, she'd have to work like a dog up to and including the launch, but that wasn't it. This wild, breath-stealing excitement was about more than just a job promotion.

She didn't want to want Zac…damn, she refused to want a man who blithely made decisions about her life without even asking her. A man who didn't want her the way she wanted him to want her.

And yet he'd kissed her. Flirted, even. Didn't that tell her something?

She tossed the notebook on her desk. Zac had crossed the line, invading her private life—a shameful, personal part of it—without invitation. Embarrassment and anger flared up, replacing the fleeting desire. She'd been forced to grow up too early, the responsible one in their fractured family, until she'd been fostered out at ten years old. Relying only on herself had become a way of life. She didn't need saving.

Not even if her personal white knight was Zac Prescott.

Three

As befitted his top-end income bracket, Zac traveled in style all the way, from the flights and airport car service to the accommodations. Normally Emily took secret delight in their business trips, in the unfamiliar luxury she could wallow in, albeit briefly. Outwardly she was perfectly composed, but inside her stomach jittered with glee each time, just like a kid on her first plane trip.

But this time was different—*she* was different. She was acutely conscious of every inch separating them on the flight south, of each small movement as he shifted his arm on the rest, when he brushed away that lock of hair while bent forward, concentrating on work. The way he took her overnight bag with a smile, shouldering it as they made their way to their waiting car. Even their "adjoining room" status at Sydney's five-star Park Hyatt on Circular Quay took on new meaning.

When they both got into the elevator and he pressed the top-floor button, she felt his interest, his eyes lingering for seconds too long.

"New suit?"

Startled, she darted him a glance. "No."

"Shoes?"

"No."

He paused then said, "There's something different about you."

"Maybe it's my absence of rose-colored glasses."

She hadn't meant to make him laugh. And in this luxurious harborside hotel, with the cloud of serious circumstances hovering in the background, it was a relief to see his normally animated face crease into humor.

"Does this mean," he said with a quirk of an eyebrow, "you've forgiven me for butting into your life and paying off your debt?"

"No."

"Even though I've handed you my highly-sought-after Point One account?"

Her eyes narrowed. "Is that why—"

"No." The truth lay in his direct gaze. "They're two unrelated issues. You can do this job without worrying about you or your sister's safety."

Man, why'd he have to put it like that? She pressed her lips together and stared at the ascending floors. Her objections were beginning to make her sound like an ingrate, and he knew it.

He returned his attention to the numbers, hands in his pockets. He was still smiling when they got off on their floor and he indicated she lead the way. They paused at their respective doors, Emily making a big deal of digging the keycard from her pocket.

"I'll see you in an hour," he said as she finally shoved the door open.

She nodded like she had a thousand times before, knowing he'd be knocking on her door a minute to the hour, ready to throw himself into work. But when she stumbled into the familiar surroundings of her premier suite, pulled in her bag and closed the door, heavy tension came crashing down, forcing her over to the cream couch. With a groan, she collapsed into it.

Acute and painful awareness. That's what it was. He moved

and she flinched. He spoke and she felt a burst of desire spike her heart rate. And when he inadvertently touched her, she had to bite her tongue to swallow a frustrated groan.

You have got to get a grip.

Toeing off her shoes, she shoved her glasses up and rubbed her eyes. Work. This was work. She'd had no trouble focusing on it before. And now it was more important than ever. Zac had enough confidence in her to oversee the launch of Point One instead of outsourcing to a more highly qualified event-planning company. Whatever his motives for paying off Jimmy's debt, he wouldn't jeopardize his company or his reputation in order to do it.

Which meant she owed it to him to do her job.

Emily sensed Zac's mood change the moment they walked through VP Tech's huge glass doors in affluent North Sydney. They cut a silent path through the hushed foyer, all polished marble floor, chrome-and-leather fittings and subtle lighting. His posture signaled an impending battle even though his expression gave nothing away. Yet no matter how tense she knew he was, he still spared a smile and a greeting for the front-desk secretary and security man as they passed. Emily noted their surprised glances before his pace increased and she almost had to run to catch up with him. His haste, his irritation, all spoke volumes.

Do it quickly, then run. Don't get caught.

The words were so clear her mother could've been standing right there, slurring in her ear, her eyes glassy with drugs and bourbon. With an inward gasp Emily pulled up short, just in time to avoid Zac's broad back as he stopped at the elevator bay.

She was nervous for him, and that sent her heart into a jarring rhythm. Even as she covered up with efficient aplomb, readjusting her jacket over her hips and shoving her glasses back up her nose, she needn't have bothered. Zac was staring at the ascending elevator numbers with single-minded concentration, a frown creasing his brow.

They rode up forty floors in silence, and when the doors slid open onto what was obviously the executive level, an imposing man stood awaiting them.

Zac's expression abruptly shut down.

Cal Prescott was the taller and broader of the two, with dark, lush features that spoke of a Mediterranean heritage. In comparison, Zac's face was more angular, more aristocratic, and coupled with his lean frame and tanned Nordic skin, the differences were a sharp and distinct contrast. Stepbrothers, so different in appearance, yet sharing an innate air of authority and confidence.

"Cal." Zac finally offered his hand, which Cal took firmly. Then suddenly Cal enveloped him in a hug.

Emily watched them closely. When Zac finally extricated himself, awkwardness was etched as clearly as permanent marker over his entire body.

He took a step back and cleared his throat. "This is Emily Reynolds, my assistant."

Cal smiled, thrust out his hand and said, "A pleasure, Emily."

Emily could name only a handful of Zac's clients who gave her the courtesy of a handshake. Having Cal Prescott, heir to the VP Tech fortune and Mr. One-Click himself, pay her the subtle respect threw her. And judging by the look on Zac's face as their eyes met, it threw him, too.

Without missing a beat she recovered, returning the shake with a nod. "Same here, Mr. Prescott."

"Well, let's go into the conference room." Cal clapped a hand on Zac's shoulder. "Victor's on his way up."

"We're not staying."

Cal paused, hand dropping. "Why not?"

"Because I have a business to run and frankly, threatening me with press coverage to get me here was childish. Whatever game Victor's cooked up, I'm not playing."

"Victor threatened you?"

"Via voice mail."

"Great. Typical Victor," Cal snorted. "Well, come in and

you can tell him yourself." And he swept open the conference doors.

After Zac finally sat at the long boardroom table, eerie déjà vu crept over his skin with dark foreboding. Cal's odd welcome aside, nothing had changed in this place. Yet *he'd* changed. The years he'd spent carving out his own niche, finally free from Victor Prescott's suffocating influence, had given him new life and opened his eyes to new possibilities, new horizons.

It had made him who he was.

"So how've you been, Zac?"

His older brother sat opposite, the innocent question coated in loaded expectation. Zac studied him carefully. Cal had been his one and only regret when he'd walked out. He'd suspected his defection would cost him Cal's respect, but he still hadn't been prepared for the man's total ostracism.

So when Cal's immaculate yet impersonal wedding invitation had arrived in August, he'd been thrown for a loop, those old wounds threatening the peace he'd worked so hard to create. He'd declined the invite but still that perfidious Prescott blade managed to draw blood.

"Business is great," Zac finally said. "Buyers are flocking to the Gold Coast, thanks to Sydney's outrageous land tax."

"And yet I hear you've got a new property venture down here."

He nodded. "Apartment blocks in Potts Point."

When Cal's gaze landed on Emily, she returned it with a polite smile before opening her notebook, ready to take notes.

Her familiar cool professionalism was like a shot of Valium in the arm.

"Where are you staying?" Cal asked.

"The Park Hyatt on the Quay."

"Nice." Silence fell, and awkward seconds stretched by until Cal finally said, "Are you free on March the fifteenth?"

"Why?"

"Because I'm getting married. Attempt number two," he added with a self-deprecating smile.

"What happened to—?" Zac clamped his mouth shut. He didn't need to know.

"You didn't see the write-up in the papers?" At Zac's curt head shake, Cal looked oddly irked. "Ava fainted, got taken to hospital. We're putting it off until after the baby's born in January."

The automatic refusal fizzled on the tip of Zac's tongue, his hesitation furrowing Cal's brow.

"Congratulations, Mr. Prescott," Emily automatically responded, her fingers flicking through her schedule book. "Zac, you have a meeting on the thirteenth—" to her credit, when she looked up and caught his expression she didn't even stumble "—but that's not confirmed," she added diplomatically.

"You're going to turn me down *again?*" Cal said in disbelief.

What the hell was going on? Cal's thunderous silence over the years had screamed everything words couldn't. And now in the space of a few months, he'd not only called twice but was inviting him to his wedding again?

Then Victor strode in and all conversation ground to a halt.

Like all great businessmen, Victor Prescott commanded the room by his mere presence. "Reputation, authority, attitude and entitlement—make like you have them and people will give you respect," he'd always said. Zac swallowed heavily. He couldn't remember a time when Victor's little decree of wisdom hadn't been on the tail end of every life lesson, every business deal he'd made.

The sour pill of irony was that he'd called upon it more times than he cared to remember these last three years.

Yes, he was free of all that tension and conflict. Yes, he knew who he truly was. But that didn't stop the suffocating expectation from surging up to tighten his chest and quicken his breath.

"Dad," he said now, forcing his voice into neutrality.

"Zac." Victor made a point of leaning over the table and offering his hand. Zac returned the handshake, then sat back down.

"Look, I have a meeting this afternoon," Zac said without

preamble. "So I'll make this quick. You've got me here. What do you want?"

Victor paused, his eyes going from Zac then to Cal, who gave him a faint nod.

"I told you—as soon as you sign the papers, you'll be VP Tech's new CEO. Of course, you'd start as cochair on the board," Victor said, ignoring Zac's scowl. "Then, after six months' probation, getting to know the business, our products and clients, you'll take on the position of CEO. That means you'd—"

"Hang on," Zac lifted an impatient hand, then glared at Cal. "You actually meant what you said last Thursday?"

At Cal's nod, Zac speared Victor with his gaze. "You're CEO. Where are you going?"

"It's time I took a step back."

No way. "You're retiring?"

"Sort of."

"Victor…" Cal began, but paused as Victor stared back. Something passed between the two men, then Victor finally let out an aggrieved sigh.

"I had an operation a few months ago. I'm fine now," Victor shrugged off Zac's look, "but the doctors advised I should cut back on my hours."

"I see." Zac looked to a suspiciously silent Cal. "And what about you?"

"Cal has a family to think of," Victor said coolly. "He doesn't need the pressure or stress."

And I bet that just pisses you off. "And I do?"

"Zac," Cal began, but his younger brother's glare silenced him.

"After all those years," Zac said, "those brutal hours working yourself half to death, you're passing up the top job?"

The look on Cal's face was unreadable. "As Victor said, I have a family now."

This was unbelievable. "So you both thought I'd fall over myself to step into the breach? That I'd embrace this opportunity to return to the Prescott fold?"

He couldn't—wouldn't—hide the sneer in his voice. Latent

anger bubbled up, burning his throat. Once he'd desperately needed his father's approval, but Victor's lies and manipulation had pushed him over the line. Way, way over the line.

Zac had walked away from it all without a drop of guilt.

I can't go back to that.

He rose swiftly, back rigid. "No. Find someone else."

"Zac!" Victor rose too, preventing his escape with one swift step forward. "At least think about it. You owe it to—"

"Don't. Say. Another. Word," Zac ground out as the past swirled his vision, shrouding it in a patchwork of shadow and bright, painful light.

"You're a Prescott whether you like it or not," Cal said calmly behind him. "It's part of who you are. So is this company."

Zac spun back, a dozen furious comebacks tangling his tongue before he chewed them down. "That was your dream, Cal. I never wanted it. And I'm sure as hell not going to be *guilted* into it."

And then he stalked out the door, Emily close behind.

As the elevator glided down, Emily chanced a glance at Zac. She'd known this meeting was the last thing he'd wanted, but the struggle now etched on his face spoke of so much more.

He took a deep breath, then another. If that was her, she'd be a quivering mess on the floor. Not Zac—he dealt with conflict, breathed it out and then moved on. He didn't let things get to him, which was why he was so perfectly comfortable in his own skin.

It was a quality that fascinated as much as it attracted.

As the doors slid open, Zac surged forward, long strides devouring the corridor. Yet as they made their way toward the exit, he gradually began to ease up. First, his rigid back and tense shoulders loosened an inch. Then, that furious march turned into his familiar rolling gait. When he nodded goodbye to the front desk, his jaw had relaxed. Finally, as the doors swooshed open and they stepped out onto sun-filled Berry Street, whatever lingering traces that remained had fallen away.

"We're meeting with the Point One team in an hour," she reminded him.

"Good." He glanced at his watch, then at his mobile as it started to ring. He pocketed it. "Let's get going."

"Zac! Wait up."

They both turned as Cal emerged from the glass doors, breaking into a jog to catch up. "I need to talk to you."

Emily glanced at Zac. He gave her a quick nod, his expression stiffly cautious. "I won't be a minute."

Zac waited until Emily had reached their car parked a few spaces down before he turned back to Cal. "I thought I made myself clear upstairs."

Cal pocketed his hands and shifted his weight. "Very. And I don't blame you." His surprise must've shown, because Cal let out a small laugh. "You don't think I know how Victor operates? Do you have any idea of the crap he's been dealing out these past few months?"

"Yeah, thanks for including me."

"Don't be a smartarse. Whatever Victor's faults—and we know he has many—he's had a rough time. He—"

"I don't want to know, Cal. I left all this behind, in case you've forgotten."

"Yes, you did."

Irritation flared at Cal's subtle jab. "What's that supposed to mean?"

"You left—not once but twice. The first time I get—you were eighteen, you'd scored a place at that university in Sweden. You needed to do stuff for yourself, to stand on your own feet. But the second time, after you'd graduated, you were home one week, gone the next. No calls, no e-mails. What the hell do you think *I'd* think?"

Zac scowled. "Would it have changed anything? You were on Victor's side, you always were—"

Cal's foul curse snapped Zac's brow up. "You're my brother, Zac. You owed me an explanation."

"Victor thought I owed him, too, and look how that turned out." Cloying memories wound their way around his chest, choking his lungs. "And hey, if we're laying the blame here, why didn't you pick up the bloody phone before now and call *me?*" He snapped his head back to the car, refusing to feel guilty about the fleeting remorse twisting Cal's face. "I've got to go."

"Zac…"

He turned and marched off toward the car, toward Emily, and away from the gut-wrenching emotions of his past.

Four

Seven. That's how many times Zac checked his phone, then ignored the call. Throughout their two-hour meeting with the Point One Sydney team in the hotel's private meeting room, Zac's attention had been distracted by that phone, which was so unlike him.

"Are you okay?" she asked casually when the meeting finally broke up and she began gathering up the files.

"Huh? Yeah. Fine." He firmly stuck his phone back in his pocket. "Do you have any questions so far?"

"Not yet. Thanks," she added when Zac relieved her of the document bag, hefting the long strap onto his shoulder. "We have our site inspection at four—shall I order lunch up?"

He nodded absently, his mind a thousand miles away, and Emily wondered if his thoughts were on the business at hand or still stuck back at VP Tech.

When she returned to her suite, his mood had rubbed off, dimming the enjoyment of room service, distracting her thoughts as she went over the paperwork again.

Finally, at three o'clock, she gave up. As she leaned back in the couch, pulled the band from her hair, then smoothly retied it, a sudden thought occurred.

The laptop glowed back at her. *I could just...*

No. She slammed the computer closed and crossed her arms. Zac had never discussed his family, which meant that part of his life was off-limits. She wasn't about to violate that trust now by trawling through the Internet in search of salacious—and probably highly inaccurate—details.

Yet thanks to this morning, her curiosity had begun to grow.

She'd never seen Zac so wound up, barely able to keep a lid on his simmering anger, which meant something major had happened. Something big enough to make him walk away from his family.

She rose, suddenly restless, and stalked over to the huge sliding doors that led onto the balcony. The tinted glass warmed her palms, a familiar sensation that brought to mind another time, another place. Another kind of heat.

With her forehead resting on the smooth window, she allowed herself a brief moment of indulgence, a moment to recall Zac's mouth, his scent. His ability to make her forget everything in her past and just be. With him.

Finally, she straightened, dragging a long breath in. *Enough.* She'd been appalled at the thought of Zac digging around in *her* life. Getting involved in his family problems was unprofessional. It had nothing to do with her.

Nothing.

When they reconvened in the foyer at three-thirty, she was relieved to see Zac back to his normal self. Yet even as they talked work during the entire drive to Potts Point, Emily still found herself thinking increasingly unprofessional thoughts during the lulls.

She was worried about him. This thing with the Prescotts had gotten under his skin, affecting him in a way she'd never seen before. The most difficult of clients hadn't elicited even half the reaction he'd given this.

"We're here."

As Zac pulled up into a space, Emily's gaze automatically went to the window.

Building plastic and chipboard covered the ground floor. Leaning forward, her gaze went up…and up, and up. From what she'd read, the complex was twenty-five stories high, twenty levels of private apartments, a fourth-level gym and indoor pool, a laundry level, three more for businesses, and a ground floor restaurant, coffee shop and café.

And Zac had put his faith in her to launch this to the Sydney public.

"Coming?" Zac was on the sidewalk, peering steadily in at her.

"It'll be full-on getting it all ready by December." She scrambled out, barely faltering as he rounded the car to take her bag.

"Yep."

"Long hours, late nights…" She smoothed her jacket then retrieved her bag from him.

He nodded. "For a while, yes."

Irritation threaded her blood, her partly demolished wall teetering as one brick reappeared with a solid thunk. "I've drafted a preliminary list of requirements—staff, budget…"

"Sure. E-mail me when it's finalized." He swept one arm toward the service entrance. "They're meeting us in the penthouse suite."

Emily straightened her shoulders and nodded. She'd said yes to this job, had given her word. It wouldn't be forever. Even if she couldn't get into Queensland University by second term, she'd still end up repaying Zac by then.

You can do this. You've honed professional *to a fine art. You're an expert at focusing on work.*

And she would *not* stress about Zac Prescott.

As the Sydney team made their way through the freshly painted top-floor penthouse apartment, Emily studied them again, filing away their names and positions for future reference. The structural engineer, the acoustic consultant, the fit-out specialist. But it was Sattler Design, Sydney's leading brother-and-sister interior design duo, that captured her attention. Steve and Trish Sattler were walking, talking ex-cover models—Steve with rangy good looks and artfully messy hair that only added to his urban sophistication. He was a perfect foil for Trish, with her long, glossy mahogany mane and big brown eyes that frequently focused on Zac with entirely too much interest.

Zac, to his credit, didn't pick up on that, instead conducting himself as professionally as always. She had to give him points for that, if not for the way he didn't entirely discourage Trish's overly friendly body language.

Her boss was unlike any man she'd met: trustworthy, honorable, loyal. She actually liked him, which was saying something. He couldn't help it if all those attributes oozed a "come here" aura that attracted women of all ages.

She glanced up from the schematics just in time to catch Trish's look. She was studying Zac's profile with almost lustful relish, a small smile hovering on her lips. When she caught Emily looking, she merely raised one eyebrow, giving her a woman-to-woman smile. Without acknowledging it, Emily returned to the plans.

Point proven right there. Another ex-girlfriend-in-training. She fielded a handful of those calls each week.

From the twenty-fifth floor they went systematically down, addressing outstanding issues until they ended up in the plastic-covered foyer of a soon-to-be authentic Balinese restaurant.

Meeting over, Emily shook everyone's hand with a smile and a nod. From the corner of her vision she watched Trish approach Zac.

"I just wanted to thank you for this wonderful opportunity, Mr. Prescott," she began, a wide smile on her perfectly made-up mouth.

"Zac, please."

"Zac." She practically purred out his name. Emily narrowed her eyes as she checked her phone messages.

"Sattler Design's reputation precedes you, Miss Sattler."

"Trish, please."

Trish, please, Emily mentally mimicked, scrolling through her calls with single-minded intent.

"Are you free for dinner? Steve has another client, but I thought you and I could discuss the finer points of our brief, to get a firm handle on what you really need."

Oh, please. Emily nearly rolled her eyes at the double entendre but noted that Zac had pulled out his phone again.

"No, I think everything's looking pretty good at this stage. Emily?"

"Sorry?" Emily blinked innocently as both sets of eyes fell on her.

"Do you have any issues you need to raise with Trish?"

Yes. You're only one in a long line. She smiled and shook her head. "Not right now. But I'm sure we'll be talking later."

She watched Zac shake hands, thanking them for coming. The look on Trish's face didn't crack, but Emily knew the woman was reconnoitering, already working out another way to achieve her goal. It was a familiar dance, one that had begun as an amusing weekly anecdote she related to her sister. But now it had slipped from amusing to tiresome. Especially since…

She pulled herself up short with a frown.

Especially since you kissed him?

Yes.

He was talking to her and she was nodding, giving the outward appearance of actually listening. But inside her heart pounded, her blood racing at breakneck speed while her brain buzzed annoyingly.

Okay. So this is just a physical thing. You've been celibate for close to two years. Of course you're reacting to the first man who's shown any interest in you since…Jimmy.

Ooh. Bad comparison.

"Emily? You okay?"

A hand on her shoulder stopped her thoughts. She blinked up at Zac, at the concern in his eyes. Expressive olive eyes designed to make short work of a woman's will.

A pulse of irritation spread through her belly and she quickly jerked her jacket back into place. The stiff collar suddenly chafed.

"Just thinking about Point One. It's…different from your usual."

"There are only so many mansions you can build before you need a bigger challenge," he answered with a smile, pulling open the glass doors for her.

"True. A challenge is good."

He slid in the car after her, clipping on his seatbelt. "You up for it, Emily?"

His eyes mesmerized her, part amusement, part determination. Suddenly the air in the car got way too warm.

"Yes." Her voice came out way too breathy. Her cheeks heated as his lips spread into a grin, and she quickly coughed, warmth swamping her limbs. "Yes," she added more firmly. "I am."

"Great." With that devilish smile still in place, he shoved on his sunglasses and started the car.

Five

"Dinner at six downstairs." The note had been pushed under her door, signed with a large "Z" at the bottom.

She'd planned on eating alone in her room, going over the files and refining her action plan, not sharing an intimate meal with Zac. *No, not intimate.* A working dinner. They'd talk business like they had a hundred times before. There'd be schedule discussions, costings, launch ideas. There would be no hand-holding, no seductive looks, no footsie under the table.

Just work.

Ignoring that tiny swoop of disappointment, she walked firmly into the dining room at two minutes to six, shoulders back, eyes straight ahead.

The Harbour Kitchen & Bar was prime waterfront dining, with floor-to-ceiling folding glass doors and an open-plan kitchen so the diners could watch their meals being prepared by the chef. Its clean lines and quiet elegance sent a shot of confidence and calm into her bones.

But when Zac spotted her from the window table he'd secured and smiled, her body tensed up.

He pulled out her chair, seated her with effortless aplomb. She murmured her thanks as her heart thumped, making her skin twitch uncomfortably under her suit.

"Still in your work clothes?" He asked, reseating himself.

"Yes." *I'd rather be out of them. With you.* She swallowed quickly, glancing from his broad, jacketless shoulders to the spectacular harbor view outside. That one brief summary was enough for her to note his loosened collar with tie still in place.

"Great view," she murmured as the sun's low golden beams spread wide across the sparkling water, dousing the Opera House's white sails in a similar glow.

"Always is." From the corner of her eye she saw his gaze barely leave her before he picked up the menu.

Discomforted, Emily did the same, noting over the stiff gilt-paper the way his shirt cuffs skimmed perfectly tanned hands, hands that bore the scars of hard labor yet still looked clean and touchable.

She'd always liked a pair of strong hands.

Aaaaand…she was staring. Great.

She hauled her gaze up to his face before quickly glancing away. Well, *that* was such a tempting distraction she refused to look any more than absolutely necessary.

"I never knew you'd been married."

That dragged her attention back. "It's not something I talk about."

"So what *do* you talk about?" He casually unfolded his menu as she frowned. "Come on, Emily. You know practically everything about me, especially after today."

"That's not true."

"Well, what do you want to know?"

Oh, do not go there. "I know enough." She tipped her menu up, but Zac was having none of it. With one finger he gently lowered the barrier, forcing her to look at him.

"You organize me, feed me, ensure I have what I need, when I need it. You're also privy to the inner workings of my private life and now, my family. You're my work wife."

"Your what?"

He grinned at her alarm. "My work wife—a work-based partnership between a man and a woman. You haven't heard that expression before?" She shook her head and fixated on restraightening her perfectly straight cutlery as he continued. "I'd thought that, after working together for so long, I was a friend of sorts. Someone you can trust."

Her head snapped up. "Someone who took charge of my life and paid off my debts without asking?"

Was that a flash of hurt flickering behind his eyes? Contrite, she bit the inside of her bottom lip, embarrassment flooding her cheeks. "I'm sorry. That was rude."

The corner of his mouth tugged up. "I guess I deserved it. For not asking you first."

Zac watched her war with that, the struggle from his apology showing in those dark blue eyes, in her luscious mouth now thin and firm.

Man, it was like getting blood from a stone! He tried a different tack. "I overstepped, and I apologize."

"Okay."

He studied her, trying to get a handle on that closed expression. "Friends?"

As he watched, her lashes began to blink out a rapid beat. "Okay," she repeated, her voice soft and low, before she quickly took a sip of water.

Zac rested his arms on the table, locking his fingers thoughtfully as the waiter approached.

After they'd ordered, he watched her straighten the cutlery—again—then reposition her water glass.

He'd seen her glide through countless business meals, unruffled and professional. But now…things had changed. He'd changed them by violating her privacy, crossing the line by, oh, about a thousand miles.

Yet the inexplicable urge to dig deeper, to find out who Emily Reynolds really was beneath that unflappable facade, urged him on.

"It must've been tough being married to someone like—"

"Zac." She breathed out his name, almost as if it pained her. "Please don't."

"Don't what? Express sympathy? Regret that your ex hurt you? Sometimes," he added slowly, "the ones closest to us can do the most damage."

He fully expected her to shut down then and there, but instead her eyes filled with something…*almost vulnerable*. Then she glanced away. "Yeah."

Interesting.

She flipped her glass over. "I think I'll have that wine now."

Zac poured the golden liquid as she switched the topic to the Point One project. He knew she was doing it to gain control, to lead their conversation into nonpersonal waters. So he let her, until they'd finished their main meals and the wine was all gone. Then the dessert arrived.

"Thank you." She beamed up at the waiter as he placed a berry-topped baked cheesecake in front of her. When she picked up her fork, her lips curving in delight, Zac's heart rate began to pick up.

"You like cheesecake?"

"Love it. That little French patisserie across the street from Valhalla does an amazing one." She rolled her eyes. "Chocolate fudge. To die for."

Then she slid a small forkful of cake between her lips and his brain shorted.

"How…" It took all his willpower not to groan. "How did you meet him?"

"Who?" she mumbled past her mouthful.

"Your ex."

Her fork clinked down on the plate. She spent a few seconds swallowing before clearing her throat.

Zac sighed. "Look, I don't want you to think my money came with conditions. But I'd like to know. If you want to tell me. Apart from your sister, I'm guessing you don't confide in a lot of people."

The look on her face told him her internal war went beyond

the standard issues. When she finally replied, her words were deliberately measured. Cautious.

"My story isn't that interesting. I was twenty-three, young and stupid and in love, or so I thought. Jimmy turned out to be a liar and a cheat and then he died."

"I can't imagine you ever being stupid."

Her short laugh surprised him. "Oh, you'd be surprised."

They both sat in silence, eyes locked, until the seconds lengthened. And in those seconds, he sensed a tiny chink in her armor—nothing groundbreaking or defining, but something definitely positive, however small.

It sparked a glimmer of quiet confidence.

She finally broke eye contact to stare at her plate. "He drowned. For a surfer that's kind of ironic, don't you think?"

"I'm sorry."

Her expression hardened as she reached for her water. "Don't be. I just wish he was alive so I could kick his sorry, freeloading ass."

Zac waited as she downed the dregs of her glass.

"You really want to know," she finally said, her eyes glinting in challenge.

"Yes."

Her brow rose. "Fine. I met Jimmy three years ago at a Brisbane nightclub where he was singing in a band. He fancied himself a rock god—he got heaps of mileage off that cool 'struggling musician' chestnut. The kicker was, he was pretty good. But he lacked discipline and motivation, and the band finally dumped him out after one too many no-shows."

Zac just nodded, unwilling to break the moment.

"The last time I heard from him was when he signed the divorce papers, over a year ago. Now I know why. He was too busy working out ways to steal my money." She paused at the look on Zac's face. "What?"

"I was just thinking—" He hesitated, then went on tactfully. "I don't see it—you the nightclub type, marrying a musician."

Her eyes turned stormy. "Because I'm so organized and straitlaced?"

"You like order," he clarified. "But yeah, it does seem out of character."

Emily's heart twisted a little. Her curt confession hadn't satisfied his curiosity as she'd hoped. Her chin went up. "Maybe that was my little rebellion," she added, staring at her wine glass. "Emily the rebel, that's me. Or maybe I just—" *Wanted to be loved.* She bit off that last bit, mortified. She'd thought herself in love with Jimmy. No, that was wrong. She'd hoped. Desperately wished. Just like with all the others.

"What?" Zac asked.

"Nothing."

"Maybe…you just wanted to let your hair down for a change."

She scowled, a nerve well and truly touched. "You don't—"

"—know you?" His expression remained inscrutable. "I know you can't leave for the night until your desk is completely clear."

She waved that away. "You've seen my desk a thousand times a day."

"You deny yourself hot chips for a ham-and-salad sandwich."

"That's—"

"You love pink and blue but you wear black all the time. You're no-frills—you don't care for a lot of makeup or jewelry. Your hair is naturally blond, but you get highlights every two months." His gaze swept over her head, then across her face before coming to rest on her mouth. "You smell like ginger and a warm summer weekend." His voice became rough. "You taste like—"

"Stop!" She blinked. "How do you know what…." She paused blankly until her brain finally caught up. "You remember."

His smile curled with male knowledge. "So do you."

"But you—"

"I was being gentlemanly, waiting for you to say something. When you didn't, I thought it was one of those things that Must Not Be Mentioned Again."

She opened her mouth but her words jumbled together. With a swallow she tried again. "I didn't mean to..."

"I know."

"It was just..."

"I know."

"It won't—"

"Emily," he barked, a little too sharply. She clamped her mouth shut. "Enough with the apology."

The look on her face was so appealing, all flushed embarrassment, that Zac suddenly wondered what she'd do if he leaned in and kissed her.

"It wasn't even a kiss. More like a brief..." she glanced at his mouth, "brush of skin. A non-kiss."

That soft sigh she ended on hit Zac in all the right places. It revved up his blood, quickening his heartbeat into a familiar thud of arousal.

He gritted his teeth, battling for control. Yet when he thought he'd finally regained it, she had to go and chew on that full bottom lip. It wasn't a big thing, just a couple of perfect white teeth worrying the curve of her mouth for a brief second before she dipped her head and picked up her dessert fork. Yet his body jolted, her tiny reaction forever imprinted in his brain.

"Go on a date with me."

Her fork paused halfway up to her mouth. "What?"

What the hell are you doing?

He leaned in closer and unashamedly breathed in deep, drowning out that inner voice with her delicious scent. "Go. On. A. Date. With. Me."

A look of sudden horrified surprise bloomed before she smoothed out her expression.

"Very funny." She put her fork down and shoved the plate away.

"I'm not joking."

"Sure."

He frowned. "I'm not."

"Stop it, Zac. It's not funny."

"I'm not laughing." Man, her denial was beginning to nettle him.

She stared at her plate again, concentrating on edging it further to the side. "I'm sure there are a thousand other suitable women who would—"

"I'm asking *you.*"

She glanced up, her brows dipping down behind those heavy-rimmed glasses, and he had the sudden urge to ease them off her face.

"Why me, when I'm…"

He smiled at her small self-directed gesture. "When you're trying so hard to hide behind bland suits and sensible shoes?"

When her face flushed pink and her gaze shot past his shoulder, he silently cursed.

"Because," he continued more gently, "despite your best efforts, I find myself attracted to you."

"Because of a non-kiss?"

And your sweet curvy a— You can't say that! "Yep."

Blinking quickly, she refused to meet his eyes as she removed her napkin from her lap. "We work together." She began to fold the cloth efficiently on the table.

"So?"

"It's not professional."

"Says who? I'm the boss."

"Exactly. People will talk." She finally looked at him, her eyes unsettled.

"At the risk of repeating myself—so?"

"I owe you money."

He leaned back in his chair and silently studied her as she went on.

"And you've just paid off my ex's gambling debts, given me a raise and—"

"How long have we worked together?"

"What kind of—"

"Close to two years, right?"

"Yes."

"And in that entire time have I given you any reason to believe I'd blackmail you—or anyone—in that way?"

She paused, those lashes fluttering at his growing irritation. "I didn't mean to insult you."

"Well, you have."

"Look, Zac," she took a breath and leaned forward. "This is coming out all wrong. I appreciate your offer, but—"

He scowled. "You *appreciate* my offer?"

"I mean, I'm flattered, naturally—"

"Really."

"No, really. Any woman would be thrilled to be asked out by you."

"But you're not."

She shook her head. "I am *so* not your type."

He leaned in, which made her pull back. "And what is my type?"

"Oh, tall. Leggy and gorgeous. Rich. Any one of your ex-girlfriends fit the bill." She paused then added, "Trish Sattler fits the bill."

Emily studied Zac's frowning face—a beautiful, angular, all-male face—from behind the security of her glasses. Seriousness rippled off him in waves, his focus squarely on her. It was a look that made movement impossible, that dissected and disarmed.

Oh, my Lord. Her heart skipped a beat. "You *are* serious," she finally managed.

"Deadly."

"You *do* know there's a betting pool going on in Payroll? Who your next bed partner's going to be?"

His hand went to his nape, ruffling the hair there. "Okaaaaay…?"

"And that doesn't bother you?"

He shrugged. "Not really. What's your point?"

Was she thrilled? How about terrified. Shocked. Tempted. All of the above. But…

"This is not good," she muttered to herself.

Zac sighed. "The money thing again?"

"How can that not be an issue?"

"It just isn't. That was something a friend would do. This—" he flicked a finger between them "—is something different entirely."

"I see." Now her skin was tingling in earnest. She glanced away.

"So? What do you think?"

"I think…" *I think you're crazy, actually having this conversation aloud.* With a deep breath, she dragged her eyes back to his. "Workplace affairs always change things—when it goes wrong, it will go *really* wrong."

"What makes you think it'll go wrong?"

"Because it always does."

He paused, giving her a strange look. "Speaking from experience?"

"No." But as she watched him quirk up a disbelieving eyebrow, she swallowed thickly.

She leaned back in her chair, her mind churning. Even through everything—the parents from hell, the sexist boss, the numerous failed relationships—she'd kept believing, had clung tooth and nail to optimism, to the chance that love was out there somewhere. Despite the six-year gap, she'd been the strong one, keeping her sister AJ afloat when they were kids. She'd refused to use her sexuality as a career jump. She'd started over in a new city.

Yet had all those setbacks managed to steal more than money, self-respect and trust from her?

Had she turned into one of those cynical, hard-assed man-hating females?

"I'm not like your ex, Emily."

She smoothed down the tablecloth once, twice. "No, you're not."

"So…?"

"So what happens if it's a disaster?"

His mouth quirked. "We're adults. *If* it's a disaster, then we spend a week or so in awkward silence, then go back to being work colleagues. We'd do our jobs, you'd pay me back that money, and you'd go back to school."

You are not actually giving this serious thought?

She abruptly rose. "I have to…go."

Zac got to his feet. "I'll walk you to your room."

"That's not necessary."

"It is."

"No."

As she glared at him, the corner of his mouth curved. "I don't believe it."

"What?"

"*You're* giving *me* that look."

"What look?"

"That don't-mess-with-me-mate look." She frowned, which only made him chuckle. "You give it to all our difficult clients. I call it the rottweiler look—because no one's going to get past you without some serious backup." His warm hand seared through her jacket as he guided her out the restaurant.

"Nice. Did you just call me a dog?"

His laughter rang out in the elegant foyer, turning a few heads. When they paused at the elevator bank she tilted her chin up, exasperated at his amusement.

"You did!"

"I said your attitude was *doglike*. Big difference."

The doors slid open and they got in, Zac pressing the button before settling into the corner, his elbows resting on the railing, taking her in with a lazy smile. Emily steadfastly kept her eyes on the ascending floors.

When they arrived at their floor, Emily surged out, desperate to escape the confinement of that tiny space.

When she finally got to her door, she dug in her jacket pocket for her keycard, painfully aware of Zac at her shoulder.

She swiped the card once, then twice. The light remained red.

With a soft mutter, she tried again.

Still red.

"Here, let me." He took the card from her fingers and swiped it.

Red. He tried again.

"Can't we just go through your room?" Emily said impatiently.

"We could, but—"

"Then let's do that."

He glanced at her, shrugged and pulled out his keycard.

The lock green-lighted them on the first attempt, an irony that wasn't lost on her. Then he shouldered the door open, sweeping his hand in to allow her entry first.

With back straight, eyes ahead, she entered his room, walking swiftly across the living area to the connecting door. She opened it, then tried hers.

"It's locked," she said with a frown.

"I know."

Why hadn't she thought of that? She turned, only to find Zac with arms crossed, studying her in silence.

"So why didn't you say something?"

"I tried, but you were hell-bent on running away from me."

She blinked. "I wasn't running away!"

"Right." He unfolded his arms, then, to her consternation, reached for her glasses.

"What are you doing?" Instinctively she grabbed his arm, but the unexpected heat of his skin jerked her back. It was all he needed to claim his prize.

He inspected her glasses, looking through the thick lenses before pulling out a handkerchief from his pocket.

"You're shortsighted."

"Yes." She frowned as he brought her glasses to his mouth then breathed thickly over one lens.

It felt like her entire insides tightened with unexpected delight.

He began to polish the glass, a mischievous smile tilting his lips as he watched her squint at him.

"You don't need to…" She broke off as his lips parted again, mouth opening in slow deliberation before his hot breath frosted the glass.

What would it feel like to have those lips, that mouth, that breath on her skin?

Even with Zac so horribly out of focus, she could still make out that grin that told her he knew exactly what she was thinking.

Her belly flipped, warmth flooding her limbs.

"You should really leave these off."

"I need them to see." She blinked for emphasis. "Everything's fuzzy otherwise."

He moved and suddenly Zac-in-soft-focus became Zac-in-sharp-definition. "This better?"

She leaned back, desperately trying to ignore the warm singing of blood coursing through her body. "Uh…no…"

Before she could say another word, he put a hand on her nape, pulled her forward and kissed her.

Surprise held her still for a heartbeat, until heat surged into her chest where it swirled and dipped in delicious expectation.

His warm mouth was firm and skillful. He kissed her like he'd been practicing this all his life, a kiss that told her he knew what he was doing, knew how to please a woman. A kiss that melted her bones and quickly turned her on in a thousand different ways.

Through the haze of swiftly building desire, she felt his body move, and suddenly he was pressed up against her, heat spilling out to infuse them both.

Years of sexual frustration surged up, scorching her from the inside out as their breath and lips merged. She let out a groan, knew he'd felt it when his mouth curved against hers…just before he gently eased his tongue inside.

Oh. Wow. Emily let out a shocked squeak, which quickly petered off into a breathy sigh. She was vaguely aware of him gently palming her cheek, his thumb caressing her jaw, but she was too caught up in the divine sensation of his mouth making love to hers.

The hard insistent throb of his manhood began to grow between them, solidifying the reality of their location. Gradually, like wading into consciousness from a deep dream, she became aware of Zac pulling back.

It was, she realized groggily, her eyes at half-mast and her mouth still puckered, the most delicious few minutes of her entire life.

"Emily."

Her eyes sprang open, looking directly into his olive ones, dark with desire and amusement.

She swallowed thickly as the heat rose in her face. "I…can't. I just can't."

"Emmm—"

She ducked her head and practically raced for the door, eyes downcast. Zac surged forward but was too late—the solid thunk in her wake felt like the full stop to his unspoken sentence.

"—ily." He finished softly to the closed door. With an aggravated sigh he shoved his hands on his hips, then raised his head heavenward and scrunched his eyes shut. *Damn.*

Six

He stood there for what felt like ages, reining in his body, forcing it to relax through gritted teeth.

Until the small tap.

He yanked the door open. She stood in the doorway, blinking and squinting. She'd undone her jacket, revealing a white shirt tucked into a skirt that inadvertently emphasized curvy hips and a defined waist.

"My key works but I need—" Zac gave her no time to finish the sentence, instead grabbing her arms and firmly pulling her inside, kicking the door shut with one foot. Then he pushed her up against the wall and kissed her.

She offered a tiny protest, one that abruptly snapped off when his lips collided with hers, her breath in his mouth, her scent everywhere. It teased and tormented, that innocent gingery-appley smell that made him want to rip her clothes off and bury himself inside her.

Instead he yanked her jacket down her shoulders, then pulled her shirt from her waistband, desperate to feel skin.

Yes. He groaned approvingly, closing his eyes to fully

appreciate her smooth torso as it arched forward, arms pinned behind her back by her jacket, skin silken heat beneath his palms. Beautiful. Just beautiful.

"This needs to come off," he muttered into her mouth, tugging at her shirt.

Her breathless agreement was all he needed to wrench those damn buttons apart and tug the shirt from her shoulders.

Emily finally managed to struggle free of her jacket, her eyes flying open as his hands continued their exploration. He overwhelmed her, filling her skin, her pores with hot desperate longing.

This. This was what she craved. What she needed. And when he bunched her skirt up around her waist before easing her legs apart with his knee, she groaned from sheer pleasure.

Pleasure that exploded into a thousand tiny sparks of need when his hand dove into her knickers and intimately cupped her curls.

She would've fallen if he wasn't pinning her to the wall with his mouth, his hands, his hard thigh. And when his fingers slid through her warm slickness, brushing over hot flesh to unerringly find her taut sensitive bud, she groaned, wrenching her mouth from his.

It was too much. Too hot. Too...

"Zac," she got out. "What are we doing?"

His other hand clasped her chin, dragging her face back to him.

"I'm touching you. Now take your hair down."

With shaky hands she did as he asked, pulling her hair free from the severe knot. The strands fell down her back and shoulders, across her face, and he reached up a finger to gently brush them from her eyes. Those all-seeing, all-knowing eyes were almost black with desire, his breath hot as it fanned over her cheek.

"Let go for me, Emily."

She seemed to have lost all ability to think. Each single heartbeat echoed, blood racing through her body like a wall of flames.

She managed to get out a small nod, then a sigh when Zac let out a rumble of triumph and covered her mouth with his.

Then his finger slid inside her and her world ground to a breath-stealing halt. When she thought she might pass out from pleasure, he swiftly took charge, setting up a steady stroking pace that quickly began to swell and grow.

Her entire body screamed with joy. He'd set her skin on fire, his fingers dipping inside before easing out to smooth over her engorged bud. Over and over, again and again, until she whimpered beneath his mouth, a ragged plea for relief tearing from her lips.

He suddenly shifted, bracing himself, pressing her hard against the wall. Then his tongue was in her mouth, echoing the erotic glide of his fingers deep inside her, and she couldn't hold back any longer.

Zac felt the exact moment she went crashing over the edge. He gritted his teeth, desperate to hold on to that thin thread of control so he didn't embarrass himself and follow her.

Her hot wetness as it flooded him, the sheer beauty of her face frozen in climactic joy, nearly did him in. With a racing heart and an almost unbearable throb in his groin, he held on, waiting until Emily stopped trembling, until her breathing regulated and he finally registered her hands on his shoulders, pushing him back.

"Emily?" He tried to meet her eyes, but they were averted to the floor, her face flushed in acute embarrassment.

"I came back for my glasses," she muttered.

In the wake of his stunned surprise, she pulled away, quickly refixing her clothing.

The air was warm and thick with that familiar musky scent of sex, the silence complete as he forced his body into some semblance of control.

Her clothes were rumpled, shirt hanging loose and buttons askew. Her mouth was still puffy from his kisses, her hairdo now falling in gentle waves around her shoulders.

She looked so damn delicious, like a lush, slightly debauched angel made for love, that all he wanted to do was take her to bed and worship her body all night.

But her expression barred him entry, her stormy eyes rife with confusion. So, with careful deliberation, he pulled out her glasses and placed them in her outstretched hand, folding her fingers around them while he battled with the siren's call.

"Good night, Zac."

All he could do was nod, staring as she turned and practically ran from his room.

The lock clicked into place just before he ground out a groan full of pure frustration.

Emily sat on her darkened balcony, staring at the glittering Sydney harbor lights spread before her.

What on earth had she just done?

Her breath faltered again for about the millionth time that night, her thighs flush with excitement.

Zac had paid off her debt, given her this Sydney account and offered his services as a lover. He was the textbook definition of the answer to all her problems.

And now this. He'd been on her, inside her. Touching her in the most intimate of places while she broke apart beneath his hands and lips.

Things like this just didn't happen to her. Not ever.

Men were for fun. No emotional entanglements, no responsibility. Her declaration to AJ felt like a year ago, not just a few days. The irony would have made her laugh if she weren't so torn in a dozen different directions.

With a frown she pulled her tracksuit jacket tighter and studied the sparkling waterline, her eyes tracing the Opera House's illuminated curves against the black night before dropping down to the table where her notepad and pen sat.

She was a big girl. Sure, the thought of facing Zac after tonight made her squirm with embarrassment, but she'd gotten through worse. And if his date offer was still on the table, she still had to logically dissect it.

Since the age of fifteen, she'd made all her major life decisions after carefully listing the pros and cons. With one major exception. She clicked the pen button up then down. *Jimmy.* He'd been charming and confident, so persistent he'd thrown her for a loop.

Expensive shoes or a flashy car were impulse buys. Marrying Jimmy had been hers.

C'mon, babe. Live a little on the edge, huh?

She grimaced. Her ex's enthusiasm for all things spontaneous had chipped away at her caution, made her doubt everything she'd thought herself to be. He'd tried to change what she now realized was in her very bones.

So what was better—going into a relationship with improbable hopes of love, or with realistic expectations that it would just be for mutual pleasure?

Picking up the pen, she drew a line down the center of the page, wrote "Pros" in one column, then "Cons" in the other.

A few minutes later, she stared at her list.

Pros—one, she was single. Two, she needed a fling to erase the leftovers of Jimmy's betrayal. Three, Zac was a great lover. Four, if it crashed and burned, she was leaving in April. Probably.

Cons—one, he was her boss: it'd not only look bad if it got out at the office, but could she handle going through the stress of workplace gossip again?

No.

Two... She nibbled on the end of the pen. He had a bevy of gorgeous ex-girlfriends, ones she couldn't hope to compete with.

Sighing, she took a gulp of coffee from her steadily cooling cup, then scribbled "3" in the "Cons" column: *Leaving in April,* before sitting back in the chair and scrutinizing the list in silence.

You don't do impulsive. It isn't you, remember?

The irony of that statement warred inside as she recalled what had happened next door. It had been good. No, not good. Amazing. Mind-blowing.

And she wanted more.

Somewhere along the line she'd lost herself. Once upon a

time she'd liked dressing up and going dancing. But now she was always working. She had no friends to speak of, unless she counted AJ's. And a hot date when she looked like Miss Moneypenny every day? Right. She'd not only disguised her physical appearance but had become entirely wrapped up in playing the part, too.

And here Zac was, a tempting way to break free from that. Even if it was only temporary.

"Look, you're totally looking at this the wrong way," AJ reasoned when Emily called her sister a minute later. "Stop thinking of sex as one of your fairytale romance novels that ends in marriage."

Emily scowled. "What's wrong with—"

"You're both attracted to each other, you're both single, and you're not hurting anyone. Keep it a secret at work if you want—it'll add to the excitement. And Zac's a no-commitment guy, perfect for you right now. It'll be fun. A *lot* of fun. Which is something you're due for after…well…after the crap that was our childhood," AJ finished diplomatically.

Her uncomplicated, straight-talking sister always knew how to get to the heart of the matter.

Yet that thought didn't comfort her as she finally headed inside to her empty bed.

Saturday passed in a round of meetings that included a working lunch before Zac gave Emily the afternoon off while he met with a potential client.

Delighted at the unexpected windfall, she pulled on jeans and walking shoes and spent a few pleasant hours shopping along Pitt Street Mall before wandering through Skygarden, then the Queen Victoria Building.

When she finally made her way back to the hotel, she'd bought the latest Debbie Macomber novel, a frangipani-scented candle and a Swarovski crystal butterfly for AJ's growing collection.

Emily called for room service, then packed away the last of her clothes. She and Zac had spent the morning with other people, no time to exchange awkward glances or ruminate on what last night meant. If it meant anything at all. To her critical eye Zac had appeared exactly the same, commanding those meetings with his usual aura of professionalism, neither overtly or covertly avoiding her.

He was discreet.

As she went over her action plan for the Point One launch she devoured a club sandwich, then a decadent pistachio crème brûlée with biscotti. With the last bite she rose from the table, leaving the computer as she stretched out her back.

It was seven-thirty, and while she'd worked later countless times before, something inside urged her to call it a night.

So she did, closing the laptop with a decisive snap before grabbing her iPod and padding over to the balcony.

With a smile and a deep cleansing breath, she drew the heavy curtains apart to reveal the breathtaking harbor sunset, pausing for only a second before opening the doors and stepping outside.

Behind the hotel the blood-red sun hung heavy in the sky, bathing the Opera House in shards of amber and orange as Zac sat in cool, darkening silence.

As a teenager he'd studied the color, the form and play of shadow and light, across Elizabeth Bay a million times from his bedroom window. He'd sketched a bunch of those houses, an apartment or two, a uniquely styled building. Where were those sketches now?

Long gone, he suspected, recrossing his ankles on the low patio table and taking another sip of beer. At eighteen he'd traded in Australia for Sweden, refusing an automatic placing at Sydney's University of Technology to study architecture at Lund University. Victor had hit the roof then cut him off without a penny.

His hand tightened on his glass as familiar bitterness swooped in on black wings.

The man may have been a legend in business, but Zac knew the true Victor Prescott. A liar. A hypocrite. An unyielding, stubborn, unforgiving sonofa—

A small sound to his right had his hairs standing up, and when he glanced over, the entire world took that moment to pause.

A row of terra-cotta pots divided their shared balcony, and with light spearing from her suite, he could clearly make out Emily's figure a few feet away.

She leaned forward, hands crossed casually over the railing. The snug pink long-sleeved T-shirt accented her waist and generous hips, soft tracksuit sweats clinging to her rounded butt. His eyes traveled leisurely over those generous curves until they came to rest on her bare feet.

Then she shifted her weight and leaned into the balcony, treating him to a view of her beautiful bottom.

His mouth went dry. *That would fit perfectly in my hands...*

Memories of last night flashed past—her soft skin and warm limbs, her gentle sighs of pleasure teasing and taunting as his body stiffened.

Then she began to hum.

He blinked, surprised, as her head started to bob, then her shoulders swayed. Her humming became indistinguishable words, something about "party" and "starting tonight"...

She actually had a nice singing voice, kind of smoky and breathy. He grinned when he spotted the earphones, then finally recognized the song. He'd never pick his assistant as a closet Lionel Richie fan.

She suddenly turned, eyes closed, a small smile on her face as she began to dance.

Good God, she was absolutely luscious. Her hips swiveled, shoulders swayed. He choked out an appreciative groan. She made his blood race and his breath stutter. She filled him with a burning need to touch, to kiss, to taste. A dangerous need.

His drink sloshed over the rim of the glass as he abruptly dropped his feet to the floor with an audible thump.

And still she moved, her grin wide, mouthing the words as his vision began to glaze over.

Then his phone rang.

He grabbed it from the table, seizing a ragged breath as he jammed his finger on the off button. Too late.

Emily had yanked the earbuds out, her wide eyes skimming the shadows until they finally settled on him.

"Zac?"

Busted. He sighed. "Yeah?"

"Were you…" Her self-conscious hesitancy was so endearing that he couldn't help smiling. "Watching me?"

"Yep."

"Uhhhh…" She threaded, then unthreaded her fingers until she realized what she was doing and dragged her palms over her thighs.

"'Dancing On the Ceiling'?" he teased. "You like the eighties, huh?"

He fully expected her to turn tail in a haze of embarrassment. Instead she surprised him with a chin tilt and a nod. "It varies. Lionel Richie, Michael Jackson, Duran Duran. Some Prince. 'Baby I'm a Star' is great running music."

"You run?" He tried to stop his eyes from skimming down her legs. He failed.

"Most mornings."

He shifted in his chair and crossed an ankle over his knee. "I must admit I'm more of a commercial rock guy."

"Oh, you don't know what you're missing." She palmed her iPod, wrapping the ear buds around her hand. "One of my major year-twelve assignments was comparing the relevance of eighties music to the political and socioeconomic climate at the time."

She'd never cease to amaze him. "Wow, that's, uhh…"

She chuckled. "A challenge? I knew my music teacher had a thing for retro." Her eyes creased mischievously. "She gave me an excellent grade."

"Clever."

They grinned at each other, until Zac's phone once again shattered the moment.

"I'm…" She glanced back to her suite. "I should go and take a shower. You'd better get that."

He turned his phone off and stood, pinning her eyes with his. "It can wait."

He walked casually to the balcony. Even from this distance he

could see caution warring behind her eyes, reminding him of a
day long ago when he was living in Sweden. A cat had suddenly
appeared around his apartment block, wary of the kindness of
strangers. Yet beneath those almond eyes there had been an
almost heartbreaking desperation for affection.

He'd eventually worn her down with a mixture of food,
patience and space.

"Come here."

"Why?" she squeaked out.

His grin spread wider as he heard her breath catch nervously
in her throat. *That makes two of us, sweetheart.* "So I can kiss
you."

"Ahhh…."

Impatience propelled him over those terra-cotta pots before he
finally managed to tamp on the brakes less than a foot away.

The breath rattling in Emily's throat threatened to choke her
as Zac's hard body came into unhurried full-on contact with
hers.

Shock hit first, and she instinctively recoiled. But as his arms
snaked around her waist, heat quickly engulfed her. She felt like
melting into him, all commanding, six-foot-two of hard muscle
and hot skin. Muscle she wanted to touch and knead, skin she was
aching to taste. A body she wanted to claim and to be claimed
by.

Yet the blunt reality of having Zac up close and personal, his
groin pressing hard into her belly, kept her frozen to the spot.
Her back arched, hands clutching his arms, almost as if she'd
changed her mind and decided to stop him.

Which was ridiculous. She didn't *want* to stop him.

Then his lips went to her neck, tasting her racing pulse, and
all thought crumbled as need took over.

Hot, solid male. Heady, musky scent. Arms that wrapped
around her, strong and protective. She registered it all, her body
twitching with remembered delight.

She gulped and squeezed her eyes shut as his mouth drew soft
kisses along the length of her neck.

Yes. Oh, yes. Emily let the pleasure of his mouth pull her under as his hands cupped her cheeks.

Beads of sweat pooled down the small of her back, her body singing with anticipation as his lips stroked, caressed, teased hers, before firmly pushing them apart to boldly explore her mouth. His small murmur of appreciation filled her with pleasure and she leaned in closer, desperate to feel him.

A sudden craving thundered through Zac's veins, making his groin swell, forcing his breath out. She tasted so good, felt even better. Her lush breasts pushed up against his chest, an erotic teaser of things to come. Chaos swirled behind his eyes as he continued to kiss her, running his hands over her arms, to her waist, then leisurely over the curves of her rounded butt. She moaned in his mouth, ending in a gasp as he roughly pulled her closer.

"Can you feel that?" He growled beneath her lips.

She got out a muffled affirmation, a kind of half sigh, half whimper that fired his blood even more.

Gradually he pulled back, taking in her languid, desire-filled eyes, her thoroughly kissed Cupid mouth. Images of her wearing nothing but that expression sent an urgent bolt of heat straight to his erection.

With a thick swallow, he said roughly, "Emily. Look at me."

She blinked, breath hitching, before reluctantly dragging her gaze to his. Those thickly lashed, wide blue eyes, shining with vulnerability and uncertainty sent a jolt of protectiveness into his heart.

"You can feel how hard I am but you can't meet my eyes?"

The corner of her lip dipped inward, those teeth worrying the swollen flesh. "Zac," she breathed out, her grip tense on his biceps. "I need to—"

He placed a finger over her lips. "Just one kiss. Then you can go."

With eyes at half-mast she sighed, her warm breath grazing over his skin, stoking the flames below. When her hands skimmed up his arms, goose bumps rose even as his skin heated. "Okay."

The surge of victory melted into desire as he claimed her mouth once more, her decadent curves pressing into his arousal.

They kissed for long minutes, until he felt her begin to pull away. Everything screamed in protest, his groin throbbing unbearably, but he let her go, his fingers loosely trailing down her arm as she turned away.

She didn't glance back. If she had, she would've seen the burning need on his face, need echoed in every rigid muscle as he stood there with only the mild November night as relief.

As her door slid closed, he muttered a dozen colorful curses under his breath before grabbing his empty glass and storming back inside.

It was only then that he realized someone was at his door. And given the energy with which the caller was thumping, they'd been there for some time.

He stalked to the door and grabbed the handle.

"Zac. It's Cal."

His hand stilled as he glanced through the peephole. "What do you want?"

"Victor was really sick, you know," came the muffled reply.

"What?"

Cal paused. "You're not answering my messages. Can we not talk through a door?"

With a muttered curse, Zac yanked the door open.

Cal's palms were up in a conciliatory gesture. "I didn't come here to start a fight."

"So what are you here for?"

"A truce. An olive branch. Whatever it takes."

Zac's hand dove into his hair, guilt, anger and a tiny, faint hope churning together to make a huge confused mess in his brain.

"So can I come in?" Cal asked after a moment.

Zac shrugged, turned and stalked over to the bar.

Cal closed the door behind him.

"I've got nothing to say. Everyone knows VP's yours."

Cal's expression was a mix of chagrin and apology. "Yeah, well, let's just say becoming the next Victor Prescott isn't what I want for the rest of my life." His expression softened then. "The baby's due in January and I'm getting married in March. I'd like to have an actual relationship with my wife and child."

The rest of that unspoken sentence lay between them, reluctantly bonding the two men for a long moment. As a boy, Zac couldn't remember a time when Victor hadn't been coming from or going to a meeting, the office, a business trip. Up until he was seven, when his mother had abruptly left, he'd grown up in an absent-father home, albeit a fantasy home filled with more toys, gadgets and electronics than a kid could wish for. He couldn't blame Cal for wanting a normal life.

Cal finally broke the silence. "We need to sort this VP mess out."

Zac eyed him carefully as he wrenched off the cap of a long-neck beer and tossed it in the sink. "I don't have a mess. You do."

"You're a Prescott. It's yours, too."

"You keep saying that like it means something to me."

"It should."

"Well it doesn't. I stopped being part of the family a long time ago."

"Oh, for God's sake, what the hell did he do to make you so damn cynical? To turn your back on everyone who—" With blazing eyes, Cal bit back the last words, hands on his hips, before averting his gaze with a derisive snort.

"Have you asked him?" Zac asked slowly.

"He won't talk. You won't talk." Cal glared. "No one will bloody talk."

"Cal…" What could he say? To Cal, Victor was a savior, marrying his mother and transporting them from a life of hardship and struggle to wealth and privilege. Cal worshipped Victor, and Victor had basked in the glow. Long ago, Zac had furiously resented that connection, the attention that should have rightfully been his. Cal had been determined to prove himself, the boy with the razor-sharp mind who dissected, then rebuilt computers for fun. Of course he and Victor had bonded over that. Then there was Zac: a quiet thinker, a lover of visual arts and drawing. While he'd been seething with teenage angst and rebelling against everyone and everything, Cal had developed what would eventually become One-Click, Australia's number-one software package.

Zac was an adult now, with an adult's understanding and perspective. It wasn't his place to destroy whatever bond Cal and Victor had, no matter how terrible a father Victor had been to his own flesh and blood.

"It's...in the past, Cal," he finally got out.

"Bull. It's still happening." Cal put his hands on his hips, a direct challenge. "It started ever since you took off overseas to study."

It had started long before that, but still... "I was eighteen. Nearly ten years ago."

"Yeah."

"Cal..." The thick warning was clear. "Don't push it. You won't like what you hear."

Cal's humorless laugh startled him. "Nothing Victor does surprises me anymore. He's stepping back from the company, donating to charity, talking about investing in small business. And this from a man who tried to marry me off instead of telling me the truth about his tumor."

Shock jolted Zac back a step. "What tumor?"

"Victor had a brain tumor," Cal said softly. "He actually died on the operating table. For a while there, we didn't know if he'd make it."

What the hell was he supposed to do with that? Past and present swirled into a dozen churning emotions, humbling him. "Why didn't anyone tell me?"

Cal's expression was astute. "Would you have taken my call?"

Would he have? A surge of guilt and cold, hard truth flooded Zac's conscience. Probably not. "Is he...?"

"He's fine now," Cal said firmly. "But you know what he's like—Victor manipulates, that's what he does. It doesn't mean the company should suffer for it."

Neither man spoke for a long while.

"Okay," Cal finally conceded. "You don't want to talk to me. After the last few years of silence, I don't blame you."

"Cal—"

"No, I get it. *I* wouldn't want to talk to me," he added with a twist to his mouth. "Can we just put that aside for now? I need your help. I might not want the top job, but that doesn't mean I want to see the company crash."

Guilt twisted inside. "So you're really giving it up."

"There's more to life than working."

"Jesus, don't let Victor catch you saying that."

Both men laughed, a welcome moment of levity.

"Look, mate." Zac began. "Me and Victor—" Cal shook his head, but Zac forged on. "It's a complicated, toxic relationship, you know that. I had to get away."

"And not one call. I know," Cal added at the look on Zac's face. "I didn't, either."

"Yeah." Zac reached into the minibar and pulled out another beer, offering it to Cal. "So we're both crappy brothers." He flicked his head to the sofa. "Want to sit?"

For one second, caution warred on his stepbrother's face. He'd put that there when he'd walked out all those years ago. That realization made Zac's jaw clench.

"If you want me to," Cal said.

Regret seeped into Zac's bones, the years they'd lost gaping wide. He'd done this, had driven cracks into their once-amiable relationship so that Cal no longer trusted him.

That was wrong.

"Please," he said gruffly. "Sit."

They drank too much, stayed up too late and, Zac thought fuzzily as Cal left around 2 a.m., probably said way too much.

The alcohol had done its job and taken the edge off, relaxing them enough to openly discuss the company while studiously avoiding any personal stuff.

Lying in his bed, hands behind his head, Zac lazily blinked at the ornate ceiling frescos, the beer buzz still warming his veins. Was it before or after they'd shared their fifth drink and memories of one tenth-grade Julie Jenkins and a see-through shirt that he'd suggested advertising for a new CEO and floating the company on the stock exchange?

Cal had nearly choked. "An outsider *and* going public?" He finally got out, wiping beer from his chin.

"Yeah."

"Victor would never go for it."

Zac had shrugged. "Then you have a problem."

They'd sat in silence until Cal's phone rang. From the soft dip in his voice to the way his face had relaxed before he turned away, Zac knew exactly who was on the other end of the line. Ava, Cal's fiancée. Which, for some reason, had made him suddenly think of Emily. Curvy, luscious Emily.

With a groan he flipped to his side, punched the pillow and glared at the shadows through the half-open bedroom door.

Emily—now probably asleep—in the room next to his.

Emily, who'd kissed him so sweetly his body got hard just thinking about it.

Did she sleep on the left or the right side of the bed? On her back or front?

What did she wear to bed?

Stop.

Yet his body ignored him, his groin slowly stirring to life as a myriad of pictures flashed behind his eyes: Emily in a skimpy bra and knickers. Emily in high heels and black garters.

Emily in his boxer shorts…

With a growl, he flung the sheets off and swung from the bed. There'd be time to do it right. He'd been patient, he could wait a little longer.

But now, a cold shower couldn't.

Seven

Their 9 a.m. flight was delayed by an hour. Emily had always laughingly joked about AJ's belief in omens, but right now, seated next to Zac in Virgin Blue's executive lounge in Sydney's departure terminal, she wasn't amused.

More time in his presence, more time to feel awkward and embarrassed.

More time to rethink her decision?

On their drive to the airport Emily had shamelessly used her phone as a buffer. She'd talked with the Valhalla staff about the Point One project, texted ones who couldn't be reached...and yes, faked a few, too.

Tiredness nipped at her heels as she stared at her phone, reading the same e-mail for the fifth time. A night in the most heavenly bed in all the world and still she couldn't sleep. Her brain had teased her with various scenarios of Zac there beside her, touching, kissing, making love to her.

She frowned, reached for her cappuccino and took a sip before glancing over at Zac, who sat directly opposite.

His expression was hidden behind expensive sunglasses, but

she was directly in his sightline, even if he was busy with his text messages.

"Cal stopped by last night," Zac said suddenly.

Emily looked up. "Really?"

A small pause, then, "I suggested floating the company and bringing in a new CEO. Cal didn't outright refuse."

"That's good."

"Only if he can convince Victor."

"And the wedding? You're free that weekend," she reminded him.

"Not sure. There's lots of…" He hesitated, as if searching for the right word. "Baggage."

She nodded. "Sometimes it's better to go forward than to step back."

"Exactly." His gaze tripped over her, studying her expression (she'd gone for inscrutable), her mood (professional yet distant), her clothes (hmmm…yeah). Dark gray jacket, long skirt, plain cream shirt, sensible kitten heels.

Gray. Plain. Sensible. That's what he saw, what everyone saw. And before that kiss, she'd accepted it. How could she not, when she'd actively cultivated the facade?

But now…

He'd obviously seen something to warrant his attention.

A small twist of pleasure caught her unawares, but then their flight was announced and the moment was broken.

Twenty minutes passed, an excruciatingly long time to be on the edge of her seat. They'd boarded in silence, Zac's normal businesslike wall of confidence marred with underlying tension—tension that melted away as soon as the plane took off.

The sudden pressure drop and stomach-constricting momentum eventually eased. Yet Emily remained tense, completely aware of the man next to her, ostensibly reading the morning paper. Tension that had everything to do with last night's kiss and the dilemma she was now in.

How could she focus on her job when all she wanted to do was have Zac naked?

He turned the page and she jumped, crushing a soft curse under her breath.

He was too close and he knew it. How could he not know it after what they'd done?

She shifted her leg, angling her body toward the aisle, away from him, with casual subtlety.

Business class and still not enough room. She sighed and refolded the complimentary gossip magazine, staring at the sensational headlines without seeing them, before shoving it in the seat pocket.

The flight attendant hovered past, offering coffee, which Zac took with a smile. When he withdrew with the cup, his arm passed way too close to her chest.

She held her breath as her heart began to thump, fingers stiff on the armrest. He placed the glass in the holder between them, his hand brushing hers.

She blinked and slid her gaze sideways.

A small smile stretched his mouth…and what a mouth it was. A mouth made for kissing, with soft lips and strong teeth and— One eyebrow went up and she nearly groaned aloud. Then he leaned in and gently covered her hand with his warm fingers, and she barely managed to muffle her surprise.

"Zac—"

"Emily."

"You're…" She glanced furtively back over her shoulder. "You're holding my hand."

"Yes, I am."

His leg shifted, bumping into hers, and she nearly leaped from her seat. "Now you're—"

"Touching your leg. I know. And you know what else?" He dipped his head conspiratorially, beckoning her with his finger. With a thickness in her throat she bent forward. His warm breath swooped over her cheek and her stomach fluttered. "I think I'll have to kiss you."

His firm disclosure shocked her immobile, her eyes transfixed on his lips as they inched closer to hers.

"You can't—" she managed to choke out.

"I can." His mouth curved, the frankly seductive look in his eyes forcing her breath out in excited little puffs. "I will."

"But—"

Her protest gushed out on a sigh when his lips brushed over her cheek, searing her skin. He feathered his mouth across her cheekbone, the barest of touches, before coming to rest by her earlobe. That warm breath sent flaring heat down through her body, curling around her stomach, her thighs, before ending in her toes.

"Someone could see…" she whispered desperately.

"Yes." His teeth nibbled on her lobe and she bit her lip to stifle the whimper of pleasure.

"We…" She swallowed. "We can't do this here."

His lips skimmed the tender point where her ear met her neck. "So name the time and place."

Oh. Her breath hissed in as she struggled to vocalize what she'd been fantasizing about these last few months. Now, faced with the certainty of Zac's interest, it made her list seem… Cold. Businesslike.

He must have taken her lack of response as hesitancy, because he gently added, "Tonight?"

Tonight? She squeezed her eyes shut as his mouth moved back across her cheek in a sensuous trail of warm breath and soft lips.

"You…have that thing with Josh Kerans tonight."

He paused, an irritated frown marring his forehead as Emily opened her eyes. Yet his hand still captured hers, sending a trembling anticipation through her bones.

"Right. Client get-together at his beach house. You should be there, too."

"Why?" She pulled back, the heat in her cheeks beginning to ebb.

"Because he's a client and he invited me. And now I've invited you."

She shook her head. "This isn't…no."

"This is work, Emily, not a social outing. Jason, Mitch and June will be there." He smoothly reeled off some of Valhalla's key staff. "And your involvement with Point One means people need to see you as more than just my assistant. And I go, you go." To take the sting from the demand, he gave a small smile. "Networking is a necessity. But I promise—" his lips curved, turned slightly wicked "—I'll make it up to you tomorrow night."

His husky murmur, full of lustful promise, made her nerves groan. The air crackled dangerously between them, doing something hot and exciting to her insides. It forced Emily to swallow, but still she couldn't look away from his eyes, those dark, sultry depths that said, "I'd like to do things to you and I know you'll enjoy them."

"This has to stay out of the office," she finally blurted out. Clearly, from the look on his face, this was not what he'd expected her to say.

His mouth curved. "There goes my sex-on-the-desk fantasy."

"I mean it, Zac." At her stern look, his humor fled. "It's not you they'll talk about. You're the boss—you won't be the one labeled."

His eyes narrowed. "Why does that sound—"

"It doesn't matter what it sounds like. There can't be any secret looks, any off-the-cuff comments, any touching. During the day we're professionals."

He remained silent for so long that Emily's head began to spin from the breath she held.

Finally, he nodded and said, "I'll pick you up at eight tonight." And calmly reached for another newspaper, unfolded it and began to read.

Emily stared blindly down the crowded isle as excitement zinged through her blood. How on earth was she going to survive Monday—let alone tonight—without thinking of the coming evening?

At least, Zac thought ruefully, her skirt was above the knee—the only concession she'd made to the evening. It was still black.

It was still distorted with a boxy jacket. And she still had on a pair of horrible clunky heels.

He *had* said it was work. So he remained silent on the twenty-minute drive to Kerans's Broadbeach Waters luxury apartment, the only background noise coming from his iPod plugged into the dash.

But when he pulled into the cul-de-sac, cut the engine and saw her studying the partygoers with a frown, he paused.

"Ready?"

She took too long to commit to that nod. Her hesitation told him what she wouldn't—couldn't?—voice.

"It's a warm night. You might want to lose the jacket," he said casually.

She gave him a look that told him she knew what he was up to, but still she unbuttoned her jacket, then slipped it off her shoulders.

Her silky short-sleeved purple shirt shimmered beneath the streetlights, revealing tanned arms as she pulled the door open and got out.

When he'd rounded the bonnet, she was nervously smoothing down her skirt, a skirt that now hugged her hips, emphasizing her generous curves and indented waist.

Behind the glasses, irritation brimmed in those blue eyes. But there was also a little fear. Fear of the unknown. Fear of being judged.

He knew what that was like, even if it'd been years since he'd allowed himself to feel that emotion.

He glanced around: they were alone with only the streetlights above as witnesses. Unable to resist, his hand went to her face, but paused when she quickly rocked back. Her brow creased.

"Emily."

With great reluctance she met his eyes, her expression shuttered.

Then a car door slammed and the moment was gone. She stepped back. "We should go in."

He wanted to say more, but what? That for the first time in

his life he wanted to ditch work and instead spend the evening kissing her all over? *That* would not go over well.

Slow it down, mate. You don't want to scare her off.

He nodded, trying to ignore the growing desire warming his blood.

"Let's go."

The opulent dozen-bedroom, two-story apartment was a Valhalla triumph. Zac's signature—huge windows with intricate personalized frames and sconces that showcased the view—presented the expansive Broadbeach Waters in all its glory. Beyond the buzz of conversation, the sharply dressed and expensive-smelling people, the subtle ceiling lights and the strains of a Mozart concerto, the stunning sunset streaking across the sky commanded Emily's attention.

Red sky at night, sailor's delight.

She frowned at the childhood rhyme before glancing curiously at the assembled crowd.

Men and women greeted each other, drank champagne and chatted animatedly. Here were the über-rich in serious socializing mode. Yet how could they not notice the glorious blue-red-navy spectacle of a Surfers sunset?

She watched small waves lap up against Kerans's luxury yacht tethered at the boat ramp, studying the cerulean water before she sensed someone approaching. Zac. Only he had the power to send her body tingling on high alert.

She turned to him. "This is amazing, Zac. Another great job."

"Thank you. Champagne?" He offered the cold stemmed glass. She took it with a smile, then sipped to cover her nervousness at his direct scrutiny.

"It's—"

"Zac! You're here! *Hur mår du?*"

Delicious. The word died along with a tentative smile as a silky voice cut through the surrounding chatter. A tall, dark-haired woman stalked through the crowd, her black, sleeveless catsuit flaunting an extremely fit physique. Around her neck hung two silver chains, the handful of fashionable dangly charms chiming melodiously below a pair of impressive breasts, their curves revealed by a half-lowered zipper.

Haylee Kerans, the client's daughter. And—Emily's grip tightened imperceptibly on her glass—one of Zac's many ex-girlfriends who didn't accept the words *break up* lightly.

As Zac turned to greet Haylee, Emily stood there awkwardly, listening to them converse in melodious, singsong Swedish.

Then Haylee linked her arm through his and swung her gaze to Emily.

"Kan du talar Svenska?"

At Emily's blank look, her smile seemed to take on a condescending smirk. "You can't speak Swedish? Oh, you should. Such a *musikal* language—but then, Zac's half Swede, so I'm biased." Her striking face creased with deliberate thought. "I shall have to teach you...Emma, right?"

"Emily," Zac interjected. Emily didn't miss the way he'd firmly extricated himself from Haylee's grip.

"Oh." Haylee's eyes suddenly narrowed. "Zac's gatekeeper. You field all his calls."

Emily blinked in surprise. What, it was *her* fault Zac was an expert on moving on? Irritation bubbled up but she quickly got a handle on it.

"I'm Zac's assistant," she said calmly. "He directs, I do."

One of Haylee's eyebrows went up as her gaze swept Emily from head to toe, a silent, insulting inspection that had her flushing. But before she could formulate any kind of comeback, Zac intervened.

"Any idea where your father is?"

The younger woman's expression quickly transformed as she looked back to Zac, a perfect smile that looked a tad too bright to Emily's thinking.

"Where he normally is." Haylee nodded into the crowd. "Over near the bar, surrounded by his mates and talking business. Zac." Haylee ran a teasing hand up his arm. "You should call me. We could go for a drive in that *smaskig* car of yours."

She leaned forward, proffering her cheek. As politeness

dictated, Zac went in for the kiss, but at the last minute she turned and his mouth landed firmly on hers.

"For later," she purred, pulling back, then shooting Emily a triumphant glance.

When Zac steered Emily away, her back was rigid beneath his hand.

"She'll 'teach me'?" she muttered.

"Ignore her," he commanded as they steadily made their way across the room.

"Oh, I intend to. I'd rather take swimming lessons from a shark."

He grinned, then looked fleetingly over his shoulder. The now-unsmiling Haylee still stood where they'd left her, one elegant finger tapping rhythmically against her champagne flute.

He'd never understand women. Haylee had been fun for a month or two—impulsive and unconcerned with looking perfect, unlike many of his other exes. And growing up with wealth meant she'd been unfazed by his billion-dollar reputation. But gradually, her attentiveness had begun to chafe. Where was he? Who was he with? When would he be back? She'd gone from fun to serious, hinting about "a more permanent living arrangement" and casually wondering aloud when she'd get to meet his family.

His cue to backpedal like an Olympic champion.

"Sorry," he muttered.

"For what?"

"For putting you in the middle of that."

She shrugged, keeping pace with him as they wound their way through the crowd. "I've handled worse."

"Really?"

She paused, forcing him to stop dead too. "I answer your phone, Zac. I field a handful of ex-girlfriends' calls every week. I've been screamed at, cajoled, threatened. Some even beg and cry."

"You're joking."

"No."

The truth was reflected in her expression, prompting a frown.

But when he opened his mouth, someone clapped a hand on his shoulder.

"Zac. How was Sydney?"

When he turned to Joe Watts, Valhalla's chief engineer, his expression was neutral.

Emily stood calmly by as they chatted, fully aware of his arm, his shoulder close to hers, fully aware he could touch her at a moment's notice—but she knew without a doubt he wouldn't. This was work, and she had drawn the line. Plus...

She glanced around the room, her eyes coming to rest on a familiar catsuited woman, the center of attention in a group of men. Haylee's little display only underscored her need for the line. The billionaire's daughter didn't seem the type who liked competition. She was also someone who could make life uncomfortable with one calculated conversation with her father.

Yes, Emily realized as she watched Haylee's gaze devour an unsuspecting Zac more than once as the minutes ticked by, Daddy's little girl would come first, despite Zac and Josh's professional business relationship.

She quickly excused herself and made her way to the bathroom.

Eight

They drove home the same way they'd come, with the soft strains of music alleviating the distinctly uncomfortable silence.

Zac had sensed a change ever since their first kiss. It was as if he made her nervous somehow. Unsure. So unlike the Emily he knew.

It was oddly gratifying, knowing he could ruffle those perfect feathers, that he had this kind of effect.

He stole a glance as she stared out the window. She'd unbuttoned her shirt to reveal an elegant collarbone and smooth skin, demure yet extremely tempting. And she'd done something with her hair, loosened it up so that small strands floated around her jawline, bringing emphasis to that lush Cupid's-bow mouth.

"A lot of people are interested in Point One," she said suddenly.

The compliment he'd been reworking lay preempted in his mouth. She was still in work mode. And right now, he was her boss.

Damn. He nodded. "How are the plans coming along?"

"I've already talked with Michelle from Publicity." She crossed her legs and kept her focus ahead, out into the dark night. "If those ground-floor businesses are in by the end of November, we can utilize them for the December launch. We've already presold half the apartments. Which means we have ten left, plus five spare offices," she said as they turned off Pacific Highway and left onto Duringan Street. "I expect those to be filled in the next few weeks."

"And the launch?"

"Final estimate by tomorrow."

He flicked her a smile. "Great."

"And…" She paused as the car smoothly took the corner, passing Currumbin Surf Club on the right.

"I'm waiting on a call from Queensland Uni, to see if I can start my course in second term. April."

"They let you do that?"

"Depends on the circumstances. And I worked out a plan to pay you back."

"There's no hurry." He glanced over at her but couldn't read her expression.

"I don't like owing people money."

They finally turned into Emily's street and he pulled the car to a smooth stop at the curb. When he cut the engine, the Porsche's throaty purr died out, leaving a heavy silence in its wake.

Dark clouds hid the moon, distorting her face, making it difficult to read her expression. And he really, really wanted to know what she was thinking.

He snicked open his door and the interior light came on. Then he slowly turned, giving her no choice but to look at him.

Her face was half in shadow, half in light. An apt description for someone who guarded her secrets so very carefully.

She was the complete opposite of every woman he'd dated, someone who hadn't been born into wealth and didn't run in the same privileged circles. Yet she could handle any situation he'd thrown at her, from boardrooms to client parties to fending off clingy exes. So why did he feel the sudden urge to protect her?

"Emily."

Ignoring her startled murmur, he curled a strand of her hair around his fingers, savoring the silkiness before gently smoothing it behind her ear.

"Yes?"

He hesitated, oddly tongue-tied.

Admit it. You've been spoiled by all those other women—bold, confident women who knew what they wanted and came right out and said it.

No, not spoiled—bored. Cynical, even.

It'd been a long time since he'd had to put a concerted effort into a seduction.

That thought gave him pause. And as he sat there, trying to work out a tactful follow-up, she blinked, her lips parting slightly. The light streamed over them, revealing the tip of her tongue as it touched the inside bottom lip before she closed her teeth on it.

With an inward groan he slid his hand around her neck, cupping her head and tangling her hair.

Then he pulled her in and kissed her.

It was just as sweet, just as delicious as before. Her pouty lips beneath his, soft and pliant. That scent…conjuring up freshness and innocence. And her warm breath that came out in a gasp before lengthening into a murmur of pleasure.

His body stirred, sparked into life by one simple kiss.

He explored her mouth, tasting the curves, the creases, her soft tentative tongue that at first shied away, then bit by bit returned to tangle with his, until his blood began to pound in earnest and his breath became ragged.

He groaned. *Stop.* But Emily's fingers were teasing the hair on his nape, her gentle, almost hesitant touch only stoking the fires higher.

He had to stop before it got out of hand.

With a supreme effort he reluctantly broke the kiss, easing away with a regretful growl. She frowned and her eyes snapped open.

His groin tightened. Her blue eyes were dark and heavy with

desire, her damp mouth bruised with kisses. He could hear her rapid breath—or was that his?—as she pulled back.

"Tomorrow night," he got out, knowing his voice was thick with lust, knowing it wouldn't take any effort to have her here, now. "My place."

When she glanced away with a quick nod, the light revealed a flush on her smooth cheeks as she scrambled from the car.

Tomorrow night. His body was already keyed up just thinking about it as he followed her out.

"Thanks for the ride."

"My pleasure." He lingered on that last word, crossing his arms and leaning back against the car, taking a warped delight in her flustered expression.

She turned and headed for the stairs without a backward glance, and Zac was rewarded with a view of her gently swaying bottom and hips as she ascended. When she paused at her door, she finally turned to give him a nod, then unlocked the door and went inside.

By the time he was back in his car, her living room lights had come on, the soft glow warming the darkness as he started up the engine.

He reluctantly pulled away, heading back into Surfers while fervently wishing away the next twenty-four hours.

The sun was barely peering over the horizon as Emily laced up her joggers, did a quick stretch on her porch, then headed off down the beach.

Running was an uncomfortable, sweaty, muscle-aching affair. She hated it while she was in the middle of it, but she liked having done it. Liked that it kept her relatively healthy, that it was free and right on her doorstep. And with her headphones on, no one bothered her. She gave a few brief nods to the regulars, a smile for the Japanese tourists who'd never seen a Gold Coast beach before. And with the wild angry beat of Nirvana reverberating in her head, she could block everything out as she jogged south along pristine Currumbin Beach.

Her daily run took her through the half-filled Currumbin

Surf Club car park and Elephant Rock, then down past a bunch of sleek beachfront mansions, many of which Valhalla had been behind. Behind the grassy dunes she could see roofs, sometimes a window or two, or a glimpse of backyard as she pounded out each step on the hard, ocean-compacted sand.

An hour later, sweaty yet energized, she took her stairs two at a time, her legs throbbing with the effort.

Prior to the weekend, lots of things had been on the periphery. Now she was hyper-aware. Like instead of pulling her hair into its usual smooth bun, she looped it back into a soft ponytail. And instead of her usual lip-liner-and-balm that served as lipstick, she picked up a soft plum Revlon gloss AJ had bought for her birthday.

Two changes, two tiny things that seemed unimportant but made her feel a little more confident. And confidence meant control.

It was all about control.

It was unlikely anyone would notice, she reasoned as she walked into the office foyer. The barista at Bennetti's hadn't. Nor had the building's security. And certainly not the other workers as she crammed into the lift that sped them up to Valhalla's offices.

She had set her bag down, placed the coffee on her desk and turned on the computer before she noticed Zac's mobile phone and the sticky note on the keyboard.

"In a meeting," it read.

She placed the phone to one side, crumpled the note then opened her electronic scheduler, looking up as the mail clerk pushed open the door, smiled, then dropped a bundle of mail on her desk.

When Zac's phone beeped, indicating an incoming text, she glanced up from the keyboard.

A number not recognized in his list of contacts.

A new client? She quickly activated the touch screen and brought up the text.

"Did U get my picture last nite?"

She sat back in her chair, jiggling her leg in thought. Clients sent Zac "before" shots of their houses all the time. So why didn't he have this particular caller in his contacts? Come to think of it, *picture* was an odd word. Why not *photo*?

The phone beeped again and she nearly jumped out of her skin.

"This 1's better. Call me, K?"

When she clicked on the attachment, shock froze her fingers.

It was a very different Haylee—kissing for the camera, striking a sexy topless pose in a red G-string and garters.

Emily swiftly placed the phone on her desk, heart pounding. Her fingers twitched like she'd seared them on the stove, her breath jamming hard against her ribs.

Zac hadn't…? No, he wasn't like that. But…

He always gave his office number to the girlfriends, never his mobile. She slowly palmed the phone, then located the list of incoming calls and scrolled down. Haylee's number appeared between three and five times a day. During the weekend, she'd called him over a dozen times. If she'd sent texts, Zac must've deleted them.

Her hands were surprisingly steady as she placed the phone on her desk. Which meant there was only one rational explanation—Haylee was stalking Zac.

Work well and truly forgotten, she linked her fingers behind her head and tipped back to focus on the ceiling.

Think about it. You've met the woman. You know Zac. What else could it possibly be?

When Zac returned an hour later, she was mentally prepared.

"Any calls?" he asked with a smile as she handed him the mail and his phone.

"Cal called again."

His smile dimmed. "And Victor?"

"No. But Haylee texted your mobile."

He frowned. "What did she want?"

"It was a photo."

Her expression must've given her away because his eyes

darkened before he muttered something under his breath. "Sorry. I thought I'd dealt with it. Leave it with me." And he turned towards his office.

"She's stalking you."

He paused in the doorway then slowly turned back, shaking his head. "No. Haylee's just a little…"

"Crazy?"

"Attached," he amended with a short grin. "I let her down gently, but obviously she's taken that as an invitation to try harder."

Zac was never rude—it was her job to buy the breakup flowers, which he always sent with a personal note. Which was why, she suspected, so many of his exes just couldn't let go. Emily sighed. "Shall I get you a new mobile number?"

"Good idea." He nodded and tossed the phone. She caught it smoothly. "Are you ready to give the update on Point One?"

"Sure." She grabbed a file and rose.

She presented her concise report smoothly, ticking off most of the items on Zac's mental to-do list. Then she reminded him he had a conference call at two and asked about his lunch preferences, all while placing a steaming coffee mug by his elbow.

When he reached for it, he accidently bumped her hand.

She made a small sound, as if he'd shocked her. And when her eyes darted up to his, a throb of anticipation spread through his blood at the reluctant desire in those blue depths.

Then she glanced away. "Sorry."

He sucked in a breath, sharp and ragged. How much of an ass was he to have this gorgeous woman sorry for wanting him?

She nodded to the open door. "Megan from Accounts is here."

"New hairstyle?" he asked.

She scooped up the contents of his out tray and stepped back, clutching the papers to her chest. "Yes," she said.

"I like it."

She frowned, those glossy lips flattening. "That's not why I did it."

His grin called her a liar even as he remained silent.

She cleared her throat. "Shall I send Megan in?"

"Sure." Then he added, "I've got inspections this afternoon, but I'll be home around seven-thirty."

His statement hung in the silence, the subtext clear. Anticipation zinged his nerves as she glanced nervously to the door and the waiting Valhalla worker outside.

She gave him a short nod, then left.

Through his open door Zac caught the exchange—Megan commenting on Emily's new hairstyle, Emily thanking her—before Megan was standing in the doorway with a smile.

"Got a minute to sign off on the Christmas bonuses?"

He motioned her in. It was time to get back to work.

Emily sat heavily at her desk, then quickly flicked open a folder. Nervousness punctuated each flip of the page, until one finally tore at the corner.

Her hands stilled. Control. She breathed in deep, eyes closed, then let it out. *I am in control of what I do and say. It's just casual. You can walk away at any time.*

Instead of taking comfort in that mantra, it began to sound a lot like her mother's petulant whine.

Her eyes sprang open. Her schedule was still open on the computer, listing today's urgent tasks for Point One.

Right. She could either continue to moon over Zac, letting the anticipation of tonight cripple her day. Or she could get some work done.

What's it to be, Emily?

With her back straight, she picked up the phone and started dialing.

Nine

By firmly blocking out everything but work, Emily managed to get through the day with her sanity intact. It also helped that Zac had left around 2 p.m. and wouldn't return.

Apart from a few comments about her hair—all from women, she noted—and calls from both Cal and Victor, the day remained busy but uneventful. At seven she turned off her computer and locked up the office, deliberately leaving it too late to change her mind and go home.

At seven-fifteen she parked around the corner from Zac's street, killed the engine and sat in the eerie silence. As his assistant, she had full access to his elegant beachside house and his security codes. Yet she'd never had to use them for anything other than work purposes.

This was her point of no return. If she did this—

No. AJ would kick your butt for second-guessing yourself like this.

Her fingers tapped on the steering wheel as the sun gradually lengthened the shadows.

It was time.

Just as she placed a hand on the door, headlights suddenly blinded her through the rearview mirror. She hesitated, and a second later a sleek dark car drove slowly by.

Emily watched the sporty coupe crawl down Zac's street, past his house, then suddenly accelerate, leaving the distinctive scent of diesel fumes in its wake.

She shook her head then took a deep breath. Then she grabbed her handbag and scrambled from the car.

If Zac could've done a hundred and twenty down the packed Pacific Highway he would've. *Too slow, too slow,* his heart seemed to thump as the traffic sluggishly chugged along, only to stop again at the lights.

Gray clouds gathered overhead, heavy with impending rain. The steering wheel complained beneath his grip. He wanted her in his arms right now. Wanted to feel her mouth on his, her warm breath, her yielding skin.

Wanted her legs wrapped around him.

That mouthwatering thought had dominated his last few hours. He'd come that close to canceling his last meeting because of it.

Now he glared at the time—seven-forty—and softly cursed. "Come on, come ooooon…. Finally!"

Within five minutes he was home, the movement-sensitive porch light flicking on as the garage door slid up and the first fat drops of rain began to fall.

He grabbed the packages on the front seat, locked up and went through the inner door, tossing his keys on the entrance table as he strode down the hall.

He paused in the living area and placed the takeaway bag on the table.

"Emily?"

His voice echoed through the spacious silence, disappearing into the lengthening darkness.

"Yes?"

He turned. Her back was to his huge ocean-view window, the

steely clouds, turbulent sea and gently falling rain providing a dramatic backdrop to her shadowy figure.

"You've been shopping?" she asked as he flicked on a lamp.

"Food." He noted the firm grip on her handbag, held like a shield in front of her. With one finger he lifted the other package by the thin handles. "And these are for you."

She frowned. "You didn't have to buy me—"

"I wanted to. There's a difference."

"Zac…"

"Just try them on. If you don't like them, I'll take 'em back. Please," he added with a smile.

She blinked and her fingers tightened around her bag handles, eliciting a leathery squeak of protest. Then she sighed. "All right." She took his offering, carefully avoiding any contact.

"Go on up," he said, nodding to the iron-and-polished-mahogany stairs. "I'll bring up the food and drinks."

Emily took the stairs slowly, highly aware of Zac's gaze following her ascent.

She paused at the top, the small entrance stretching out into what was obviously Zac's loft bedroom. She barely registered the dark furniture, the photos adorning the walls, the beautiful bay window revealing another perfect view of the Pacific Ocean. Her heart was pounding way too hard to notice anything except the rumpled bed jutting from the wall.

It was massive, covered in a wine-colored spread with mossy-green piping, black pillows tossed casually against the simple iron headboard. The covers had been dragged from one side, which told her two things. One, he didn't have a housekeeper. And two, he slept on the left.

Zac's bed. Where he slept. Where he and other women…

No. She turned away, coming face-to-face with her reflection in the full-length mirror. This was *her,* right here, right now. Zac was a good guy. Sure, he loved women—a *lot* of women—but he treated them with respect. He didn't cheat or lie to get them into bed.

Her head reeled as she dropped her handbag on the floor, then slowly placed the designer-boutique shopping bag on the bed.

With trembling fingers she yanked her shirt free from her skirt, then plucked open the buttons until it hung loose on her shoulders. She'd packed a toothbrush, deodorant and condoms crammed in with a handful of bra and knicker sets, choosing anything remotely seductive while visions of Zac's gorgeous ex-girlfriends taunted her selection. But now, standing half-dressed in front of his unforgiving mirror, she hesitated.

He'd bought her a gift...most likely lingerie. Men were predictable like that.

She stared at her reflection. She'd picked out a red lacy bra this morning, but the thing had itched so badly she'd quickly swapped it for her favorite white cotton one with tiny blue flowers.

She pulled off her shirt, hands on her hips and studied the bra in the mirror. Clean, pretty. But still white cotton.

Swiftly she grabbed the shopping bag, frowning when she pulled out a simple white shoe box with Martinez Valero in blocked roman lettering.

Shoes. So...*not* lingerie?

She peeled the lid back, expecting something red, high and flashy—stripper shoes.

But the gorgeous strappy-sandal creation nestling in black velvet sent her feminine heart beating faster. With a gasp, she reached in and reverently pulled out one shoe.

It wasn't the tiny rhinestone-encrusted buckles that got her, nor the four-inch white-satin-covered heels. It was the fluttery arrangement of sheer silver organza petals that fell along the white leather T-strap from ankle to toe.

"Oh, my—" They were gorgeous. Quickly she toed off her black office shoes, then reverently slipped on Zac's gift.

After buckling the straps, she straightened.

Her breath caught at the sight. Wow. By some miracle her legs looked longer. She hiked up her gray skirt to mid-thigh then turned side-on. Yep. Legs definitely longer. And skinnier.

"Magical shoes," she breathed, staring at her wide-eyed reflection until her eyes came to rest on her bra.

She quickly fished out that morning's reject from her bag, swiftly got it on, then stepped back, surveying herself with a critical eye.

It was too small. The cups barely held in all that boob. She tugged, then dug her hand in, repositioning her breasts. Nope. Still about to pop out. With a resigned sigh, she focused on her hair, pulling out the ponytail, then tipping her head down to fluff it up.

The sight that greeted Zac as he padded soundlessly up the stairs stopped him in his tracks.

Emily, her butt in the air, shaking out her hair, skirt hiked up to reveal shapely muscular thighs, curvy knees and a pair of strong calves. Deceptively long legs that complemented the shoes perfectly.

But then she straightened and placed her hands on her hips, and he nearly dropped the wine.

A smooth torso, hands on her flaring hips, emphasizing an hourglass waist…and then, the most magnificent pair of breasts he'd ever seen. The lush mounds were encased in a fire-red bra, the cups sweeping so low they barely concealed her nipples.

His breath came out in a strangled gurgle and Emily whirled, wide-eyed.

As he stared, a flush spread slowly across her cheeks, hands fluttering as if deciding whether to cover up or not. Blood began to pound thickly, expectantly.

"Don't move."

She froze, fingers laced demurely in front while he took in his fill.

He ran his gaze unhurriedly down her lush body, paused on the shoes before coming back up to meet her eyes with a satisfied grin. She met his gaze, as if daring him to comment.

The only thing that gave her away were those fluttering lashes.

With slow deliberation he placed the takeaway bag and bottle of wine on his armoire. "Do you like the shoes?"

She moved, her weight transferring onto her back foot. "I

do," she got out after clearing her throat. "They're absolutely beautiful."

So are you, he wanted to add, but sensed that such an obvious compliment would only make her more nervous. Instead he poured the wine and offered her a glass.

Trepidation slowed her approach. It amused him to see his normally unflappable assistant so wary, so out of her depth. Dressed in a skirt, a bra and a pair of high heels.

It also flared something deeply male inside, firing his blood and quickening his breath.

She was all his for the night.

Oblivious to his heated thoughts, she took the glass, murmured her thanks, then took a sip. But when he reached out to run a finger over the curve of her bare forearm, she jerked back.

"Sorry," she muttered, first wiping the wine from her hand, then dragging a finger up the glass to catch the rest.

"You missed a bit."

"Where?"

"Here." With a firm hand he pulled her to him, leaned down and gently licked the drops from her bottom lip.

Her breath strangled out, her eyes fluttering closed.

Zac grinned. He took a sip of his wine before placing both glasses down and going in for another kiss.

Warmed from Zac's mouth, the semisweet liquid slipped past Emily's lips and she groaned, swallowing.

His hands on her arms firmly pinned her as he deepened the kiss, spiked with the bite of alcohol and flamed by need. Her breasts began to throb, pushed up against his chest, and she let out another groan when he wedged one hard thigh between her legs.

So hot. So, so hot.

Through the haze of desire, she felt him nudging her backward, and suddenly her legs met resistance. The bed.

They both went down, his grip tempering their fall, lips still tasting, teasing. The satin cover gave her goose bumps until Zac swept his hands over her stomach—her most sensitive spot—and she shivered in earnest.

At his deep chuckle, she forced her eyes open.

He was above her, that lock of too-long hair flopping forward, giving him a rakish edge. She couldn't make out his eyes in the shadows, but as his palm slid firmly up her belly, the slant of his mouth revealed the utter seriousness of his intent.

After months spent lusting after *the* Zac Prescott, he was finally here, in bed and touching her. This amazing, gorgeous man wanted *her*.

Then his hand cupped one breast, his thumb finding her hardened nipple, and all thought fled. The half-curve of his smile twisted the hard knot of desire inside her.

With slow deliberation, he peeled down one bra cup and her puckered nipple sprang free. His mouth swiftly covered it, the damp heat a mixture of joyous delight and shocking intimacy.

When his teeth gently scraped the sensitive flesh she gasped, her back arching, longing spreading deep into her belly, then creeping lower, fanning the blaze of arousal.

He nudged her back up on the bed, settled himself between her legs, then proceeded to lavish undivided attention on her breasts. He stroked the swelling curves, then teased the nipples into hard nubs with first his fingers, then his mouth. A myriad of sensations burst like small zaps of electricity over her skin, forcing her breath into a ragged gasp.

"Zac. Please…"

"What?" His grin was too innocent as his mouth closed over her breast. And his tongue…oh, lordy, his tongue danced a wicked rhythm over her painfully engorged nipple.

"Can…you…ahhh…"

"Keep going?" His thumb stroked her other nipple and all she could do was squeeze her eyes shut, arch back and let the sensations ride her. "Stop?"

"Yes…no… It's…" Her breath strangled out as he licked the hard nub, then gently blew on it. *Too wonderful. Too amazing. Too…*

"Too much," she managed to gasp.

"Hmmmm." When he pulled back, her eyes sprang open. With infinite concentration, he slid his hand down, over her belly, skimming the indentation of her belly button, to finally stop at her waist where her skirt had bunched.

Panic spurted as he rocked her hips, gently easing off her skirt. She hadn't had time to change into anything remotely seductive, but as he peeled off her skirt to reveal white cotton bikini knickers, she needn't have worried. His eyes were glued to her face, watching her expression, her reaction.

Like the one she obviously made when he cupped the most intimate part of her and a wave of heat roared over her skin.

He grinned again. "Too much?"

Without waiting for an answer, he ran a knuckle over the elastic waistband before gently sliding inside, his ragged groan as he tangled in her curls a mix of delight and need, mirroring hers.

The urgency in his bruising kiss was unmistakable, his lips, his tongue making her drunk with desire. She couldn't resist when he nudged her legs farther apart, his skillful fingers easing firmly inside her with a purely possessive growl that rocketed through her blood. She was so very aroused, so very wet for him. And he knew it.

When Emily's tongue tangled gently with his, it nearly sent Zac over the edge. Her teasing hot mouth, those luscious breasts pressing into him, combined with the slick warmth enveloping his fingers. He couldn't wait any longer.

With a groan he wrenched away, feet hitting the floor as he ripped off his shirt, then fumbled with his belt and zipper.

He pulled down pants and boxers, cursed as they got tangled in his shoes and socks, then finally kicked them into a corner of the bedroom with a grunt of frustration.

Emily's soft laugh dragged his attention back to the bed, but as soon as they locked gazes, amusement fled.

Those suits had a lot to answer for, hiding such a superb body beneath their severely cut angles. Perfectly rounded breasts that filled a man's hands. A curvy body with taut velvet skin. And a pair of strong muscular legs that would wrap firmly around a man's waist as he drove deep inside, again and again.

Swiftly he reached for the bedside table, pulled out a row of condoms and ripped one open.

He rejoined her on the bed, hooking his thumbs in her knickers and yanking them down, grinning as she gasped.

Desperate need bubbled up, quickening his movements as he nudged her legs apart with his knee, then took his position. And then, with a dizzying breath, he drove deep into her heat.

She gasped again, but this one felt as if it'd been wrenched from her very soul. Her back arched, head back, neck exposed and vulnerable.

He grasped her face in both hands and kissed her, urgent and hot, his blood throbbing, filling her up as he paused, fighting for dominance. Then she mewled beneath his lips, her hips bucking gently, urging him to continue.

With teeth clenched, he began to move.

Exquisite sensation. Hot friction. His breath raced, his heart pounding so hard he thought it'd explode through his chest. He thrust deep and was rewarded by Emily's hiss of pleasure, her whisper of delight ramping up his lust to breaking point. She moved with him, meeting him all the way, her hands on his hips, her ragged breath in his ear. When he gripped her butt, angled her up and plunged deeper, she cried out, her teeth sinking into his shoulder.

Just when he thought he couldn't get any hotter.

Her tiny bite stung, his skin slick with sweat and their loving. Her hips tilted up to him, her legs wrapped around his waist.

"Zac…"

She was staring right at him, her cheeks flushed, that lush mouth open in an expression of pure eroticism. "I'm…it's…"

"Hold on," he murmured against her lips as he increased his pace. She did as he asked, her legs tightening around him as she buried her face in his shoulder.

From deep inside he could feel her muscles contract, the threads of orgasm building. With a groan he went in for another kiss, unashamedly stealing her sounds of pleasure with his mouth, pulling them inside, then breathing them out.

Then it happened. With a thick cry she threw back her head,

her breath ragged and harsh. Deep inside her muscles squeezed, and in a sudden rush of incredible pleasure, he couldn't hold on any longer. With his fingers digging into her flesh, he finally let go, the scalding lust engulfing him on one almighty wave as he clawed his way through the hot depths.

The orgasm racked Emily's body with almost unbearable force. He filled every dark corner with pleasure, and her entire body shook from the force of it.

Elation bubbled from her throat as her body shuddered. She'd never been this close to this kind of…bliss. Yes, that's what it was. She felt completely alive and totally, completely spent.

"Wow." She didn't realize she'd said it aloud until Zac pulled back onto his elbows and met her eyes with a satisfied grin.

"Thank you." He gently swept her damp hair back from her forehead.

They were plastered together from the chest down, still intimately connected. Inside, she could still feel the deep erotic pulse of him, his heartbeat echoing hers. Yet his simple act of stroking her hair had her whole body in a flush, her skin tingling, wanting more.

She'd been without intimacy for way too long. And now she was overloading on it.

As if sensing her change, Zac slowly rolled from her, back onto the pillows, hands resting lightly on his forehead. And a few minutes later, with the musky scent of lovemaking still lingering, she finally heard his slow, deep rhythmic breathing.

She was glad he was asleep. It made escape easier.

Cautiously she eased from the warm bed, groped around the floor for agonizing seconds until she found her clothes, then quickly dressed, all the while with one eye on Zac.

It would be so very easy to crawl back between those sheets, back into his arms. Her body ached in a dozen intimate places, a satisfied, languid ache that eventually made up her mind.

No sleepovers. No weekends. No personal talk.

She'd made the rules, now it was up to her to follow them.

With bags in hand she crept down the stairs, across the cool living room and out the front door without looking back.

Ten

You could learn a lot about a woman by the way her hands moved when she talked. Some waved them animatedly, some used touch either subconsciously or with deliberate effect. And some liked to keep their own personal space. Emily, Zac realized, was one of the latter. She made a point of avoiding any physical contact. No brush of the fingers when exchanging files. No accidental arm contact in the elevator or corridor.

At first he thought it was her steely determination to keep that line drawn, but she retained the personal boundary even when they were alone in his office.

He stared at his closed door, then down at the remnants of his devoured lunch burger before shoving it all in the trash.

It shouldn't matter. It didn't matter. Her response was a pointed reminder of his position—him boss, her employee. Yet last night they'd been more. With him buried deep in her wet warmth, her legs wrapped around his waist as they rocked in that age-old rhythm.

Yeah, it had been much, much more.

With a soft curse, he ripped his mind back to the present. A hard-on at work was the last thing he needed, not when he had to deal with a hundred other things—like the upcoming Point One event. And then there was Cal, Victor and the whole VP Tech debacle.

He shoved back his chair and stalked to the door, yanking it open.

"Reschedule my one o'clock," he said, knowing his voice came out too harsh. "I'm going out."

Emily nodded and picked up the phone. "Will you be back for your three-thirty?"

No questions, just acceptance. Her composure rankled, her once-valued hyper-efficiency now just another thing that drove him crazy.

"Yes."

He couldn't escape the building quickly enough, the sudden desire to get behind the wheel and drive urging him on.

So he did. He drove north, up the Gold Coast Highway, then turned right onto Waterways Drive and followed the signs to Seaworld. He passed Palazzo Versace, the Sheraton Mirage, the various takeaways.

On the way he made a few calls and set up more meetings. He succeeded in not thinking about Emily or last night until he passed Seaworld itself, until the road became narrower, the surrounding vegetation thicker.

The western arm of Gold Coast Spit appeared on his left, the sandy peninsula and watery inlet filled with yachts and recreational fishermen. The road continued, through the trees that formed part of Main Beach Park, until the Spit car park appeared.

He pulled in, gravel crunching beneath the tires, and cut off the engine. The classic AC/DC song abruptly ceased, giving way to the familiar sound of pounding waves through the trees and sand dunes ahead.

Easing from the car, he breathed deep, last night's rain salty and wild on the air. He loved this spot, even more than the small strip of private beach that flanked his house.

He grabbed a bag from the boot and pulled out a wetsuit before heading toward the small board-rental shed. Ten minutes later he was jogging down to the beach toward the flags, a surfboard under his arm.

An hour passed before he finally called it a day, collapsing on the warm sand to let the sun dry him off.

Depending on which direction you faced, you could see the high-rises of Southport, the wilds of South Stradbroke Island or straight out into the vast Pacific Ocean. He'd been surfing here for years, had spotted whales, been caught in powerful storms that were a stark reminder of the power of nature and fragility of life.

How could he keep this thing with him and Emily out of the office when all he wanted to do was rip off her clothes? Hell, even in her usual office getup and those awful clunky shoes, he *still* wanted her. Yet if he wanted to keep her in his bed, he'd have to keep their after-hours affair a secret.

He hated secrets. Secrets turned people into liars, and he liked lies about as much as secrets.

With a grunt, he finally stood, his toes digging into the grainy sand as he made his way back to the car.

The soft swoosh of the glass door drew Emily's eyes up from her computer screen. Zac strode in, looking tanned and windswept. When he dragged a hand through his hair, leaving peaks in its wake, her heart did a little flip.

"Your father called."

His brow dipped as he paused, hands going to his hips. "Right. Thanks."

"You didn't give him your mobile number?"

"No."

Emily paused, feeling as if she were missing something. "He says you're not returning his calls."

"I know." Zac continued toward his office, his mouth grim, shoulders rigid. She grabbed up some papers and followed him in.

He stood behind the huge desk, his yellow smiley stress ball in one fist as he gazed out onto Broadbeach Mall.

Squeeze, release. Squeeze, release. They'd all had a laugh when one of his more difficult clients had given him that by way of apology. Everyone knew—especially the client—that Zac didn't stress.

Squeeze, release. Squeeze, release. His profile was the very definition of contained frustration combined with deep thought.

"Do you want me to give him a message next time he calls?"

Startled, he turned to her. "No." He tossed the stress ball back onto his desk. "I'll call him."

"But you don't want to."

His silent frown told her she was right, even though he'd rather she not be.

"Zac, whatever happened between you and your father—"

"—is not something I want to talk about."

The shutters slammed down so abruptly that Emily took a step back. With warm cheeks, she said, "I understand that. But when I was ten, my sister ran out, and I spent thirteen years not knowing if she was dead or alive. When she finally found me, do you think I still cared about all those stupid arguments we'd had years before?"

His eyes widened in brief surprise, weakening the frown.

What are you doing? Shut up, shut up, shut— "People make decisions based on emotion, not what's logical," she said quickly. "That's how they make mistakes. And if Victor's trying to make an effort you should at least hear him out."

She snapped her mouth shut, suddenly appalled. Then without another word, she spun and headed out the door.

Emily slapped her notepad on her desk before taking a deep breath. She didn't know what was worse, revealing that small nugget from her past or Zac acting as if last night had been a complete fabrication of her overactive imagination.

Well, she couldn't take those words back now. But was it enough to sway him?

With a sigh, she sat heavily in her chair. Yes, he had to

maintain their professional boss-employee front to throw off any suspicion. But did it have to feel so real?

She clicked through her e-mails absently.

She'd finally managed to deflect Zac's familiar non sequiturs that made her totally aware of herself as a woman, and then he went and did a one-eighty. After last night, she'd been prepared to fend off any intimate comments, to remind him they were at work and should act appropriately. But that had never materialized.

What had happened to the flirty, good-humored Zac of before, the guy she'd been able to keep separate from her personal life?

The vibe was all wrong. He was painfully polite. No, more like… She chewed the end of the pen thoughtfully. Disinterested.

Because she'd finally succumbed to his charms, slept with him, and now the chase was over, he wanted to move on?

"Emily? Do you have a minute?"

She didn't have to turn to know he stood at the door: his eyes burned a hole in her back. Instinctively, she straightened, clicking off her screen saver to reveal the Point One schedule.

"Actually, I'm in the middle of—"

"This is important."

She stilled, hand on the mouse, then sighed in resignation. *Here it comes.*

He remained standing as she walked in, then closed the door softly behind her. Her senses barely had time to register his familiar aftershave, that warm radiating body heat as he walked past her to take a seat behind his desk.

She sat, crossed her legs and waited.

He stared at her in silence. And to her credit, she stared right back.

"I don't want this to be awkward between us," he finally said.

"Awkward?"

"Us working together, given our…arrangement."

"I don't feel awkward." She gave him her best "restrained and composed" look. "Do you?"

"No."

"Because if you want out, I'll understand."

"Do *you* want out?" His eyes narrowed.

"I asked first."

A wry grin creased Zac's face. "What are we, in eighth grade?" Then more seriously, he added, "I don't want out."

Well, so much for your theory. "Well, neither do I." Her chin went up as she met his eyes, firmly ignoring the little cheer her body made.

"Good."

"Fine."

They both paused, Zac scrutinizing her with the same intensity he reserved for a particularly difficult problem.

"Do you think I'm over my head with the Point One event?" she suddenly blurted out.

He leaned back in his chair. "What do you think?"

"It's a challenge."

"Which is what you wanted."

"Yes."

"What you've done so far is good, Emily. And we're a team here—use the staff to get whatever you need done. And keep me posted." His smile was brief. "And while we're in the office, it will always be about work. This is a Valhalla project," he added. "I know it's yours, but it's also mine. We both make this work and we both benefit."

With a nod, Emily rose to leave.

"Emily."

She paused, glancing back at him.

"Are you free tonight?"

And just like that, last night came flooding back, playing away in her mind like an erotic movie taken off pause. Despite herself, she felt excitement tingle her skin.

"Yes."

His mouth curved and suddenly he seemed like Zac again. "Then I'll see you after eight."

"Sure." She left his office way more discomforted than she'd gone in.

Eleven

The precedent was set for the next two weeks. Zac remained cool and professional during office hours. He always asked if she was free that night. Emily always said yes, except for the weekends. Those days were hers alone.

At night Zac spent hours exploring her body, learning what turned her on, what made her cry out in passion or sigh with delight. He focused on her pleasure, skillfully bringing her to the brink of bliss night after night, then taking them both over the edge. And in the early hours of the morning, Emily crept from his bed and returned to her own, exhausted. She made sure she always got to work on time, despite her growing need for sleep and the ever-present ache between her legs.

And she never let anything remotely personal slip again.

"Any plans for Saturday night?" Zac casually asked when their Friday afternoon meeting had broken up.

"Work. And I might get in a book and a bath."

She ignored the glint in his eye, then the small frown when she reiterated her plans after they were alone in his office.

Yet on Sunday, after she'd slept, read and bathed herself into boredom, she dressed in a pair of gray track pants and an old baby-doll T-shirt and opened up her laptop.

As she put the finishing touches on the launch for Point One and finally pressed "save," a deep sense of satisfaction engulfed her. *This* is what she should've been doing every weeknight instead of indulging in the joys of mutual sexual pleasure. This was her career, her life. Do this well and there was no telling the kind of contacts she'd make when it came time to set up her business.

Her hands stilled over the keys.

She hadn't thought about that in…days. Weeks, even. She hadn't heard back from the university to confirm her second-term enrollment. And, she realized with shock, she hadn't gone chasing it, either. Carnal pleasure had taken priority, pushing her goals from the limelight. And Point One had firmly kept them in the darkness.

You got caught up in the sex.

She leaned back into the sofa, grabbed a throw pillow and cradled it in her lap.

And the intimacy. And actually feeling desirable and wanted without there being an ulterior motive. For Jimmy she'd been a meal ticket. For her ex-boss, a conquest. And the others had come with their own unique baggage. Not one guy had wanted her for *her*.

Sure, she may have been clueless when it came to boyfriends, but she'd made sure to bank every single one of her paychecks. She'd always understood the power and freedom money represented.

So what would happen after Point One launched, when her debt to Zac was paid, when she got into her course?

You'll go forward with your life. Moving on, no looking back. Just like Zac always moved on, with the next eager female.

Thoughts of him with another woman sharing his bed, doing the things they'd done, suddenly made her want to gag.

She rose, threw the pillow across the room and headed for the kitchen. Grabbing the half bottle of mineral water from the fridge, she poured it into a wineglass and gulped it. The bubbles fizzed on the way down, followed by a sudden desperate need for normalcy. Her apartment, AJ, her job. They were normal, they were stable. Not this…this…crippling self-doubt.

Yet her mind was still buzzing hours later, her dreams peppered with gorgeous women vying for Zac's attention, her mother's cold, lined face and an empty room where the Point One launch party should have been.

She woke before dawn, a strange feeling pooling in the pit of her belly. After checking all the faucets, the locked front door and windows, then the lights, she texted AJ, then crawled back into bed.

No good.

It wasn't about her mother: she had no idea if Charlene was still alive, let alone where.

The Point One project?

She ran over the details in her head. No. Everything was on track, the prospectus was out, buyers were calling their sales division and the invites for the launch were going out today.

Yet something wasn't right. She rolled over onto her tummy, grabbed her glasses, cracked open the venetian blinds behind the headboard and squinted out into the predawn light.

Number seven's German shepherd was barking, as usual. Number ten had left her porch light on again. But other than that, nothing.

It had to be Zac—or more specifically, the way she felt about Zac. She knew what his life was like, the kinds of women he attracted. Who wouldn't feel inferior compared to the likes of Haylee Kerans and Trish Sattler?

With a sigh, she dragged herself up and pulled on her jogging gear.

The sun rose halfway into her run, the only other beach activity three lone fishermen and some surfers suiting up in the parking lot.

The office was empty when she got in. Zac had a site inspection that morning. A common occurrence, yet discontent dogged her routine.

AJ finally returned her text and Emily ticked it off her mental list, turning on the computer, then syncing up with Zac's schedule as she grabbed her coffee. The distinctive aroma made her mouth water, but before she could take a mouthful, the office door opened.

"Hey, Em." Zac's chief accountant, Megan Hwong, always reminded Emily of actress Lucy Liu—exotic, poised and confident. "Here's those budget figures you wanted." She put a file on the desk, then perched her Armani-clad hip on the corner with a smile.

An expectant, knowing smile.

Emily blinked. "What's up?"

Megan tipped her shiny black-bobbed head. "Just wanted to see something."

"What?"

"You."

"Why?"

Megan leaned in with a grin. "To see if last week was a fluke."

All sorts of scenarios sped through her mind. "Sorry?"

With an elegant hand, Megan gestured at Emily. "A nice hairstyle, a little lippy. You've even ditched those awful jackets," she added, eying Emily's sweater-and-skirt ensemble. "We reckon there's a man involved."

"What? No!"

"Wow." Megan pulled back with a grin. "Denial, much?"

Emily took a deep breath then said more calmly, "There's no man—it's getting warmer and I felt like a change and…and who's we?"

"Oh, Kerri and Bob," she supplied, naming the Accounts team. "Nice necklace, by the way."

Emily glanced down at the dozen long silvery strands of beads tied into a low knot. "Thanks. A late birthday present to myself."

"See? With an eye like that, I knew there was a fashion diva inside, dying to get out!" Megan grinned. "You should come shopping with the girls on Saturday."

Surprise stilled her for one second before she realized Megan was serious. "This Saturday?"

"Sure. Early Christmas shopping." She mock eye-rolled with a smile as she stood. "I'll e-mail you, okay?"

"Okay."

As the door clicked shut, silence engulfed the large office. After all her gentle refusals to social invites, all her deliberate avoidance of personal relationships in the workplace, it took just one, an invitation to shop with one of the most stylish women in Valhalla, to spark something inside, the part of her that longed to indulge in being a woman again.

She stared at the glass door as doubt surged. Was it coincidence that the offer came on the heels of Megan's casual reference to a man?

Emily gathered up some papers, walked into Zac's office, then shut the door, leaning up against the solid wood as her mind leaped to a thousand different conclusions, all of them bad.

Finally she straightened and went over to Zac's desk. No. Megan wasn't into subterfuge, unlike some. She'd asked, Emily had answered. Case closed.

Her reflection stared back from the huge tinted windows. She saw a twenty-six-year-old blonde in standard office wear—a long black skirt, sensible shoes, panty hose, short-sleeved baby-blue sweater.

She placed the papers in Zac's tray, then stepped in for a closer look. The sweater was cashmere, the V-neck showing off her collarbone, the long dangly beads drawing the eye down. She turned to the side, then front on. The material clung over her hips, a thin black belt defining her waist. Short capped sleeves showed off toned arms. With a frown she smoothed the sweater down over her belly, then her bottom.

Have I lost weight? Have I—

The door suddenly opened and she whirled, cheeks flushed. Zac.

Their gazes met and held for a heartbeat, then two. Despite herself, she felt her breath hitch as memories crammed her head.

Soft touches. Demanding kisses. Hot skin, sweaty with passion...

She felt the instantaneous heat pool low, then fan upward as he stood there, his eyes grazing her body with a slow smile.

"That color suits you," he finally said.

"Thank you."

"But I hate the shoes."

Her chin went up, a sharp reply at the ready, but his grin somehow negated her irritation.

"Maybe that's why I wear them."

One dark eyebrow lifted. "First you make a point of saying your new hairstyle is *not* to impress me, and now you're wearing shoes you know I hate?"

When he walked steadily toward her, she forced herself to remain exactly where she was. *Good, that's good. Don't show him you're affected, or how that boyish grin makes him way too irresistible.*

He stopped, so close she could see tiny flecks of gold in his olive eyes, the creases in his bottom lip as he continued to grin at her. And there was his scent, a mixture of shaving cream and some subtle aftershave that always seemed to scramble her senses.

"How was your weekend?" he asked softly. When his gaze dropped to her lips and remained there, she gave an inward curse.

Damn you, Max Factor, and your To-Be-Kissed Pink gloss.

"Fine."

"Good." It didn't sound as though he was pleased, but she let that go.

"What happened to your meeting?" she asked, determined to uphold that professional veneer.

"Rescheduled." He reached out and plucked something from her sweater sleeve, his fingers briefly brushing her arm before he withdrew. "I just sent you a text."

She nodded, letting silence command the room.

He leaned in and to her dismay, she jumped, her hip bumping into the desk.

He smiled, his mouth close to her ear, his cheek not quite touching hers but radiating warmth all the same. "Did you need something?"

Can I make a list? "Ahh. No."

"You sure?"

His breath brushed over her lobe, sending scalding heat through her veins. And when his tongue followed, she bit her lip to stop the groan from escaping.

"You don't need this?"

His mouth nibbled at the spot where her ear met her neck, then slid down her jaw.

"No…" she managed to croak out, frantically trying to ignore her body screaming *yes!* through every nerve.

"Or this?" He trailed one finger over her collarbone, then slowly into the valley between her breasts, carefully watching for her reaction.

"Zac, you can't."

His grin was full of wicked knowledge. "I can. I have."

"We're in your office," she got out as his finger edged around her bra cup, eventually finding her hard nipple. His other hand came around to the desk and settled by her hip, pinning her there, possessive yet allowing escape if she so chose.

His heat, his breath, the need in his eyes threatened to overwhelm her thoughts.

His finger rhythmically stroked her nipple, producing little shudders that she struggled to quash. His mouth—that wondrous, skillful mouth—curved, teasing her into acquiescence with one smile. And the intense heat from his body engulfed her, spinning her thoughts, negating her halfhearted protest.

She swallowed as arousal pulsed beneath her skin. No matter how hard she tried to keep their arrangement after-hours, her body betrayed her every time. Since Friday night she'd been alone, three nights that suddenly felt like three months, and now she craved him like some illegal drug.

Suddenly she didn't care that they were in his office or that she'd been the one who'd demanded secrecy. All she wanted was for him to kiss her, take off her clothes and make love to her in that plush leather office chair.

Her phone shattered the moment, the two-time ring muffled through the door before it went to voice mail.

With a gasp she twisted, away from his drugging heat, away from her weakness.

She glared at him as she quickly adjusted her glasses then smoothed down her sweater. "I told you, Zac—not in your office. What would've happened if someone had walked in?"

"Then they would've won big on the office pools."

His shrug, such a casual dismissal of her concerns, sent indignation surging. "What?"

"I know everything that goes on in this company, Emily." He crossed his arms. "The current odds of you being my next conquest are about three hundred to one."

"Three…"

As she floundered with embarrassment, his smile dropped. "Look, don't let it worry you. No one cares—"

"*I* care."

"Why?" He crossed his arms. "Why does it bother you so much what other people think?"

The familiar hot pulse of shame engulfed Emily as he stood silent, awaiting her reply. Yet she had none to give him, none that would keep him at the distance she so desperately needed him to be.

"Because I refuse to be judged on anything other than my work. And now I have to get back to it." And she was out the door.

If he hadn't had back-to-back meetings, Zac would've gotten to the bottom of whatever was really bugging Emily. As it was, he spent most of the day thinking about the deeper reason she'd been so upset and how he was going to broach the subject again.

They'd actually started becoming friends. No, not friends. The things he wanted to do to her were not friendly at all—they were downright dirty. For three long, frustrating nights he'd spent way too much time thinking about her skin, her lips, her warm, accommodating body. After such a solid beating, his restraint had lapsed that morning and he'd been unable to keep his hands off her.

You're lucky she didn't call it off then and there.

When she'd texted back a simple "can't" to his request to meet that evening, his first thought was to drive over to her place and demand to know what was going on. Yet he knew that would force her away, and that was the last thing he wanted.

So he ate Thai takeaway at home alone, absently wondering what Emily would say to a proper meal in a proper restaurant. Somewhere public where he could show her off, with candlelight, music and dancing.

She'd shut you down and you know it. So stop complaining.

Dissatisfied, he finished his food, shoved the dishes in the washer, then picked up the phone.

Time to deal with VP Tech.

He hung up thirty minutes later, flush with—not exactly victory, but close enough. Cal had been working on Victor, and while the suggestion to float the company had died in the water, he'd been making headway with advertising the CEO position. They could utilize VP Tech's young, hungry executives and keep everything in-house. Progress, yes, but Victor still wanted Zac involved, a prospect Zac refused to even discuss. At the moment, Cal was their go-between, a situation Zac felt half guilty, half grateful for.

Desperate for physical exertion, he grabbed his gym bag and headed out, taking two hours to run, row and heave weights at Surfers' twenty-four-hour gym. Yet after he showered and changed, then got back into his car, his body still hummed with energy, his brain still fixated on VP Tech.

He needed to really lose himself, not just force his muscles into screaming agony. And he knew exactly what to do.

Twelve

Emily swung her front door open but instead of the pizza delivery guy, Zac stood there, his arm resting casually on her doorframe.

"Let's go out."

She blinked. "What?"

"Out. Somewhere dark, with loud music."

"I'm… I'm…" He stepped over the threshold and she instinctively moved aside. "Expecting a pizza," she ended lamely as he paused in her living room.

He turned to face her, hands on his hips, one eyebrow raised. "Wow. Really living the high life."

"I'm also working."

She crossed her arms, refusing to let his appraising dissection of her casual sweats and bare feet affect her.

"I've just been on the phone with Cal about VP Tech and now I need to let off some steam. I thought you might like to join me."

She swallowed. *Admit it. You're thrilled you're his first choice and he came all this way to ask you. You want to go.*

And, her doubt demons added, *he could always ask someone else if you turned him down.*

"What about the pizza?" she blurted out.

His mouth tweaked. "I'll wait for it while you go change."

"I'm not sure—"

He silenced her with a kiss, a deep, blood-pumping kiss that made her legs weak and her brain fuzzy. "Emily," he finally murmured, a scant inch away from her bruised mouth. "I'm sure. We'll go someplace no one will recognize us. Trust me."

What could she say to that?

They were at Heaven, one of Surfers' popular nightclubs famous for dance music, decently priced drinks and top-notch security, and despite the weeknight, the place was packed. True to Zac's word, it was a place where no one cared who you were and how much you earned. Emily glanced around the strobe-lighted dance floor. A place where you could relax without being watched or judged. Zac could've taken her to any of a dozen private clubs frequented by the super-rich and beautiful, yet he'd picked this one.

Was it for her benefit or his?

She didn't care. Because right now the familiar, sexy throb-throb beat began to seep into her skin, teasing, tempting, making her body ache with sudden longing.

Come dance, the music beckoned as the lights flashed and the crowded dance floor moved as one. She shifted from foot to foot, suddenly desperate to get out there, to let her hair down and just enjoy the music.

Then Zac locked eyes with hers and everything seemed to fade into watercolor at the edges. For one second, the short velvet skirt and glittery silver tank top she'd dug from her closet felt way too undressed. But when he grinned, offered his hand and said, "Let's dance, gorgeous," all her self-consciousness melted away.

Linking her fingers in his, he led her to the dance floor, the heavy bass warming her blood and tingling her skin.

Bodies were everywhere, dancing and laughing, and when

the current track suddenly morphed into a familiar Beyoncé hit, the crowd roared, then surged forward, sweeping them up into the vortex.

Zac found a space near the shadowed stage and pulled her close, mashing her body up against his from thigh to collar. Emily's body responded instantaneously.

"It's not that kind of dance," she murmured, sucking in air as his arms looped possessively around her waist.

"Don't care."

His breath fluttered against her neck, delicious and warm, and slowly they began to move.

Emily laid her cheek on his chest and squeezed her eyes shut, letting the music and heat wash over her. When she was with Zac, just like this, everything else seemed unimportant. It was like closing a door, a door that held her past, her problems and her doubts at bay.

He made her feel wanted. Needed. Like she was some powerful sexual goddess in control of her destiny.

His hands slid up her back, over the bumpy fabric of her tank, his fingers teasing the soft skin under the straps. And all the while, the crowd spun crazily around them, the music echoing her rising heart rate.

"Hey, Zac! I thought it was you! How are you?"

She felt him reluctantly pull away, and when she turned, a tall, gorgeous blonde stood beside them. Emily blinked, astonishment suddenly giving way to the burn of unwelcome jealousy as the woman dropped a brief kiss on his lips.

If her smile was too stiff when Zac introduced them, he didn't seem to notice. She nodded politely as fear and irritation solidified in her stomach, the snapshot of this stunning creature kissing Zac burning away in her mind as she overtly flirted with him.

When the woman finally left, Emily was ready to pull out those glossy blond hairs one by one.

"Who does she think she is?" she muttered under her breath as she glared into the crowd. She'd obviously seen the way she and Zac had been dancing, yet she'd kissed and flirted with abandon.

She glanced up to see Zac watching her intently.

"Josie works for Scandinavian Airlines," he offered. "I met her on a flight to Europe."

"Was she—" Emily bit her lip, refusing to voice that damning question. It made her sound needy. Childish. Jealous.

But Zac had her all figured out. He reached for her, dragging her back into his embrace. Her breath surged out as anticipation began to sluggishly chug through her veins.

"Was she a girlfriend? No." He paused to study her, his eyes way too perceptive even in the strobe-lighted darkness. "Why?"

She couldn't tell him. Couldn't say that she was burning with jealousy, that the mere attention from another female sparked ice-cold fear in her stomach.

"Your exes have no concept of boundaries," she said, then ended on a gasp as his palms slid boldly over her bottom.

"She wasn't my girlfriend. But you're right," he murmured, backing up and taking her with him until they hit the edge of the dance floor. "They don't."

The massive stage curtains fell like a dark cloud at their backs, the shadows swallowing them.

His lips found her neck. She shivered as his breath tripped over her sensitive flesh, his mouth shockingly hot as he began to sway in time to the sensual beat of a familiar chart topper.

The heavy bass swirled, the throbbing pulse filling her chest, her throat. She could feel it vibrate through every muscle, echoing in Zac's heartbeat as his chest pressed up against her.

"Maybe coming here was a bad idea," he whispered.

Her heart skipped. "Why?"

"Because of this." He moved and his hard arousal pressed into her stomach.

She groaned, and for a moment she wished she could remain like this, warm and protected. But then the lights flashed, illuminating the bar crowd for less than five seconds, before dropping them back into darkness. And in those seconds, Emily caught a figure in the throng, staring straight at them.

She stumbled but Zac steadied her. When she glanced back, Louie Mayer was gone.

The enjoyment of the night fled. She couldn't concentrate on the music, on Zac's warm body flush against hers, not now.

"Can we get out of here?" she said softly.

Zac's eyes darkened, then with a short nod, he took her hand and they began the slow process of plowing through the dancers.

Emily lay on Zac's soft sheets staring at the ceiling, knowing she had a dopey smile on her face. Who wouldn't grin like an idiot when she'd just been completely and thoroughly loved by Zac Prescott?

"You okay?" Zac murmured in the moonlit darkness.

"Fine." She turned to him, propping her elbow on the mattress, her head on her hand. "But your stairs are tough on the back. And I think I have a splinter in my butt."

His grin flashed, sending a bolt of heat through her blood. "So next time, you can be on top. In fact…"

He reached for her and rolled, and she went willingly. Her body still sang with their previous lovemaking, but that didn't stop her heart from picking up in anticipation.

They lay there wedged from chest to knee, Zac effortlessly cradling her weight. Gently, he brushed her hair back, tucking the long strands behind her ears, before tugging her down for a kiss. A soft, tender kiss that made her chest contract with a longing so deep, so sudden, that it made every bone dissolve with joy.

In that moment, she completely understood why all those women wouldn't take no for an answer. Zac Prescott was like a drug. Her body burned for his touch, his skilled hands, his sinful mouth. And when they weren't together, like this, he was all she could think about.

"What do you want me to do?" His breath was warm in her ear, his lips nibbling on her lobe. She stifled a groan and sat up, her brain thick with yearning.

Her heart did another little leap as she stared down at him. Her knees firmly bracketed his waist, her bottom wedged on his abdomen. This was real. He was real.

So why did she get the feeling it could all come crashing down in disaster?

"Emily?"

Zac reached out to grasp her waist. She was like some ancient goddess of fertility, with that womanly hourglass figure, the indented waist, the gentle belly curve. And those breasts…

He reached up and palmed them, each luscious swell of generous flesh heavy in his hands.

His groin began to stir again but he ignored it, instead taking the time to thumb those rosy-budded nipples, grinning when her breath hitched and her eyes began to close in dreamy pleasure.

"What do you want me to do?" he repeated thickly. As his thumbs continued their rhythmic stroking, she began to quiver.

"Just…just…"

"Yes?"

"I don't…"

She wiggled in frustration and he swallowed a groan. "Look at me."

His command brooked no refusal. She sighed, slowly opening her eyes. The dark arousal in those depths made every muscle constrict with lust.

"You're in charge, Emily. Tell me what you want me to do."

Just when he thought he couldn't be more turned on, her white teeth nibbled on her bottom lip, the tiny pink tongue briefly flashing out to lick the spot.

A new round of flames scorched across his skin, sending his heart rate sky high.

"I want…" The warm flush spread across her cheeks as she blinked. "I want you to kiss me. All over."

With guttural triumph deep in his throat, he flipped her, pinning her to the mattress. He slid a knee between her legs, then dragged in a breath at the damp heat pooling there.

"You're wet."

She tipped back her head and closed her eyes with a mutter

of assent, and he grinned. Shocking her gave him no small amount of pleasure. Seeing her flush, watching those lashes flutter nervously, all told him he affected her, that she wasn't as indifferent as she pretended to be when they were in the office.

Oh yeah, it pleased him greatly.

He cupped her mound, the curls tickling his hand, and she dragged in a breath.

"I'm going to kiss you, Emily."

Another murmur, another sigh.

"First, your mouth." He pinned her face with one hand, the other still resting possessively between her legs.

When Zac's lips came down on hers Emily couldn't hold back her sigh of delight. Of all the things she'd missed about being intimate, kissing topped the list. Yet every other kiss paled in the wake of Zac's. He started tender, almost gentle, but soon it deepened into something hot and breathless. When he pulled back she whimpered, no longer caring how it made her sound, just needing his lips on hers.

"Relax." His mouth went to her jaw, curving into a smile against her skin. "You wanted to be kissed all over, right?"

"Yes." Although she was quickly regretting her request, because his still hand between her legs had become an almost unbearable distraction.

"So let me kiss you."

For endless minutes he lavished attention on her neck, then her breasts, before slipping down to her belly button, his hot breath creating a shivering path across her skin.

She knew where he was headed. Every nerve screamed with anticipation. Yet when his mouth closed over the most intimate part of her, the sudden shock wrenched her off the bed with a gasp.

He murmured gently and repositioned himself, cupping her bottom firmly in his palms before applying himself to the task of pleasuring her.

She couldn't breathe. Couldn't think. Couldn't do anything except feel…his strong hands, his teasing hot tongue, his warm breath. Even his chin, dusted with stubble, intimately grazed across her swollen flesh, creating an almost unbearable friction.

She squeezed her eyes shut as the ripples of ecstasy began to build. And Zac kept right on going, his tongue swirling around her hardened bud, his mouth kissing, sucking, teasing her into incoherence.

The trembling began, first in her legs, then her body, then suddenly the orgasm crashed, wave upon wave of rapture forcing a whimper from her lips.

Behind her eyelids everything went a shimmering, iridescent black. Her body twitched like she'd been shot with a thousand volts, skin throbbing with awareness. Through the thickening euphoric haze, she realized Zac had returned to her, his mouth a shocking musky combination of her passion and his desire.

Her blood throbbed through her veins, echoing deep within as Zac smoothly eased inside her, joining them in the familiar lover's dance.

He groaned, bathing her in need, before he opened his eyes and that heat-laden gaze locked on hers.

It was the ultimate act of intimacy, him moving deep inside, making love to her while their eyes held. Zac saw her every expression, every tiny move, as he slid out, then with a wicked grin, firmly back in. He heard every gasp, every murmur. And soon he was ready to explode, nerves raw from her erotic gasps of pleasure. When he finally went over the edge, she followed a moment later, their cries of release echoing off the bedroom walls.

Emily tried to catch her breath, but Zac's weight pinned her down.

"Too heavy?" he murmured, his breath tickling her ear.

"A little."

He rolled, taking her with him so she was on top, half sprawled across his chest. Beneath her cheek she felt the strong pounding heartbeat, his crisp hair teasing her skin.

This. Right here. If everything collapsed into dust right now, she wouldn't care.

The minutes ticked by, the only movement when Zac reached down to cover their cooling bodies with the sheet.

"I heard back from admissions," she eventually said.

"You got into uni."

"Yes."

"That's good."

With a smile she slowly rolled off him to settle on her back. *So why do I feel so…calm?* "Better than good. It's…" She blinked, struggling to define the burning need she'd never had to quantify until now. "It means progress. A goal achieved. It's something I've wanted for a long time."

The silence settled around them, until Zac shifted and sheets rustled softly.

"Did you like living in Perth?" he said softly.

"Not really." She moved to her side to face him, tempering her curt reply with a small smile. "Nice city, great beaches. But I prefer Queensland."

The moonlight reflected his serious gaze. "What about your friends? Family?"

"What about them?"

He said nothing, until she finally let out a sigh.

"My mother's brother died and left me his place nearly three years ago. So I moved." She shifted her weight, drawing the sheet firmly around her. "My sister AJ lives in Robina. Everyone else is…gone."

He studied her in silence. There was something serious and honest in that look. It told her whatever she chose to reveal would remain between them. And more important, he wouldn't judge.

So instead of throwing up those familiar defenses she lay back, stared at the ceiling and answered him.

"When I was seventeen I started temping for an agency in Perth." It was easier to talk in the dark, where his all-seeing eyes couldn't drag out any more than she was willing to give. "It was good money and interesting work, but eventually I wanted something permanent. So I applied for an office manager's position at Hardy, Max & Taylor."

"The accountancy firm? That wasn't on your CV."

"No. I quit after six months."

"Why?"

She was a good liar, although not as good as AJ. To get through their childhood, to survive, lying had been a necessity for the Reynolds girls. But *needing to* and *wanting to* were two different things.

"One of the managing directors cornered me on the balcony at the Christmas party and tried to feel me up. Not only was I a 'hot piece with a great rack'—sexual harassment was alive and well in corporate Australia."

Zac made a small noise, a cross between a curse and a growl. When she turned, his profile squeezed her heart. He was angry—no, *furious*—and trying to rein it in.

"Did you report it?" he ground out.

"No." At his puckered brow, she sighed. "I was twenty-two. I had no money, no power to take on one of Australia's leading private companies. Someone would've leaked my complaint and then the TV stations would've been all over it. I didn't want that kind of publicity. And anyway, it wasn't such a big deal. He didn't actually *do* anything."

"That's bull and you know it."

Abruptly she sat up, dragging the sheet with her. "Don't make this into some big emotional speed bump, Zac. I kneed him in the groin, he threatened sexual misconduct, so I quit. End of story."

"So you're saying that didn't have any lasting effect?"

"What do you want me to say? It didn't stop me dating, although my choice in men was poor to say the least. It didn't stop me marrying Jimmy," she snorted self-deprecatingly. "It didn't stop me living my life."

"Right. A life that involves secret sex with your boss?"

Zac abruptly swung from the bed, the cold floorboards on his bare feet barely registering.

"You're angry."

His jaw tightened as he glanced back to her rigid figure. "Damn right I am."

"So…what? Are you saying you want to change our arrangement?"

"I'm saying," he snapped on the bedside light, then yanked on his boxers, then his pants with sharp jerky movements, "that once in a while it'd be nice if we went out somewhere. Together, in public, instead of sneaking around like our sex life is some big covert operation."

"What about tonight?"

He shoved his hands on his hips. "That hardly counted. I'm not ashamed of us—are you?"

Zac knew his words hit home the second her breath hissed out. Her pale face humbled him, tiny barbs of guilt thickening his throat.

"Look, Emily…"

"No, you don't have to say anything." She slid to the other end of the bed, taking the sheet with her. "I… I think I should go."

"You don't have to—"

"I do." She gathered up her clothes, adding, "it's late," as if that explained everything.

"Stay."

Her face froze in an expression he couldn't read.

"I can't." She made it to the foot of the stairs. "I'll see you at the office tomorrow."

Thirteen

It was as if last Monday night had happened in a parallel universe.

Every day that week Emily brought him lunch, organized his clients and performed exactly like the efficient assistant she was. No secret glances, no tensing up when he accidentally brushed her arm. Every time he opened his mouth, her cool blue eyes remained professional and distant.

She remained in the office after he left for the night, always working. He didn't text her to come over and she didn't offer. Yet after a few days he wondered if he should've pressed the issue instead of letting it ride, because he had no idea what to say or what he could do to fix this. Her wall of silence shut him down before any words could form.

Despite her aura of back off, she still distracted him. Her black suits had finally given way to skirts that now skimmed her knees, tucked-in tops and thin belts emphasizing every dip and curve of her luscious body. To anyone else, her perfectly suitable office attire wouldn't have rated a second glance. But to Zac, who knew exactly what was under those silky shirts and soft-to-touch sweaters, it blurred the line between demure and obscene.

He'd fantasized a hundred different ways to peel off those clothes.

"So, who are you two backing?"

Daniel from HR stood at the door, the racing form in his hand. Zac didn't miss the way Emily quickly backed away from his desk, pulling the files she held protectively against her chest.

"The race. The Melbourne Cup?" Daniel said with a grin. "We're in conference room three—thanks, Em—with nibbles, drinks and a flat screen. We just need your bets."

Emily glanced at Zac, then back to Daniel, before she gave the younger man a smile. "Come on through and I'll get some money."

He'd forgotten about the Melbourne Cup, the biggest day in Australian racing, when the whole nation stopped to watch a horse race. It was a major social event in practically every business, and Valhalla was no exception. And, he thought later as he made his way to the conference room, Emily had a real talent for organizing people. As Valhalla's unofficial social director, she was the one everyone came to to organize birthdays, retirements, the annual Christmas party. More importantly, she'd jumped into the Point One launch with expert efficiency, and was currently on target and under budget.

She'd make a damn good life coach.

He mingled with his employees, chatting comfortably but always with one eye on Emily. A few times she caught him looking and every time, glanced away.

It took thirty minutes to circulate and get to the spot where she stood, but he did so with purposeful deliberation, waiting until she broke off a conversation and approached the table laden with food.

"Are you free tonight?"

A casual observer would have missed how her outstretched hand stilled briefly before she finally took the tiny quiche and popped it in her mouth. But Zac knew he had encroached on her personal space, from the way her eyes blinked to her fingers gripping the wineglass she held. Tension radiated out like an invisible force field, yet he still itched to brush back a strand of hair that had escaped her ponytail, to test the soft skin of her cheek.

Common sense overrode desire, even though he hated holding back and his muscles ached with the effort.

"You have a client dinner." She solved his conundrum by efficiently sweeping back the offending lock of hair. "Eight o'clock at the Palazzo Versace."

He frowned, mentally reshuffling.

"And I'll probably be working," she added, taking a sip from her wineglass. "The launch is less than five weeks away."

He stared at her elegant profile. "Right." The subtext was glaringly obvious. He'd crossed the line and she was backing off.

Her mobile phone rang then, which was his cue to move away.

"This is Emily."

He went over to the food, selected a celery stick and thoughtfully chewed.

She paused. "Hello?"

Another pause, then she frowned and clicked the phone off.

He moved back, ignoring her fleeting glance. He was in her space and it annoyed her.

Well, good.

She took a sip of wine, the silence between them growing as everyone buzzed with pre-race excitement. Would she say something? A thin smile flattened his mouth. Probably not.

Just then Jenna Perkins, one of his junior architects, walked over, and she gave the woman her full attention, nodding and smiling in the appropriate places. And when someone turned on the TV, he finally conceded, giving her the space she so obviously wanted.

Emily glanced at Zac's retreating back, determined not to let that swoop of regret get the better of her. She should've put the brakes on long before now, but she'd been caught up in the sex. Amazing sex.

She'd been obsessed with their illicit nights, enthralled by Zac's lovemaking. He applied himself to the task of pleasing her with uninhibited enjoyment, and while she secretly reveled in every single second, she'd crept from his bed, anxious and flustered, way too many times. And after that incident in his office, she needed to take control.

"I must be out of my mind," she muttered, shoving a cracker in her mouth and crunching down.

"Sorry?"

Emily glanced up into Jenna's quizzical face.

"Nothing. Just talking to myself. What were you saying?"

"I said—"

Emily's phone rang again. Another hang-up.

Jenna gave Emily a gentle shoulder nudge. "I was just asking about Zac...if he's seeing anyone?"

Emily swallowed back a choke. "Why? Are you interested?"

"Dating the boss? Please!" Jenna laughed, waving her glass for emphasis. "That'd just be too weird. And anyway I'm twenty-two and he's what...thirty?"

"Twenty-seven."

"Yeah, too old. No, I was just asking a question." She nodded to a guy across the room and smiled.

Emily followed her gaze. "Mal's in charge of the office betting pool, right?"

"Hmmm?"

At Emily's cryptic silence, Jenna turned innocent brown eyes on her. "What? Noooo..."

"Jen." Emily sighed. "You know how I feel about that."

"Come on, we're only having a little fun." Jenna rolled her eyes. "Zac doesn't mind."

"Betting on the boss's sex life is not my idea of fun."

"Whatever." Jenna downed the dregs of her wine with one gulp. "Jeez, you'd think *you* were one dating him the way you protect him."

Emily stared at Jenna's retreating back, her mouth open in a surprised little "Oh."

* * *

An hour later, Emily made her way back to the office. She'd picked a long shot, only one of three horses left unclaimed on the office sweeps, and no one had been more surprised than she when Total Surrender had actually won, putting a nice three hundred dollars in her pocket.

She'd laughingly accepted the congratulations and gentle ribbing before leaving everyone to finish the food and wine. Work output would be close to zero for the remainder of today. But not for her. There were simply too many things to do to justify bunking off for the rest of the afternoon.

Total Surrender. She unlocked Zac's office with a soft snort. Very apt, her winning horse. Definitely not a predictor of things to come, not when she'd put her foot down and Zac had backed off. Yet the sense of victory she'd expected to feel hadn't materialized.

She walked in the door, paused, then tilted her head with a frown.

Something wasn't right.

She sniffed the air, noting an unfamiliar scent—musky and thick, definitely not Zac. Another worker, perhaps?

Except for the cleaners, no one else had the keys.

Quickly she tested the locked drawers. Still locked. She skimmed over the blueprint cabinet. Nothing missing.

Then she went to her desk.

Inside the top drawer, next to her stapler and spare pens, a note was taped. It said cryptically, "Look out your window."

Zac was still at the party, so it wasn't him. She walked hesitantly to the office window, drew the blinds aside and stared down into busy Broadbeach Mall.

Their corner office afforded her an expansive view, from the monorail tracks stretching from the Oasis Centre to Jupiters Casino across the busy highway to the traffic-ridden roundabout directly below on Surf Parade. Nothing seemed amiss in the restaurants and eateries in the mall below. At twenty floors up, she wasn't sure she would see anything. Unless…

Her gaze snapped up, to the Sofilel Broadbeach hotel windows directly across. Almost at eye level, a sign was taped to a window.

"Just you. Where you buy your morning coffee. Ten minutes."

A thin thread of panic shot through her bones until outrage quickly overtook it. Someone had been in here, in her work area, in her things. Were those hang-ups a part of this, too?

That anger gave her courage, straightening her back and drawing her mouth into a thin line of determination.

Seven minutes later, she stalked into Bennetti's. After scanning the few customers and two staff, her gaze landed on a familiar figure sitting at a secluded table, casually sipping a short black.

When Louie Mayer's oily smile spread across his face, she swallowed a spurt of fear.

Showing fear gives them the upper hand. Another one of her mother's little life truths. Emily grimly smoothed back her perfectly contained hair. *Thanks, Mum. Handy advice when dealing with crims.*

"You're looking good, Emily." Louie smiled, easing back in his chair as he frankly appraised her. Suppressing a shudder, she gave him her best haughty look.

"Your boss got paid, if I recall. What do you want?"

The man really was huge, she realized as he stood and pulled out a seat for her. When she shook her head, he frowned and remained standing, his arms crossed, the black cotton T-shirt stretching taut until she was sure it groaned.

"Looks like you got a good thing going at work, huh?"

Emily frowned. "What?"

"Oh, just that you seem to be enjoying some personal after-hours attention from Zac Prescott."

His dirty smirk made her want to slap him. Her fingers jerked before she purposefully relaxed them.

"That's none of your business."

His grin spread wider and a gold front tooth glinted in the light. "Ah, but it is. Very much my business." He leaned in, and Emily was suddenly enveloped in a cloying musky aftershave.

"Your rich boyfriend ponied up Jimmy's debt quicker than a teenager sculling a beer at Schoolie's week. Which tells me a coupla things." He paused, eyeing two blondes as they walked up to the counter. His eyes lingered on their butts as he continued. "One—you and he are more than coworkers, especially now I've seen you both in action. And two, he has cash to spare."

White-hot panic made her heart surge. "You're blackmailing me?"

"I wouldn't say that." He reached out to stroke her hair, but she flinched away. The amusement in his smile fled. "Call it an investment. You pay up every month, and the papers won't get to hear about Zac Prescott's private life, starting with him boning his secretary and his 'compulsive gambling problem.'"

"But you took the last of my money! I don't have—"

"Use your brain, blondie." His eyes hardened. "You're sleeping with a multimillionaire. That doesn't come for free."

Her heart beat loudly in her ears, deafening her to everything else. For one split second, she could imagine herself doing actual physical harm to another human being.

She pictured herself surging to her feet and running. Running away from this café, away from this man's threats. Away from everything.

She'd started over before, she could do it again.

You can't run. Not this time. She breathed deep, once, twice, forcing calm into her limbs, her brain.

She had to stall him.

"I need time," she finally said.

Mayer shrugged and glanced at his watch. "You've got a week. I'll be in touch." And with a wink and a pat on her shoulder, he walked out.

Zac was out at a site inspection, not due to return today. Everyone else was either still in the conference room or pretending to work. The hall was abuzz with chatter and laughter, so no one noticed Emily leaving at four-thirty.

She couldn't stay at the office, not when it'd been breached so easily. Grilling the security guard and watching video surveillance hadn't brought her much joy, so now she sat in her Toyota in the basement car park, mulling through her options.

Her body buzzed with alternate flashes of outrage and panic, her skin tight and itchy. Her foot jiggled nervously on the clutch, her fingers clicking the brake button in and out, in and out, before she suddenly realized what she was doing and shoved her hands under her thighs.

She didn't want to go home. What she really wanted to do was press "rewind" and start today all over again. She couldn't afford to pay off that criminal, not even with her increased paycheck. And asking Zac for money? She'd rather earn it busking on Broadbeach Mall.

She shivered, remembering Mayer's fingers on her arm, the way his eyes had insultingly appraised her, the dirty tilt to his mouth.

She rubbed her arms then crossed them. That awful aftershave still lingered in her nostrils, taunting, smothering. It was a reminder that she was trapped, a pawn for someone else to manipulate.

No.

Her hands shot out and she grabbed the steering wheel, hard. *I will not be a victim. I will not let that thug win.* Determination surged up, charging her body with renewed energy.

He'd given her a week. Could she think of something in that time?

She *had* to.

Her phone beeped suddenly, pulling her from her focus.

U free later? My place @ 11—2 late?

It was Zac. The only person who'd been honest about what he wanted from her, who didn't lie and manipulate. A man who hadn't given up, who disoriented her with just one kiss, who made her forget the entire world when she was in his bed. Her own personal form of escapism.

Which was what she needed right now.

She returned the text, familiar eagerness heating her skin.

I'll be there.

Zac had just walked through to the living room when he heard the key in his front door, then the lock snick open.

The lights clicked off, plunging him into darkness.

He whirled. "Emily?"

The instant the figure moved from the door to the window, a dark silhouette against the full moon glimmering through his open window, he knew it was her.

Dressed in some sort of long coat?

"What are you wearing?"

She said nothing, just flicked on the small reading lamp. The soft light speared out, bathing her in gold from head to toe.

Zac's mouth went dry.

Her hair was piled up in a tousled mass, a few strands brushing her collar, one curling seductively over one eye. She was skillfully made up, her eyes wide and mysterious, her eyebrows shaped into a come-hither arch. And her mouth...

He swallowed, knowing he was staring but unable to look away. Her luscious Cupid's-bow mouth was painted a deep red, the full bottom lip in a slight pout that conjured up all sorts of erotic images.

He couldn't breathe.

She took one slow step forward, then another, hips swaying as her heels clicked on the polished floor. He glanced down. Red stilettos with a peek-a-boo toe. Long red and black ribbons that looped around her ankles, then tied in festive bows at the sides. He'd bought her those last week.

She paused a few feet away and his eyes went to her hands, to the belt she was slowly untying.

"What are you..?"

"Stop talking."

As she plucked open the large buttons on her coat, her gaze

firmly on him, he could feel anticipation building, bubbling up to heat his blood, shred his breath.

She was stripping. For him.

Unable to move, much less think, he watched her peel away one lapel, revealing a black satin strap over one bare shoulder.

He finally tore his gaze up to meet her eyes, and what he saw crushed his lungs. Even after everything they'd done, touched, tasted, she still looked uncertain.

How could she not know how desirable she was?

Man, she could bring him to his knees with nothing more than a look from those intelligent eyes. She undid him, turning every bone in his body to mush.

With a sharp inhale, almost as if she was dragging in courage, she grasped both lapels and pulled the coat apart.

A groan rattled in his throat.

The black push-up bra firmly cupped her breasts, creating an erotic valley between. He looked his fill, spotting a tiny diamanté flower perched in the center, winking in the light. Then his gaze crept lower, to the black bikini knickers tied at her curvy hips with two jaunty bows. A thin silver chain looped low around her waist, ending in a string of tiny stars hanging just below her belly button.

A rocket surge of lust sped through his blood.

Her body was flawless. Every curve was designed to be touched, every dip a perfect place for his tongue. From the silky smoothness of her thighs to the pebbly roughness of her pink nipples, there was not a section of her skin he hadn't tasted. If there were any imperfections, he'd yet to see them.

Why did she always bring out the caveman in him?

"Emily…"

Her mouth wavered, fists still bunched on the coat, flashing him. "Zac?"

Control was way overrated.

He surged forward with a rough growl, grabbed her by the lapels and slammed his mouth down on hers.

He kissed her hard and deep, a kiss born of frustration, of

passion, of desperate need. He wanted her to know exactly how keyed up he was, how much he wanted her.

Her soft exclamation muffled against his lips as she pressed up against him, her breasts hot and eager. He knew she could feel his arousal, his groin hard as it pressed into her belly. Somehow they made it across the room, but the stairs proved too much and he stumbled, sprawling backward on the steps with Emily on top.

"Ah, what the hell," he muttered as he pulled the coat from her shoulders, trapping her arms behind her. She grinned, all wicked and wanton, her hair tumbling over her shoulders.

He reared up to capture her lips and they tangled for long, sensuous moments, breath heaving, blood thumping.

Then the intercom buzzed.

"Zac…" She mumbled beneath his lips.

He pulled back and caught her soft earlobe between his teeth, grinning when she gasped.

Just as he went in for another kiss, the intercom jarred in his brain again.

He groaned. "If it's not someone bleeding from a major artery, I'm ignoring it."

Her small burst of laughter shook her body, sliding her against him. The breath he sucked in was sharp and painful.

"Hurry up and tell them to go away," she said, peeling away from him with a smile.

"Don't move." He rose, stalked over to the door, and with eyes fixed firmly on her near-naked body reclining on his stairs, slammed his fist on the intercom. "What?"

"Hi, Zac."

The woman's familiar purr cut through the air, dousing the moment like an Antarctic wind. With one sharp movement, Emily dragged the coat around her and stood.

Zac chewed back a curse. "What do you want, Haylee?"

"You never replied to my e-mails."

Emily's eyebrows shot up, hands going to her hips. Her indignation would've been humorous if he weren't so irritated.

"We broke up, remember?" he said.

Her sigh echoed over the intercom. "Look, can I talk to you for a moment? It's important."

Zac glanced back to Emily, but all she did was wave a hand, tie her belt, then walk into the kitchen.

His decision.

Emily watched from the darkened kitchen window as Haylee stalked up to the front door. She'd gone all out, dressed in a shiny leather miniskirt, thigh-high stiletto boots and a sheer blouse that left her naked underneath as she passed under the porch light. Her hair shone, the Cleopatra fringe adding sexy mystery to a striking face and dark makeup.

Gorgeous, confident and sexually aggressive.

Emily's insides cramped as she turned away.

She heard the door swing open, then Zac's curt, "What do you want, Haylee?"

There was a long pause, too long. Emily chewed on her lip. *Eavesdropping is a bad idea. Bad, bad.* Before she could convince herself, she quickly scooted back to the window, gently prying the venetian blinds apart.

Haylee had her hands on her hips, one hip thrust forward, chest out, her bold expression a mixture of smoldering and come-here. Emily swallowed. The woman knew how to command the moment, she'd give her that. But Zac...well, his entire crossed-arms posture just gave off waves of irritability, eyes firmly fixed on Haylee's face.

"I had to see you."

Zac frowned. "What for?"

"Do I need a reason? We were good together, Zac."

"I told you. You have to stop this."

Haylee responded with a pout that looked artfully practiced for maximum effect. "Do you really want to make me say it, baby? Because I will."

Zac sighed. "Haylee..."

"I know I can convince you to give us another chance. I want you, Zac. Right here, right now." When she moved in, pressing up against his chest, a thin film of fury cleaved Emily in two, leaving her breathless. Her nails dug into her palms yet she remained motionless, balanced on a knife edge.

Zac had hold of Haylee's wrists and was firmly pushing her away, his face marred by a deep frown.

"But I don't want you. Not now, not ever. Stop harassing me. Stop calling my office. Stop everything."

Then he dragged his impersonal gaze down her body. Emily almost felt sorry for the woman. She recognized the lost-all-patience-and-was-done-being-polite look. And so did Haylee, judging by her shocked expression.

"You're turning me down?" she spat out, yanking her arms back. "How dare you? Where the hell do you get off? I can name at least a dozen guys who'd be willing—no, *thrilled*—with what I'm offering."

Zac crossed his arms. "Then by all means, take them up on it."

Her eyes narrowed, darting past his shoulder. "It's someone else, isn't it? You've got someone else in there."

"That's none of your business."

When she surged forward, Zac's arm shot out to bar her way.

"Hey. Hey!" Haylee yelled into the house, straining against Zac's arm. "You do know you're only one skank in a long line? When Zac's finished with you, he'll just drop you for some other easy lay! Hey!" She squealed as Zac grabbed her shoulders, pivoted her, then gave her a small shove.

After a brief stumble she whirled, fury twisting her face into ugly lines. "Don't you touch me."

"Leave. Now."

With a foul curse and a rude gesture, Haylee spun away, then stalked down the path.

Wow. Emily pulled away from the window, then returned to the living room. Zac stood with his back resting on the closed door, concentration creasing his forehead.

"That was…" Emily began.

"Unfortunate." He sighed and pushed off from the door, his hands going to his hips.

"Do you think she'll make trouble for you?"

"With the clients? I doubt it." Zac shrugged. "But Josh…"

"You don't need Josh Kerans's business."

"No. But he is an extremely influential man."

"So are you."

"Yeah, but…" They both knew what he meant. Rich, workaholic father, spoilt daughter. It wasn't hard to do the math.

"Well." She took a breath. "If there are any problems, you can't argue with an eyewitness."

He paused, an odd expression on his face. "You'd do that?"

"Yes."

The look in his eyes blew any niggling worry from the water. And when he smiled, her heart melted.

"Come here."

She went willingly, eagerly into his arms, met his lips with a sigh of satisfaction, letting his mouth and hands cleanse the moment.

She didn't want to think about anything she'd said or done these past twenty-four hours. Zac filled her senses, her mind and soon, her body. And right now, it was all she needed.

Fourteen

Emily never thought Jimmy's old gambling contacts would've come in handy. But after a few calls and a few pointed tugs on the heartstrings, she had the most likely places Rafe Santos—aka "Joe"—would be, including a description from a former band member.

It was late Friday night, a night for revelry, dancing and shadowy assignations. After checking out five different nightclubs and two strip joints, she'd seen more than her share of excitement.

Last one. She glanced up at the familiar pink neon proclaiming Romeo's and sighed. This was one of the clubs where Jimmy's band had once played. Same indifferent young thing at the entrance, collecting her entry fee, same mirrored walls and ceilings. Same huge bouncer at the foot of the stairs. But this time, as she passed by, the man's eyes latched onto her barely contained breasts straining against the leather bustier, lingering on her until she reached the foot of the stairs. Knowing her butt encased in a short, tight denim skirt now commanded his attention, she forced down her distaste as she clicked up the neon glass stairs in her red-and-black ribboned stilettos. The closer she got to the top, the more heavily the frantic dance music pulsed in her throat and belly. Her head began to throb with the beginnings of a headache. *Focus. You're here to bargain with a bookmaker, hopefully so he will drop his blackmail attempt.*

Strobe lights, loud music and heat from dozens of sweaty dancers simultaneously hit the moment she paused at the top of the stairs. The place was cavernous as she remembered, with a split-level dance floor, a stage area and a massive bar that spanned the entire length of the room. And past the bar, in the shadows, a handful of circular lounges were cordoned off by waist-high smoky glass, a VIP area where special guests could observe the action yet still remain private.

And there Rafe Santos was.

She pulled her shoulders back, took a deep breath as a slick-looking guy in an expensive suit sidled up.

"Hey, babe, howsabout you and me—"

She didn't stick around to hear the rest of his suggestion. With her gaze firmly on her quarry, she made her way across the room, ignoring the looks, shrugging off a couple of propositions. She stared right at the group in the private booth, at the guy lounging on the comfy love seat, his arm around a stunning blonde.

As she approached, Santos flicked his gaze over her, then back to the guy standing with his back to Emily. He held up a finger, silencing his bodyguard, then returned to her, his eyes sidling up and down her body in all-male appreciation.

The guard turned with a frown. "This is a private booth," he said, stepping forward. "You need to—"

"John."

One word from his boss and he froze, a comical snapshot of menacing indignation. Santos went on smoothly. "You would send a pretty girl away without knowing why we've attracted her attention?"

The bouncer gave her the once-over with a bored look in his eyes. "You always attract women, Mr. Santos. This one isn't worth—"

"I think I'm perfectly capable of deciding who is worthy of my time, John."

Now that she was here, with one of the city's most powerful bookies a few feet away, panic began to set in. *The man is a criminal. Just what are you going to do? Who do you think you are?*

The guard's smug expression reflected all her unspoken doubts and fears as he edged aside, allowing her entry with only the tiniest of space. Her arm brushed his and she barely managed to stop herself from recoiling.

Confidence. You ooze confidence. This is just another role to play. Emily shut everyone out and put all her focus on the man she'd come to bargain with.

He's not much older than me, was her first thought. Her second was he was an extremely good-looking man. With a smooth-shaven head and dark coffee skin spread over broad cheekbones, Rafe Santos was an exotic blend of Australia's multicultural heritage. Filipino, Pacific islander…possibly some Italian in those frankly compelling eyes. He was impeccably dressed in a deep navy suit and a silk tie, ankle casually crossed over one knee as he lounged back in the sofa and appraised her.

"Can I help you, Mrs. Catalano?" he asked smoothly, the rich, cultured voice flowing over her. It was a charismatic, built-to-seduce voice, one Emily could dispassionately acknowledge without succumbing to its charms. Beside him, one arm possessively around his shoulders, the blonde woman shot her a look of haughty distain. Emily ignored her.

"You knew I was coming?"

"An attractive woman is in my clubs asking for me and I make a point of finding out who she is." His smile was all charming seduction. If she were any other woman, if he weren't a criminal who didn't exude barely leashed danger, it would've worked. "I knew your husband—"

"My ex-husband."

His mouth thinned into a smile but his eyes cooled—a powerful man displeased at being corrected. Emily swallowed. "Jimmy was a regular," he went on, taking a drag from his cigar.

"A little too erratic for my tastes, but still, good for business. Pity he died."

"Yes."

His eyes never left hers as he took another drag. "John, go and bring some more wine."

"Yes, sir."

"White, I think. Something from the Margaret River." He uncrossed his legs and eased forward, resting his elbows on his knees. "Join me for a drink. And sit." He gestured to the sofa.

Ringed by two impassive bodyguards, she could do nothing but acquiesce. He smiled as Emily slowly sat on the sofa. "A good Australian wine is so much better than overpriced French champagne, wouldn't you agree?"

She nodded, her tongue stuck to the roof of her mouth. As he studied her intently, she slid back into the lounge and crossed her legs. It eased her already-short skirt up even higher and spread Santos's grin a little wider.

"I need to ask you a favor," she began.

"Ahh. A favor for a pretty girl. I like the sound of that."

She swallowed down her apprehension. The way she worded her request was of the utmost importance. "Can we speak privately?"

He raised one eyebrow. "But we are."

She glanced at the bodyguards, at the hostile blonde. "Not entirely."

He paused, his teeth flashing in the shadows. "Intriguing. Helena."

The blonde rose elegantly, then stalked out, followed by the guards, who repositioned themselves a few feet away, this time facing the club crowd.

With a silent prayer, she began. "I know you're a powerful man, Mr. Santos. An influential man. I respect that. And I thank you for your patience while I sorted out Jimmy's debts."

"And I thank you for your prompt payment." He eased back in the sofa, hitching his elbows along the back of the seat.

Emily nodded, nerves strung out like ragged ribbons on a breeze. "So I'm wondering…" She breathed out slowly, blinked, then took a breath. "I'm *asking* you to withdraw your current request."

His eyes narrowed through the thick plume of smoke coming from his lips. "Which is?"

She met his gaze unwaveringly. "That I pay you to stay silent about my relationship with Zac Prescott."

He was still for a moment, picking her apart with ruthless efficiency.

"I see."

He took another slow drag from his cigar, blew, then watched the smoke hover gently in the thick air. Emily felt her heartbeat emphasize every dragging second, thump-thumping hard in her chest and drowning out the heavy music.

"And what did you bring to bargain with?"

His eyes slid over her face, breasts, then her legs with disturbing familiarity. She forced herself to remain still, forcing down the surge of disgust as his mysterious gaze finally reached her feet. His wolfish grin spread, spearing ice into her veins. What *had* she brought, except herself?

Suddenly Santos's focus snapped up and into the crowded club. "I think we have a visitor."

Emily turned and stared past the wall of guards to the approaching figure.

What on earth was Zac doing here?

"Nice to see you again, Mr. Prescott." Santos smiled, then nodded at the bodyguards to let him pass. "To what do I owe this pleasure?"

Zac's glacial eyes grazed over Emily, taking in her skimpy attire and expanse of leg in silence, before he returned to Santos. "I came for Emily."

Emily blinked. "You were following me?"

"I got an anonymous call."

She frowned, glancing back at the now-silent Santos as he studied his cigar tip.

When he finally met her eyes, his cold expression revealed nothing. She was the first to glance away.

"Emily." Zac's firm command brooked no refusal yet she remained seated, glaring at him.

Santos sighed. "If you two are going to fight, could you please take it elsewhere?"

"No." Emily spun back to him, desperately trying to ignore the overwhelming presence an angry, six-foot-two Zac made. "I came here to talk with you about…what I'd mentioned before," she added cryptically. Then she looked up at Zac. "Go home, Zac. Please."

"Only if you're coming with me."

"This doesn't concern you."

"I think it does."

"How do you know?"

"He's right," Santos drawled. "If I was blackmailing you to keep silent about your affair, then he has a right to know."

"What the—?" With a growl Zac surged forward, but a beefy hand clamped down on his shoulder. Emily shot to her feet the exact moment he whirled, ready to do battle, but Santos's sharp, "Enough!" froze everyone in their tracks.

"Miss Reynolds. You and Mr. Prescott may go now."

"But what about—"

His expression blanked, those dark eyes icing over, and Emily's pulse jumped in alarm. "I am not concerned with how you paid your debt, Miss Reynolds, just that it was paid. Blackmail is not my style. It's a very messy business with no guaranteed return, not to mention dangerous to my health. I like my life too much." He nodded, his small smile doing nothing to assuage her nerves. "I thank you for bringing this issue to my attention. Rest assured you will not be getting any visits from Mr. Mayer again. Understood?"

Emily nodded slowly. "Yes."

"Let's go," Zac murmured, firmly taking her wrist.

She rose shakily, relief flooding her limbs, but before she could escape, Santos's hand was on hers.

She whirled, wide-eyed, as she met his eyes.

"If you ever get bored with playing it safe…" He caressed her knuckles, smile widening as Emily felt the blush rise up.

Zac's hand tightened around hers, a deep warning rumbling in his throat. Santos flicked a glance at Zac, shrugged, then let her go, his chuckle quickly swallowed by the music.

"What the hell were you thinking?" Zac hissed, taking her elbow as they exited the club into the warm night.

She wrenched back and ground to a halt. "I was thinking I could get him to change his mind."

"Dressed like that?" He bit off a curse, dragged a hand through his hair. "It was dangerous and stupid, Emily. What if something had happened to you? What if—"

"Nothing did."

"But what if it *had?* You were being blackmailed. Why didn't you come to me with this?"

"Because *I* needed to fix it. Jimmy was my mistake, okay? My lapse in judgment, my stupid decision."

"And you're damned lucky it worked out the way it did. Bloody hell, Emily, just what were you prepared to do?"

They glared at each other, teetering on a thin tightrope. The awful truth lay in his furious gaze, laced with worry and concern. It squeezed the fight right out of her.

She took a step back. "I… I don't know. I just thought—"

"Don't do that again." He gripped her arms, tight. "Don't put yourself in danger and don't—" The gravity of the situation they'd just left crushed Zac under its weight, her confusion tangling his words. What the hell was he trying to say?

You're mine.

His expression must have given him away, because her eyes suddenly widened, a spark of lust rending the air. With a thick, frustrated growl he captured her mouth with his.

Emily's surprise quickly melted into need as her body instantly responded, lips automatically parting, her breath hitching as she grabbed his shoulders and kissed him back.

It was an angry kiss, one born of frustration and worry and desperate desire. And she matched it, letting all her tension go in this frantic meeting of breathless gasps and hot mouths.

When he finally yanked back, his heaving chest matched hers.

"No secret is worth that, Emily. Do you hear me?" He tunneled his hand in his hair, glaring out into the night. "This was about us. Not just you, not just me. At least give me the courtesy of telling me before you jump in to try and fix something."

He clamped his mouth shut as a bunch of revelers approached, moving aside as they stumbled and laughed by. Staring at their backs as they made their way into the club, he said curtly, "Where are you parked?"

"Around the corner."

He led the way, walking the short distance in cool silence.

When they finally reached her car, Emily fished for the keys in her tiny handbag, face warm, feeling utterly stupid in light of Zac's argument.

He was right. What had she been thinking? She'd gone there full of bravado, ready to bargain, but what could she have done if Santos had demanded something more?

She blinked, furiously dashing away half-formed tears.

"Emily." She jumped when Zac placed a hand on her arm, yet summoned enough courage to meet his gaze.

"Is there anything else I should know?"

I think I love you and I'm scared. Every relationship I've ever been in gets ruined. I don't want to lose you when I leave Valhalla. All those doubts and more jostled for position, but instead she said slowly, "You should go to your brother's wedding."

He sucked in a breath then rolled his eyes heavenward, muttering something incomprehensible. "Not that again?"

"You need to."

"No," he said. "I don't."

She leaned back on her car. "I see the way you react every time you deal with your father. You get all tense and jittery, like someone stuck a key in your back and wound you up too tight. He's been calling for the past few months and yet you refuse to talk to him. Look." She sighed, putting her hands on her hips. "I admit what I did tonight was thoughtless and stupid, but at least I did *something*. I faced the problem."

He said nothing, just stood there with a hard jaw and hooded eyes in the pale streetlight, thumbs hooked in his belt loops.

Finally he said, "When I was seventeen, I told my dad I wanted to study in Sweden. So he pulled considerable strings to get me into Sydney University instead. I left anyway and he disowned me. Just like that." He clicked his fingers for emphasis.

She knew verbatim his career highs and triumphs, knew he'd gotten his degree from the exclusive Lund University. But she hadn't a clue what had driven him to the other side of the world.

"So why did you return?"

His response came easily, as if he'd been expecting the question. "Five years is a long time. It gives you distance and clarity. And Australia has always been my home. I thought coming back would change things. I thought he'd changed."

"But…?"

"Victor Prescott is—" He scowled, pausing to kick at the chipped curb with one toe. "A brilliant businessman. A clueless father. My mother left when I was seven." He sucked in a breath, his troubled expression suddenly hardening. "I remember begging her to take me, too, but instead she left me with a man who divorced her within weeks, then destroyed every photo of her I had."

Emily's heart went out to him. "Oh, Zac."

"Yeah."

Zac crossed his arms. Damn. He'd let this go, had moved on. Yet somehow the bitter betrayal still clung like sticky cobwebs inside.

"Did you ever go looking for her?" Emily was asking softly.

He wrestled with the memories, indecision warring. But Emily's expression, eyes wide and open in the pale light, somehow comforted him. He trusted her with his most confidential business transactions, so why would he not trust her with this?

"Between study and classes, every spare hour I had, I looked. But she'd vanished and I barely had enough money to live, let alone offer as an incentive. Then, after I returned to Sydney I got a letter from her lawyer telling me she'd died and left me all her money." He paused, catching the mixture of poignant sadness and understanding fleet across Emily's face before her expression cleared.

It was enough for him to continue.

"You know what the worst thing was? While I'd been studying, my mother had been alive and well, living on a small farm in the next town." He clenched his fist briefly then let it go. "So Victor and I argued and I nearly punched him out. Not my finest moment," he said with a humorless smile. "I surfed my way around Australia with the money she'd left me, trying to forget who I was, who my father was. Then I started Valhalla."

Emily was silent for a moment, digesting that information as things slowly clicked into place. His confession answered so many questions, put a lot of things in perspective.

"Zac, I am so sorry," she began. "But I still think you need to do this. There's nothing worse than regret, thinking you should've done something differently. Trust me, I know."

His gaze turned astute as he searched her face. "What do you regret?"

"Lots of things." She jingled the keys. "It doesn't matter."

He stilled her hand, his fingers warmly covering hers. "It does, otherwise it wouldn't get to you." He tipped her chin up to meet his eyes. "So it matters to me."

"I don't…" Lord, she was so tired of maintaining the walls of silence. Making love with Zac made her forget the truth of who she was and where she'd come from. For a few hours she could be someone desirable, someone wanted.

Someone loved.

Yet how would that change if he knew who she really was and how she felt about him?

So instead of answering, she leaned in, grasped his neck and dragged him down for a kiss. He frowned, resisting, but when she gently pushed apart his lips and slipped her tongue in, he yielded with a frustrated mutter.

They kissed, out in the open, on the darkened street where anyone could have seen them. Emily didn't care. All she cared about was the here and now, Zac's hard, warm body pressing her up against the cold car door, not the ghosts of her shadowy past.

"Let's go," she finally murmured. "I'll meet you at your place."

"Emily…"

"Please." She lifted large eyes to his, unashamedly using every seductive trick to sway him.

He stepped back with a groan and dug in his pocket for his car keys. "Hurry."

They made love frantically, barely getting their clothes off and making it to the bed before he was on top of her, then inside her. She cried out, thrusting her hips up, wanting this, wanting him.

When they came, it was like a violent explosion, with tangled limbs, racing breaths and crashing heartbeats.

Finally, they lay replete in his bed, Zac nuzzling her neck as their bodies cooled.

"Hungry?" he murmured.

She shivered. "Starving."

"Then let's eat."

When he slid from the bed and the cool air rushed over her damp skin, she wanted to weep.

He must have caught her shiver because he gently pulled her to her feet, bringing her flush against his naked chest. Still warm, she realized, her palms automatically going to those firm muscles, gently sprinkled with dark hair. Then, to her surprise, his arms went around her, he buried his face in her neck and inhaled deeply, like he was imprinting her scent on his brain. As if she was truly desirable and he couldn't get enough of her.

He placed a soft cotton robe around her shoulders, tying it in front before giving her a wink. "Stay here." And he headed for the stairs.

They ate picnic-style in the middle of his huge bed, devouring crusty bread, dip, olives and four different cheeses. She'd expected to be uncomfortable, eating seminaked in Zac's bed after what they'd just done between the sheets. But instead, they shared stories about their respective houses and the local wildlife that dropped in on occasion.

Emily finally reclined on the pillows with a groan, an odd feeling of contentment seeping into her limbs.

"I can't fit any more in."

"Not even cherries?" He held up a bag with a grin.

Emily grinned right back. "No."

He rattled the bag. "Just one?"

His boyish charm worked its magic: with a dramatic sigh and an eye roll, she sat up and stuck out her hand. "All right."

"Nuh-uh." He plucked off the stalk then beckoned. "Closer."

She leaned in a few inches.

"Closer."

Another inch more, straining from her cross-legged position.

His gaze darted to her neckline and he sucked in a sharp breath.

Emily glanced down and noticed the robe had parted, revealing more than she cared to. Chomping down on a soft groan she dragged the robe closed.

Suddenly the comfortable moment disappeared like vapor in the air, replaced by something warmer, more heated. Intimate.

Zac crooked his finger. "Closer," then stuck the ruby-red fruit between his lips, eyes dancing.

She hesitated for one breath, maybe two. But the temptation proved too much.

Her hands went down to the mattress as she eased her legs out, shifting until she was on all fours. Zac's gaze turned quizzical but his smile remained, the cherry sitting ripe and tempting between his lips. But when she leaned forward, gave a mischievous grin and started to crawl toward him, that smile slowly dropped.

His gaze fell to her neckline, then snapped back up to her face. Oh, she knew what she was doing, all right. The heady feeling of empowerment was like a shot of pure adrenaline through her veins as she eased her way forward, finally stopping a breathless inch away. His ragged breath bathed her cheek as she paused, her mouth close but not touching the cherry offering. His whole body glowed warm, like someone had lit a fire inside. It reflected in those eyes, all-seeing eyes that probed hers, studying, cataloging, waiting for her next move—almost relishing it, judging by the way his expression tensed as she exhaled gently before inching her mouth closer.

When she latched onto the cherry and gently bit into the flesh, he choked out a throaty groan. She grinned and eased back, chewing as the deliciously sweet juice coated her lips.

The moment solidified with sudden clarity as Zac battled through the steadily growing waves of lust. Emily in his robe, her hair tousled and falling around her shoulders, the neck gaping to reveal generous breasts. Her bright blue eyes, twinkling with mischief.

And one bright-red drop of cherry juice shimmering on the curve of her bottom lip.

Her tongue was nearly out before he acted, dipping his head to steal the juice, licking, then sucking her swelling bottom lip. Her answering groan was like gasoline on glowing embers.

They sat there, joined only by a kiss, one that seemed to go on forever. Sweet, sticky, exploratory cherry-kisses in between soft laughter and knowing smiles. But then the mood changed, the kisses becoming deeper as their breath mingled, tongues tangling.

She tasted of cherry juice, white wine and olives. Zac breathed deep, dragging in the musky reminder of their lovemaking combined with the remnants of their meal. Senses reeled as his body weighed in, his groin demanding action.

It took superhuman effort to pull back from her heavenly Cupid's mouth. Her small whimper, eyes wide and dark with arousal, shattered him.

He quickly rose and stuck out his hand.

"Come with me."

His rough command made Emily shiver. Without hesitation she took his hand.

He led her into the master bath, soft bedroom light spearing into the darkness, illuminating a massive chrome and white-tiled extravaganza complete with skylight and huge corner spa, another view of the Pacific Ocean serving as the backdrop.

When he went to turn on the light, she stopped him. "Can people see in?"

His mouth quirked. "What do you think?"

"I think…no."

"Ah, but do you know for sure?" He peeled off her robe with expert hands, backing her up against the sink until her bare bottom hit the cold tiles.

Her shock drowned in a groan as his hands went to her arms, pinning her as his mouth descended. With a tiny click, he'd flicked the lights on, bathing them in a soft golden glow.

"Does it bother you, Emily?" He asked between hot kisses. "That anyone could walk along the beach and see us together? Or is it…" She gasped as his hand slipped between them, fingers going straight to the core of her heat. "Exciting? Arousing?"

"Yes." He knew her body too well, knew when she was eager for him. His rough chin grazed her neck, his mouth dipping to capture one swollen nipple.

She whimpered, hips jerking as lust exploded, those exquisite sensations quickening her blood.

"Wait, my sweet," he whispered, before grasping her shoulders and turning her to face the mirror.

She stared at her shadowed reflection, a wide-eyed, disheveled reflection, naked and bent over at the waist. Behind her, Zac swept a hand over the curve of her bottom, then across her back, his eyes heavy with desire.

"So beautiful," he murmured, before glancing up to see her watching him through the mirror. His eyes locked on hers, lingering, and suddenly Emily knew what he was waiting for.

"Yes," she breathed.

His mouth curved into a sensual grin.

Emily's breath caught when he grasped her hips and nudged her legs apart with one knee, only to explode out as he swiftly entered her from behind.

Ohhhh… The wicked delight of his hot naked flesh in hers, their eyes locked through the mirror, shadow and soft golden light shafting across his face, freezing his expression in a moment of ecstasy.

Everything felt suddenly too hot, too sensitive, yet Zac couldn't withdraw. She surrounded him completely, her hot warmth, her pliant body beneath his hands. Inside and out.

He rocked back, slowly withdrawing, and her breath hissed out. "Zac…"

His name on her lips, pleading, wanting him, nearly sent him over the edge. Instead he gritted his teeth, took hold of her hips and began to thrust.

She was exposed and vulnerable, yet she held his gaze through the mirror, bold, languid eyes watching as he made love to her.

That only turned him on more. When he eased the pace to drive in deeper, she hauled in a stuttering breath, eyes closing, head back as she braced herself on her elbows and went with the rhythm. She rocked with him, completely in sync, and it was all he could do not to lose it then and there. Instead he bent forward and wrapped his arm around her waist, planting long, languorous kisses along her spine as he quickened the pace. He felt her shudder, then gasp. And all of a sudden, she cried out, her eyes springing wide open.

When he felt the orgasm quake through her, her entire body clenched in exquisite torture around him, he finally let go, their cries echoing off the tiles.

Eventually they shared a hot bath in that massive spa, lazily washing each other between wet kisses. Then Zac wrapped his arms around her and dragged her to sit between his legs. They languished in the bubbles, his chin on her shoulder, his hands absently stroking her arms.

Emily breathed in the damp heat, the curls of steam smelling faintly of sandalwood and vanilla, and wondered if the moment could be any more perfect—lying wet and naked with the man she loved.

The frightening realization dawned just as the fiery red sunrise began to streak across the sky.

She was in love with a man who was only supposed to be temporary. A physical distraction only.

She squeezed her eyes shut, determined to hold on to the moment instead of facing the reality for what it was.

Yet how could she not think about reality when Zac's hard body was pressed against her back, his hands splayed possessively under her breasts?

"Come with me to Cal's wedding," Zac said softly, breaking the silence.

Emily paused, squeezing her eyes shut. "Why?"

"Because I want you there."

And I want to be there. More than anything. Instead, she bit her lip and remained silent.

At her silence, he gently turned her to face him, water swirling as she went. "Look, you're my assistant. No one's going to question you being with me."

Great. "It's not that."

His expression told her he wasn't convinced. "So...?"

So why did it feel...bad? As if she was breaching the line they'd drawn. She was his bedmate, not his girlfriend. They didn't share anything except their bodies.

Not true, a little voice inside reminded her. *There's trust. Professional respect. And he knows things about you, private things, and he's still here.*

Yeah. But if he knew all of it, he'd run a mile.

"It's your brother's wedding, Zac. A private family gathering. Surely they wouldn't want—"

"I want." He reached out and pulled her in, his mouth dipping down to hers. "There's no one else I'd trust to be there."

Conflict warred briefly, until his lips skimmed hers and desire swiftly replaced it. Her eyelids sagged. *Where's your list when you need it?* Yet for the first time, she felt no urge to list those pros and cons because there was only one answer in her heart.

She was sick of letting fear and doubt shape her actions. He needed her. She'd be there.

"Okay," she breathed. "I'll go."

"Good." He finally kissed her, yet despite the warm tenderness, trepidation still oozed through her body like an ever-growing toxic spill.

Fifteen

"Why is it," AJ said casually as they ate lunch at Madison's in the Oasis Centre as the March heat scorched the sidewalk outside, "that no matter how many problems a relationship is having, couples can still overlook them to have sex?"

Emily followed her sister's eyes to the far table, where the guy and girl they'd been covertly watching argue were now deep in a passionate kiss. "Is that a question or a statement?"

AJ turned her bright blue gaze back to Emily. "I'm talking about you and Zac."

"And *I* don't know what you're talking about."

"Rubbish. You love him. And I'm assuming he has feelings for you, given the fact he's been your knight in shining armor at least twice now. But you haven't really talked, have you?"

"We don't have that kind of relationship."

"Right. Let's recap, shall we?" AJ crossed her arms, pinning Emily with a firm look. "The Point One launch was a huge, glittery, publicity-laden hit. You made the man heaps of money and provided an in-depth report in favor of his new events division. He gives you a pair of the most amazing Louboutins for Christmas, which, by the way, are worth hundreds. Then you pick me over Mr. Yummy for the holidays. So okay, I'm flattered—" AJ shook her head with a comical look of disbelief "—but in God's name, why?"

"I told you," Emily muttered past a forkful of salad. "After the launch, I think people were beginning to suspect something."

"Oh, please. You've been together for..." she mentally calculated "...close to four months—"

"—twenty-one weeks."

AJ's brows went up with a smirk. "And it's just sex, huh? Right. I think you're just grasping at straws. Maybe you don't *want* it to work out." She smiled as the waiter refreshed their empty water jug and the teenager smiled back, flushing as he left. Emily shook her head.

"How do you do it?" she asked, changing the subject.

"Do what?" AJ tossed a long lock of red hair over her shoulder and returned to her club sandwich.

"Make men fall at your feet."

"Good genes, I guess." She grinned, her mouth full. "Our mother was gorgeous before the drugs and booze ruined it. But back to you—why didn't you say something to Zac at the Point One launch?"

"You're kidding, right? I barely had time to breathe, let alone deal with any personal issues."

"Okay, then...your New Year's Eve party? A perfect time after you've had a few drinks, loosened up..." AJ wiggled her eyebrows. "And there's that midnight kiss...?"

Emily shook her head. "We were in the penthouse suite of Point One—"

"Sounds promising."

"—surrounded by Valhalla staff," Emily finished pointedly. "We all ate, drank and watched the fireworks over Sydney Harbour. I avoided Zac—" or had he avoided *her?* "—went shopping with Megan and her girlfriends on the Sunday after, then came home a few days later."

AJ snorted and sat back in her chair. "That's just dumb. Why hasn't he said anything?"

"Er, probably because he's fine with the way things are?"

"How could he be? What's not to love about you?" AJ's righteous indignation made Emily smile. "And why haven't you asked him?"

"You know why. I'm gutless about this stuff. I don't want to spoil the time we have left by ruining it. And anyway, I *know* him. Zac loves women. He never falls *in* love with one."

AJ tossed down her sandwich and reached for a napkin. "Well, now you're just not giving the guy enough credit."

"We agreed it's just about sex."

"Since when is something 'just about sex'? He makes you glow, Em. Look at you." She eyed Emily's floral shift dress with approval. "All this *and* a decent pair of shoes. There's hope for you yet."

Emily rolled her eyes. "Thanks."

"You're welcome." AJ gently shoulder-bumped her sister. "And we both know it's more than clothes and looks. People can change—just look at me."

Emily grinned despite herself.

AJ grabbed her water glass with a leisurely smile. "If a juvie runaway can come back from the brink of a glorious criminal career—" she waved her glass theatrically "—her sister can find a good guy who truly deserves her. Right?"

Emily shrugged, pushing a piece of tomato around on her plate in silence.

AJ sighed and covered Emily's hand with hers. "Em. This isn't something you need to pro-con, okay? Sometimes you just have to listen to your heart and leap right on in, regardless of the consequences. And—" she arched her eyebrows before spearing Emily's tomato with her fork "—that stupid office betting pool means squat when you're leaving in less than a month."

Half an hour later, Emily avoided her reflection as the elevator returned her to the office. AJ had a point. Well, she amended as she unlocked the office door, AJ *always* had a point. But this time, Emily began to wonder if she was actually right.

She sat at her desk, then placed her purse in the drawer.

The months leading up to the Point One launch had flown.

Two weeks prior, she'd relocated to Sydney to oversee the preparations, and even with that temporary move she'd felt the keen stab of loss. Sure, she'd spent those fourteen days living and breathing work, yet with the breaking dawn, in the split second she struggled from deep sleep to slow awareness, she'd felt it in the huge hotel and the cool sheets: emptiness.

It was almost painful, the launch night. She'd watched Zac circulate, his powerful presence and barely contained elation commanding her eyes every time she glanced over. And when he'd singled her out, praising her work and congratulating her in front of that rich, influential crowd, his perfunctory kiss had seared a path across her burning cheek.

Hours later, just before sunrise, his exhilarating euphoria had only heightened their passionate reunion.

Tell him how you feel.

With a sigh, Emily grabbed a notepad and pen, then checked her phone messages. After noting the calls, she flicked the page and slowly drew a line down it, filling in the two columns with the familiar "pro-con."

Every night her body rejoiced in his arms. During the day, the cracks had begun. The strain of the facade was beginning to tangle with her mind, winding her up into a tight mass of nerves.

Yet in public Zac was flawlessly—almost effortlessly—the epitome of the platonic boss.

What if she put it out there and he responded with indifference? Pity? A polite "thank you"? Worse, what if he called their arrangement off? She swallowed a spurt of panic. If time had flown these last few months, the weeks she had left would surely drag if he rejected her, especially when she'd agreed to go to his brother's wedding in two days' time.

Which reminded her... She clicked open a folder on her computer. She had to make a recommendation to the selection panel for her replacement.

When the office door swooshed open she glanced up, head crammed full of things to do, a pleasant smile on her lips.

That smile froze as a uniformed policeman walked in.

His bars indicated someone high up…a senior sergeant, or maybe a local area commander. Nervousness hit her stomach as she darted through worst-case scenarios.

Keep calm. Act normal. She gritted her teeth. Great. Now she was channeling her mother.

"Can I help you, Officer?" she said calmly, shoving those memories aside.

The cop tucked his cap under one arm. "Is Zac around?"

"Let me check. Can I get your name?"

"Senior Sergeant Matthews."

Emily rose fluidly, walked over to Zac's door, knocked, then went in.

"You have a policeman here to see you," she said when he dragged his gaze from the computer screen.

He glanced past her shoulder and the small frown quickly spread into a smile.

"Tim!" Zac rose, hands braced on the desk. "What can I do for you?"

As the policeman walked past Emily, his expression grim, Zac's smile slowly dropped.

"Close the door behind you, thanks, Emily," Zac said.

She did as he asked, then returned to her desk. Dread pooling in her stomach. This wasn't about her. It couldn't be.

And yet… She drew in a short breath. Something more serious than, say, a parking ticket would warrant a personal visit from a Senior Sergeant.

She heard Zac's muffled exclamation. Moments later, the cop emerged, his mouth flattened into a severe line.

Emily watched him leave, then swiveled back to Zac. His head shaking in disbelief as he stared at the papers in his hand.

"What's wrong?"

He pivoted and she quickly followed.

"Haylee issued me with an AVO." He slapped the restraining order down on his desk, one hand on his hip.

"What?" She swiftly closed the door.

"An Apprehended Violence Order."

"I know what it is." She paused, struggling to remain calm

as outrage scorched the back of her throat. "This is payback, for the night she turned up at your house."

He crumpled up the papers, hurling them across the room with a foul curse, but when she made a move toward him, the radiating waves of fury brought her to a stop.

"She's lying, Zac. We both know you didn't do anything."

His jaw clenched, eyes blazing. "That won't matter—the accusation alone will be damage enough. I have to call Josh." Zac had picked up the phone and was dialing.

"Zac," she said louder. He ignored her.

She moved, swiftly cutting off his call, eliciting a furious scowl. It was painful to watch him struggle to get a handle on his emotions. Despite everything in her past, every crappy thing that had happened to make her who she was, she'd never wished she could turn back the hands of time so fervently as right now.

"I was there, remember?" she said. "And I'll sign whatever needs to be signed as your witness."

His expression changed as the words sunk in. "You'd do that?"

She nodded. "Yes."

"Why?" He frowned. "After we've gone to such lengths to keep us a secret?"

Because I love you.

Fear slammed into her with such a force that she took a step back, desperate to avoid his gaze. Instead she homed in on the discarded AVO.

"Because it's the right thing to do." She walked over, picked up the papers and began smoothing them out, seeking calm in the rhythmic movement.

Zac stared at the papers she held out, his thoughts spiraling. She was actually going to step up and risk her privacy, possibly unveil her personal life to be scrutinized and gossiped about.

Yes, he wanted entry into that private room, but not like this.

He shook his head and took the papers. "No."

"What do you mean, no?"

"I have a solicitor. He can deal with it, make it go away."

"How?" Her hands went to her hips. "You have to go to court, unless she decides to drop it—which I don't see happening. She's a woman scorned, Zac, and she wants to hurt you. And she'll do that by hurting your company."

"You're giving her way too much credit." He tossed the papers onto his desk. "Now, if you'll excuse me, I have a call to make."

When she just glared at him and refused to budge, he glared right back. Yet beneath his irritation, a shot of admiration sparked. Her cheeks were flushed, eyes dark with righteous anger, her hands on her shapely hips, one leg thrust forward. Damn if she didn't look absolutely adorable right now.

"Emily," he began.

"Fine." She sighed before whirling and stalking out the door.

As expected, Josh Kerans was unavailable. So Zac called Andrew, his solicitor, who directed him not to approach Josh or Haylee. When Emily stuck her head in and asked for a long lunch, he nodded absently before trying to get back to business.

But a horrible feeling hijacked his thoughts, encroaching into work. He hated doing nothing, yet nothing was exactly what Andrew had instructed him to do. "Lie low for the rest of the week," he'd said. "Go to your brother's wedding. I'll get us an expedited hearing date and we can refute everything in court."

Which didn't placate him one bit.

They boarded their Sydney-bound flight early Friday morning, then an hour later switched at Sydney for the small country plane that would take them west to Parkes.

Emily remained silent as they drove through Gum Tree Falls, then down the dirt road to Jindalee, the outback spa resort where Cal and his fiancée were holding the ceremony. Sure, she'd anticipated Zac's mood wouldn't exactly be joyous, but this complete emotional shutdown was ominously disturbing.

Twice, she'd asked, "you okay?" and he'd replied with a nod and a short "yeah."

Which did absolutely nothing to calm her worries.

Finally, at the end of a long dirt road, Jindalee appeared. The homestead sprawled across the land, the green corrugated iron roof glinting in the sun atop large slabbed and roughly mortared walls. The iron porch railing was decorated in loops of white and silver-blue organza, sprigs of silvery gum-tree leaves serving as bouquets in between. Large earthenware pots filled with banksias and waratahs flanked a blue carpet that ran across the small grassy yard, up the stairs and stopped at the huge wooden double doors.

Past the main homestead she caught a glimpse of the skeletal frame of a massive extension. To the left, another blue carpet led to the wedding marquee and beyond that, a handful of guest suites.

When Emily opened the car door, the late-afternoon heat slammed into her, stealing her breath. She paused for a moment, then exited, the familiar strains of classical music floating in on the warm breeze.

"Mozart's Concerto for Two Pianos," she murmured, shoving a loose lock of hair behind her ears.

Zac looked up as he took their bags from the boot, the first real look since they'd started this trip.

"You like classical music?"

"I like Mozart," she replied, shouldering her handbag. "I saw *Amadeus* about a billion times. I'm told it was my uncle's favorite movie."

"The one who left you the apartment?"

She nodded. "I never knew my mother had family until his solicitor contacted me." She closed the car door with a solid thunk. "From what the neighbors tell me, he was a pretty good guy. He used to watch movies with Kitty from One B every Saturday night."

She let him digest that little piece of information as they mounted the steps. Then the doors swung open and Cal and his wife-to-be stood in the entrance.

Emily watched Zac smoothly make his way through Ava and Cal's warm welcome and the inevitable wedding-guest introductions. If his smile appeared too tense or his shoulders too rigid, she said nothing. Just having him here was a major step.

They were shown to their rooms, two elegant side-by-side suites decorated in cream and gold with a huge four-poster bed in the center. As Zac placed her bag on the bed, Emily's gaze slid over the opulent coverlet, the whispery canopy. It was so massive, so in-your-face, it felt like a huge elephant in the room. It tauntingly reminded her that everything had changed.

She hung up her suit pack, the wardrobe door blocking her from Zac's view.

"What time's the ceremony?"

"Seven." He dragged off his tie, then undid the top button of his shirt, the tanned skin at his neck forming a tempting V. She swallowed.

"Are you going to talk to Cal and Victor?"

"I can hardly avoid them."

"That's not what I meant."

He gave her a small smile. "I know."

She let it go, instead flipping the top of her suitcase open. Why on earth had she said yes to this? This was a wedding, a celebration joining two people in love. If that wasn't a slap in the face, what the hell was?

"I'll let you unpack."

One glance was all it took. One glance to see the uncomfortable tension riding his body as he stiffly grabbed his bag and made for the door, and her reason became clear.

She was here for Zac, to be whatever he wanted her to be this weekend—his date, his support, his emotional sounding board. He trusted her with his family secrets, a trust that simultaneously humbled and shamed her. What had *she* trusted him with?

She was sick of hiding—behind unspoken truths, behind awful work clothes. Even behind the possibility of a broken heart. She'd spent years protecting herself, making decisions based on fear.

She sank to the bed, staring unseeing at the closed bathroom door, at the polished golden handles and white glossy wood until spots danced before her eyes.

A mixture of dread and excitement rushed in, making her

limbs tremble. She was actually going to do it. After the wedding, after the reception. She'd pick her moment and then…

Then she'd tell him how she felt. Damn the consequences.

Sixteen

"Callum Stephen Prescott, do you take Ava Michelle Reilly—"

Emily's eyes skimmed over the bride, a shimmering, smiling vision in off-the-shoulder white satin, a tiny tiara of diamonds holding back waves of black hair, and her throat caught. Well, what do you know—brides *did* glow.

Then she looked over to Cal. Dark and gorgeous in a sharp gray dress suit and sky-blue cravat. But it was his expression that held her: a rapt look of such happiness and pride as he gazed on Ava that it actually made her breathless.

She swallowed thickly, forcing back unexpected tears.

"You okay?" Zac whispered beside her with a frown.

She nodded, unable to speak.

When he silently offered her his handkerchief, she took it and carefully dabbed under her eyes. "It's just a little…" Fanning herself with her hand, she gave a short, self-deprecating laugh. "I've never been to a wedding before."

"Really?"

"Shhhh!" An impressively decked-out woman to their left frowned. Emily gave her a watery smile, mouthing an apology.

Zac bent in, his lips close to her ear. "What about your own?"

She sighed, her eyes fixed on the beautiful picture Cal and Ava made as they recited their vows. "We signed papers at the town hall. Hardly cause for tears of happiness."

When Cal and Ava finally kissed, their joy was so palpable everyone laughed, then began cheering as the kiss just kept on going.

She shook her head. "I didn't think it would be so...so..."

"Emotional?"

"Exactly." She offered him his hanky back and he took it, eyes never leaving her face. She smiled nervously. "What?"

"I love your shoes."

She choked out a laugh. "Thank you for them. I think I'll concede I'm hopeless when it comes to buying footwear."

He glanced down at her feet, at the soft leopard-print high heels, the tiny pearl strands looped around the ankle. "Did I tell you how beautiful you look?"

She flushed. "You don't need to."

"I want to."

With a grin and a wink, he swung his gaze back to the ceremony, leaving Emily to swallow the lump in her throat. Hope bloomed low in her chest, a tentative bud curling around her heart. "Zac..."

Their conversation was cut short by the arrival of the bride and groom. As Cal and Ava accepted congratulations, posed for photos and smiled their way through the small gathering, Zac couldn't keep his eyes off Emily. She was no longer his conservative, efficient assistant. Dressed in a short flippy lemon skirt, a silky white tank and a cap-sleeved tangerine-colored cardigan that emphasized her womanly curves, she was elegant yet mouthwatering.

She'd even ditched her glasses. Her hair was swept up at the sides, the blond curls tumbling down her back. Unable to help himself, he ran a hand up her back, tangling his fingers in the soft waves.

She glanced up at him and her mouth stretched into a smile, her eyes shimmering from still-damp tears.

And that's when it happened.

The sounds of the wedding, the nesting rosellas, the clink of the caterer putting down the final settings, everything just fell away. His heart leaped as emotion slammed into him with such power it left him struggling for breath.

He was hopelessly, totally in love with Emily. His assistant, who couldn't stand a messy filing system. Who harbored a secret love of cheesecake and mocha lattes. Who accessorized her desk with hot pink and sky blue. Who danced in the dark. Who had woeful taste in shoes yet chose lingerie that made his eyes roll back in his head. Who kept her past locked down, allowing no one entry.

He'd never been so hell-bent on discovering what made a woman tick. She was more than just a challenge: those tiny pieces of information she doled out just made him hunger for more. He'd managed to piece together the basic framework, but she hadn't offered more than he'd asked.

Craving movement, he went in search of the circulating waiter. He was fully aware he was living on borrowed time. She was leaving Valhalla next month, and by leaving the company she'd also leave him.

No going back, just moving forward. Like she'd been doing all her life.

So where the hell did that leave him?

He watched in brooding silence as his stepmother approached Emily. Emily returned her smile, and soon they were deep in conversation. Unbidden, Zac's mouth tugged up. Isabelle had a way of putting people at ease, which he suspected came from her honest, working-class background, devoid of the polished sheen of wealth. His gaze lingered on Emily's face, the way her eyes creased when she laughed, the way she held her hips, one forward, one back, her back straight.

Then Victor joined them and familiar panic snaked through every muscle, urging him forward.

"You're Zac's assistant and his date?" Victor was asking as Zac approached with two glasses of champagne.

"Yes." She glanced up at Zac, smiling her thanks as he offered her a glass.

If Zac hadn't been watching the man so carefully, he might've missed that brief expression. But when their eyes met, Zac knew.

You're sleeping with your assistant.

The faint aura of censure accompanied an eyebrow raise, judgment quickly masked behind an impassive expression.

Zac scowled. Nearly thirty years old and he was still proving to be a letdown, tainting the exacting standards of the Prescott name.

His fingers involuntarily tightened on the glass stem before he downed the contents like water.

Well, Dad—screw you.

"I'm starting uni in April," Emily said.

"Doing what?"

"Small-business degree. I'm going to be a life coach."

Victor's bushy eyebrows went up. "A what?"

And here it comes. Zac shoved a hand in his pocket, forcing back an irritated growl.

"A life coach. You help clients determine their personal goals, then help them achieve them," Emily said.

"Like a career consultant, darling," Isabelle explained. "But more…"

"Broad," Emily added with a smile. "Holistic."

"Right. And there's a demand for it?" Victor asked.

Zac frowned. He'd been expecting Victor's usual halfhearted interest laced with thinly veiled skepticism. Instead it sounded as if the man was almost…interested.

"A huge demand," Emily said. "And it can be business-oriented, too—large corporations, government departments have life coaches under long-term contracts, which means a steady client base." She glanced at Zac. "Working at Valhalla has given me some excellent experience in the field."

"I'm sure it has." Victor's face was the epitome of politeness, yet annoyance still wound its way around Zac's chest. He had no doubt his father knew more about Emily than even she did. He was hard-core through and through, leaving nothing to chance, no sudden surprises lurking in the background. He knew this because of the way Victor watched Emily when he thought no one was looking. A calculated study, as if weighing up his options before deciding on appropriate action. The look was as familiar to Zac as every traffic light along the Gold Coast Highway from Surfers to Broadbeach.

It was Cal's wedding, for heaven's sakes. He should be happy for his brother. Dammit, he *was* happy. The man had everything—a lovely wife, a cute baby and a burgeoning business out here in Sydney's far west. Yet every time he spotted Victor, every time he thought about dealing with VP Tech, he cramped up. Like now.

"You two need to talk," Cal had said earlier in his suite. "Despite whatever he's done, he has changed. Hell, he's even agreed to consider our suggestions. Once he realized it'd give him more time to focus on his new pet projects—"

"I didn't come here to discuss business, Cal."

"Right." Cal had lifted one eyebrow as he tied his cravat with smooth precision. "So what did you come here for?"

"You're my brother. You're getting married, remember?"

"And Victor is your father. You can't ignore him forever."

"That's what Emily says." Zac muttered, absently fingering the wedding bands Cal had entrusted him with.

Cal straightened his cuffs. "Smart girl, that."

"Yeah." He couldn't help but smile. "She is."

When Cal finally held out his hand, Zac dropped the rings in his palm. "Ready?" Cal said.

"Are *you* ready?"

Zac saw the look flicker in Cal's eyes, his chest imperceptibly swelling as he nodded. Who would've thought his cool, workaholic brother would get emotional at his own wedding?

"Mate, I've been ready for months. Let's go."

Now, as the sun finally set and everyone gathered under the wedding marquee for the reception, Zac hung back on the porch watching the proceedings. Lounging against the railing, cast in the half shadows of the dying sunset and nursing a drink, he watched the man who was his father make his way slowly through the throng, smiling as the local townsfolk congratulated him in breathless awe, bailed him up to chat or simply bathed in the cast-off glow of a billionaire legend.

Victor actually smiling?

He took a slow sip of his drink. Maybe the surgeons did more than remove a tumor.

When Victor finally broke away, strode up the steps and disappeared into the house, Zac swallowed the last of his champagne, clamped a lid on his emotions and pushed off the railing. Perfect timing.

Yet just as he approached the door, he heard a voice from inside.

"Oh, I'm sorry!"

It was Emily—he'd recognize her voice anywhere.

"No, my fault," Victor returned. "I've actually been looking for you."

Zac hesitated, curiosity overriding purpose.

"For…?" He heard the smile in Emily's voice.

"I find your business venture very interesting."

"Really?"

Wow. Victor making small talk. Zac stayed still, wondering where the conversation was heading.

"And you're actually quitting work to study?"

Zac frowned. Victor never asked a question he didn't already know the answer to.

"Yes," Emily said slowly.

"That's a bold move, considering the current economic climate."

"I know. And uni fees aren't cheap."

"How's your start-up capital?"

"I have enough," she said cautiously.

"Which means you don't. Most small businesses fail within five years, you know."

"Yes. Mr. Prescott—"

"Emily. Let me cut to the chase. I don't know what Zac's told you about me—"

"Zac doesn't talk about his family."

"Really."

Zac could imagine Victor's raised bushy eyebrows, a picture of skepticism.

"Really. I work for him. We don't…have that kind of relationship."

"But you *do* have a relationship."

There was a slight pause, then Emily said, "I don't think that's an appropriate question."

Despite himself, Zac grinned. *That's my girl.*

Victor snorted in amusement. "No, I guess it's not. So let me get to the point. I'd like to offer you this."

Another pause, a small rustle and a gasp.

"That's a lot of money, Mr. Prescott," Emily said faintly.

Zac's grin fled.

Unthinkingly he surged forward, shoving open the doors in one almighty heave. In the long hallway, both Victor and Emily turned as one, a perfect visual of surprise. It took only one second for Zac to register the check in Emily's fingers, her flushed cheeks, Victor's scowling countenance.

"What the hell do you think you're doing?" He grabbed the check, staring down at the bunch of zeros before returning slowly to a now-inscrutable Victor.

"Zac," Emily said calmly. "Your father was just—"

Zac rounded on his father. "Just couldn't help yourself, could you, Dad?"

Victor crossed his arms. "If you just slow down one second, everything can be explained."

"Maybe you should take this out of the hall."

Zac whirled at the sound of Cal's voice. He and Ava stood in the doorway holding hands, wearing twin expressions of concern. Behind them, a hushed blanket of whispers spread across the wedding guests who'd stopped to blatantly stare at this exciting development.

Zac gave a curt nod and strode past them, into the reception area.

He struggled, trying to rein in his fury, but it was a losing battle. The past surged up to scorch his throat with painful, crushing memories and a desperate desire to be free of Victor's suffocating influence.

The doors closed, underscoring the moment with finality.

"I've had enough of secrets. He," Zac stabbed Victor with an accusing finger, "was offering money to Emily. A lot of money."

Emily gasped. "Just what are you implying?"

Zac raised one eyebrow, glaring at Victor. "Why don't you tell them, Dad?"

"Zac…" Cal warned.

He ignored his brother, instead turning to Emily. "Were you going to take it?"

Are you completely insane? Her wide-eyed stare mirrored that thought, her mouth dropping for one second, just before she snapped it closed and placed her hands on her hips.

"What do *you* think?"

Of course not. He pulled his back straight, struggling with the dark ghosts of his past, but the automatic answer on his tongue was a second too late.

"You," she breathed, giving him a glacial look, "are an idiot, Zac Prescott."

With supreme dignity she turned on her heel and strode for the door.

Zac swallowed in disbelief. *What have you done?* "Emily. Wait."

As Cal opened the door, she turned back to him, eyes eerily calm, expression neutral. "You need to deal with your family, Zac."

Then she was out of the room, and Cal closed the door behind her.

No. This was wrong. Zac surged for the door, but Victor's voice stopped him in his tracks.

"She's right, you know," Victor said calmly. "You can be an idiot."

Zac felt the fury burn from the inside out as he rounded on the older man. "You do not get to—"

"Shut up, Zac," Cal butted in. "Let him explain."

"What's there to explain?" Zac lashed out. "He was giving her money to walk away because she just wasn't good enough for a Prescott. That's the kind of stuff you do, Dad, right?"

At everyone's frowns of confusion, Zac laughed, the bitterness hot in his throat. "'Money always talks loudest.' Isn't that what you've always said, Dad? You paid Mum to leave, just like you did a bunch of my unsuitable girlfriends. And let's not forget you bought me a place at Sydney uni, right?"

"I think," Ava gently said from the door. "I should go and check on Emily." When she took her husband's hand and squeezed it, Zac's anger deflated.

"Ava…" His gut pitched in self-disgust. "It wasn't my intention to ruin your wedding."

She waved a hand. "Not ruined, just…made it more entertaining. It seems we've started a tradition." Her lips curved as she and Cal shared a joke before she nodded. "Just don't kill each other, okay?" With a smile she swept the doors open, then closed them firmly behind her.

The room plunged into thick silence. Zac glowered at Victor, memories and past grievances fusing to form a heavy stone in his gut. *I dare you, Dad,* he glared. *I dare you to deny the truth.*

"Look, most of those girls were more interested in themselves than in you," Victor began.

"Way to go, Victor," Cal muttered and threw himself down into a one-seater.

Zac scowled. "So that made it okay, Dad? You had no right."

"I had every right! I was protecting you!"

"From what? From leading my own life? From my own mother?"

"She was sick, Zac!" Victor exploded. "You were barely a year old when I came home one day to find you alone in the bathtub! God knows what would've happened if I hadn't been there."

Zac sucked in a breath, the icy shards piercing his heart. "No."

"Yes. She couldn't cope—with a baby, with being my wife, with the constant scrutiny and attention, the expectations that entailed."

Victor's craggy face creased for one second before he quickly composed himself and went on.

"She wanted to leave and I let her go. The settlement was generous."

"And then she disappeared."

"Yes."

"You know," Zac said, "it took me a long time to come to terms with what you'd done." He dragged a hand through his hair. *Liar. It's always been there, eating away at you.*

"I kept the truth about your mother from you, and I'm sorry." Victor's brow dipped and he stepped back, a sudden picture of remorse. "I didn't want you to think it was your fault she left."

"But you never explained *anything*. I asked, but you either ignored me, said 'she's not coming back,' or changed the subject. Jesus, Dad, you not only tossed her things out, but destroyed every single photo!"

"I was angry," Victor ground out. "And okay, in retrospect, I should've handled it better. You were a withdrawn, solitary child, and your mother was not well."

"So you just cut her loose?"

"No!" Victor barked. "Your mother just wanted privacy. So I let her go on the condition she got help and you stayed with me. Yes, I was angry. Yes, I blamed her for a long time. But there was nothing more I could've done. She didn't want to be found—not by you, not by anyone. And my job was to make sure you were safe and well taken care of."

"I needed a *father,* Dad." When Zac felt his voice crack, he stopped, swallowing thickly. "But you were always working. I didn't need the latest PlayStation, I just needed *you*. I needed you to tell me the truth, to let me make my own mistakes. I needed—"

He choked, the past saturating every corner of his mind, overwhelming, suffocating. He shoved one hand through his hair, head downcast. *Dammit, mate. Get. It. Together.*

With gritted teeth, he finally lifted his head. "Do you know I've never heard you say 'good job, son'. Not once."

Victor frowned. "I'm sure I—"

"Not once."

Victor's craggy face reddened. "Then I'm sorry, Zac," he said stiffly.

Zac's eyes widened as they met Cal's, mirroring stunned surprise.

"And I don't want VP Tech," Zac added, on a roll. "I design houses, Dad. I love my job and I'm bloody good at it. I just don't understand why you're so hell-bent on involving me in a company I have absolutely no interest in."

He paused, the cool air stilling as both brothers waited for Victor's answer. When no one said anything, Zac glanced at Cal. His brother just shrugged.

"Because it was the only way you'd ever talk to me," Victor finally said.

"What's wrong with the phone?"

Victor's eyebrows shot up. "You refused to take my calls. It took a threat to get you down here."

Damn. Zac scrubbed one hand across his face. The man had a point.

They both fell silent until Victor said, "Look, after I was diagnosed with that tumor, I began thinking about things…regrets, mostly. How I'd do things differently. And you topped the list, son." He smiled, a thin humorless smile tinged with remorse, before exhaling heavily. "The way I handled things with you was inexcusable. My major regret."

Shock rooted Zac to the spot as reality suddenly tipped sideways. This was crazy. Victor didn't apologize, much less talk about his feelings. What kind of world was it where Victor Prescott recognized he was wrong?

The same one where Cal gave up the Prescott legacy, apparently. And one where Emily walked out on him.

Emily. He paused, breath shallow and garbled. What the hell had he done?

"So what was that check for?"

Victor crossed his arms. "My new project. I'm looking for a few good small businesses to help off the ground. I offer silent financial partnership, they do the work, and we both benefit."

Zac glanced at Cal, who nodded. "He's right."

"And if you hadn't burst in," Victor added, "I would've explained that to her."

Zac studied his father with a critical eye. His hair was thinner, grayer. There were darkening circles under his eyes, eyes that normally held such authority and command but now were simply those of a man who'd experienced life and all its ups and downs, had worked murderous hours for something he passionately believed in.

Looking at the man with whom he'd fought so hard for so long, he realized that now that everything was out in the open, he was more sad than angry. Sad that things had turned out the way they had, sad for all those lost years.

It didn't hurt quite so much. For once, his mind was clear with purpose.

Zac shook his head. "She wouldn't have taken it."

"Hmmm. Well." Victor slowly loosened his tie with a sigh. "I *was* trying to do something nice."

Zac's eyes narrowed. The past had taught him to refute it. Argue. Deny. Yet the truth lay heavy in the air, truth that couldn't be denied or ignored.

For the first time in a long time, Zac actually believed him. It was a start, however small.

He gave Cal a contrite look. "Sorry about messing up your wedding, mate."

"You didn't. And I'm not the one you should be apologizing to," Cal said pointedly.

Zac nodded. Could he be a bigger idiot?

He surged for the door, grabbed the handle and wrenched it open. "I've got to be somewhere."

Seventeen

When Zac's phone rang as he strode along the path to the guest suites he had half a mind to ignore it. But then he glanced at the display. His solicitor. "Andrew."

"I texted you but you didn't call back."

"Sorry. Patchy reception," Zac said. "What's up?"

"Good news," Andrew said. "The AVO's been dropped."

Zac paused, rubbing his temple as relief washed over him. "Mate, thank you. I really owe you for this one."

"Oh, it wasn't me. When I fronted up at the station, it'd already been taken care of."

Confused, Zac thanked him again, then hung up. The only way that could've happened was if Haylee had withdrawn the charges. Which meant...

He pounded on Emily's door, a faint thread of relief mingling with overwhelming trepidation the longer the seconds grew.

Finally, the door opened and Ava stood there. She said nothing, just gave him a small smile and a pat on his arm and left.

Emily was zipping the top off her suitcase and shoving it open. Seeing her flushed and barefoot, her shoes kicked across

the room, quickened his heartbeat, forcing every single thought
from his brain.

She barely glanced up when he gently closed the door.

"Leaving?" Zac said softly.

"Well, I hardly think it's appropriate to stay, do you?"

In silence, he watched her scoop up a pile of neatly folded
clothes, then stuff them into the bag.

"Emily." He paused to clear his throat, then started again.
"Look, I—"

"You don't have to explain yourself, Zac." She kept right on
packing, refusing to meet his eyes. "That's quite okay."

"No. It's not. Can you—" He frowned as she disappeared into
the bathroom. A few seconds passed before impatience sent him
to the door, only to barely avoid a collision when Emily came
barreling back out.

When he grabbed her arms, she gasped.

He dropped his hands. "Can you stop for a second and just
talk to me?"

She took a step back, her toiletry bag pressed up against her
chest, her eyes cool. "About what?"

"About what an idiot I am."

His lips tweaked encouragingly, but hers remained flat.

"Okay." He grasped her arms more gently this time, and felt
the tiny shiver she tried to suppress. Slowly, he guided her from
the doorway, across the room and down onto the solid pine chair
before taking a seat next to her on the edge of the bed.

"I hesitated back there, I admit it. And my only excuse is…
well." He sighed with a shrug. "Okay, I have no excuse. I'm
sorry."

She finally met his eyes, giving him a thorough going-over.
"You actually thought I'd take the money? After everything that's
happened?"

"Not for one second," he said firmly. "It was just shock, seeing
Victor pull that stunt. I choked and I'm sorry. He's used money
as a bargaining tool all my life, and watching you two at the
reception, chatting so easily—"

"I was doing that for you."

"Me?"

She tossed her toiletry bag on the bed and eased back in the chair. "Calming the waters. Putting your dad in a good mood. For you."

He started. "I didn't realize."

"Well, I was." She firmly crossed her arms and legs, the overt body language telling him he wasn't out of the woods yet. Not by a long shot.

"And did you go and see Haylee for me?"

A small frown passed fleetingly across her brow. "No. I saw Josh."

The look on his face tilted her chin up. "I offered to help, you refused. So I called Josh's assistant and found out where he was having lunch."

"What did you tell him?"

"The truth. We talked about a few things. Apparently Haylee's been acting out since her parents' divorce last year. She has a bit of a problem letting go of her exes."

"She…"

She stared at him, daring him to make an issue of this. Hell, he should be delighted to be in the clear, but instead, all he could think of was that she'd sacrificed her privacy to help him.

This time, she'd been the one to charge in and save *him*.

And by doing that, she might as well have taken out a full-page ad about their relationship. Which had to mean something. Surely it meant something?

"You really are quite extraordinary, do you know that?" he murmured with a smile. "What on earth would I do without you?"

She stilled, her bright blue eyes capturing his for long, agonizing seconds before they suddenly began to flutter.

"I'm sure my replacement will do a great job," she said softly.

"That's not what I meant."

They stared at each other as the air practically crackled with unspoken words. But as Zac took a breath and opened his mouth, Emily got in first.

"My mother was a cokehead, a drunk and a welfare cheat," she blurted out. "I don't know who my dad was—my mom had an affair with some guy, then went back to Pete, my stepfather. AJ is actually my half-sister, six years older. My mother taught us to shoplift when I was five. When we got caught, Charlene and Pete did a runner and we were shipped off to the Department of Community Services, then foster care when DOCS couldn't find any relatives to take me. I was ten." She paused, gauging his stunned silence before continuing. "AJ ran off and I didn't see her again until I was twenty-three, when she tracked me down through my uncle's obituary. Yes, I've had it tougher than some, but I would never take money from your father. Never."

She finally stopped to take a breath, clamping her mouth shut. Yet past her defensiveness, the bright eyes that held his so steadily, Zac could see the turmoil. Turmoil that had been shoved down deep, then covered over by hyper-efficiency.

Chaos, uncertainty and disorganization—they all scared the crap out of her.

"I'm not telling you this for sympathy," she added quickly, her face reddening. "I just… I thought you should know."

His silence, his expression laced with concern and sympathy, ripped at Emily's composure, the walls she'd built crumbling as she wrestled with tainted memories. Her mother's booze and drug-soaked hangovers, the constant hunger-filled days. Charlene and Pete screaming at each other. The dead-of-the-night departures. Too many goodbyes.

She hadn't planned on saying this much, but it was like her mouth had yanked the steering wheel from her hands and had floored it. Zac did that to her, made her feel crazy, out of control. He'd invaded her life, challenging her self-preservation, demanding she open up to him, and now she couldn't reconstruct her defense no matter how hard she tried.

"I'm a foster kid who was given up by her parents—no wonder I suck at relationships. For years I kept everything in a suitcase. Ready to leave in minutes. It took me ages to actually buy furniture. I've never…" *Felt I've belonged anywhere. Until now.* She swallowed, her stomach fluttering.

His expression softened.

"Your past doesn't define who you are."

"But it does influence you. You know that. Which is why I said yes to you. It was about sex, not emotion."

He flinched as if she'd landed a physical blow. "Do you think that's all we are?"

Her breath hitched. "Isn't it?"

His expression was a tangle of emotions she couldn't quite unravel. "You tell me."

This was it. He wanted the truth and she'd never lied to him before. But instead of leaping into that abyss of uncertainty, she took a shuddering breath. "I find myself—" she glanced up at his unreadable face, then quickly away "—wanting more. Feeling more. Look, the fact is, I think I'm in love with you, and it's a strange, scary thing. But this doesn't have to mean—"

She ended in a squeak of surprise as Zac surged forward, ending up on his knees before her.

Her wrists captured by a pair of strong hands, silenced by those intense eyes as they searched her face, she could see the dark edges of his pupils, the small lines bracketing his mouth.

"Emily." He paused to breathe in deep, his eyes closing for a brief second before they returned to hers with burning intensity. "I know there's comfort in predictability. And I know you hate chaos and disorder. But that's what love is—it's crazy, unpredictable and full of mistakes."

"Look, you don't know... What?" She frowned. "Are you saying... What *are* you saying?"

"I said," he slid his hands down to capture hers, "I love you." He gave a wry snort. "I've actually been in love with you for months."

She was totally and utterly speechless.

"Em? Sweetheart?" He gently shook her hands, his mouth curving into a slow smile. "Can you say something?"

"No one's said that to me in a very long time."

Zac drew in a long breath. Lord, she was amazing. She may be compact, fitting under his chin, yet the power she wielded was infinite. She could destroy him with a few mere words.

"Then let me repeat it. Emily Reynolds, I love you. I love the way you're so hyper-organized, I love the way you blink and chew on your lip when you're nervous…the way you're doing right now," he added with a grin. "I love your loyalty, your sense of right and wrong. And—" his mouth swooped down, so close he could feel the warmth from her cheek on his "—I love kissing you, making love to you. I love every single inch of your gorgeous body."

All the words Emily had prepared, silently rehearsing over and over in her head, disappeared into a delicious haze as Zac kissed her slowly, tenderly, thoroughly.

When he finally pulled back, his hands still cupping her face, swelling elation threatened to choke her. It was like she'd been soaring a thousand feet off the ground.

"Do you want to add anything?" he murmured, eyes dark with flickering arousal.

"I think I found someone to fill my position."

His laugh rumbled through her, shaking her entire body. "I don't think anyone could ever do that, my love. And while we're on the subject of you leaving…"

"Yes?"

His arms tightened around her. "You should at least consider Victor's offer. He knows a good investment when he sees it."

"Really?"

"Yes." A myriad of emotions passed over his face until he settled on one Emily recognized. Peace.

When his lips gently met her upturned mouth again, it was like their first kiss all over again. Desire rampaged through every vein, arousing her, filling her with such a need that she thought her heart would explode from it.

Was it possible to be any happier right now?

"Marry me, Emily." His lips moved across her neck, little flares of heat on her skin. "I won't lose you. Be my wife."

Yes. Yes, it was.

Her breath hitched as she pulled back and stared into his face. His eyes may have been languid with desire, his mouth curved into a sexy smile, but his expression was deadly serious.

This was so much more than she ever deserved. Ever expected. Ever hoped. Joy surged until she was sure her face would crack from the huge grin.

"You're not going to lose me. And yes, I will marry you."

In between laughter and a few tears, they kissed again, until suddenly, kisses were no longer enough.

Their clothes were quickly discarded, the bedcovers yanked off, and they fell to the mattress in a tumble.

"I love you, Emily," he murmured, loving the way her eyes widened and her full mouth curved.

"And I love you, too, Zac."

And then, suddenly, words were no longer necessary.

* * * * *

A sneaky peek at next month...

Desire™

PASSIONATE AND DRAMATIC LOVE STORIES

My wish list for next month's titles...

2 stories in each book - on £5.30

In stores from 16th December 2011:

☐ Have Baby, Need Billionaire – Maureen Child

& The Boss's Baby Affair – Tessa Radley

☐ His Heir, Her Honour – Catherine Mann

& Meddling with a Millionaire – Cat Schield

☐ Seducing His Opposition – Katherine Garbera

& Secret Nights at Nine Oaks – Amy J. Fetzer

☐ Texas-Sized Temptation – Sara Orwig

& Star of His Heart – Brenda Jackson

Available at WHSmith, Tesco, Asda, Eason, Amazon and Apple

Just can't wait?

Visit us Online

You can buy our books online a month before they hit the shops! **www.millsandboon.co.uk**

1211/

Have Your Say

You've just finished your book.
So what did you think?

We'd love to hear your thoughts on our
'Have your say' online panel
www.millsandboon.co.uk/haveyoursay

- Easy to use
- Short questionnaire
- Chance to win Mills & Boon® goodies

Special Offers

Every month we put together collections and longer reads written by your favourite authors.

Here are some of next month's highlights— and don't miss our fabulous discount online!

On sale 16th December   On sale 16th December   On sale 6th January

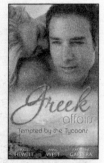